CHILD OF THE MERSEY

Kitty Callaghan has plenty on her plate. Since her mother died when she was just a child, she's cooked, cleaned and scraped to make ends meet for her drunken father and her headstrong brothers. Rita Kennedy, living with her husband under the roof of her spiteful mother-in-law, is desperate for their own home. Perhaps that will help them get their marriage back on track? For the two women, and others like them on Liverpool's dockside, the threatening clouds of war will bring heartache and tragedy. It will take courage, and ties of friendship and family to see them through the dark days of war.

CHILD OF THE MERSEY

CHILD OF THE MERSEY

by

Annie Groves

Magna Large Print Books
Long Preston, North Yorkshire,
BD23 4ND, England.

British Library Cataloguing in Publication Data.

Groves, Annie
    Child of the Mersey.

    A catalogue record of this book is
    available from the British Library

    ISBN   978-0-7505-4070-4

First published in Great Britain by HarperCollins*Publishers* 2014

Copyright © Annie Groves 2014

Cover illustration © Colin Thomas

Annie Groves asserts the moral right to be identified as the author of this work

Published in Large Print 2015 by arrangement with HarperCollins Publishers

Magna Large Print is an imprint of Library Magna Books Ltd.

Printed and bound in Great Britain by
T.J. (International) Ltd., Cornwall, PL28 8RW

My adorable grandchildren Emily, Abi, Daniel,
Jack and Hollie
The Future.
Thomas, Michael and Mathew
Our Heavenly Stars xxx

ACKNOWLEDGEMENTS

Many thanks go to my wonderful agent Teresa Chris, my editor extraordinaire, Kate Bradley, and the magnificent team at HarperCollins who all give so unstintingly of their time, expertise and brilliant advice, and without whom these stories would remain locked on my hard drive.

To my friends, Ian, Paul, John, Ali, Jackie, Dee, Frank, Emma, Lee and Michael, the Tuesday Writers of the May Logan Centre who review with alacrity. *Never Give Up!*

PROLOGUE

September 1930

'Mam?' Eleven-year-old Kitty Callaghan edged further into her mother's bedroom. Unusually, the clean but faded curtains were not yet open, and in the dim light Kitty could just make out her mother lying on the bed. Ellen's head was to one side, as if looking down at something, and a small, barely perceptible sound was coming from her direction.

It had gone noon but there was no dinner ready. When Kitty and her brothers, fifteen-year-old Jack and ten-year-old Danny, came home from school and the shipyard there was always something hot to eat, even in the summer. Kitty did not know where her dad was. Maybe he was out looking for work – if he had not got a start on the dock that morning.

'Mam? Mam, are you all right? Are you sick?' Rising panic caught Kitty's throat as she inched towards the bed. When her mother did not answer, fear made Kitty's heart beat faster.

If she opened the curtains, Mam would wake with a fright, which Kitty knew would make her cross, but Kitty could not see properly in this gloom. Her attention struck by an unfamiliar sound, she made up her mind.

Unhooking the wire that threaded through the

13

top hem, Kitty drew back the faded curtains. They slipped along the wire with ease, and then she placed the wire back onto the nail so they did not sag in the middle. Her mam liked everything tidy and said saggy curtains had a poverty-stricken look about them.

'I'll get you a nice cup of tea, Mam,' Kitty said brightly. 'I'll take the afternoon off school to help you out with the baking if you're not feeling up to it.' Her mother was not the strongest of women, Kitty knew, even though she was always on the go, taking care of everyone, especially Dad.

It would be nice for her to have a day in bed. She deserved a bit of peace and quiet. Only this morning she said her legs felt like they did not belong to her. Kitty had laughed and wondered to whom the legs did belong. Her mam said some funny things sometimes.

'Let me wait on you for a change, Mam. I'll fetch you that nice hot cup of tea,' Kitty said. 'You'd like that, wouldn't you, Mam?'

Turning, Kitty looked again towards the bed, not used to seeing her mother lying down, doing nothing. Usually she was scrubbing out or, more often, making bread and cakes to sell, just to keep body and soul together when Dad was out of work.

A chill came over Kitty and almost without realising it she found herself inching closer towards the bed, almost drawn by an invisible force. Moving slowly, her eyes took in the motionless shape of her mother; the bloodstained bed a deep crimson and her mother's hand that cradled a quietly mewling bundle, itself huddled into her mother's still form.

'Mam...?' Kitty's voice wavered. 'I'm here. It's going to be all right. I'll get you help.' Kitty saw her mam's half-opened eyes fixed on the new-born baby in the crook of her arm. Quickly now, she moved towards the infant. Its tiny mouth was puckered, searching for sustenance.

Kitty reached towards her mother's hand, taking it in her own. She let out a small cry of shock; her mother's hand was as cold as a stone. The dawning realisation that her new sibling's quest was futile was starting to overwhelm her and she dropped her mother's hand, unable to bear the coldness from a hand that had once been so warm. The hand that had stroked her with such tenderness; that had held her own reassuringly thousands of times... The motion seemed to distress the child further, and even in her fear Kitty still took in the fact that the infant was a little boy, his face screwed up in frustration and whose cry was growing more strident with each breath.

'Mam! Mam, wake up!' Panic screamed through Kitty's mind and body, even as she shook her head in denial. She wanted it to be five minutes ago when everything was fine. She stood rooted to the spot, her hands trapped under her arms, hugging her body, her legs refusing to move.

'Mam?' Kitty's trembling voice was barely above a whisper as she began to shake uncontrollably. The thought that her beloved mam was dead was too much to take in. She would get the doctor and he could give her something to make her better, couldn't he?

'No...' she groaned in despair. 'Mam, please don't go... Don't go, Mam. Everything will be fine... I am here now ... I'll be good...' Into her mind sprang the recollection of days when Dad had no work and no money, and her mam, at the end of her tether, said she felt like running miles away.

'I'll get the doctor... I'll get Aunty Doll...'

Still, there was no sign of any movement in her mother's curled-up body. As hot tears fell freely down Kitty's cheeks, she rapidly blinked them away. It was too late and she knew it. Her beautiful, kind, hardworking mam could not hear her any more.

Kitty lifted her mother's marble-cold hand again and curled its icy fingers around her own, she held it to her face and then gently bent down and kissed her mother's soft cheek. Her hair around her face felt like the softest down. Desolate, Kitty knew without a doubt that her cherished, much-loved mother was beyond anyone's help.

What was she going to do now? Mam was dead! A scream of anguish escaped her lips and drowned out the cry of the infant, whose tiny purple fists balled in fury, showing no regard for his mother who had made the ultimate sacrifice to bring him into the world.

Quickly coming to her senses, Kitty scooped the newborn babe from her mother's lifeless arms and wrapped him in a threadbare sheet she retrieved from the dresser drawer. Scurrying from the room, Kitty headed towards the stairs, almost tripping in her haste to be out of the house.

'Aunty Doll! Aunty Doll!' she cried. 'Please help me!'

Frank Feeny, hands in pockets, flat cap pushed to the back of his dark brown hair, whistled a happy tune as he turned the corner of Empire Street. At fourteen years old, he had just received his first pay packet from the Co-op, where he had worked for the past two weeks, and was looking forward to handing it over to his mam.

'Kitty? Kitty!' When he saw the distress on the face of the young girl whom he treated like his own kid sister, he broke into a run. She was clearly crying as she banged her front door shut.

'Kit?' Frank called again. 'What's the matter? What have you got there?'

Empire Street contained only ten houses, five on each side. From the dock road corner, there was the Sailor's Rest public house opposite a disused warehouse, and at the 'top' end, opposite the stable where Frank's dad kept his horses, was Winnie Kennedy's general shop, next door to the happy home he shared with his family and where Kitty was now heading.

Everybody knew everybody around here – you couldn't scratch your nose without somebody commenting on it – and some of the country's richest men walked the same street as the poorest. Ship owners were only a stone's throw from the working class and the families who lived hand to mouth.

The ships, the factories, the warehouses were proof of a thriving port; the noisy clang of dockside machinery, the rattle of trains taking goods to every part of the country, and beyond. The overhead railway at the bottom of Empire Street carried dockers, clerks, businessmen and everyone in between. Like any other port, it knew villainy, roguery, had sinners and saints; and everyone looked out for each other because that is what they had to do.

The kids stopped playing their games of hop-scotch in the midday heat, while their mothers, sitting on the little walls that separated each door-step, ceased fanning their faces with newspapers, to gawp at young Kitty darting across the street, carrying a bundle of sheets in her arms.

Kitty needed help. Frank's legs, normally whip-pet-fast, felt as if he were wading through mud to get to her.

'What you got there, girl?' He lowered his handsome face to look inside Kitty's bundle.

'Frank! Get your mam, quick!'

Horrified, he saw the bundle Kitty was carrying was bloodstained, but he could not voice the ter-rible questions that were racing through his head. Thankfully, his mother, Dolly, had seen Kitty's approach and was now hurrying out to her, wiping her wet hands on her full-length flowered pinny.

'Jesus, Mary and Joseph!' Dolly cried when she saw the infant in Kitty's arms. From her forehead to her ample bosom and over each shoulder, she made the sign of the Cross. 'Whose is this?'

'It's me mam's. What am I going to do, Aunty Doll?' Kitty's dark eyes, stricken with horrified shock, looked to the woman who was as familiar as her own mam. She could always run to Aunty Doll, her mother's best friend.

'Where is she, Kit? Where's your mam?' Dolly said the words slowly, as if dreading the answer.

'Aunty Doll, you've got to help me.' Kitty felt

her stomach heave; she was going to throw up right there on the street. 'Me poor mam's dead!'

The world of women and babies was a closed book to Frank but all he knew was that Kitty needed him, so he gathered her and the baby into his arms. There was something about Kitty; it was often said about her that she was an old head on young shoulders but Kitty was still only a child and he was determined to offer what comfort he could.

Dolly shuddered, horrified to think of her best friend, Ellen, suffering on her own as she must have done. The babe hadn't been due for some weeks yet, so Ellen's labours must have come over her very quickly – too quickly even for her to cry out and for one of the neighbours in these cramped back-to-back houses to hear her. As Dolly eyed the screaming infant and the quiet, grave face of young Kitty, she reminded herself that death was no stranger to these parts, Folk were poor, and doctors and medicine were for those that could afford them, which wasn't many in Empire Street. A mother of five children herself, Dolly took the struggling child from Frank's nervous arms, holding the infant boy to her breast. Her ease and experience must have been felt by the child because he stilled immediately.

'Poor little mite,' she observed. 'You couldn't have had a worse start. But we'll make it right, won't we, Kitty?' And she took Kitty's shaking hand and led her back to the house. 'I'll look after them, Ellen.' She raised her eyes to heaven and knew the time had come for her to keep the pact she and Ellen made all those years ago.

Dolly vowed to do all she could to help Kitty and her family. It would be difficult enough for any woman in a family of men, who were not used to fending for themselves, but Kitty was only a slip of a girl, despite being mature for her years.

The day after Ellen's death Dolly rose early, full of resolve to help her best friend's only daughter. She lifted the newborn from the dresser drawer that rested on two straight-backed chairs, where he had slept in blissful ignorance, waking only to be fed.

Poor Ellen – Dolly made her usual sign of the Cross – God rest her weary soul, she would want her family kept together. However, that would not happen if it were left up to that feckless waster Sonny Callaghan...

Dolly had no compassion for Sonny Callaghan. He had been bad for Ellen from the day he met her. He was a dreamer who made gossamer promises. Beautiful but totally insubstantial and impossible to keep. He was more likely to be found in the pub squandering what he had earned rather than looking after his family. Ellen had ended up charring and taking in washing to supplement her meagre housekeeping, which more often than not never made it back from the pub on a Friday night.

'Bah,' Dolly told the sleeping infant, whose sooty lashes rested on peachy cheeks, 'he's a fool and your darlin' mam paid the biggest price for loving him.' She walked over to her bedroom window and looked out across the street where women huddled together, talking. Most likely discussing the future of the Callaghan children, thought Dolly.

'It's little Kitty who needs my help,' Dolly told the sleeping child in the soft soothing tones of her Celtic homeland, 'for it's she who has it all to do now.' Ellen had taught the young girl everything there was to know about keeping a clean house and making good, cheap, wholesome food, but Kitty, skinny little snapper that she was, could not manage a feckless father, two growing brothers, and a newborn babe all on her own. Furthermore, there were things that men knew nothing about. Dolly took a deep breath.

'But I have it all in hand, Ellen,' she said to the cerulean sky, as white cotton wool clouds ambled by. 'I will make sure Kitty will not have to shoulder the burden on her own. There are plenty here to help her.' The women of Empire Street coped because they had to. Their men were seafarers, away for long stretches, and it was up to the women to keep body and soul together, and maintain hearth, home and family. These women, however, were a lot older than this poor eleven-year-old girl.

Sonny Callaghan walked with a sombre, somewhat rolling gait to stand behind the horse-drawn hearse bearing his wife's coffin, accompanied on either side by his young sons, Jack and Danny. Dolly suspected that Sonny Callaghan had taken more than a little Dutch courage to get him this far. Kitty followed a few steps behind, holding on to Dolly's arm for support. Dolly handed the youngest of the Callaghan children to her daughter Rita. The small dockside street was filled with friends and neighbours, as well as a smattering of family from the little Irish village of Cashalree, 'over the water', where Sonny had married the beautiful and much-missed Ellen.

As the grieving procession moved off, Rita took the baby indoors out of the way. She was going to look after him until the chief mourners returned from burying his mother at Ford Cemetery. The boy did not have a name yet.

'Everyone came out to support them,' Dolly said later when the mourners had all gone home and she was back in her own house. She sighed and looked around the table to her loving family, all seated and quiet for once.

Pop, her husband of seventeen years, nodded in agreement. Rita, their eldest, was a good girl; unbidden she rose now and went to make a pot of tea. Then there were the two boys, fourteen-year-old Frank, handsome like Pop, and twelve-year-old Eddy – the quiet one; she did not know who he took after considering that most of the family could talk the hind legs off a donkey. The youngest were ten-year-old dance-mad Nancy, followed by Sarah, who at six had a wise head on young shoulders. Now, Dolly thought, her family would grow even bigger because of the pact she and Ellen had made all those years ago.

'I'll look out for yours if you look out for mine,' they had promised each other, and Dolly would do it gladly; anything to stop Ellen's family from being split up and the children put into a home. She would not let that happen for all the ships on the Mersey. Her family were the beat of her huge, generous heart. There was always room for a few more.

'The whole street turned out except the widow, Mrs Delaney, I noticed,' said Dolly, 'and who would wonder?' She nodded at nobody in particular. 'Ellen's death will surely take the shine off the professional widow now.'

'Do you think so, Doll?' Pop, always the peace-maker, smiled at his wife.

'I've never seen a woman more eager to get into widow's weeds – her husband's been dead donkey's years, and that woman is still parading around in her black. She reminds me of old Queen Victoria.' There was a small silence, everybody still touched by the sadness of the funeral earlier. Pop thought of how he would feel if it was his own beloved Dolly that he'd had to bury that morning. He pushed the thought away, and was glad of the distraction when Rita brought in a tray of cups, saucers, a pot of tea and a huge plate of freshly made ham sandwiches.

'Aunty Ellen will know she left her family in good hands with us,' Rita said, patting her mother's shoulder. Dolly nodded. Rita always knew the right thing to say; she was going to make a smashing nurse. 'But,' Rita added with a half-smile, 'calling Mrs Delaney names won't bring her back.'

'I know, and I'm sorry, but I can't believe that old crow didn't come to pay her respects. Just makes me mad, that's all.' Dolly sniffed into her handkerchief. 'Poor Ellen didn't deserve to go the way she did.' She got up from the table. 'The one thing I can do for her now is look after her family, and I will.'

'We know.' Pop rose, too, put his arm around his wife's shoulders and gave a sad smile.

'I will make sure her little ones know they can come here anytime.'

'They know that already, Mam.' Rita passed her mother a cup of tea. 'I've put a little drop of something in that to help you sleep.'

'We will not be starting that caper,' Dolly said indignantly. 'Strong drink has never passed my lips before, except at Christmas, and it won't do now.' Rita took the cup from her mam while, out of Dolly's sight, Pop passed his daughter the bottle of whiskey, surmising what the eye did not see the heart could never grieve over. Unbeknown to Dolly, she had drunk umpteen cups of tea today laced with a slosh of the old country.

'Poor Kitty,' Dolly lamented. 'She's tied to that house as sure as any married woman – and she's not even old enough to leave school.'

PART ONE

CHAPTER ONE

August 1939

'Kit, it wasn't me! Honest to God.' Eight-year-old Tommy Callaghan looked over to where his older brother Danny was just sloping off towards the back door. 'It wasn't my fault. So you needn't look at me like that.'

'Don't be so impudent, Tommy. I'll see to you later.' Kitty stood near the shelf in the kitchen with a half-empty tea caddy in her hand. She shook it a few times and peered inside. Then, after wiping it on her pinny, she replaced the lid and put it back on the shelf. Turning, she watched in frustration as Danny slipped smartly out of the door, quickly followed down the back yard by their father.

Tommy, however, was not so fast, which enabled Kitty to grip the collar of his shirt, almost choking him in the process of dragging him back into the kitchen. She never raised a hand to Tommy, as a rule. If she stared at him long enough he always told her the truth. However, now, finding half the housekeeping money gone, she was sorely tempted to knock him into the middle of next week.

'Aar 'ey, Kit, you know I've got a sore throat,' Tommy complained, giving his collar an exaggerated tug. His face was the picture of self-pity.

'Come here, you little horror. You don't have to

sound so hard done by. You are going nowhere.'
Pots hissed and bubbled on the rickety stove and
the heat of the kitchen combined with the sizzling
late afternoon sun creeping into the house was
making it oppressive, but Kitty wasn't going to let
that stop her getting her hands on Tommy. She
stooped low so as to be eye-to-eye with him and
said very slowly, 'Now tell me, Tommy, who took
the money out of the tin? The truth. I'll wait, but
not for too long.'

Her brother Jack had given her the housekeeping money only this morning and now half
of it was gone. It would be a toss-up between
paying the rent and buying food, and as the rent
man was now calling on a daily basis because
they were three weeks in arrears, she really didn't
have a choice.

Kitty's thoughts were racing ahead now. Losing
half the housekeeping money meant she would
have to go over the road and try to persuade Mrs
Kennedy to let her have a bit longer to pay her
'tick' bill. Either that or grovel for the lend of a few
bob to pay the bill, and then there would be interest to pay on top, and everybody knew that Winnie
Kennedy was the last woman on earth you'd want
to borrow money off. Her exorbitant repayment
rates were not the only reason either. Kitty surmised she took great delight in giving sancti-
monious lectures to poor unfortunate women who
could not pay – in front of other customers, too.

Kitty felt so sorry for the recipients of these self-
righteous sermons, vowing never to get into that
situation if she could help it. However, her own
credit bill had accumulated to a frightening

amount because of Nancy Feeny's wedding. Kitty had offered to make the three-tiered cake as a wedding present, and it had seemed a good idea at the time. She hoped it would go some way to showing the Feeny family, Aunty Dolly especially, how grateful she was for all their help over the years.

Aunty Doll had been good to her and Tommy, who had been a newborn baby when their mother died, practically raising them in those early years while they were still grieving. She would not dream of asking Aunty Doll to pay for the cake now.

'What money?' Tommy asked as a thatch of dark hair, so like their mother's, flopped down onto his forehead and into those innocent-looking, adorable blue eyes. Kitty swept the fringe from his face. He could wrap her around his little finger usually, but not today. He was getting away with far too much these days.

'The housekeeping money I keep in the tea caddy! C'mon, spit it out before it chokes you. Who took the money out of the tin?' He was stalling now and she knew it. Well, she had all night; she would get the truth out of him by hook or by crook.

After a long pause, during which Kitty was staring down at him as if she could read his mind, Tommy said reluctantly, 'I didn't see nothing ... exactly.' He paused. 'I just saw our Danny – or was it me dad...?' Tommy stopped talking, rolling his eyes around the room before latching on to two lines of condensation racing down the distempered wall. He suddenly found them very interesting – anything to avoid Kitty's piercing eyes.

Kitty took a long deep breath. 'Were they at the tin?' she asked with all the patience she could muster. 'Tell me the truth now, Tommy, or I'll have to tell Jack, and you know what he said when you were throwing stones at the barrage balloons on the dock?' Kitty always knew when Tommy was telling the truth. 'He said he'll have you evacuated whether there's a war coming or not.'

'Don't tell our Jack, Kit! It wasn't me, honest,' Tommy said hurriedly. He knew that their older brother would not be best pleased that somebody had been helping himself to the housekeeping that he brought to the house every week. Jack did not see eye to eye with their father and although he didn't live with them any more, he made sure they didn't go short of much and helped out any way he could. He liked to be certain Dad and Danny gave Kitty their share of the housekeeping, too. Nobody back-chatted Jack.

'I won't bring your name into it if you tell me the truth.'

Kitty remembered the night Jack left. Even now, it made her insides shrink when she recalled her fear. He and Dad were nose to nose. Dad was drunk – as usual – and Kitty could see Jack was using every ounce of self-control to stop himself hitting his father. His huge fists, curled tightly at his side, were shaking with such rage his knuckles gleamed white.

Jack had left school at fourteen to go out to work at the local ship manufacturers, and had done the best that he could to help Kitty out since their mother had died. But year after year, watching his

out of the room. 'If you carry on I'll go and live at Aunty Dolly's. I will, I swear.'

Jack turned to Kitty. 'You'll not have to worry about going to Dolly's, our Kit. I'll save everyone the trouble.'

'What do you mean, Jack? You can't leave us – how will we manage?'

'I've been meaning to tell you, but it's never the right moment. I've taken a job in Belfast, training as a shipwright in the Harland and Wolff shipyard there. They'll give me a good tuition and when I come back I reckon I'll be able to read and write as good as anyone.'

Sonny Callaghan didn't have the nerve to meet his own son's eyes and Kitty knew that he was ashamed of his earlier outburst. But men had pride, didn't they, and he would rather slit his own throat than apologise. Kitty felt the tears well up and suddenly the thought that her beloved brother was leaving was too much to bear. She threw herself into his arms. 'Oh, Jack. What will I do without you?'

'I'll send home every penny I earn, Kit, and in a few years I'll be back and be able to help better by being a qualified shipwright.' He held her to his chest and said gently, 'You couldn't have two men living together that don't agree. It's asking for trouble. But I won't let you down, Kit, you'll see.'

So Jack was gone for three years, but he was true to his word, his money arrived for her every week at the post office and when he came back three years later he was a changed man. Bigger, leaner, stronger, and Kitty could see her father could no longer safely poke the bars of Jack's cage.

Jack still came for his tea now and then and he and his father had reached an uneasy truce, but it pained Kitty to know that things would never be the same between them.

Kitty tried to banish the terrible memories from her mind. 'Look at the cut of you,' she admonished Tommy, and her tone was more abrupt than she intended. Still gripping the back of Tommy's collar, she pushed him towards the brown stone sink.

'Before you sit up to your tea, you can have a good wash. You're filthy!' Turning on the single copper tap, Kitty let the cold water run into an enamel bowl and felt Tommy squirm. Nevertheless, she did not intend to let him get away. 'I'm ashamed of you.' She added hot water from the big black kettle that was always on the boil. 'You're a disgrace, running around like no one owns you.' She knew she was being a little harsh but she had to keep a tight rein on Tommy, otherwise he would get out of hand. A bobby from Gladstone Dock had brought him home earlier in the week for shooting pigeons with his catapult.

'But, Kit ... I've been washed.' Tommy's muffled protest went ignored as she threw a clean, though threadbare, towel around his shoulders. Dipping his head over the sink Kitty said, 'You could grow spuds in those ears, and that tidemark is bigger than the one on Seaforth shore.' Scooping warmed water into an enamel cup that their dad usually drank from, she poured it over his head.

'I got washed last night,' Tommy protested, his voice echoing into the sink. He was finding it impossible to wriggle free of Kitty's strong hold.

34

'And this morning?' Kitty asked, taking a remnant of old towel now used as a flannel, and slathering it in Lifebuoy carbolic soap, before vigorously rubbing at Tommy's two-tone neck.

'I didn't get dirty in bed,' Tommy exclaimed with haughty indignation, 'so why do I need to get washed twice in the same day?'

Kitty sighed and shook her head. 'Getting washed wakes you up and makes you smell nice,' she answered.

'I don't want to smell nice.' Tommy sounded most put out. 'I'm not a cissy.'

Kitty could not help but smile, but still ignored his protestations. Then, after scrubbing Tommy's neck, she said firmly, 'Just put your filthy hands in that bowl.'

'It's freezing!' Tommy barely dipped his fingertips into the cloudy water in the enamel bowl. 'I'll get pneumonia.'

'You'll get more than that if you don't put your hands in,' Kitty said, 'but there'll be no tea until you're clean.'

Tommy was certain of one thing: even though he had never known a mother's firm hand he had not missed out. Kitty was mother enough for anyone.

'I mean it, Tommy. If you don't change your tune, Jack will make sure you're with the first lot to be evacuated and who knows where you'll end up?' Kitty knew her little brother hated the thought of being away from home if war was declared.

'Do you think there will be a war?' Tommy asked. It would be so exciting, he thought as he rolled the block of red Lifebuoy soap around his hands, inhaling the carbolic scent. When he had enough lather, he blew bubbles through the O of his finger and thumb.

Kitty said nothing; the thought that there could really be a war made her shiver. The newspapers and the radio could talk of nothing else but that evil man Hitler, with his silly moustache and his mad ravings. But as far as Kitty could tell, there was no taste for war in Empire Street. The memory of the Great War and the terrible toll it took on the country's men was still felt and could be seen all around them. Women like Mrs Delaney who still wore her widow's weeds. And men like poor Joe, with his one leg and half of his face missing, who sold matches on the street corner.

And what about her brothers Jack and Danny? The thought that they could be sent off to fight in some far-flung place horrified her – they were so young. And what about Dolly's boys, Frank and Eddy, they'd have to go too, wouldn't they?

Frank Feeny...

Kitty was unaware of the smile that played on her lips as she thought of Frank Feeny and the slight blush that crept into her cheeks. Frank had been like a brother to her and he surely only thought of her as a sister. So why had he started to creep into her daydreams with his deep blue eyes and his hair the colour of molasses sugar?

But her thoughts were interrupted and she quickly released her strong grip on Tommy's collar when she heard the sound of heavy boots on the linoleum. To her surprise, a line of local men all entered through the front door that opened out onto the street and made their way through her kitchen towards the back door. Kitty's mouth opened in a big O as the men filed quickly past her.

'Sorry, Kitty,' said Mr Donahue, who lived at the bottom of the street. He was followed by Danny and her father, who hurried behind him out of the back door, down the yard, past the lavatory and disappeared to the narrow alleyway beyond.

Pushing Tommy to one side, Kitty leaned her hands on the sink and, perching on tiptoes, looked out of the narrow window. Her heart was racing now. What had Danny and her dad been up to this time?

'Sorry, Kitty.' Sid Kerrigan, marrying Aunty Dolly's daughter Nancy on Saturday and looking every inch the spiv with his Brylcreemed hair and his sharp suit, joined the moving line of men to the back door. He furtively dropped a pack of cards and a handful of coins into her pinny pocket, and Kitty guessed that an illegal gambling ring had been running. The bobbies must have got wind of it; either that or they'd stumbled across an illegal game of pitch-and-toss, usually played in the narrow alleyway, commonly known as 'the jigger', that ran between the Callaghans' house and Pop Feeny's stable.

Kitty's suspicions were confirmed when, moments later, she heard another set of heavy boots running through the kitchen. She was furious that her home had been used as an escape route but she would rather have been struck down by a bolt of lightning than dob them into the police. You didn't do that sort of thing on

37

Empire Street.

A hefty police constable, looking as strong as one of those new air-raid shelters, his truncheon raised at the ready, hurled himself into Kitty's scullery and nearly upended the three-tiered wedding cake that she had finished decorating only that morning. Trembling in all its white-pillared glory, it looked about to lose the tiny bride and groom that sat neatly on the top. Kitty, imagining her hard work was about to smash to the floor, saw red.

'Here, what do you think you're doing?' She thrust out her hand and, in the blink of an eye, saved the cake from certain destruction. Having steadied it back onto the stand, she pushed her chin forward only inches from the bobby's face and her determined expression told him he was out of luck if he thought he was going to take the shortcut to an arrest today.

Tommy stood watching, his face lit with delight. With a bit of luck Kitty would forget all about finishing his wash.

'We have reason to believe—' the bobby began.

'I don't care what you've got, you've got no right to come crashing into decent people's homes. If you haven't got a warrant you're not going any further, so get out of my kitchen and leave us honest folk to our work, will you!' With that, slightly built as she was, Kitty pushed back the surprised constable and urged him down the lobby and out of the front door. Slamming it shut, she dusted her hands and vowed that she would have more than a little word with Danny and her father when they deigned to show their faces again.

'And you...' Kitty arrived back in the scullery, looking menacingly at Tommy, 'get those hands washed. Your tea will be ready in five minutes.' Tommy washed his hands in double-quick time. He was not going to argue with Kitty when she was in this mood. If asked, he would not be able to describe the rising admiration he now felt for his sister. She was only a slip of a girl, but she had the courage of a lioness.

'We were just having a game of pitch-and-toss in the back alley, there...' Danny stilled the hunk of bread that was heading towards his mouth and nodded towards the wall that separated the house from Pop Feeny's stable. Danny and his father had crept back into the house while Kitty got the dinner onto the table. It was a simple meal of beef suet pudding with boiled potatoes and cabbage. Money for food was often scarce but Kitty was adept at stretching her housekeeping money out and she had inherited her mother's talent for cooking as well as for watching the pennies. She could often be found at the local market on a Saturday evening, haggling with the stall-holders and usually getting the best prices.

Kitty hadn't forgotten about the incident earlier but the worry over the housekeeping money was still unresolved and she bore down on her younger brother.

'I don't care about the game. What about the money in the tin?' she asked Danny, who let out a long exasperated sigh.

'That was just a loan, Kit. You know I'll put it back before the rent man comes.'

'It's a bit late for that. He's been and I've paid him and now I've got nothing left.' Kitty knew this wasn't true, thinking of the money that Sid had popped in her pinny, but she wasn't ready to let Danny off the hook. Her hands were in their usual position on her hips and she leaned towards him. She wanted answers, not excuses.

'You haven't?' Danny's pale face was a picture of disbelief. Kitty nodded.

'He promised he'd be our lookout, but he was nowhere to be seen.' Danny nodded towards young Tommy. 'I was on a winning hand when the bobbies came. Someone scooped all the stake money – I'm not sure who but I'll soon find out.'

'A fat lot of good that will do me.' Kitty was angry now. 'What am I supposed to do when I have to go into the shop and tell old-misery-on-the-hob Mrs Kennedy that I don't have the money to pay me bill?'

Kitty would tell him about Sid Kerrigan dropping the money into her pocket later, but for now, he could sweat. Danny had a job as a stevedore on Canada Dock but he ducked and dived, did a little bit of this, and a little bit of that, and up to now he had stayed just the right side of the law, but sometimes only by the skin of his teeth. Kitty worried how long it would be before his luck ran out and there would be no going back. She noted her shifty-looking father, his head buried in the *Evening Echo*, making no attempt to meet her eyes. How was she ever going to instil some morals in Danny if his father only encouraged him in the opposite direction?

'I'll get your money,' Danny said in a reassuring

voice, trying to calm Kitty down. It wouldn't do to get her all steamed up before he told them all his news. It was going to be bad enough once he told her. He was going to join up!

'Well, you just make sure you do, Danny Callaghan, otherwise you'll be going to visit Mam up in heaven – if they'll have you! We do not have the money to throw away on fines if you are caught gambling, Danny.' Kitty took the plate from under his nose, refusing to acknowledge his look of disappointment that told her he had been about to mop up the remaining gravy with his bread. She stacked the plate on top of the others on the battered wooden tray. 'I warned you not to bring trouble to this door, Danny, and I mean it.' She gave her younger brother a murderous look.

'I told our Tommy it would be worth a couple of coppers if he kept dixie,' Danny said, as if his brother's failure to keep a lookout for the law was the reason they'd got in this mess.

'Don't blame Tommy – you had no right,' Kitty fumed. 'I am trying to bring him up decent. The way Mam would have wanted.' She was taking no lip from Danny now.

Danny knew, judging by the determined look in her dark eyes, that Kitty was not in the mood for being soft-soaped. As she impatiently shoved a fine wisp of dark wavy hair behind her ear he took a chance and said, by way of explanation, 'You know what it's like, Kit: payday on the docks the lads wanted a little flutter. Percy the Greek was nowhere to be seen, so they decided on a game of pitch-and-toss. But where was our Tommy, who was supposed to be lookout...?'

41

'Tommy was here with me, where he should have been, and not with you lot of scallywags picking up bad habits.'

'It wasn't my fault,' Tommy whined. 'I had a sore throat.'

'Another one?' Danny's brows puckered. 'You'll have to get him seen to, Kit.'

'If you two didn't gamble and drink our money away, I might be able to afford a doctor.' Kitty looked at her little brother. She didn't know whether it was his bad start in life but Tommy had a very weak chest and still seemed to pick up whatever was going. The summer months saw an improvement but they'd had a few close shaves with him in their time and Kitty worried about him constantly.

'All right, Kitty, that's enough now.' Her father tried to assert his authority, which she respected when he was sober. It was a different matter when he was falling over drunk, as he would have been if the dice school had not been scattered.

'How am I expected to bring Tommy up the right way with you two leading the example?' Kitty asked her father. 'If it wasn't for Jack and me, goodness knows what would have become of him. I don't know where me mam got you two from, but it was definitely the same place!'

'Sorry, Kit,' her father and her brother said in unison, and as usual, she relented.

'I don't want to get a cob on with you,' she said as if talking to young children, 'but you both squander what little money we have.' She'd only own up that she had the money in her pocket after the pub shut. They could live without it for once in their lives.

'Jack won't be happy, will he, Kit?' Tommy said piously, giving Danny cause to glare.

'Mam would be horrified.' Kitty knew the mention of her mother always brought a wave of contrition. 'And if you bring the bobbies to this door again, either of you,' she said, pointing at them with the knife she was about to put on the tray, 'I *will* tell Jack.'

'Sounds like she's at the end of her tether,' Danny whispered to his father when Kitty took the tray out to the scullery.

'I heard that, and I am,' Kitty called. Then coming back into the room and nodding to Tommy she said, 'You go and have a lie-down, you look awful.' She looked at his untouched plate of suet pudding.

'I wouldn't mind a bit of a lie-down,' he said without complaint, so unlike him as he loved to be outside.

'Is he sickening for something?' Danny asked, his eyebrows meeting. Kitty tilted her head to one side to get a better look at Tommy's downturned face. These things came on so fast with Tommy and they disappeared just as quickly sometimes.

'I'll go now if that's all right, Kit?' Tommy said, getting up from the table and heading to the stairs.

Kitty's eyebrows rose. He must be sick if he was taking himself to bed. 'Go on,' she said more gently. 'I'll bring you a drink up soon.'

'Ta, Kit,' Tommy said, looking miserable. Then, in a low voice, milking his sister's sympathy for all it was worth, he added, 'It was probably making me get that wash that did it.'

'What's the matter, Spud?' Jack, just coming through the door, was surprised his little brother did not raise a smile when he produced his weekly comic.

'He's not feeling well; he's got another one of his sore throats.' Kitty felt guilty for scolding Tommy earlier. 'I got a couple of lemons from the shop. I'll make him a hot drink.'

'In this weather!' Tommy exclaimed in a croaky, despondent voice. 'I'll melt.' Then, without another word, he climbed the stairs to the middle bedroom he shared with Danny. Dad had the back room since Mam died, and Kitty had the big front bedroom containing just a single bed, a small table for the alarm clock and a chest of drawers for her meagre amount of clothing.

'That's a lovely cake, Kit,' Jack said, taking off his cap, his jacket slung over his shoulder. He and his father nodded warily to each other as Jack entered the kitchen. 'Did you make it?'

Jack was now a well-paid shipwright at Harland and Wolff's foundry and marine repair works in Strand Road.

Every payday Jack put his wages on the table, and Kitty gave him back his spends. Not once did she hear him complain. Work had been scarce for Danny and Dad, and Jack was often the only one providing. Kitty supplemented the coffers with the odd catering job, and made delicious wedding or christening cakes, but although everybody around came to her, she could not charge inflated prices to people she knew were in the same boat as herself.

'Aye,' Kitty answered proudly, gazing at the

cake she had moved to the sideboard for safety. She could feel her face flush warmly; it wasn't very often she got a compliment in this house. 'I'm going to take it over to Aunty Dolly's later.'

'You've surpassed yourself, Kit!' Danny smiled.

'Will you stay for your tea today, Jack?' He didn't always, and Kitty sneaked a look at her father whose head was still buried in the *Echo*.

'Would be a shame to waste it.' He answered her after a pause, and gave her a grin. It must have been one of their good days, thought Kitty, and pulled a seat out for her brother, taking his cap and jacket and hooking them on a peg behind the door.

'If you wait until I've finished my tea,' Jack said, sitting down to the table for his evening meal, after which he'd go back to his digs, 'I'll carry it over for you.'

It would be nice to have a chat with Aunty Dolly and Pop. Maybe, he thought, trying to suppress a warm smile, Rita would be there too...

CHAPTER TWO

'It's only us,' Kitty called up the narrow passageway everybody referred to as a lobby, following Jack, who was carrying Nancy's wedding cakes in three individual boxes, which Nancy had purchased specially from George Henry Lee.

'Come in, Jack, and you, Kit.' Rita shooed the sleeping cat off the chair and Kitty was surprised

45

to see the kitchen almost full.

'Oh, Mam, you didn't tell us Kitty was bringing the cake over. Put it on the table here, Kit, so we can get a good look at it,' said Nancy.

'Hello, Jack, how are you?' Rita, married now to Charlie Kennedy, gave a friendly smile as she tried to disengage her son, who was six years old, and his five-year-old sister from her skirt where they were playing a chasing game. There was only fifteen months between the two children and Michael was the image of his mother, with flame-red hair, though his eyes were hazel, unlike her green ones. Megan's hair was fairer and she favoured her father's looks.

'All the better for seeing you, Rita.' Jack gave her a warm smile. Despite herself, Rita felt herself blush. She and Jack went back a long way. Before she married Charlie, she and Jack had been walking out together. But that had all been a long time ago, she reminded herself. They'd been little more than kids. Now she was married to Charlie with two children. It was best to look forward and not back.

'It looks like you've got your hands full there, Rita,' Kitty said as she placed one of the boxes on the table ready for the family inspection. She felt nervous suddenly. She did hope they liked it. Nancy especially.

'They never give me a minute.' Rita's laugh was easy-going, practised, and Kitty marvelled at her ability to snap on a smile at a moment's notice. 'I don't know what I'd do without them, though.'

'They're thriving, Rita, and it's a credit to you,' Jack said.

Rita found it hard to meet his eyes and brushed off his compliment. 'Thanks, Jack, they're good kids. Let's hope there isn't a war. I couldn't bear to part with them.'

Thinking of Tommy, Kitty knew exactly what she meant. If Mr Chamberlain decided that this country was going to war with Germany, the children were to be taken away to a place of safety. Kitty had heard the mothers talking in the shops and in the streets around. Many said that they would send their children away to God only knew where only over their own dead bodies. Others said that their children's safety must come before any personal considerations. It was a choice no mother wanted to make.

'It's lovely to see everybody here,' Kitty smiled as Jack placed the two bigger boxes on the table.

Pop and Dolly nodded with proud appreciation of a full house. 'Only our Frank missing,' said Dolly, 'but he'll be home tomorrow if he can get leave.'

'I'd better be off, Dolly. Good to see you all. I'm looking forward to a slice of that cake on Saturday.'

'Bye, Jack. Mind how you go, now,' Rita said, as Jack made his way to the door.

'You too, Reet,' Jack replied as their eyes met. Rita looked away quickly and then he was gone. But she was aware that Jack had used the same shortening of her name that he'd always done. Jack was the only person that Rita would allow to call her that.

'Have a seat, Kit.' Eddy scraped back his chair and offered it to Kitty. A merchant mariner, he had managed to get leave for his sister's wedding.

'Hopefully he will get here before Saturday,' Dolly said, pouring tea into another two cups while Kitty's heartbeat fluttered at the mention of Frank Feeny.

'You're looking well, Kit.' Eddy's friendly smile flashed white against a rugged, windblown complexion, enhanced by three years of sea voyages.

'I'm fine, Eddy.' Kitty took the cup of tea from Dolly and sat at the table. 'How's yourself?'

'We docked yesterday. I'm joining a new ship down the Pool on Monday.' He sounded excited and Kitty couldn't help but notice the pained look on his mother's face. Kitty knew young men like Eddy were joining the services because they could not get jobs, but around here many had always gone away to sea. The thought of war made her feel sick. There were two million unemployed in this country and it seemed that joining one of the Forces was the only one way to get a decent day's work. She knew that naval forces had been marshalling for months and the local docks had provided anchorage for ships of many nations.

'I've got salt water in my veins, like Frank ... and Pop, of course.' Eddy looked over to his father, a Royal Navy veteran who had seen action in the Great War. Although he did not talk about it much the proof of all he had been through sat on his handsome face. The dark eye-patch he wore was a daily reminder.

'You'll have best bitter running through your veins on Saturday,' Pop laughed. The Feeny house was always lively and full of laughter.

'You know,' Pop whispered to Eddy, out of

Dolly's earshot, 'your mother never talks about it but there are bags of sugar and tins of stuff all over the house. She doesn't want to be caught out if the worst happens. There's talk of rationing if war breaks out.' Everybody was quietly preparing for war, it seemed.

'Are you going to save me a dance on Saturday, Kit?' Eddy asked, slow, slow, quick-quick, slowing in circles around the room, making Kitty laugh loudly. 'Go on, Kit, will you?'

Kitty, nodding, agreed.

Eddy and his older brother, Frank, had always treated her like a younger sister, larking about with her just as they did with Nancy or fifteen-year-old Sarah, the youngest of the Feeny clan. The thought of any of them, especially Frank, going to fight an enemy – risking their lives – gave her chills.

Neither of them had serious relationships, but Frank seemed more the type to play the field. He always said there was enough of him to go round, and why stop at one, which brought howls of protest from his sisters, who maintained he would get himself into trouble saying things like that.

The more outgoing of the Feeny brothers, Frank had courted a great many girls on his travels – so he said – and Kitty had no cause to doubt him. Now she sat ramrod straight, holding tightly on to her teacup like a shield. What was it they said about sailors – a girl in every port?

Please come home alone, Frank. The sun dipped behind a cloud and the room grew darker for a moment, the gloom temporarily mirroring Kitty's feelings when she recalled the last time Frank had brought a girl home to Empire Street. Kitty did not know who the girl was, nor did she ask Rita about it. She had seen Frank come down the street with the pretty girl, obviously taking her home to meet his folks. Kitty thought they looked like a couple of film stars. Frank, being his usual friendly self, waved to Kitty, sitting on the front step after cleaning the house from top to bottom and worrying where the money for the next meal was coming from. Frank's girlfriend, dressed in a fabulous camel-hair coat with wide, turn-back cuffs and large buttons, waved too, making Kitty feel dull and dowdy by comparison. To her shame, Kitty did not wave back, pretending not to notice; instead she got up, went inside and cleaned up all over again, all the while fighting back hot tears and wondering where they had come from all of a sudden.

'Oh, Kitty!' Sarah exclaimed, bringing Kitty back to the present moment. 'Would you look at that beautiful cake! I've never seen such a work of art – and it is a work of art, to be sure.'

Nancy, the bride-to-be, was dumbstruck by the sight of the beautiful cake.

'You have done yourself proud with this one, Kit,' Dolly said, while Nancy threw her arms around Kitty and gave her a hug so tight it took the breath right out of her.

'Gloria is going to be so jealous when she sees this cake,' Nancy laughed. Gloria was her best friend and chief bridesmaid, and like many best friends they were always in competition with each other. The Feeny women gazed at the exquisite latticework and perfectly crafted white roses, so wonderfully sculptured with the finest icing sugar they looked perfectly real.

'Mine was nowhere near as good as that, and I paid a fortune for it,' Rita joined in, eyeing the three cakes with obvious admiration.

'Well, we couldn't expect the poor widow to put her hand in her purse, could we?' Dolly was unable to confine the sardonic words.

'Nancy's wedding will be smashing, Aunty Doll,' Kitty said, thrilled that they liked her creation and equally sure they would enjoy eating it. 'You'll have nothing to worry about, just you wait and see.' She smiled as Dolly rippled with unashamed pride.

'I'll not have Madam Kennedy looking down her nose and finding us wanting.'

'Hell will freeze over before she'll lay on a spread!' Rita laughed, knowing everybody was aware of her mother-in-law's miserly reputation. 'Anyway, I'll be off now before Charlie gets in from work.'

'You'd better make tracks, he'll be coming down the street pretty soon.' From her window Dolly could watch her son-in-law's daily arrival home with amusement. The insurance salesman, his bicycle clips wrapped firmly around his trouser legs, always sat far back on the saddle, riding his cycle down the street like a powerful Norton motorbike. 'Madam Kennedy didn't have cause to complain at your wedding, Rita.'

'And she won't have any reason to carp at Nancy's either.' Rita knew her mother had been saving for months for this day, and she was proud of her family's generous nature.

'I'd sooner starve than ask her to help me out, moneylender or not.' Dolly's nostrils flared with disdain.

Kitty sighed. Some of us have no option, she thought, knowing she would shortly have to go cap in hand to Mrs Kennedy and grovel for a loan.

For, as much as she had rescued the money that Danny and her dad almost gambled away, she still did not have enough to rig out Tommy, who was one of Nancy's ushers. He was going to need a new pair of trousers and shoes, not to mention a new shirt and tie.

'Right then,' said Rita, 'I'll have to be going now, Mam. As it's my and Charlie's anniversary I've made a special tea with sherry trifle for afters.'

'Oh, that sounds lovely,' said Pop. 'Can I come?'

'You might as well, Pop,' Rita laughed. 'Mrs Kennedy will be there.'

'In that case I don't think I'll bother, but give her my regards.' Pop rolled his eyes to the ceiling. Rita had never heard him say a bad word about anybody, not even the old dragon Winnie Kennedy, her own mother-in-law.

'You'd think she'd leave you alone on your anniversary!' Eddy said. 'Or even better, Charlie should have taken you out instead.'

'We're saving for a deposit, Eddy.' Rita pulled her son's socks up as she was talking. 'We'll never get a house if we waste our money on nights out.'

'Maybe he'll win the money for a deposit,' Nancy said. Rita's look of confusion told her she had said too much so she added suddenly, 'Let's go into the parlour,' linking her arm through Kitty's, 'and we'll see what's what.' Amidst the bustle of Rita and the two kids leaving, Nancy, Dolly and Kitty went into the parlour. Kitty eyed up the room, which Pop had decorated in preparation for the wedding, and decided the top table would look better under the window. They wanted everything just right.

'The wedding cake could go there,' Kitty pointed to the imaginary table, 'with Nancy's bouquet in front ... and then we could have the groom's family over here...'

'You can say what you like about Kitty Callaghan...' A deep, melodious voice coming from the direction of the parlour door made Kitty's insides turn to jelly, '...but she knows how to put on a splash.' Kitty's head whipped round and that familiar feeling of pleasure tingled through her at the sound of Frank Feeny's velvety voice. She only just managed to hold on to a gasp of delight at the sight of him, and heaved a sigh of relief when Dolly rushed past her to throw her arms around her elder son. It gave Kitty the chance to drink in his compelling presence.

Frank had grown from a gangly six-footer to a strong, handsome man. Confidently self-assured without being cocky, he was a petty officer in the Royal Navy and the only man whose tanned good looks had ever made her pulse race. Kitty stepped back and, as the lid was up, leaned on the piano keys, causing a plinkety-plonk, which almost turned into a tune as she tried to retain a little dignity.

'Give us a song then, Kit!' Frank laughed, dropped his kitbag on the floor and almost hugged the living daylights out of his mother.

Kitty reluctantly lowered her gaze; she had been staring, intentionally, of course. However, she did not want him to think she had lost her marbles...

'You said you wouldn't be home until Friday. You're a day early,' Dolly cried when she got her breath back.

Frank looked comically sad before turning his gaze to Kitty. 'Hello, Kit, maybe you'll be glad to see me?' His dark blue eyes lingered just a little longer than necessary before he gave Kitty's arm a playful squeeze. 'Those muscles are still a bit puny.'

'You look well, Frank,' Kitty said shyly, hoping her cheeks were not glowing, and felt the surprising sting of happy tears threaten. Annoyed with herself for the way a hot colour always rose to her throat and neck when Frank was around, she said in a mock hurt voice, 'They are not puny!' Her eyes widened and she blinked back the unshed tears. He would be a good catch for some lucky girl one day. If that girl could drag him onto dry land long enough, that was.

'How long are you home for?' she asked, feeling her colour rise even more.

'Listen to her, Mam!' Frank pretended to be hurt. 'I've only just stepped through the door; you tell me you don't want me home for another day and Kitty's trying to get shut of me.'

'No, I didn't mean...' Kitty was tongue-tied now. 'I just meant... I didn't mean...' Then she saw his handsome, mischievous eyes dance and she laughed, relieved. 'Oh, you, Frank...'

'I get you every time, Kit.' He squeezed her arm again and Kitty, reluctantly, shrugged him away.

She had to get back to Tommy; if he was feeling better he would be out in the street and she would never get him in.

'I'll be going then, Aunty Doll... Glad to see you home again, Frank,' Kitty said, blushing to the roots of her hair and pushing a damp curl back under her turbaned headscarf. She headed for the parlour door.

'Was it something I said?' Frank gently caught her arm and his eyes, the deep colour of a tropical ocean, sparkled when he smiled. Kitty could see her reflection in them, he was so close. For a moment, she felt as if they were the only two in the room. A small cough from Dolly brought her out of her reverie and Kitty began distractedly to tidy together the things she had brought over to show her: the small bride and groom to go on the top tier of the cake, the sprig of white silk flowers to adorn the bottom layer.

'You'll have a lot to catch up on,' she said shyly. 'I don't want to intrude.'

'You could never do that, Kit.' Frank's voice, lower, gentler, even a little solemn now, caused her to smile self-consciously. Feeling flustered, she dropped the small bride on the floor and bent down to pick it up, as Frank did the same. They knocked their heads together gently, and Kitty put her hand to her own. She felt her cheeks must be crimson now. Frank laughed softly and touched her forehead where they had bumped into each other.

'You all right, Kit? I haven't given you a concussion, have I?' He handed her the little model of the bride. 'Here you go, pretty as a picture.

Just like you.'

Kitty thought that Frank looked so handsome at that moment and her heart was bursting with so much emotion and embarrassment that she could hardly bear to look at him. Mumbling her excuses, she departed the Feenys' parlour quicker that a hare round a race track – as their Danny would say.

If she had known Frank was coming home on leave she would have ... what? What would she have done? Washed her hair? Left her turban off? What would be the point? Kitty knew that he was joking when he said she was pretty. She had never seen him look at girls like her. She was not one for wearing lippy and rouge. Living in a house of men, she had never given a thought to such things. Therefore, what hope was there of Frank Feeny seeing her as anything other than another sister? Relieved to be back outdoors and away from Frank's unsettling presence, she smiled: fancy having all these daft notions. It was amazing what an imminent wedding could do to your head.

Outside in the sunshine she breathed deeply, trying to calm her racing heart. Oh, he was a joker, that Frank Feeny, she thought dreamily. The girl who got him would be the luckiest girl in the whole, wide world.

Now Dolly called from the doorway as Kitty was just about to cross the road. 'Kitty! Hang on a minute!'

She stopped and turned round.

'Here, you put this in your purse. You've earned it.' Kitty opened her mouth to protest when Aunty Dolly raised her chin, a sign that she would not take 'no' for an answer and the matter was closed. When Dolly had hurried back into the house, Kitty looked down at the roll of pound notes and gasped in surprise. There was enough for Tommy's clothes and his shoes.

'Oh, thank God for you, Aunty Doll,' Kitty whispered as her throat tightened, bringing a tearful sigh of relief. The extra money would allow her to get a little present for Tommy's birthday too. He would soon be nine years old.

'How are you feeling, Tom?' As soon as she was back, Kitty took her young brother another drink and this time she also brought some Ashton & Parsons Infants' Powders. Dolly had said it would work wonders and even if it did not, at least Tommy would feel as if something was being done. Sometimes mind over matter was the best cure, she'd added.

'I'm feeling much better now,' Tommy said, eyeing the powder on the end of the teaspoon.

'Well, just in case you still feel a bit under the weather, have this.'

Tommy did not look keen. 'I know you wouldn't poison me deliberately, Kit,' he said, wrinkling his nose and taking the powder.

'You'll be as right as rain,' Kitty smiled, 'and tomorrow we are going out to buy you some new clothes for the wedding.'

Tommy's eyes were wide in amazement. 'Truly, Kit?' Tommy had never had new clothes before; they were usually second- or even third-hand from Cazneau Street market. Kitty, smiling, nodded.

'I'm feeling better already.'

'Right, well, it's about time I shut that front

door. It's been open all day and the pub's cat keeps wandering in.' As Kitty made to close the door, she saw Nancy's best friend and chief bridesmaid-to-be, Gloria, arm in arm with a dashing Royal Air Force officer in immaculate uniform. They made a lovely couple.

'Going somewhere nice?' Kitty asked, friendly as ever.

Gloria's crimson lips parted to reveal perfect teeth. 'We're going to the Adelphi and then on to a jazz club.'

'That sounds lovely,' Kitty said, wondering what it must feel like to be dressed in beautiful clothes and taken somewhere as posh as the Adelphi Hotel. Still, she would not dwell on the matter. What she never had she couldn't miss. Although, somehow ... she did.

Gloria watched over the rim of her champagne glass as Giles, her debonair escort, beckoned over the maitre d'hôtel in the swish lounge of the fashionable Adelphi.

Giles whispered something into his ear and the waiter nodded and accepted the folded note Giles slipped into his hand. Gloria did not catch what he was saying above the sound of the band playing.

'Certainly, sir,' the waiter answered. 'I can arrange that for you.'

'And while you're at it,' said Giles, 'another bottle of your finest champagne.'

'Of course, sir,' the waiter said with the reverence reserved for an officer in uniform who had plenty of cash to throw around.

'Happy, darling?' Giles smiled. He reached across the candle-lit table for Gloria's hand, his lips delicately caressing the perfectly manicured nails that matched her pouting ruby-coloured lips, which were just begging to be kissed.

'Couldn't be happier,' Gloria answered, her elbow resting elegantly on the arm of the velvet-covered chair, aware the position showed her slim neck and *décolletage* to the best advantage.

'Shall we dance?' Giles asked, eager to hold her close and feel the smooth voluptuous contours of her body against his own.

'Let's dance after I've taken my spot.' Gloria stood up, and with the fluid grace of a sensual stretching cat she sashayed across the dance floor towards the band, aware of all eyes upon her as her exquisite silver gown shimmered in the half-light. She took in the fashionable clientele with a single sweep of her lengthened lashes and a ripple of pleasure coursed through her. What woman would not want such attention? She walked with the confidence of one who knew all male eyes would be fully appreciative, regardless of the attractions of their female companions. Leaning over the rail, she whispered to the bandleader, who smiled before announcing loudly, 'Ladies and gentlemen, it gives me great pleasure to introduce Miss Gloria Arden.'

Gloria let the applause die down completely before she opened her glossy lips to sing.

War was turning from a possibility to an inevitability, and many uniforms graced the swish tables. After her first song, Gloria was encouraged to sing again and again, enjoying the attention and laughing aloud at each order to 'Sing another one!'

Eventually she held up her hand to let the audience know this was going to be her last song. Giles, although smiling and clapping enthusiastically, looked a little lonely out there all on his own. Gloria finished her set with arousing rendition of 'There'll Always Be an England', which had the audience on their feet, waving and singing along.

The applause was deafening, and Gloria felt ten feet tall as she walked back to Giles with shouts of 'Encore!' ringing in her ears. It was then that she saw, among a group of people sitting at a table just off the dance floor, Sid Kerrigan. His arm was draped around a woman who looked as if she had more money than dress sense, given the tight-fitting frock she was wearing, and he certainly didn't look like a man who was ready to marry Gloria's best friend in two days' time.

CHAPTER THREE

Rita stood back and looked at the table, resplendent with a new white tablecloth and five cotton napkins, each folded into a bishop's mitre.

She had worked hard getting the food ready for her and Charlie's anniversary. She had cooked Charlie's favourite, steak and kidney pudding, which always put him in a good mood. The suet pastry cases filled with meat in rich gravy had been steaming all afternoon. Rita had had to leave the shop frequently to check the pan had not boiled dry. Much to her mother-in-law's annoyance, in the end she'd asked if she could take the rest of the afternoon off. Mrs Kennedy was not keen on her cutting her hours short, complaining about her arthritic leg, which she did frequently. Nevertheless, Rita pointed out that it was only the second time and the first was when she'd gone into labour with Megan. It was a bonus to her little holiday that she'd popped in to see her mam and had seen Nancy's wedding cake.

Rita wanted to make the tea special for the children too, especially after the news on the wireless that the Germans were about to cross the Polish border and England, promising to stand by Poland, was now on heightened alert. Rita felt a fizz of terror run through her. How many more teas would they have together? Every one of them would be special now and she must keep her chin up for the children's sake.

You'll do, Rita thought, checking her appearance one more time. She was slimmer than the day she had married Charlie. But she'd been pregnant then.

Dressed in her best, a pale blue crêpe de Chine frock with a sweetheart neckline and short puffed sleeves, she felt wonderful. Earlier she had sent Michael to get the accumulator filled for the wireless and was humming along to the lively tune now playing. Everything was perfect.

'Is that dress new?' Charlie asked when he came in. The children were in the kitchen washing their hands and making a right song-and-dance about it, too. Rita laughed and told Charlie the dress was over five years old. 'I don't remember it,' he said, walking over to her and giving her a perfunctory peck on the cheek. Rita took this as an opportunity to pin her husband down, and put her arms around his neck. 'Aren't you going to wish me Happy Anniversary?'

Charlie was so hard to read these days and Rita wasn't really sure what reception she'd get, but she was thrilled when he placed his hand on the small of her back and ran his fingers through her hair. Rita thrilled at this rare moment of intimacy as she leaned against him.

However, the moment was short-lived when the door between the shop and the sitting room opened, and Charlie's mother entered the room like a ship in full sail. Charlie immediately pushed Rita away none too gently, as if she were contaminated in some way.

She could only imagine how it might feel if her husband were to kiss her cheek in front of his mother. Charlie never showed any emotion when she was around.

'Oh, the table looks lovely, Mam!' Megan said, her face alight with a beaming smile. 'Doesn't it look lovely, Dad?' Charlie looked at the table as if seeing it for the first time and muttered something unintelligible while Mrs Kennedy went straight to her chair at the side of the fire.

'I've been stuck in the shop having to do the evening papers on my own. We don't all have the luxury of swanning off for the afternoon.' She pursed her lips and looked pointedly at Rita.

Rita chose to ignore this dig and gently ruffled her daughter's hair, accepting the understanding smile from Megan. Where would she be without her children, she wondered.

'I'll do the morning papers and Saturday's,' Rita said, determined not to have her good mood spoiled.

'What about the wedding?' Mrs Kennedy's tone was sharp, almost accusing.

'It's not until three o'clock. I'll work in the morning and Veronica will be in to do the afternoon and the evening papers.' Veronica lived next door to Vera Delaney, worked in the shop part time, and had a soft spot for Eddy Feeny.

Mrs Kennedy did not give the table a second glance, let alone comment on it, as they all sat down to eat Rita's delicious celebratory tea...

'More trifle, Charlie?' Rita lifted the heavy cutglass bowl, her mother's pride and joy, which was on loan for the occasion. 'I said to Kitty when she took round Nancy's cake—'

'I can't believe that Kitty Callaghan has been entrusted with making that wedding cake. She'll have pilfered the money for it and substituted cheap ingredients. It'll be inedible.'

Rita silently counted to ten before answering. 'Kitty made that cake out of the goodness of her heart and never expected to be paid for it. Mum only gave her some money after she'd brought the finished cake round. Kitty's a great cook, the cake will be delicious.'

Mrs Kennedy stuck her nose in the air and wrinkled it. 'That Callaghan family are a bunch of layabouts and you should have nothing to do with any of them. That father of hers practically lives in the Sailor's Rest, and as for that Danny

Callaghan, he'll get his collar felt one of these days, you mark my words.

Rita sighed. Ma Kennedy could suck the pleasure out of just about anything, but it was a special occasion so she let it go. She looked to her children and smiled. They were good kids and her love for them had kept her from walking out many a time.

'Does she have to do that?' Mrs Kennedy asked Rita, and nodded to Megan, who was scraping her bowl clean of delicious trifle. Michael, in support of his sister, it seemed, began to scrape his bowl, too. Mrs Kennedy smiled indulgently and Rita felt her good mood slipping away. It made no sense to Rita why her mother-in-law favoured her son. She had a strong hold over her own son, for some reason, but Rita did not want her to have a hold over Michael, too, nor would she be beholden to the woman who could so easily make her life miserable.

'I hope Michael will have something new to wear on Saturday. Those best trousers are way too small for him,' Mrs Kennedy said.

'There's no money spare; his best suit will have to do for a while longer, I'm afraid. I can still let the trousers down a bit.'

'There's no way you can let him go to a wedding in those!' Rita braced herself for one of her mother-in-law's rants. 'And there's no way I'm letting the street see my only grandson going round in shoddy clothes.'

Rita looked to her husband. 'I don't think we can afford to buy new clothes for the children, can we, Charlie?'

'Megan doesn't need anything new, she's going to be a bridesmaid,' interrupted Mrs Kennedy.

Was it her imagination or could Rita feel the walls of the sitting room closing in on her? The heat was stifling. Mrs Kennedy had insisted on keeping the windows shut to keep the bluebottles out but all Rita wanted to do right now was throw the windows open and take in a big gulp of air. She felt defeated.

Looking at Charlie, she said, 'There's some money put by in the Post Office. We could use some of that,' thinking it was no wonder they were taking so long to save for a deposit on a house of their own if his mother kept coming up with schemes to spend their hard-earned savings.

'I know.' Charlie's eyes were cold when he looked at Rita. 'I was just going to suggest that. I'll get it from the Post Office tomorrow.' Charlie dropped his spoon into the empty bowl. Suddenly he was not in the mood for more trifle. He was in the mood for something else. However, that *something else* would not happen under this roof. Not with his mother sleeping in the next bedroom. Anyway, Charlie thought, he was going to see that potential new client later. Her husband, in whose firm she worked, was away a lot. She made sure he did not go without womanly comforts when he went to 'collect her premium' every Thursday. She was lonely and looked forward to his visits. He was doing her a favour really.

'I have a bit of business tonight, so I'll be late.' He did not look at his wife, only to his mother, who nodded and smiled while holding her bowl out for Rita to refill.

'You have to work tonight, of all nights?' Rita protested, as her earlier anticipation vanished to be replaced with utter disappointment.

'I imagine it would be difficult to have any savings at all if you did not work so hard.'

'Nigh on impossible, Mum,' Charlie patted his mother's hand, 'and I don't know where we would be without your continuing support.'

Rita breathed a heavy sigh. It was just like Charlie to side with his mother. She couldn't remember a time when she didn't feel like an unwelcome visitor under Mrs Kennedy's roof. Charlie's father, Mr Kennedy, had died of Spanish flu when Charlie was just a child and he had never known his father. As a result he and his mother seemed joined at the hip. She wondered if the walls of the room really were closing in, or if it was just her over-active imagination.

'I'm sorry, Charlie...' Rita stretched her hand across the creaking bed and Charlie turned his back to her. They slept in the front room above the shop overlooking Empire Street, the bedroom that had once belonged to Charlie's parents, and Rita hated it. His mother slept in the next room and the walls were paper-thin.

'Maybe all this overtime you've been doing,' Rita whispered, 'will take us a step closer to having a home of our own.'

'Shut up, Rita. She will hear you!' Charlie replied through gritted teeth.

'If we had our own place...' Rita inched tentative outstretched fingertips across the mattress towards him. However, the tone of his voice stopped her short of actually touching him. She stared at his back, ramrod straight as he sat rigidly on the side of the bed. She knew Charlie had had an unsuccessful journey to his client, and was not in the mood to make love to his wife now. However, that was nothing new.

'I'm tired... It's work... The threat of war...' *You name it and I'll use it for an excuse.*

There had been a time when he couldn't wait to get Rita into bed. Normally he enjoyed a little contest to see if he could get a woman to give herself to him. He'd had his eye on Rita for a while before he'd bedded her, her flame-red hair and flashing eyes, along with her shapely figure; her rounded breasts swelling beneath her clothes. Rita was younger than him by a good few years and she'd had eyes only for that Jack Callaghan. Then when he went off to Belfast or wherever it was he'd gone Charlie had seized his chance. She'd been easier to bed than he thought and her willingness to succumb had surprised him. At the time her passion and hunger had only inflamed his desire for more. But then she told him she was pregnant and he had paid tenfold for his little weakness. Usually, once he caught what he wanted he soon lost interest. He loved the challenge, the chase. But Rita had well and truly caught him out. There was no way he could leave her in the lurch like he could the others before her. His trouble was he had broken the golden rule and brought trouble to his own doorstep. The shame would have killed his mother if their name had been muddied. So he had done the 'decent thing'. Now he couldn't bear the sight of

Rita. Sometimes his urges would get the better of him when his 'home visits' were a little quiet. Then he would take her just how he wanted her.

That new woman he was bedding near Southport had him by the balls, thought Charlie. She was playing him like a good 'un. Her husband owned a large engineering firm in Bootle and she was his accountant. With the threat of war, it should have been so easy to secure the deal. However, Mrs Smallfield was playing cat and mouse.

The thrill was certainly in the pursuit, Charlie thought, knowing he would secure the policy – a big one even by his company's standards. However, Mrs Smallfield wanted more than the promise of security for her husband's firm in time of war. The woman was insatiable. Except tonight!

Twenty bloody miles and for what? Nothing! No signature and not even the usual shag. Now Rita was coming over to him, unusually seductive. *She was the mother of his children, for Christ's sake!* Charlie shuddered. Perish the thought! It had been a long time. The last time she had been so eager Charlie reckoned he could have been anybody.

'There's nothing wrong, is there, Charlie?' Now she was using her feminine charms. He knew her game. She was broody, wanted a gang of kids, like her mother, and all live happily ever after. The thought sickened him.

'Go to sleep,' he mumbled.

'I don't know what to do about the children, Charlie.' Rita lay on her back listening to the late-night revellers coming out of the pub at the bottom of the small street. 'We had somebody

68

around earlier talking about evacuation.'

'Hardly surprising, Rita. Have you heard the news lately?'

'I want to do what's best for them, of course I do,' Rita could feel her heart breaking even now, 'but they missed you so much when you went on that business trip. I don't know what they would do if they didn't have either of us.'

'They'll be fine, Rita,' Charlie sighed. That brandy he'd had in the Sailor's Rest was beginning to take its toll and all he wanted to do was sleep now.

'I don't think I can let them go, Charlie.' Rita felt the sting of tears behind her eyes.

'You'll do as you are told,' Charlie snapped. 'It won't be safe around here and if the authorities say they have to go then they will.'

Rita flinched at his harsh words. If war did come then there would be many changes around here, and not just in this family. Plenty of marriages kept going only for the sake of the children, Rita knew, and hers was one of them.

'We could move to the countryside. It would be safe there.'

'Don't be so stupid, woman!' Charlie was lying on his back now, looking up at the ceiling, his fingers entwined on his chest as Rita listened to the mournful lament of a tugboat out on the river. It sounded exactly the way she felt. 'There's not a chance I could move out now.'

Leave your mother? Unthinkable! Rita did not voice her thoughts. Instead she lay motionless beside him, anxious and despondent. All Rita wanted was a home of their own, where they could raise the children and be normal. How had she ended up like this? In a loveless marriage to a man who preferred the company of his mother to that of his own wife.

In the strained atmosphere of the battleground their bed had become of late, Rita wondered silently if Charlie had ever loved her. How different things could have been if Jack had been her husband, as it was meant to be. Rita thought back to her earlier encounter with Jack. All Rita wanted was to be a good wife to Charlie but Jack's presence always threatened to release those pent-up feelings for him that she had tried unsuccessfully to bury. Why did you have to leave me, Jack? she asked herself for the millionth time.

Charlie always blamed her for forcing him to marry her because she was pregnant. Now Rita blamed herself too. If only she could turn back the clock. But no, she reminded herself, she loved both of her children though the circumstances of their conception were so different. Living here under this roof with Charlie and his mother was the price she must pay for her mistake. Marry in haste, repent at leisure, isn't that what they said? It was certainly true in her case. She must make the best of it and do the right thing by the children. Charlie was right on that score. It was up to a woman to make a marriage work, everyone knew that, and if hers wasn't working it was because she was doing something wrong. Rita vowed to try harder. Sometimes Charlie did want to make love to her, and then it was different, though there didn't seem to be much love involved either.

A creak on the landing had Rita turning to the

door. She knew Mrs Kennedy was not averse to holding a glass to the wall and earwigging their private conversations.

'Get some sleep. We have to be up early tomorrow,' Charlie said, his eyes closed.

'I had hoped you would have taken the night off, we could have asked your mum to mind the kids and gone to the cinema,' she couldn't help saying.

'Thursday is our busiest night,' Charlie said, listening to the drinkers calling good night and making a racket after imbibing their wives' housekeeping money. A part of him envied them their freedom; another part said, *Irish peasants! No wonder their kids have rickets and dress in rags.* Charlie did not voice his thoughts: Rita, being of Irish stock, would not take kindly to the criticism.

'There has been a lot of late-night business recently,' Rita said quietly.

'That's because there is a lot of war talk,' Charlie answered with a sneer. 'Those that won't hear of their children being evacuated are insuring them to the hilt!'

'Are they really?' Rita asked, horrified.

'Well, if anything happens, they can rest assured they'll have a few bob to spend in the alehouse to drown their sorrows.'

'Charlie! That's a terrible thing to say!' She caught sight of her tousled, fiery mane reflected in the dressing table mirror opposite and likened herself to a madwoman. Before she had fallen pregnant, Rita had been training to be a nurse and though she was young, she understood the stories that the women on the wards told each other when they thought no one was listening. About what went on in the bedroom and how husbands and wives were supposed to be with each other. Rita knew that she and Charlie weren't like other couples. Maybe he thought her unattractive. Charlie shrugged her hand off his arm and, feeling another wave of rejection, Rita moved back to her side of the bed.

Even if she could not make out his expression in the darkness, she knew from the unyielding position of his body that his countenance would be grim. He stretched a little but he did not turn towards her.

'Charlie, I...'

'Rita, how many times have I told you not to call me Charlie? You know it irritates Mother.' His voice was cold, so different from the light-hearted, almost loving way he had expressed his affection for her earlier.

Your mother might as well be here. Rita moved her hands from their temporary resting place on the candlewick counterpane, and pummelled the lumpy feather pillow in silent frustration.

'Why can't you just relax?' In the heat of the darkened room, Charlie's tone was belligerent now.

'I am relaxed.' Her body stiffened as she smoothed the freshly laundered, white cotton case over the grey striped pillow. 'It will be different when we get our own place.' She ignored the small but obvious stiffening of her husband's body.

The light of a passing vehicle heading to the docks arced across the mottled ceiling, filling the darkened room with glaring light. Then a sudden

72

knock on the bedroom door shattered the hush of the night.

'Charles! Charles! Are you awake?' Mrs Kennedy's strident enquiring would have woken the inhabitants of Ford Cemetery, Rita thought. If they had been asleep before his mother started ran-tanning on the bedroom door, they certainly would not be now!

'I can hear someone in the back yard!' Mrs Kennedy's penetrating voice was getting louder and more impatient.

Charlie raked his hands through his thinning floppy hair and plastered it back against his scalp. After sucking a long, slow breath of sultry night air through his teeth, he pulled on his dressing gown over his pyjamas. 'It'll be a cat, Mother, go back to bed.'

By the landing light, entering through the small window above the bedroom door, Rita could see a rivulet of perspiration trickle down his neck and knew he would never do something as outrageous as sleep naked beside her.

Another impatient knock rattled the bedroom door and Rita pulled the covers up to her chin, worried now that her mother-in-law was going to barge right in.

'What if it isn't a cat, Charles?' Mrs Kennedy persisted through the closed bedroom door. Rita knew he would go and see what was wrong; he was unable to say no to his mother.

'I'll see to it now,' he said wearily, and for a moment Rita felt quite sorry for him.

'Shall I wait for you to come back?' she asked, feeling her gritty lids scratch her eyes every time

73

she blinked. The busy day had caught up with her now. However, if Charlie wanted her to stay awake and wait for him, she would ignore the fact that she had been up since five this morning for the paper delivery.

Stealing a furtive glance at the luminous hands of the round-faced alarm clock, Rita could clearly see the glowing fingers had gone way past midnight.

'There is no point in both of us being awake.' Charlie's answer was brusque, his back towards her.

He did not turn round when Rita said tentatively, 'We wouldn't be disturbed if we had our own place, Charlie.'

'Enough, woman!' he snapped, and she flinched at the ice in his voice. 'I won't be long.' He sounded preoccupied, as if talking to a stranger. 'Just go to sleep.' Charlie's voice was sharp. Final. It brooked no inducement to further intimacy, and Rita experienced that awful stomach-churning emotion that always seemed to accompany their bedtimes. She quickly fastened the buttons on her nightdress, pulling it down over her hunched knees.

'Good night then, Charlie,' she whispered, trying to retain a small crumb of dignity. However, he did not reply as the bedroom door closed firmly behind him. Turning towards the fireplace wall, Rita wept silent tears as she wondered if there was anything she could do to make their marriage happier.

'*Just go to sleep.*' He had never been one to raise his voice, as that would show he had feelings he could not control. Control meant everything, and Rita knew he simmered constantly. His resentment bubbled away but never erupted into a full-scale shouting match, like some of the people around here. Passionate people, who got things off their chests, and got on with their lives. They did not harbour grudges and resentments. They certainly did not feel sorry for themselves.

As her mind drifted back and forth, sleep eluded her. She wanted to do something out of the ordinary... Make love in a huge verdant field, sandwiched between the earth and sky, feel the scratch of sand on her back, or wallow in the crash of waves. She wanted to...

Oh, what is the use of having those feelings now? Rita silently raged, throwing herself onto her stomach. Nothing would come of it. How she yearned for strong arms to hold her and to hear soft words whispered in her hair. She was only twenty-four yet she felt as undesirable as a dried-up shell of a woman. Rita knew that she could make Charlie happy if only he would allow it. But she must try harder to stop thinking about Jack.

'Ta, love,' Rita said without lifting her head, as the flat-capped dockworker handed her the coins for his *Daily Mirror*. Quickly she continued on to the next customer impatiently waiting to be served.

'I see all the lights are on at number four.' Mrs Kennedy was looking out of the wide shop window and doing not much else.

'It's not unusual for the light to be on in Mrs Faraday's parlour this early,' Rita answered, serving the morning papers two at a time now, knowing the dockers were eager to be on their way.

'She's always pottering about at odd hours.'

'But isn't it strange that she should have every light on, upstairs as well as down?'

'I don't know.' Rita nodded her thanks to another customer. 'I haven't got time to stand around and ponder.' Last night's interruptions had left her feeling unsettled. Charlie had not looked worried by what had indeed turned out to be an intruder. In fact, thought Rita, when she looked out of the window some time later he and the intruder looked quite friendly, laughing as he passed something to Charlie. However, having overslept, neither she nor Charlie had time to discuss it this morning. Rita was getting through the customers in record time. She had been serving them so long she knew by heart what they wanted, which was just as well with Madam Kennedy too busy gawping out of the window to help her.

The men were all racing to get into the queue for work on the dock, situated at the bottom of Empire Street. There were always more men than there was work for them. Like cattle, they would be wedged into the shed-like building, known as the Pen, hoping to be hired for the day. If they were not lucky they would be back in the afternoon to go through the process all over again.

Empire Street's three-up, three-down terraced houses were the last in a long line of streets leading down to the dock road. The air smelled of soot even in summer, mingled with the odours of imported Canadian lumber from the nearby dock and timber yards, petroleum products, heavy horses, and foodstuffs from countries all over the globe. The River Mersey was the gateway to the world. From the shop Rita could hear the derricks and cranes that swung over ships and the heads of men who toiled for a pittance, loading and unloading the vessels of every shape and size.

As she worked she could hear the sounds of ships coming in and going out again, of tugs blowing on the river, while disinterested gulls screamed disdainfully overhead, swooping for any bits of food they could get. The sound Rita loved best of all was the clip-clop of hoofs on cobbles as huge, heavily laden carts were pulled by powerful horses over the uneven setts between the castellated walls along the dock road. Pop was a carter and this was the sound she had grown up listening out for.

Rita, rushed off her feet with trying to get everybody served and out of the shop as quickly as possible, could see that her mother-in-law was doing nothing to help, and nor was she looking after her children. The thought of her children now tore at Rita's heart.

If war was imminent, and the children were to be evacuated, away from their mother for the first time, should she not be spending every possible precious moment with them?

'Next!' she called, not raising her head, already folding the morning paper while reaching for Old Holborn tobacco.

'D'ya think Chamberlain has saved the day?' Pop said, hurrying into the shop.

'I'll tell you what, Pop,' said one of the dockers. 'I would not trust that Hitler any more than I'd trust my missus to open me wage packet.'

'Put that on my slate, girl,' Pop said, picking up the *Daily Post* as he hurried towards the shop door.

Rita's eyes rolled to the cracked white ceiling, from which hung naked electric light bulbs on twisted cables, when she heard her father's ready laughter dissolving into the warm summer air as he hurried out to his team of two huge Clydesdale horses waiting patiently outside.

'You haven't got a slate!' Rita called to his disappearing back, knowing her mother would have an apoplectic fit if she ever thought her husband was getting credit from her nemesis, Mrs Kennedy.

'Good luck in the Pen, love, hope you get a start today...' Rita said as the fingers of the clock stole around to five to seven. She watched the blue-grey cloud of tobacco smoke rise from the departing dockworkers like steam from restless horses as the air resonated with the beat of steel toe-capped boots. Preparations for war, a subject never far from the lips of every hard-working customer lately, were all around them now, with brick shelters built in the middle of streets. Gladstone Dock was a base for transatlantic escort ships and minesweepers, which were now gathering, and Rita heard men talking of an anti-U-boat fleet based here, too.

Whatever would become of them all? Few families around here harboured romantic ideas of the sea, surviving unquestioningly by their wits. They were resilient because they had to be. Rita was proud to be among these people, with large, loving, exuberant families, with ties that were strong. They could rely on good neighbours and sometimes the Church. Being tough was not only a way of life but also an obligation. To care for their neighbours came as naturally as breathing. She knew instinctively how important this would be if war came.

'It says here Mr Chamberlain's gone to America today,' a man waiting his turn said.

'Good on him,' said the impatient docker ahead of him. 'D'you think 'e'll bring a few jobs back for us?'

'Good morning, Rita.' Jack Callaghan, head and shoulders taller than the last man to leave the shop, smiled at Rita as he neared the counter. Jack did not have to stand in line in the Pen like the others. His time in Belfast meant that as a shipwright he was highly qualified and his job was full time.

'Morning, Jack. Tell your Kitty I'm ready to slice the ham when she wants to bring it over.' Rita was determined that she would remain in control of herself around Jack. It was time she grew up and stopped dwelling on the past. Her life was with Charlie now.

'Will do, Rita,' Jack smiled. He knew that Rita had a new life now and despite Charlie being a wrong 'un – Jack was no stool pigeon, but he would love to tell Rita the things he had heard about Charlie Kennedy... If Kennedy ever hurt her, Jack thought, as he picked up his usual packet of Woodbines with his morning paper, he would hunt him down like the cheating dog he was.

'Can I get you anything else, Jack?' Rita's hand brushed his as she gave him change. Jack smiled and, looking into her eyes, he shook his head. It was nothing, Rita thought. She had touched many gnarled and calloused hands this morning.

However, none of them left the tingling fingertip sensation that Jack Callaghan's did.

'Our Frank's home, Jack!' Dolly called as she passed the shop doorway. 'I'm just on my way to the butcher's to get some nice steaks. Oh, I'm so glad he made it home in time for the wedding.'

'Glad to hear it, too,' said Jack. 'Tell him I'll be over at dinnertime after my shift.'

Dolly nodded. Frank and Jack had been lifelong friends so she ventured into the shop and said in a low whisper, 'He told us last night he could be called back to sea at any time. I'm beside myself with worry...'

'He'll be fine, Dolly,' said Jack as he walked towards the shop door. 'Only the good die young.'

'Oh, go on,' cried Dolly theatrically. 'You'll be worrying the guts out of me.'

Rita knew her mam was thrilled to have her sons home together but also worried at what was ahead of them, and Rita could only imagine what she was going through.

Jack laughed and said in an upbeat voice that made them feel a bit better, 'Tell the boys I'll be in the Sailor's Rest after tea. We'll give Sid a good send-off on his last night of freedom.'

'Boys, indeed!' Dolly said, laughing as her attention wandered to Mrs Kennedy, who was leaning on the counter reading a magazine. 'Does she ever do any work?'

Rita laughed, too, knowing that standing idle was anathema to her mother.

'Shh, Mam, she'll hear you.' Rita straightened the remains of the morning papers.

80

'Can I get you anything in the butcher's?' Dolly could not let go of the motherly reins completely.

'We're having fish, *because it's Friday*,' Rita said pointedly, and her mam gasped with shock. Catholics did not eat meat on a Friday.

'Oh, Rita, why did you have to go and remind me? My head's all over the place with this wedding.' Dolly gave a disappointed sigh. 'I was looking forward to a nice bit of steak, too. Now I'll have to have finny haddock.'

'And Dad?' Rita asked as Mrs Kennedy gave a disdainful sniff at the interruption and took her magazine to the private sitting room on the other side of the adjoining shop wall.

Dolly waited until the woman, not much older than herself, climbed the three wooden steps with exaggerated difficulty and closed the connecting door behind her. 'Given that he's got an elasticated conscience, he'll still have the steak but pretend it's Thursday.'

'You'd better hope Father Harding doesn't decide to visit,' Rita grinned.

'Your father will do his usual disappearing act out the back door as the priest walks in the front,' Dolly answered, 'and he'll take his steak with him. Oh, well, fishmonger's, here I come.'

'Ta-ra, Mam,' Rita called, watching through the large glass window as her mother scurried away. With so much going on, Rita did not have the heart to heap any more worry onto her mother's shoulders so she kept her worries about the children being evacuated to herself.

There was just one possible bright star on the horizon, however. Rita knew Dolly would be

81

thrilled if she took up her nursing career again, and maybe – just maybe – that could happen. It was too early to say anything yet but Rita hugged to herself the knowledge of her application for a nursing job. War was looking increasingly likely and, as she'd already had some training, she felt it would be her duty to do what she could. In fact, she would relish the opportunity. If war did break out it would give her a chance to get out of here.

Later, Sarah nipped into the shop and asked Rita if she would go next door and have a look at Mam's new suit. 'She thinks it's too young for her.'

Rita was keen to see it. The kids were having the tea she had made earlier and Mrs Kennedy was resting her imaginary bad leg – again.

'Mrs Kennedy, can you keep an eye on Charlie's dinner; I just have to go into me mam's for five minutes?' Rita put her husband's dinner of mashed potatoes, cheese pie and peas onto a pan of gently simmering water and put another plate over it to keep it hot.

'I'll look after it, Rita,' Mrs Kennedy said as Rita left for her mother's house, reasoning that Mrs Kennedy was helpful when she put her mind to it. Rita wished her good moods were a bit more frequent, that's all. If her mother-in-law was as easy-going in front of Charlie, he might be able to relax more.

CHAPTER FOUR

'Gloria!' Nancy Feeny's hereditary titian-coloured curls bounced in the afternoon sunshine as she hurried down the street in white, peep-toe wedge-heeled sandals. They would certainly have got her into trouble with her supervisor in the exclusive George Henry Lee haberdashery department if she wore them for work. However, she was not working today because of the imminent wedding and was just setting off to go into town.

Nancy was sure Gloria had heard her and she waved to her best friend. Gloria had obviously not been in work, and by the look of her evening gown and swish jacket, she had not even been home last night. Detecting a whiff of gossip in the hot afternoon air, especially if that notoriously nosy Vera Delaney saw Gloria, Nancy hurried over. For a moment, she felt a pang of envy at her friend's freedom to do as she pleased.

Nancy admired the blush-coloured square-shouldered 'swing' jacket, lavishly embellished around the neck with diamanté, that swayed around Gloria's slim hips, a gorgeous contrast to the navy-blue skirt and cardigan, teamed with a plain white blouse that they were obliged to wear to serve behind the elegant counters at George Henry Lee.

'I'm just going into town if you fancy coming with me?'

83

'Shh!' Gloria put her finger to her lips and pointed to the open upstairs window at the Sailor's Rest. Already undoing the jacket, she beckoned Nancy to follow as she headed towards the side door of the public house, where her father had been the proprietor for the last twenty years. 'I'll have to change out of these first.'

'You have been out all night, haven't you?' An incredulous laugh laced Nancy's words. 'You dirty stop-out... Tell me everything!' Gloria's silky blonde shoulder-length hair, which framed her flawless features in a becoming Jean Harlow style, still looked as immaculate as always.

Nancy wished her own despised auburn waves were as gorgeous, and hoped Gloria, her lifelong friend and chief bridesmaid, would not steal her limelight tomorrow. With an inimitable giggle in her voice and a natural wiggle in her hips, Gloria was never short of male attention. Men said they wanted to protect her, although Nancy could not think why, given that Gloria, brought up over a pub, could take care of herself very well.

'I miss us going out together,' Nancy said wistfully. Sid was the jealous kind. He did not like Nancy and Gloria spending their evenings together. Gloria liked to go to late-night jazz clubs in town, which was harmless fun really. She just enjoyed singing, and she had a smashing voice. Nancy was flattered Sid loved her so much he wanted to be with her every night he was not working shifts on the docks, and he had made it clear Nancy was not to go dancing without him. She could see Sid's point of view, too. What kind of a husband let his wife run around town at all hours of the night? Not that she ever would now. Not in her condition.

He did not mind Nancy going to see Gloria when he was having a pint in the pub, though. Gloria lived upstairs, and lately they would spend the evening going over the wedding preparations and listening to the wireless.

'Did you see Sid last night?' Gloria asked, her tone unusually abrupt.

Nancy's eyebrows puckered. 'No, he's working nights on the dock.'

'Oh, is that what he told you?'

'What's that supposed to mean?' Nancy asked. It was not like Gloria to be sarcastic or even annoyed usually. They could tell each other anything. Except... Nancy placed an almost protective hand on her abdomen...

She and Sid had decided that they would keep the news of her pregnancy to themselves. Nancy knew how people talked and he'd asked her to marry him ages ago. There was no point in filling people's mouths with gossip when they were already getting married.

'I couldn't have a man telling me what to do,' Gloria answered. 'You want to put your foot down and tell him it's not the Victorian days and he doesn't own you.'

'He doesn't tell me what to do ... well, not always.' Nancy was confused. She knew there was no love lost between Gloria and Sid. Gloria thought he was overbearing and domineering, telling Nancy what she could and could not do, and Sid thought Gloria was fast and heading for trouble in a big way. But this display of waspish criticism was surely due to her best friend being jealous. After all, who would have thought Nancy would be the first to get married? She remembered the night of Sid's proposal vividly.

Nancy told Sid she was staying in and washing her hair because he was doing night work on the docks when, in truth, she and Gloria had made plans to go to the local church dance. They had spent all their dinnertime discussing what they would wear. Getting dressed up was half the fun. Nancy favoured the Rita Hayworth look and Gloria was the image of Jean Harlow.

Nancy remembered she had just finished waltzing with Stan Hathaway from Accounts when she caught sight of Sid standing at the church door. She was rooted to the spot. Sid glared over to where she was, still in Stan Hathaway's arms. He had always had his eye for her and said so as they danced... Poor Stan, thought Gloria. He'd have to be prepared for fisticuffs if Sid got angry. She watched as Sid separated the dancers like Moses parting the Red Sea. Everybody knew how possessive he could be.

They were waiting for him to drag her out of that hall like some kind of Neanderthal. Nobody was more surprised than she was when he just took her hand and they walked silently out of the dance hall together. The next day she was still in raptures over Sid's gentlemanly conduct, slipping his arm around her waist like that and walking her home. Then Gloria spoiled it all by saying, 'Stan was bigger than him, though, let's be honest.'

However, Nancy soon wiped the smile from Gloria's face when she told her that Sid had asked her to marry him, adding that he'd told her he wasn't letting her get away that easily.

Now, though, Gloria was being all tetchy and disagreeable, and Nancy did not have a clue why. Gloria snatched a sudden intake of breath as if she were about to say something else. Then she stopped. Nancy realised that it was going to be hard for her best friend to give up their time together. Nancy would go her own married way; her life would change as she made a home and a new family with Sid, and poor Gloria would be left all on her own... It was understandable that her best friend felt no longer wanted; like a once-favourite cardigan that was no longer of any use.

'We'll have great memories of the good times, Glor. And we can still always go to the pictures during the week,' Nancy said, trying to cheer her up.

'Ah, thanks for that, Nance,' Gloria said sardonically. 'I'll look forward to it.' She knew that Sid wouldn't let Nancy move before they were wed, so there was little chance afterwards.

'Don't be like that, Glor,' Nancy said, smoothing her straight dark skirt, which fitted more snugly than it had last month. There wasn't much she could do about it now, was there?

Gloria looked at her best friend Nancy had a total blind spot to Sid Kerrigan's domineering ways and she could not understand why. Surely, she could not love such an uncouth and shady man. Nancy had been brought up in a decent family who went to church and grafted hard even when work was scarce.

'He doesn't like me going to dances and being

eyed up by other men.'

'Maybe he knows his own tricks best,' Gloria said, then put her hand to her lips, immediately regretting her slip of the tongue. It was one thing knowing Nancy was too good for Sid Kerrigan, caught up in the seedy criminal underworld she knew nothing about, but quite another to enlighten her about it on the eve of her wedding.

If only I had known sooner, Gloria thought. Sid had been having a fine old time last night in the Adelphi Hotel. Gloria recognised his lady friend, whose brother'd connections in late-night drinking clubs, and he was not keen on shifty characters seducing his sister. Gloria knew Sid was playing with fire. But what could she do about it now?

It was too late to say anything, surely. Nancy was besotted with Sid.

'Sid's very good to me. He's out looking for a house for us as we speak.'

No doubt, it would be some run-down rooms in a dilapidated old house barely fit for pigs to live in, convenient for Sid to make a few bob on the side smuggling contraband off the dock and selling it cheaply around the area. What the hell had her best friend let herself in for? Gloria was so angry she could scream!

There was one thing Gloria was certain of: the man she married would have to be very special. Her man would have money, status, and would wine and dine her in style at exclusive restaurants and... Until last night she had drawn the line at meeting in hotels.

'So, what kept you out until now?' Nancy asked, eager for details.

'I can't talk here,' Gloria took Nancy's arm, 'and ... if by any strange chance my mother asks where I was ... I slept in yours last night.'

'She's bound to have talked to my mam today already,' Nancy said.

Gloria shook her head. 'My mother seldom asks questions, especially about me.'

'You are so lucky, Glor.' Nancy linked Gloria's arm. 'My mam knows what we're doing before we even think about doing it.'

'It must be nice to have a mother who cares.' Gloria opened the side door, then, popping her head inside the passageway, she listened before leading the way up the narrow staircase.

'I'll get changed and come with you into town.'

'Well, you've got to give me every last detail.' Nancy followed in eager anticipation of a good old jangle, hurrying up the sumptuously carpeted stairs leading to the Ardens' private quarters.

Pop and his sons made themselves scarce and, disappearing into the Sailor's Rest, let the women do what they had to do the night before a wedding. Both his sons being home at the same time was a rarity these days, and Pop was in his element. Looking after them gave his lovely wife, Dolly, something to keep her mind occupied other than on what he was doing, for a change.

It was a great relief to know he could go about his ARP training without Dolly wanting to know the ins and outs of it all. Not that any of them would have her any other way; his Doll was the mainstay of the family, and he did not know where he would be without her.

Having the boys home made for lively discussions around the tea table. He smiled recalling the way each tried to outdo the other with his naval stories. He loved every minute of it. He had hoped they would take up the cartage line of work like him, get their own team of horses and be out delivering goods from one end of the docks to the other. Pop had a roving soul and loved the open road, but the rolling seas called his sons like many who lived in and around the docks and they were quick to answer. Frank had joined the Royal Navy three years ago, and Eddy had joined the Merchant Navy not long after. Both were proud they had salt water running through their veins and would not give it up for anything.

Outside the Sailor's Rest the cobbles rang with children's voices as they skipped in a rolling rope.

Under the spreading chestnut tree,
Neville Chamberlain said to me:
'If you want your gas mask free,
Join the blinking ARP.'

A young girl was sitting on a looped rope lashed and knotted to the outstretched arms of the gas lamp while her friends swung her around it. A ship's horn could be heard on the Mersey.

Pop, trying to push the anxious worry about what the war held for his family to the back of his mind, had thrown the singing children a few coppers as he passed. They scrambled in the dusty gutter, where a thrupenny bit landed on one of its twelve flat sides. Pop knew his wife hated the thought of another war, especially now her sons would both be in the front line. 'But, Pop, it's only been twenty-one years since the last war,' Dolly had cried – as if that would prevent another one. Pop took a sip of his pint while his sons caught up with old pals... What had the world learned in the last twenty-one years? Here they were, on the brink of war again. Pop had seen many terrible things in the Great War and it made his blood run cold to think that his sons would do the same. But Pop knew that his boys would stand up to Hitler, no matter what.

'Don't fret about it now, Doll,' he had said. Dolly was a strong, dignified woman, but first and foremost she was a mother. Fretting over her offspring came as naturally as breathing. 'You've got a wedding to think about.' If Dolly knew he had been humping corrugated cardboard, flat-packed coffins into the local swimming baths in Balliol Road all day she would have had a fit and refused to speak to him. However, the authorities had ordered them in case of war, and someone had to shift them...

Pop glanced at the huge round clock over the bar and wondered if Sid would get here before closing time.

Enjoying his rare night out with Frank and Eddy, Pop joined in the singing while Frank played the old upright piano. By nine o'clock, the whole pub seemed to be full of voices all happy to throw their opinions into the ring. They were all listening with interest to war stories from veterans of the last lot. By nine thirty, his sons were talking as if they would guide the British fleet to victory all by themselves, if need be. However, Pop laughed when he thought of thick heads in the morning, because tonight the only thing they were sinking was their beer.

'Here, where's the bridegroom got to?' Eddy asked when he saw Pop looking at the time again.

'This is a fine carry-on,' said Frank, 'a stag do and no stag.' The die-hard regulars standing at the bar joined in Frank's cheery banter.

'Well,' said one 'who wants to spend their last night of freedom with their future *outlaws?*'

'Don't you let my Dolly hear you talking like that, Fred,' Pop replied. 'We only got out of the house on the promise of looking after Sid...' Pop, with theatrical exaggeration, looked right and left before he spoke again. 'If she finds out he's not turned up, she'll be in here, evacuate the lot of us and have us making fairy cakes.' The bar erupted with good-natured laughter and before long Frank started a medley of sea shanties.

Much to Eddy's delight, Gloria came into the pub and silently beckoned him to the end of the bar. She was looking particularly fetching in a pale cream dress with puffed sleeves and a sweetheart neckline, and with her hair swept up in those fabulous Betty Grable curls, she looked very sophisticated.

'Hello, gorgeous,' Eddy said, giving Gloria a huge sloppy kiss on the cheek. They hugged and passed the usual pleasantries. *How long are you home? Are you courting yet? Do you fancy going to the pictures sometime?* Gloria saw the Feeny boys as welcome extensions of her own family, the brothers she did not have, especially Eddy, who always took the mick and made her laugh. But the boy next door wasn't for Gloria, she had other ideas about the sort of man who would be worthy of her.

'Eddy, listen to me,' Gloria said as he started to hum along to the piano. 'Eddy? Eddy, are you listening?' She turned his face towards her and could see by the silly grin and half-closed eyes that he was already half-cut. Eddy nodded like an adoring two-year-old.

'It's about Sid.' Gloria voice was urgently solemn now and she saw his expression change. His brow pleated and his head went up.

'What about him?' Eddy asked, alert now.

Gloria leaned over and whispered in his ear. Concentrating hard, Eddy felt his head begin to clear.

'Frank,' he said in a low voice, summoning his brother with a slight nod of his head. Frank dutifully left the piano and joined Eddy at the end of the bar.

'What's the matter?' Frank asked. Able to take his ale better than his younger brother, he was listening intently.

Eddy wagged a finger in front of his nose and said in a low voice, 'I don't want Pop to hear this, but we've to go on a mission.'

'A mission? Where to?' Frank asked. 'And why don't you want Pop to hear?'

'First things first,' Eddy answered, putting his full pint of best bitter on the bar. 'We are going to the Adelphi Hotel.'

'What? Now?' Frank asked, puzzled, and Eddy nodded. 'It's a bit late to be going into town; Ma will have our guts for violin strings if we get up to mischief and spoil the wedding.'

'She'll do more than that if she ever finds out what I've just heard.'

'Oh, aye,' said Frank, suddenly interested, 'and what was that?'

'I'll tell you outside,' Eddy offered, before letting Pop know he would see him back at the house later.

'Sailors, hey?' Pop's laughter was drowned out by the cheers of the other men at the bar, all of whom had been away to sea at one time or another. 'You can't keep good men down.'

'Thanks, Glor.' Eddy gave her a peck on the cheek, quickly followed by Frank, who did not want to miss a female hug. A cheer went up as the two brothers left the pub.

'So, what's the mystery?' Frank asked, hands in pockets, as they ambled across to the dock road. A striking pair of handsome sailors, the same height, weight and jovial manner.

'I think Sid might be in a bit of bother,' Eddy said in a low voice as they crossed over towards Seaforth and the terminus of the overhead railway. 'He certainly will be if we don't go and fetch him.'

'What kind of bother?' Frank felt his heartbeat quicken. He never went looking for trouble but if it came to visit, he was always ready.

'Gloria saw him in the Adelphi Hotel last night and again tonight. And he was not on his own.' Eddy filled Frank in on the details Gloria had told him about Sid enjoying the company of a woman whose brother, infamously, was not averse to the use of violence.

'I'm more Queensberry rules than the rough

stuff,' said Frank, who knew how to handle himself if need be. Coming from a neighbourhood where being tough was a state of mind, as well as body, you had to learn very quickly.

'And what about Gloria?' he asked. 'How come she was in the Adelphi?'

'She's a singer, is Glor,' said Eddy. 'Didn't you know? Nancy told me that she's got a regular spot at the Adelphi. She's going places, that girl.'

'Have you gone a bit soft on her?' asked Frank, nudging his brother playfully in the ribs.

'Who wouldn't be? That figure, those hips! She drives men wild.'

Frank was amused by his brother's glowing assessment of Gloria. The drink had clearly loosened his tongue.

'But I'm not daft, Frank. She'd no more look at me than she would a scrape of mud on one of her shoes. I'm not in her league.'

Frank clapped his brother on the shoulder. 'Who dares wins, Edward, who dares wins...'

The dance floor at the Adelphi was heaving with couples entwined in the last waltz of the evening. Soldiers, sailors and airmen were taking a chance to enjoy the tranquil ambience, the good music and fine wine before they were to be shipped off at a moment's notice to God knew where.

It took only a moment before the Feeny brothers caught sight of Sid Kerrigan swishing around the polished floor like Fred Astaire, obviously enjoying himself. Perhaps a little too much. They both recognised his dance partner immediately and they were shocked to see Queenie Calendar, sister of the infamous gang leader Harry Calendar, hanging around Sid's neck like a barnacle. Sid appeared to be whispering sweet nothings into her ear and she was lapping up every minute. They certainly looked like more than dance partners. Before Sid was aware of it, a handsome sailor had whisked his ravishing partner away and was twirling her around the dance floor himself.

'Oy, this ain't a gentlemen's-excuse-me,' Sid protested. Then he noticed who it was leading him off the dance floor and he gave a sickly grin. 'Oh, hello, Eddy, me old cock sparrow, where did you come from?'

'We just thought we'd escort you home, Sid,' Eddy offered with a tight smile. 'A nice fish supper and an early night would do you the world of good, don't you think?' Sid looked flummoxed but nodded all the same.

Just then, Queenie, who had extricated herself from Frank, came up to Sid, and with her hands on her hips said, 'What happened to my dance?' Queenie was all woman, with large breasts and hips that strained against her tight-fitting dress, and a mop of dark brown curls that she had pinned up in the latest style.

'I'm just having a chat with some old friends, Queenie,' said Sid, ushering her away, his face flushing as he tugged nervously at his necktie, which suddenly felt too tight.

He turned back to the Feeny brothers. 'Yes, a nice fish supper, that's just what I was saying to that nice lady over there,' Sid recovered himself quickly, 'before she dragged me up to dance. I don't have a clue who she is. Never seen her before in my life.'

'Is that right, Sid?' Eddy, level-headed now, was in no mood for excuses. He had left a full pint on the bar at the Sailor's and was not pleased about it one bit. However, his sister's good name was at stake and it was his job to make sure that Sid did nothing to embarrass her in any way.

'And your white lies are turning darker by the minute, me old mucker,' Frank advised Sid. He went on to inform his future brother-in-law about the danger of plank walking over the River Mersey. '...A man might miss his wedding day and that would never do. We have to think of the poor bride in all of this.'

'I agree wholeheartedly!' Sid nodded as the music finished. A polite round of applause filled the air, preventing any further communication as he left the dance floor.

'I am so glad you agree, Sid,' said Eddy, 'because we are taking you back to your digs now. And just in case you sleep in, our Frank is going to stay with you tonight, because that's what a best man does: he looks after the groom and makes sure the bride has a happy day.'

'There won't be any need for you to stay, Frank,' Sid began. 'I have an alarm clock and–'

'I don't mind, Sid,' Frank insisted. 'I wouldn't want you to miss your wedding day because you'd ended up on the wrong end of someone's fist.'

'I get your drift,' Sid replied uncertainly as they made their way on foot along the dock road, having stopped by the chippy for their supper.

'Have you ever seen a bloated body that's been in the water too long, Sid?' Frank asked conversationally. 'One that's been washed up many miles from where it started?' He was enjoying his future brother-in-law's discomfort. Serves him right, he thought. 'A body becomes so grey it's barely recognisable, and hardly ever reunited with its grieving family.'

'Such a shame,' said Eddy, tucking into his cod and chips out of a newspaper.

'A terrible shame,' Frank added, offering Sid half his fish. Sid shook his head. He was in no mood for a fish supper now. 'Aye,' Frank continued, 'we've seen many a good man driven to tears at the loss of his bachelor freedom. But a promise is a promise, don't you agree, Sid?' Frank smiled at his future brother-in-law, who quickly nodded.

'Our Nancy's good name means everything to the family, don't you agree?'

'Certainly,' Sid replied.

'And the life of luxury in the arms of a rich woman would never have suited you, Sid.'

'I do believe you are right, Frank,' said Eddy as they ambled along the dock road whistling a happy tune.

CHAPTER FIVE

Nancy went over to close the window in the parlour. The weather had been very hot of late although an earlier thunderstorm had cooled the air down a little. She hoped that the sun would shine tomorrow and that they had seen the last of the rain for now. The summer had been glorious, and Nancy, choosing to wear white satin shoes with her wedding dress, had not envisaged rain. She felt the electric zing of excitement shoot through her each time she thought of her wedding day. She was in a constant state of anticipation and delight. In a few short hours Pop would walk her up the aisle to Sid and happy-ever-after.

A small breeze made her shiver slightly. The sash window was open just enough to allow a gentle breeze to ripple the new curtains Mam had made on her treadle sewing machine.

Mam and Sarah had gone to bed already and the others would be home any minute. She could hear Pop's deep resonating voice in the distance, a little louder now after a few pints. It was funny how sound carried at night, Nancy thought as she smoothed an imaginary crease from the immaculate, virginal white tablecloth. She could feel the heat flood her face; it was a good thing she was getting married tomorrow. Any later and her pregnancy would start to show. This way she could hold her head up and say her 'honeymoon' baby was six weeks early.

Stepping back, she admired the room her father had decorated so well. Pop, Frank and Eddy had been to the church hall earlier in the day to pick up the borrowed tables, now set in a T shape and running the length of the parlour. Nancy could hear their voices growing louder, heralding their approach. All she had to do was close the parlour window and make haste upstairs; otherwise, she would be lumbered with making tea and a bit of supper for them all.

'She's not to know a thing about this, ever!' Pop sounded worried. 'This is never to be discussed again after tonight, d'you hear me?'

Nancy listened more attentively now. What was it that Mam should never know? She smiled: Pop said he never kept secrets from Mam, he just reasoned that it was wiser not to tell her certain things... Like his activities as a member of the Air Raid Precautions, handing out gas masks at the local school hall. She would only worry, he'd said, and worry did not sit well with Mam, Nancy knew. However, the next words stopped Nancy in her tracks and stilled her hand from pushing back the curtains to close the window.

'Young Sid made a mistake. You and Frank have showed him the error of his ways and let that be an end to it.'

What did Pop mean? What mistake had Sid made? Had he told them about the baby? Oh, she would be mortified if he had! She could not walk up the aisle in virginal white on Pop's arm if he knew she was already pregnant. That would make her look like a hypocrite. The thought that she was already being two-faced never occurred to Nancy. However, Pop's next announcement really took the wind out of Nancy's sails.

'Let's just hope Sid didn't give Queenie Calendar more than just a dance.'

Nancy had heard of the notorious Calendar family from Gloria. Harry Calendar was not a man to be messed about with, apparently. He ran a black market racket as well as owning a couple of nightclubs in town, and had his fingers in more pies than a cheap-rate pastry chef. What was Pop talking about? What did Sid have to do with Harry's sister?

'Oh, I could have smacked him right there on the dance floor in the middle of the Adelphi, Pop,' Eddy said, 'and I would have if our Frank hadn't persuaded me otherwise.'

Nancy was nobody's fool. It did not take her long to realise that Sid had been playing away and Eddy's next words told her that this was not the action of a bachelor on his stag night.

'Dancing a little too close, they were, and that was a good half an hour after Gloria told me.'

Gloria! What did she know about this? Sid would never do the dirty on her, would he? He didn't have time: he was either with her or he was working on the dock. When did he ever get time to go out with fancy women? Nancy dragged a chair out from under the table and slumped onto it before she fell down.

She could not catch her breath. The room was suddenly stiflingly hot. There was no air. She opened her mouth and tried to take a lungful but she couldn't. Instead, she heard a noise. It sounded like the wail of a wounded cat and it took a moment before Nancy realised it was coming from her own mouth. Nancy wished she could stop but she was helpless to control it.

'Nancy, love, what's the matter?' Mam and Sarah hurried into the parlour where Nancy was huddled over, her face in her hands, trying to block out the information she had heard earlier.

'Oh, Mam!' she whimpered, burying her face into her mother's shoulder as the floodgates opened and she began to sob.

'What's wrong, love?' Dolly was dressed in her woollen housecoat even in this heat, her hair, wound in steel curlers, covered by a thick black hairnet ready to be combed out tomorrow. Dolly shushed her middle daughter and patted her back, motioning for Sarah to put the kettle on in the kitchen. 'It's just nerves... Everything will be fine in the morning after a good night's sleep.'

'It won't, Mam,' Nancy wailed. 'Nothing will ever be all right ever again... And if Sid Kerrigan thinks I'm going to marry him now, he's got another think coming!' She told Dolly what she'd heard.

'But, Nancy, love, it's just one little incident.'

'You don't understand, Mam.' Nancy was almost hysterical now, great racking sobs escaping from her.

'Come on, Nancy, pull yourself together, it won't do to upset yourself like this, your face will be all puffed up for your wedding.'

'How could he, Mam?' Nancy wailed. 'I've given him everything – everything! And now all I've got to show for it is a swollen belly and broken promises.' Nancy let out another frantic howl.

Realisation suddenly dawned on Dolly and she put her hand to her mouth. 'Oh, Nancy, you've not got a bun in the oven?'

Nancy could only nod her head and continued crying bitterly into the hankie that her mother had proffered.

Deciding to leave Nancy with her misery for a moment, Dolly went and found Pop and they sat down to drink the pot of tea that Sarah had made, generously laced with a good splash of whiskey – for shock, said Dolly.

'She's got to go through with this wedding, Pop.' Dolly looked worried as she added another spoonful of sugar to her daughter's tea.

'We cannot make her marry him, love,' said Pop. 'She has a mind of her own and we have always brought them up to do what they think is right.'

'But, Pop, she's ... she's...' Dolly could not bring herself to say it,'... she's suffering the same complaint as our Rita did when she married Charlie Kennedy!' She heaved a pained sigh.

'Oh, bloody 'ell,' Pop said, looking shocked and reaching for the whiskey bottle. Pouring a finger's worth into a wide glass, he gulped it down in one. For a short while he was silent, as if mulling the situation over.

'What is it with young people today, Dolly? They don't seem to have the same principles as young folk in our day.'

'Nonsense,' said Dolly, pragmatically. 'Men and women have been the same since the dawn of time and there's nothing we can do about it. And you weren't such a paragon of virtue yourself, I recall.'

Pop had the good grace to look abashed. 'Well, that's as maybe. But they seemed so happy, too.' He sat at the table and took the cup and saucer his wife offered him. They were in no hurry to go back to the girls and Eddy just yet. 'But I wouldn't want Nancy to be unhappy... We made that mistake with Rita and look at her now.'

'I know,' Dolly answered, staring into space. 'I look at Rita sometimes and see the little girl I once had. When she thinks nobody is looking her smile disappears completely and that's when my heart goes out to her.'

'Do we want the same thing for Nancy?' Pop asked. 'Could you ride the storm of gossip?'

'She could always have it adopted,' Dolly said. 'Or I could rear it as my own.'

'Don't you think you're getting on a bit to be rearing more children?' Pop asked, shaking his head when Dolly raised an eyebrow and gave him one of her looks. He knew that Dolly would do whatever she had to do and to hell with the consequences. There were far worse things than unmarried mothers... There were unmarried mothers who had no family support behind them. 'You do what you think is best, love. I will be here to back you up. But I'd love to give that Sid Kerrigan a bloody good hiding.'

'I know you would, Pop,' Dolly said, her face set in determination. Life was a vicious circle and they all had to run to keep up. 'But you always do the right thing, in the end.'

Nancy lay in bed, her eyes closed as she listened to the sound of the family downstairs.

Mam was giving orders as good as any sergeant major, and the house was running like a well-oiled machine. There was a ran-tan at the front door.

'Sarah! Get that, will you?'

'I have to do everything around here,' Sarah called back. 'I was just making Pop and Eddy a bacon sarnie!'

'Just do it!' Dolly ordered; and Nancy could hear her sister's determined tread down the lobby before the front door opened.

The smell of fried bacon wafted up the stairs and turned Nancy's stomach. She then heard her mother walking down the linoleum-covered passage to the front door, she thanked somebody in a lower tone, and then the front door closed.

'Sarah! The flowers have arrived. Come and take this box from me! Oh ... there you are. Put this bouquet in a sink of water and splash some on these buttonholes; they look as if they're dying of thirst.'

'Hello, Gloria, love, come in...' Dolly's voice dipped and Nancy caught only part of it, '...you know I'm not one for taking any nonsense but our Nancy's got it into her head about Sid playing away with some fancy piece in that there Adelphi... I know it's a load of old rubbish... Can you talk some sense into her?'

'It's just last-minute nerves, Mrs Feeny,' said Gloria. 'She'll be fine.'

'I won't be fine,' Nancy's voice was low and lonely in the middle bedroom she had shared with their Sarah for the last fifteen years.

The freesias' sweet perfume, which Nancy had picked to go with the pale lemon roses, meandered up the stairs and sent her senses reeling and her stomach heaving.

I can't do this! She buried her head in the pillow. *How can I marry a man I cannot trust?* Nancy had not slept a wink all night. Opening her tear-swollen eyes as Gloria!s footsteps grew louder on the stairs, she had to blink a few times at the sunlight flooding the room. She could see her white satin wedding dress, with its leg-o'-mutton sleeves and modest V-shaped neckline, hanging on the wardrobe door. The bust and waistline were emphasised by soft shoulder gathers that tapered to the fitted waist panel. She doubted it would fit any more. So maybe it was just as well she was going to call the whole thing off.

'Cooee! I hope you are decent!' Gloria called from the landing.

'Come in, Glor,' Nancy said, lifting her head from the pillow.

'Do you know you look the colour of boiled putty?' Gloria said. 'But don't worry, we'll soon get you ready.'

'I know exactly what I look like and it's a million miles away from the blushing bride everybody is expecting.' The mirror told her she looked a fright. She was dressed in a blue flowered winceyette nightie, her auburn hair wound around strips of ripped pillowcase that her mam called 'rags' and that looked like wounded sausages.

'A sight to behold,' Gloria said. 'You look like you've slept on your face.'

'That's because I did.' The 'rags' were tied so tight they dragged the scalp off, but that wasn't the reason she tried to sleep on her face. 'I did it in the hope I would suffocate myself and not wake up today.'

'Hey...' Gloria said when she saw Nancy's tears flowing freely down her cheeks. She would let Nancy tell her about Sid in her own time. The humiliation was enough to bear without broadcasting it. 'Ahh, come here,' Gloria said, putting her arms around Nancy's shoulders. 'Don't worry, you'll look fabulous when Aunty Glor has done you up a bit.'

'I know you're trying to help, Glor, but–'

'Now come on.' Gloria sat Nancy on the bed. 'It's just nerves. Everything will be perfect, just you wait and see.'

'How can it be perfect? I don't even know if the dress will still fit me...'

'Why shouldn't it?' Gloria asked, nonplussed.

'Well, you see... I'm pregnant.'

'You're what!' Gloria felt her heart sink. 'The bloody rat-faced–'

'Come on, Gloria.' Nancy looked shocked. 'We both know it takes two.'

'Yes, of course, but...' How could she tell her friend what she had seen last night after this? She couldn't. It would break her heart. Now there was a baby to consider... Sid would have to make an honest woman of Nancy now. He had no choice. 'Has your dad got a shotgun?' Gloria tried to make light of the situation, knowing Nancy had to make the best of it now.

'No, but the ARP gave him a broom handle,' Nancy laughed, and Gloria joined in.

'It won't fit me, I know it won't,' Nancy said, taking the wedding dress off the hanger. She was not going to discuss Sid being with another woman last night. The humiliation was hard for her to bear and, from what she'd heard last night and just now, Gloria knew already. She was obviously only being kind and saving Nancy's face by not raising the subject.

'Just try it on now to make sure. It's not too late to alter it if need be. You will look fabulous,' Gloria said as Nancy eased her arms into the narrow parts of the leg-o'-mutton-style sleeves and slipped the loop onto her middle finger to keep the V-shaped sleeve hems taut.

'Those sleeves will show your wedding ring off a treat,' Gloria said, drawing attention to her friend's long elegant hands and perfectly manicured, pink-varnished nails.

'As long as it keeps everybody's attention away from the middle area of my tummy,' Nancy said.

'There's nothing to see yet,' Gloria reassured her.

'We only did it the once...' Nancy's colour rose from a pale cement to deep pink.

'It's too late to worry now,' Gloria said with the candour of one who did not shock easily. 'The stable door has been opened and the horse has definitely bolted.'

'I know,' Nancy sighed as her friend began to fasten the many tiny buttons at the back of the dress. 'It wasn't that much fun either... Glor, you're my best friend, aren't you?' Nancy said with a cautious note in her voice. 'And you must promise me that you'll tell me the truth.' She had been waiting for this day all her life and now it was here she did not want to go through with it. If there was one thing that Nancy couldn't bear it was the thought that Sid was playing away with someone else. She wanted to know the truth.

'Of course I will.' Gloria finished fastening the buttons and turned Nancy to the mirror. 'There, perfect, even better than before.' Nancy took in her reflection. She knew she looked fantastic even with a head full of rags.

'Come on, what is it?' Gloria said encouragingly.

'Did you see Sid with another woman? Has he

been messing me about, Gloria? I don't think I could bear it if it really was true.'

Gloria looked at her friend's tired and anxious face. Bloody Sid Kerrigan, she thought. This should have been the happiest day of Nancy's life. Oh, she could be silly and selfish all right and was often too caught up in herself to see the wood for the trees. Any girl with half a brain could see that Sid Kerrigan wasn't great marriage material. But what Gloria thought of Sid and his ways was neither here nor there now. Nancy was up the duff and that was that. Raising a baby without a husband wasn't an option in Empire Street with the likes of Mrs Kennedy making trouble. Nancy would just have to put a brave face on it and a little white lie would have to do the trick for now.

'From what I've seen, most men are vain and Sid's no different. If a pretty girl makes a pass at him he'll be flattered.' Gloria checked the buttons were all secured at the back of Nancy's dress. 'It was probably just a bit of fun before he got married. If Sid didn't want to marry you then he wouldn't have asked you now, would he?'

Gloria could see Nancy was softening up – she held her breath.

'Oh, I suppose you're right. It was probably him getting it out of his system,' Nancy said, patting the rags on her head. 'Anyway, thank God the dress still fits, I was just about to ask if you could help me alter the dress in case it needed it.'

'Not me, darling,' Gloria laughed. 'You know I've never held a sewing needle in my life. I wouldn't know which end to thread.' She did not intend to find out either; she had plans for her future and domesticity definitely did not come into them.

Nancy laughed. Eyeing her belly in the mirror, she thought she was bound to get away with it, it was only the tiniest of bumps. She thought about what Gloria had said. Maybe she was right and Sid was just letting off a bit of steam. He'd have his own wedding nerves too, wouldn't he? What Nancy couldn't bring herself to admit was that finding out that Sid had this other life had given her doubts. Did she really love him? Did he really love her? She sighed at her reflection. It was too late to change her mind now. Far too late. She could not bring that shame onto her mam.

'I'm going to miss going dancing,' Gloria said, helping Nancy out of the dress so she could do her hair and make-up. Having unwrapped the rags, she clipped Nancy's hair into a froth of curls on top of her head. 'But we can go to the pictures when Sid is on night shift. Surely he won't moan about that?'

'I'm sure he won't.' Nancy's voice was flat and she sounded unconvinced. She was moving into his mother's house after the wedding; she would always be able to depend on her mother-in-law to keep her company when Sid was on nights. Mr Kerrigan was a mousy little man who worked as a printer on the *Liverpool Daily Post* and was rarely seen as he was a night shift worker himself. Mrs Kerrigan seemed to be able to do exactly as she wished. Which was more than Nancy would...

'Right, before I put your make-up on, I'll go and see if your mam's marcel waves need a touch-up.' Gloria had always had the knack of styling hair, thought Nancy. It was such a shame to waste her talent. Gloria was just the right type of girl to be a successful hairdresser: glamorous, outgoing and friendly. Anyway, Gloria probably thought she was destined for greater things now that she had a singing spot at the Adelphi. She probably thought she was too good to be a hairdresser. Perhaps Sid won't mind if I go and watch Gloria now and again, Nancy wondered, and Mrs Kerrigan could mind the babe? Without realising it, Nancy touched her tummy gently.

CHAPTER SIX

'Talking of war,' Rita said, putting a plate of freshly made toast onto the table, 'there are posters going up all over Liverpool asking for nurses.'

'You're married, they won't want you,' Charlie said flatly, not looking up from his morning paper. 'They will only want young, single women.'

'They'll want as many nurses as they can get,' Rita answered.

'I hope you're not thinking of applying,' Charlie said dismissively.

Tears burned the backs of Rita's eyes. She so wanted to return to her chosen profession and had hoped that by introducing the subject casually, she could prepare Charlie to support her if her application was successful. She quickly headed out to the scullery where the kettle was boiling on the gas stove Mrs Kennedy had just had installed, and through tear-filled eyes she looked around her. Nothing in this room, in these premises, belonged to her. For seven years she had been cooking, washing and cleaning another woman's possessions. All she had to call her own were her children. When she returned to the table, they ate in silence.

Mrs Kennedy took her place at the head of the table while misery tore painfully at Rita's throat. She knew she had made the biggest mistake of her life when she married Charlie Kennedy. What chance did they ever have of making a normal life together while they were living under his mother's roof?

The only time they were ever alone was when they were in bed. Mrs Kennedy frowned upon a show of any form of intimacy or lovingness. Brought up in an era that purported that to spare the rod was to spoil the child, she ruled this place with contempt for everyone. Nothing Rita did was good enough for her.

'The children will want their breakfast,' Charlie said, still not looking at Rita. 'I'll call them.' His abrupt manner told her their conversation was at an end. He no longer wanted to discuss the matter of their marriage or their children or their life in general.

Rita, like the well-trained wife she was, collected the teapot from the table and went out into the scullery to refill it. She shouldn't still feel awkward talking to her husband about their hopes for the future in front of her mother-in-law, but she did.

There was a lot to do today. The first job after

breakfast was to go into the shop before it opened and slice that ham for Kitty. Just then, she noticed Jack Callaghan heading to his former home across the road. There was always something about the sight of him that cheered her. She remembered his offer to help her over with the ham. She could manage it herself, but there was so much to do... She hurried to open the shop door and called him over.

'Jack!'

The beaming sunshine promised another hot day. Leaning against the shop doorframe, Rita watched as Jack turned, smiling. The tall, dark and handsome man walked straight-backed towards her and a small fizz of excitement shot through her. Jack was straight-talking, worked hard to provide for his family and took no nonsense from anybody. In other words, he was everything that Charlie was not. When they were kids, Jack used to call for her elder brother, Frank. They were best friends and as they grew older she fancied Jack like mad on the quiet, never daring to imagine what it would be like if he asked her on a date. She could hardly believe it when he asked her to come to the pictures with him. That was how it started.

On their first night out she remembered the thrill of sitting so closely to him in the back of the Regent Cinema. It seemed incredible that he felt the same way about her as she did about him. They watched *The Public Enemy* with James Cagney. Rita, being only sixteen at the time was quite terrified by some of the violence and when Jack placed his arm around her protectively, she leaned into him, feeling like his arms were the place that she'd always meant to be. Rita didn't think she would ever forget that first kiss.

'Jack, will you tell Kitty I'll be over with the ham in about ten minutes? I'm late this morning, of all days.'

'Do you want me to take it?' Jack asked, and Rita sighed with relief. If Jack took the meat she could get on with serving the early customers. Then she had to bathe the children in the tin bath. Mentally she ticked off her chores before she could even think about getting ready for the wedding.

'Jack, you're a godsend. That would be a great help.' Rita stepped back inside the small vestibule leading to the shop door. 'I won't keep you long.'

'Keep me as long as you like,' Jack said, laughing, as Rita led him into the shop. She turned the key in the lock and pulled down the blind. The shop would not be open for another half-hour. 'I'd best keep out of our Kitty's road this morning; she'll be running around that kitchen like a headless chicken getting everything done.' His laugh was an attractive low rumble, which made Rita's heartbeat quicken. She felt unable to get that first kiss out of her mind today. All of this business with Charlie and his mother was unsettling her.

'I won't be a minute,' she said as she went into the little back room to fetch the joint and to take a deep breath to try to calm her racing heart. Jack Callaghan always had that effect on her. Rita tried to push unwanted thoughts from her mind. *The smell of Jack and the taste of him as his lips met hers, their bodies so close and the heat that came off him.* With Jack in the room, Rita felt that familiar thrill now.

'Shall I put the kettle on while you slice?' Jack's softly spoken words came from behind her and made Rita jump. He was one of the few men around here who was beholden to nobody. Since he had finished his training in Belfast he'd returned to finish his apprenticeship in engineering at Harland and Wolff in Bootle, working alongside other skilled working-class men, enjoying more security than the dockworkers. His job at the foundry and marine repair works had enabled him and Kitty to keep the family together and reasonably well fed. Scrupulously honest and less exuberant than his cocky younger brother, Jack liked to keep himself to himself. He had never married although many of the local girls would have given their eyeteeth to be seen on Jack's arm. Rita silently dreaded that day.

Rita and Jack were always friendly with each other but Rita knew, deep down in her heart of hearts, that there was unfinished business between them There were so many unanswered questions. It wasn't often that she allowed herself these thoughts but Nancy's wedding and the claustrophobia at home were starting to get to her. *Why didn't you answer my letter, Jack? Why...?*

Hoping to quell the hot colour she knew had flooded her face, Rita nodded before going to fetch the ham from the fridge. The room was tiny and held two people only just comfortably. It contained a two-ring gas burner connected to a rubber hose sitting on a small table. There was just one chair, the other being in the front shop, and the brass cold-water tap was opposite the door next to the refrigerator Mrs Kennedy had bought cheaply from 'someone off the docks'.

'I'll just get out of your way,' Rita said as she took the ham from the fridge, to see Jack with the kettle in his hand, ready to fill it. The space between the table and the wall was so narrow they were going to have a job getting past each other, without touching.

'Whoops!' Rita laughed self-consciously, raising her hands to make more room. *His lips on hers, their arms entwined...*

Jack's heart thundered in his chest. What a bloody fool he was! He should have waited outside until Rita had collected the joint. Jack tried to keep his distance from Rita but that was impossible given that they all lived on top of each other around here. He could still remember the shock when he came back from Belfast and found Rita married to Charlie Kennedy, with two young children. Charlie Kennedy of all people! But he could never stop loving Rita. That would be like asking the sun to stop shining. He knew Rita like the back of his hand and Jack could tell from her eyes that she wasn't happy. How could anyone be happy with Charlie Kennedy as a husband and with his battle-axe of a mother thrown in to boot? He had heard the rumours about Charlie, of the late night deals in the back alleys, swapping bets for money with the bookie's runner.

Jack could never be Rita's husband now, like he had once dreamed of being, but he vowed he would always be her friend, no matter what. *Why didn't you wait for me, Rita? Why...?*

But here they were, almost nose to nose. They hadn't been in this close proximity for many years.

Jack liked to think that he had got Rita out of his system but on days like this he knew he was kidding himself. He felt flustered in that cramped space, almost as if all of his feelings could now been seen on his face in close up. He had not deliberately set out to pin her against the wall like that.

'Sorry, Rita, I thought there was more room.' That sounded even worse! Now she was going to think he was criticising her shapely figure! He thought she had a lovely figure, although he really should not be looking. She was a married woman now.

'I should eat less pies,' Jack laughed, trying to cover up his awkwardness.

'There's nothing wrong with you, Jack, you have a fine physique.' *Shut up, Rita, you are making it worse*. She took a deep breath and hurried back to the shop.

She could not help the way she felt though she knew it was wrong. Was she mad to be thinking about Jack's kind, dark eyes, which always seemed to be on the verge of laughter? If it were true what people said about eyes being the windows to the soul then Jack must have goodness right through him.

Moments later Jack came back into the shop with two cups of tea and Rita suddenly realised that in all the years she had been with Charlie he had never once made her a cup of tea.

'Here you go, Rita,' Jack said with his usual, dazzling smile. 'No sugar for you, if I recall, because you once said you are sweet enough,' he laughed as he laid the cup on the wooden counter.

'Are you being sarky, Jack Callaghan?' Rita was glad he had said something she could react to and amazed that he remembered the time, years ago, when she had said that same thing.

'Not at all.' Jack took out his tobacco tin and papers and began to roll a cigarette for later, while his eyes travelled the line of glass jars behind the shop counter. After much pondering he said, 'I'll have two ounces of mint humbugs when you're ready, Rita.' He took a sip of the hot tea. 'Our Kitty loves a sweet when she's listening to the wireless of a night.'

'Oh, I think she'll be over at me mam's until late today.' Rita wrapped the ham in paper before taking the heavy glass jar down from the shelf and went over to the scales to weigh a handful of humbugs in the shiny metal tray.

'Aye, she is, me and our Tommy will save her a few. She needs all the energy she can get with our Tommy. He can be a right handful.'

'Kitty puts him in his place,' Rita said, twisting the triangular paper bag.

'She puts us all in our place,' Jack laughed. 'Have you seen our Kitty when she's got a cob on? Even Dad has to look out.' Aware now that Jack's eyes were focused on her own as if he could see right into the depth of her being, Rita could feel a hot flush rise to her cheeks. There was an intense tenderness in his gaze and she suddenly felt the weight of their past coming down to bear on her. Perhaps now was the time to ask him all of those questions?

Just then the deliveryman who brought the morning newspapers knocked on the shop door, breaking the spell.

The moment had passed. Rita was relieved. What possible good could it do raking over old bones?

'She has to, being one woman in a house of three men,' Rita said, keeping her voice light as she went to open the door for the deliveryman, who brought in the papers and then waited at the counter while Rita paid him from the till.

'I'd better take the *Dandy* for our Tommy,' Jack said, smiling. 'He'll be excited after the wedding, but it will help to calm him down to have a little read before he goes to bed.'

He has a good heart, Rita thought, handing Jack the weekly comic, which he wrapped inside his morning newspaper.

'I'll let you in on a secret,' Jack leaned forward, 'we all read it. Even our Danny and me dad, one after the other.' He laughed when Rita flicked him with a duster, showing perfectly straight white teeth.

'Is there anything else I can get for you, Jack?' Rita asked, knowing she had taken up a lot of his time this morning.

Suddenly his expression changed. He was quiet for a moment and then he said in a low, barely audible voice, 'I haven't told anybody yet, I only sent the letter this morning... I'm joining up.'

'Joining up?' A shard of shock pierced Rita's heart. 'What about Kitty?' She knew Jack was the only full-time breadwinner in the Callaghan household.

'Yes, the RAF. I'll make sure everybody's looked after. I'll set up an allowance in Kitty's name so she can collect it each week so Dad can't spend it all in the boozer.'

The country is on the brink of war. The words were going round and round in Rita's head so that nothing else would register. 'Why, Jack? Surely you are in a reserved occupation?' He was a good man. Decent. Not like... There was a moment's silence. There had been so much talk of war recently and everyone agreed that it was almost inevitable but it wasn't until this moment that Rita felt that it was really happening. The thought that Jack was certain to face battle was a terrible jolt. Rita felt her emotions starting to well up. First Jack and next it would be the children being sent away. It all suddenly felt horribly real. 'I'll be sorry to see you go, Jack.' Her voice was a whisper.

'Will you, Rita?' Unable to meet her eyes, he looked out of one of the large glass windows onto Empire Street. 'Better to be in the thick of it than worrying from the outside.'

'When are you going?' Rita could not hide the tremor that laced her words. Soon all of them would be going off to fight. Her brothers, Frank and Eddy, off to sea... Poor Kitty.

'You won't say anything to our Kitty, will you?' Jack asked, as if reading her thoughts. 'I haven't told her yet.'

'I wouldn't dream of saying anything. It's not my place.'

'I will tell her, but not until the last minute.' He lowered his head, looking contrite. 'I'm a bit of a coward in that respect...'

'You are not a coward,' Rita answered. 'I've never met a braver man.' She could feel the tight

120

stretch hurt her throat muscles and she swallowed hard. *Don't cry, Rita!*

'Any chance of being served here?' asked a woman from Strand Road. 'Me breakfast is going cold.'

'I'm holding you up.' Jack, not wanting his time with Rita to end, tapped the peak of his cap with the rolled-up newspaper and turned to the customer. 'Sorry about that, missus.'

He scooped up the joint and turned back to Rita with a smile. 'See you at the wedding.'

CHAPTER SEVEN

After the morning rush, Rita remembered the letter that had been delivered for her earlier and which she'd picked up discreetly and hidden in her pocket. Quickly she took it out and sliced the envelope with her thumbnail.

A small gasp escaped from her lips when she read the news that she had been waiting for for so long. She had an interview for a nursing post at the General Hospital on the dock road next week. A current of excitement shot through her. She had not expected to hear from Matron so soon. This must mean that war was nearer than anybody had thought.

Shoving the letter deep into her pocket Rita shivered. If war was so close, then that would mean the children could be sent away very soon. A leaflet distributed by the infants' school gave instructions about what would happen and why in the event of war, and Rita had already been instructed by the school to register the children for the evacuation scheme as all of the other mothers had been. Children under five must be accompanied by their mothers. Rita thought of Megan, only just five. How could such a small child be expected to manage without a mother's love? Please God let the children at least be billeted together with a kind and loving family like her own.

The wording was matter-of-fact. Mothers must try not to be emotional. The children must not be upset. It would be better if mothers said goodbye from home and did not come to see their children off. If war with Germany were declared, bombing raids were expected to begin at once. It was imperative to get the children away as quickly as possible, the leaflet said.

The whole country was preparing for war with gusto. The signs were all around: sandbags, air raid shelters, those huge silver balloons tethered to metal cables. Rita felt a fresh sting of tears behind her eyes. She had to be strong, but how on earth could she ever hide her anguish? She read the leaflet again. The Government was right. Taking the children away from the danger of the cities was the right thing to do. She just prayed to God that she would be strong enough to go through with it and not show the children that she was utterly devastated they would be going away.

Michael and Megan were her life. Everything she did, she did for them. If war broke out Rita knew she would lay down her life for her children. She would protect them any way she could ... but if they had to go through this terrible thing, why could they not go through it together?

The shop was empty now the morning rush was over. It was time for Rita to start getting the children ready for Nancy's wedding this afternoon. It was a good thing Sid was in a reserved occupation on the docks; but he was in the Territorials and some of them were being called up for more training.

At the breakfast table, Charlie's face was set into a determined scowl. His mother was already sitting in her usual chair at the head of the table. Rita noticed that she was having an animated conversation with Michael and completely ignoring Megan.

Rita gave her daughter a tight smile and, after making a fresh pot of tea, she poured out three cups. It was not right the way Charlie's mother favoured her grandson and all but ignored her granddaughter. It had always been this way. Rita knew Megan felt it keenly, as would any child, and she made a special effort to include Megan in everything, knowing that if they had a place of their own, both her children would receive equal treatment.

'When you have finished your breakfast we will take your dress into Nanny Feeny's and hang it up with Aunty Nancy's,' Rita told her daughter with a smile. Megan looked so pretty in the beautiful taffeta bridesmaid dress Nancy had chosen for her.

'Leave her be,' Charlie said, barely lifting his head from the *Daily Mirror*, and Rita could tell he was going to be awkward today, just by the

123

thrust of his jaw. He did not like family get-togethers – her family especially.

They all ate in silence. Mrs Kennedy did not like noise in the morning. Nor did she tolerate it at night. The children practically walked around on eggshells and Rita's nerves, as taut as piano wires, practically fizzed when Charlie clattered his knife and fork onto his plate.

'How is your leg today, Mrs Kennedy?' Rita asked politely. The older woman suffered terribly with an arthritic leg. It was unclear which one gave her the most gyp because she often forgot herself. However, Rita could see no evidence of arthritics when Winnie Kennedy stood talking for hours in the shop to Vera Delaney, one of her favourite customers.

'It's very swollen today.' Mrs Kennedy scraped back her chair with ease and thrust a perfectly normal leg on Megan's chair, causing the child to flinch and move over. 'Look, all around my ankle – it's practically blue with the swelling.'

'It looks fine to me,' Rita said. She gently and expertly turned the ankle one way, and Mrs Kennedy flinched dramatically, then, slowly turned it the other, while her mother-in-law yelped in pain.

'I'm so sorry,' Rita said. 'Sometimes it helps if you keep it moving.'

'How can I keep it moving when I can't even stand on it?' Mrs Kennedy cried. 'I only thank the Lord above that I have a loving family around me.' She patted Charlie's hand and he smiled.

Ah, so that is it! The penny dropped. Rita knew exactly what her mother-in-law was up to now.

'Heaven only knows how I would manage if I

did not have my precious son and my wonderful grandchildren to rely on.'

Not to mention muggins here, who fetches and carries, opens the shop at six every morning while you lie in bed, and works like a skivvy for a pittance.

'Did Charlie tell you I've been thinking about going back to nursing if there is a war?' Rita's innocently delivered remark made her mother-in-law's features pale, as Rita knew it would. The idea of Lady Muck doing much work was unthinkable. Moreover, if Rita were nursing, Mrs Kennedy would have to pay someone else to work in the shop. Her icy look told Rita her announcement was tantamount to treachery.

'Rita, you don't have to talk about that now. Can't you see Mum is in pain?' Charlie shot out of his chair and, holding his mother's leg so delicately, he lowered it back onto the floor and eased her foot into her slipper, reminding Rita of Prince Charming in *Cinderella*. However, there was nothing charming about her husband. He was worried in case his mother cut off the allowance she gave him each week, as she threatened to whenever she thought Charlie was about to exercise his own will.

His mother gave Charlie everything, Rita knew. She had spoiled him rotten since he was born. Apparently, even her husband had been surplus to requirements once Charlie was born, so besotted was she with her only offspring. Rita had realised one thing very quickly, though: Mrs Kennedy's leg got a whole lot worse every time there was even a hint of their moving to a place of their own, even though Charlie's icy blue eyes could not see it.

125

A black cloud of dread like a physical presence settled on Rita's shoulders and she knew she would have to fight hard to dispel it. Everybody had been talking about the threat of war for so long without anything happening. It was hard to believe anything *was* going to happen, despite the fact the Government had already sent out leaflets telling them about the effects of gas poisoning, not to mention light restrictions and evacuations, and delivering gas masks. However, there was one thing that kept Rita's mind focused on the positive, and that was the knowledge that Charlie could not evade his call-up. She would welcome war for that one reason. It would mean Charlie would have to do something he did not want to do. He would have to leave here and prove he was a man. A man who could provide for his family without going cap in hand to his mother for money.

Rita knew he did not work hard enough to earn a decent wage. He was too busy chatting up his customers, women who were susceptible to a bit of flannel. Rita had heard the stories. Some people, namely Vera Delaney, could not help but hint that there were other women willing to take Rita's place if she did not buck her ideas up.

'I need money,' Charlie said a little while later when Rita was washing the dishes in the scullery.

'But I gave you all I had before you went out last night,' Rita replied. 'What did you do with that?' She could guess he'd spent it in the Sailor's Rest.

'Never you mind,' Charlie said in a slow agitated voice. Rita prayed he would not cause a scene; she did not want the children upset, today of all days. Taking her purse from the shelf, she opened it and gave him her last ten-shilling note.

'How far is that supposed to get us?' Charlie asked. 'Are you trying to make me look like a complete idiot, Rita?' Rita refrained from telling him he could do that all by himself.

'It's all the same to me if we don't go to this wedding. So if you want to go you'd better find me some more money because I'm not asking my mother again, just so you can go to this poxy party.'

For what seemed like the millionth time, Rita asked herself how she and Charlie could have come to this. She had never seen her father look at her mother in such a cold, disparaging way, but she wasn't shocked by her husband's salty language nor his opinion of her family. He had never liked them and made no secret of it. To her, at least. However, when he was in the company of the Feenys it was a different matter. He was charm personified and it was easy to see how his female customers would be swayed into opening another policy. Thank goodness her own family could see through his two-faced charade. They weren't fools, no matter how often he said they were.

'Would you like another pot of tea, Charles?' Mrs Kennedy asked as he returned to the dining room. 'And what about you, Michael?' Rita and Megan might as well have been invisible.

'We were discussing the prospect of moving to a place of our own if the opportunity arises,' Rita said, unable to resist the small revenge.

'That won't happen now,' Mrs Kennedy said

with an assured air. 'With all this talk of war people are staying put. You can't get a house for love nor money these days.'

'I've told you once and for all, Rita,' Charlie's steely tones told Rita she had gone too far, 'we are not moving, and that's final.' The ghost of a smile crossed Mrs Kennedy's lips and Rita felt her husband's betrayal keenly. 'Now let that be an end to it.' Charlie made no pretence of their being a happily married couple in front of his mother any more. A lowly paid salesman in an insurance company, he had promised her the world at one time. He had been lying then, and his only honesty now was to promise her nothing.

If they did not get out of here soon, Rita thought, she would go mad.

'Is the happy bride up yet?' Rita smiled when her mother showed her into the parlour to appreciate the wonderful table set out with her best china and glass, all ready for the return of the wedding party later that day. The top table, where the bride and groom were going to sit, beside the three-tiered wedding cake, looked gorgeous. The house smelled like a flower garden.

'She'll be down soon.' Dolly bustled around the table, fixing a spoon here, a knife there.

'Pop, you've made a lovely job of that wallpaper.'

'I know.' Pop, never one to suffer false modesty, proudly pushed his chest out like a canary pluming its feathers. His rugged, still handsome, face held an unabashed grin and Rita noticed her mother, proud as anything, did not rebuke him for being big-headed.

'This place is fit for the King himself,' Rita added as a warm glow dissolved the sense of worthlessness her husband and his mother had fuelled in her. If her family only knew what she was going through, however... Rita squashed the thought immediately.

'Your father's been ever so busy. I wish our Nancy was moving into the parlour.'

Let us hope she does not end up like me, Rita thought. It was no fun living with the mother-in-law. However, Sid would not contemplate the idea of moving into number three with the Feeny family, even though he got on quite well with everybody.

'It's me mam,' he had said. 'She's so often by herself and she doesn't like being on her own.' Rita had rolled her eyes when Nancy, starry-eyed and pleasingly compliant, agreed wholeheartedly. It was like history repeating itself.

Carrying a cup of hot tea into the parlour and then being quickly shooed out by his mother, Frank called up the stairs, 'I've left Sid to get ready, Nance. I told him I'd be back as soon as I'd picked up my number ones.' His 'number ones' were his Royal Navy uniform, complete with brilliant white gaiters and a white silk ribbon, a naval tradition when attending a wedding.

'Our Eddy's invited a few of his pals to the wedding,' said Dolly, 'so I want it all to look nice.'

'Mam, you always have it nice. We've always been proud to bring our friends home,' Rita said with feeling, 'and they've always been made welcome.'

'Aye, well, we do our best, don't we, Pop?'

Pop gave her shoulder a little squeeze. 'That's right, girl, open the doors, let them all come in and have a gander at my lovely walls.'

'Modesty is not one of his failings, hey, Mam?' Rita laughed, all tension dissolved now.

'The table looks lovely. Kitty's worked so hard.' Dolly smiled, looking up into her husband's cheerful face, as, quite naturally, he bent and gave her a loving peck on the lips. Rita was aware of the pink colour in her mam's cheeks. She was so proud of the fact that her father could still make her mother blush after all these years. However, the moment was over quickly when Dolly gently poked Pop in the ribs with her elbow.

'Not in front of the children.'

Rita could not help but laugh.

'Mam, it's a long time since we were children,' Frank said, coming back in with Eddy, two strapping young men together.

'I am ever so lucky with my family,' said Dolly with a sigh. Rita knew her mother was making a good show of putting on a brave face, for everybody's sake.

'Perhaps it won't really come to anything, you know, Mam? Maybe the powers that be will step back from the brink?' Rita said suddenly, knowing Mam worried about what the future held for her sons.

'You mark my words, the rumours of war are all hot air,' Frank said brightly. 'Now, where's that sandwich you said you were making...? It's half past eight and I haven't been fed yet.'

'You and your stomach,' Dolly laughed. 'I don't know how I keep up with the lot of you.' Rita knew her mother loved every minute of fussing around her family. 'Let Kitty into the parlour when she gets here. She's bringing more flowers for the table.'

'Will do,' said Frank, who was always pleased to see Kitty.

'And tell your father to stop marching through every room with that broom handle over his shoulder,' Dolly said briskly. 'It's unnerving, and he'll wear out the mat.' They all burst out laughing.

'You think I'm kidding?' Dolly asked. 'I said to him, "Bert, if war does ever break out you'll be too tired to do anything about it." That soon put a stop to his gallop, I can tell you.'

'Oh, you lot really are a tonic today,' Rita laughed. Her family was just what she needed after putting up with Charlie and his mother.

'I do wish Nancy and Sid were living here, but Sid's mam is a bit nervy and Sid doesn't want to leave her in case...' Dolly stopped short of saying 'in case war breaks out'.

'She asked me what colour you're wearing,' said Rita. 'She doesn't want to clash.'

'It's a bit late to ask that now,' Dolly said, getting flustered. 'If she hasn't got hers now, she's cutting it fine.'

'She asked me last week and I forgot to say.' Rita looked a little embarrassed.

'She'll be wearing a fetching sky-blue pink,' Pop said, now enjoying a cup of tea. Dolly gave him a quizzical look and shook her head.

'I'm wearing my nice navy-blue two-piece, that new blouse I bought and ... you'll see it later,' she said.

'She's never wearing that old two-piece suit?' Eddy was aghast. 'It's older than me.'

'Take no notice,' Pop laughed. 'I rigged her out earlier in the week.'

'He took her to Bon Marché in Church Street, didn't you, Pop?' Rita said, and he nodded. 'Mind now, you two,' Rita said to Megan and Michael, 'don't go missing. We'll be going home soon so you can have a bath before you put on your wedding finery.'

'Mam, can I stay here with Uncle Frank and Uncle Eddy?' Michael asked. 'They can take me to the washing baths on Marsh Lane.'

'No, you'll never wash yourself properly and you're not making a show of me today.'

'I waited with your mother while she tried on every outfit in the shop,' Pop chuckled.

Oh, it did feel good to be home again, Rita thought. There might be only a couple of walls and an entry to separate her from her family, but number three was a world away from the Kennedys.

'I can do no wrong,' Pop sighed contentedly, 'which makes a nice change.'

'I can't remember Charlie ever going into a shop with or without me,' Rita said.

'*Modes*,' Pop said, looking lovingly towards his beautiful wife. 'Got a lovely pale blue dress and coat with navy *ensemble*.' He repeated the words of the superior saleswoman in the dress shop. 'Although I'm not sure what an *ensemble* is.'

'It's a hat, shoes and gloves,' Rita said.

'I thought the pale blue was a bit young for me.' Dolly, never still, was wiping imaginary dust from the sideboard with the sleeve of her cardigan. 'I

132

don't want to look like mutton.' Everybody spoke at once. They would love her new outfit. Mam suited everything. Considering the time they had gone to bed in the early hours of the morning Dolly looked as fresh as a daisy and Gloria had done her hair a treat.

Rita, smiling now, watched the easy way her mam and dad connected to each other in that loving, intimate way, not afraid to show their loving sides. She suddenly realised that even when she and Charlie were courting, they had never looked at each other in the way her mam and dad were looking at each other now. She could never imagine wanting to look at Charlie like that anymore. But Jack... Rita quickly banished the thought.

'Come on, Tom,' Kitty said wearily. She had been up all night finishing off the food for Nancy's wedding, turning the collar on Danny's shirt, pressing Dad's jacket, which had seen much better days, and putting a hem in Jack's new grey trousers. Then, to top it all, Tommy had come down with another sore throat this morning.

'I don't feel well,' he groaned, and Kitty had to admit he did sound like the bullfrog their Danny had once brought back from the countryside.

'Do you think you'll be able to manage the wedding?' Kitty asked, putting the palm of her hand against her brother's forehead. It did not feel too hot but she could not take any chances. 'I'll have to get the doctor out.'

'I'll be fine after a cup of tea, Kit,' Tommy croaked, and Kitty wondered if she had time to nip over the bridge to Merton Road and ask Dr

O'Malley for a bottle of linctus. She did not have the five bob for a home visit. If she paid that, then she wouldn't be able to afford the medicine. It was not yet too late to ask Mrs Kennedy for a loan, though. She was closing the shop early as she was going to the wedding, and Kitty could not bring herself to mention it to Jack, who had already spent enough this week on a wedding present from the Callaghan family for Nancy and Sid.

However, when Tommy still did not feel any better after his cup of tea Kitty was forced to come to a decision. She could not let him suffer all day. It was bad enough she was going to be so busy she would not be able to look after him properly.

'You wait here, Tom,' she said, hurrying to the door. She had no choice but to go to ask Winnie Kennedy if she had five bob to lend her. When she closed the front door behind her Kitty turned and collided slap-bang into Alfie Delaney.

'Hey, where's the fire?' Alfie laughed. 'Not that I'm complaining.' His hands remained on Kitty's slim hips where he had caught her a moment earlier. Kitty, feeling uncomfortable, wriggled free.

'I've got to get a doctor for our Tommy. His throat's bad again.'

'You don't want to go wasting money on doctors,' Alfie said quickly. 'I've got just the thing in our house. It'll fix him up a treat; he'll be good as new.'

'Are you sure?' Kitty asked. She did not like Alfie very much; he was a friend of Sid's, was far too cocky and fancied himself as a bit of a gangster. However, she did not have time to play nursemaid to Tommy today of all days, and the main thing was to get him well enough to be able to come to the wedding, and if it saved her a couple of bob into the bargain...

'As long as it's proper medicine and not some concoction...'

'Never let it be said I would put a child's life in danger.' Alfie looked highly offended and Kitty quickly jumped to cover her plain-speaking.

'Oh, I didn't mean anything by it, Alf,' she said hurriedly. 'I was just saying...' She took a deep breath. What choice did she have? Either she risked a lecture on household management from Mrs Kennedy or their Tommy would be left in pain all day. There was no choice, she reckoned.

'Thank you, Alfie. I'd be so obliged.'

'Think nothing of it.' Alfie's smile was huge. 'Just knowing you're grateful for my efforts is enough for me.' Kitty offered a tight smile when he said he would be back in five minutes with the medicine.

The linctus worked a treat and in no time at all Tommy was back on his feet as if nothing had been wrong. Kitty wondered what was in the magical elixir but as Tommy hadn't fallen down dead after taking it she felt she shouldn't worry.

'I never thought I'd ever hear myself say this, Tom,' Kitty said a short while later, 'but thank the Lord for Alfie Delaney.'

'I wouldn't go that far, Kit.' Tommy was not so impressed by Alfie's sudden healing powers but he was glad his throat was no longer sore.

CHAPTER EIGHT

Dolly marshalled her family with such military precision that even Mr Chamberlain would have been proud. She busied herself polishing glasses and arranged the flowers that Kitty had brought on the top table.

Pop poured whiskey into glasses in readiness for the male guests and a nice schooner of sherry for the ladies, knowing some of the alcohol would gladly be consumed before the wedding cars arrived.

The bride-to-be, having steadfastly refused to go to the church in her father's horse-drawn cart, even with the promise of white ribbons tied to it, waited in nervous anticipation in her bedroom upstairs.

'Just as well I budgeted for a bridal car,' said Dolly, handbag over her arm, her hat perched at a fetching angle on her marcel-waved hair.

'What would we do without you, my sweet?' said Pop. Dolly's face, wreathed in smiles, was a picture of motherly pride.

There was a slight tap on the door of Nancy's bedroom. Taking a deep breath, she called lightly, 'Come in if you've brought forty per cent proof.'

'You're in luck,' Rita said smiling as she put a glass of sherry on the dressing table. 'Mam said I'd better bring you one up.'

'I would have preferred a whiskey,' Nancy said tightly.

'Is everything all right, Nance?' Rita was concerned her sister was getting the pre-wedding jitters. Nancy shook her head and was quiet for a moment longer. Rita knew her sister was going to make a lovely bride, with her rich red curls and fresh, perfect complexion. How could she fail to make an impression? But Nancy, considered the prettiest of the Feeny girls, looked pale and drawn now.

'Put a bit more rouge on your cheeks, Nance, you look too pale.' Rita knew her sister could have had any man she chose, and she had to go and pick Sid Kerrigan. What did Sid possess that the line of countless past boyfriends did not? 'You're not getting last-minute nerves, are you?'

Nancy shook her head and gave a small nervous laugh. 'I always worried I might end up an old maid, like Miss Taylor.'

Miss Taylor, in her thirties, came from London and had recently moved in with her widowed aunt across the road. 'She doesn't look like an old maid these days – have you seen her?'

'No,' said Nancy, not really interested as she drank the sherry in one gulp before wrinkling her nose and coughing.

'She's had a perm,' Rita said. 'It's made a real difference to her.'

'Super.' Nancy's voice was flat; she did not care one way or the other.

'It's going to be the happiest day of your life,' Rita replied. 'Sid's a lucky man.'

'He's in the Territorials; he'll be called up first,

137

won't he?' Nancy said suddenly. 'I'll be on my own.'

'You and every other girl in England,' Rita scoffed. 'Anyway, he might not as he's on the docks; it's a reserved occupation so who knows if and when a call-up will come? You'll soon get over being alone if there's a dance on the go.'

'There's something I've got to say, and I know you'll give me a straight answer, Rita.'

'Go on,' Rita smiled, thinking nothing her younger sister did or said could shock her.

'Do you remember Stan Hathaway from Strand Road? He worked in Accounts, his mam and dad owned the pork butcher's on Derby Road... You remember them?'

Rita's brows pleated and she slowly shook her head.

'His mother was very pound-note-ish ... a bit like Mrs Kennedy...'

'Oh, I remember now,' Rita laughed. 'He was tall, good-looking, went to university...'

'That's him!' Nancy's eyes were dancing now and she nodded enthusiastically. 'Well, you'll never guess what.'

'Come on, spit it out.' Rita sat on the edge of the bed.

'I saw him in town the other day. We hit it off straight away. He said he had never forgotten me.' She did not look at her older sister now. 'He told me I'd got better looking since the last time he saw me.' She lifted her chin and viewed her profile in the dressing table mirror from a head-tilted angle.

'And you are nearly a married woman,' Rita smiled, knowing Nancy liked nothing better than a good compliment. It cheered her up as nothing else would.

'He's joined the air force,' Nancy said, ignoring her sister's well-intentioned sarcasm, 'which is a bit of a coincidence because Gloria's chap is in the RAF too.' She tried to keep her voice as casual as possible.

'They might know each other,' Rita said drily, thinking her sister had something she needed to get off her chest and, judging by the way she was hedging around the subject, it must be something quite serious.

'Oh, he did look handsome in his uniform,' Nancy said, ignoring Rita's little barb. 'I nearly had thoughts of cancelling the wedding.' She threw back her head and let out an exaggerated deep-throated laugh. 'And he only asked me to write to him!' Her eyes were wide now and she nodded as if to affirm her revelation. 'What do you think of that?'

'I hope you told him you're getting married!' Rita, although not a prude, did not want to see Nancy mixed up in anything that could complicate her life with Sid.

'It's not that kind of friendship.' Nancy laughed, but something was not right, Rita could tell. She put it down to nerves; her sister was a nice girl.

'Did he give you his address?' Rita suddenly felt uncomfortable. She knew Stan had always attracted Nancy with his easy-going charm.

'Only of his Forces mail. What do you take me for?' Nancy answered, colouring noticeably.

'Thank goodness for that,' Rita sighed. It had not taken much in the past for the good-looking lad to turn her sister's head.

'Anyway,' Nancy said innocently, looking down at her perfectly painted fingernails, avoiding Rita's gaze, 'what harm would it do?' What's good for the goose is good for the gander, she thought, still angry with Sid.

'Have you lost your senses, Nancy?' Rita shook her head, hardly able to believe that her sister could be so naïve. 'You're getting married!'

'Don't you think I know that? I don't need you to remind me.' Nancy, obviously vexed, turned away from Rita. 'But that doesn't mean I have to go around like a blind nun.'

Rita could see that there was something deeper at the heart of Nancy's state of mind.

'Nancy, come on, you can tell me, what's the matter? You do want to marry Sid, don't you?' Rita had heard from Sarah that there had been some rumblings of discontent over the last week, but her mam hadn't seen fit to divulge any of the details as yet to her eldest daughter. Rita figured there must be a reason why it was all so hush-hush.

Nancy, hesitated before speaking. 'What's it like, Rita? Being married to Charlie? I know he hasn't really taken to our family and likewise, but you love him, don't you?'

Maybe it was last-minute nerves, thought Rita. But what on earth could she tell her sister about her own marriage? It wasn't a good day to ask. Rita could hardly think of one single positive thing to say about Charlie.

Rita took Nancy's hand in her own. 'Look, Nance, every marriage is different from the next and what makes a marriage work can't be bottled.

The most important thing is that you love Sid. You do, don't you?'

Nancy's bottom lip started to wobble. 'I'm not sure, Rita. I know he's been messing about with other girls and well... I'm not sure I'm doing the right thing.'

'Then why on earth have you let it get this far?' Rita could see tears welling behind her sister's eyes.

Nancy didn't answer but her hand moved towards her belly where Rita could now see the barely perceptible bump that she hadn't noticed before. The penny dropped.

'Oh, Nancy, how did that happen?'

Nancy gave her sister a look and both of them laughed despite the weight of the situation.

'Silly question.' Rita looked at Nancy steadily. They both knew that it was too late now to back out. Rita's heart went out to her younger sibling and despite the fact that Nancy could be immature and self-centred, Rita knew from bitter experience that this was no way to start a marriage. Nancy and Sid were as bad as each other and both of them were going to have to grow up if they had a chance in hell of making this work. But Rita judged that this wasn't the time for lectures or tough talking.

'Nancy, no matter what Sid may or may not have been up to, you can see he adores you. He's probably just got the last-minute jitters himself. You wouldn't have given yourself to him in the way you did if you weren't certain that you wanted him for a husband, now would you?'

Nancy dabbed at her eyes. 'I suppose.'

'Exactly. You and Sid have got as good a chance of having a happy marriage as anybody and I can tell you now that as soon as that baby comes along, he or she will be the apple of their daddy's eye and he'll love you all the more for giving him a much-loved child.'

'Do you think so Rita?'

'I'm sure of it. Now come on, get yourself together, stop thinking about Stan Hathaway and what might have been and let's give Empire Street the wedding that everyone will still be talking about at Christmas.'

'Oh, Rita – thank you!' and with this, Nancy gave her sister a heartfelt hug. The Feenys weren't a very touchy-feely family, but they could rise to the occasion when it mattered.

'Right, where's Mam and Sarah?' Nancy was fussing now. 'My hair's not finished and I still haven't seen me posy!'

With this Nancy dashed out of the room, all anxieties seemingly forgotten. Rita caught sight of herself in the mirror of the dressing table. She could see the glistening tears in her own eyes and dashed them away hurriedly.

Rita thought about what she had said to Nancy. She hoped that every word she had said was true, but suspected it wasn't. *I gave myself to someone because I thought we'd be together for ever and look where it's got me.*

'Pull yourself together,' she whispered to herself out loud. That ship had sailed.

Since April, England had responded to Hitler's threats of aggression in Europe by summoning her fittest and bravest young men. Danny Callaghan was not slow to want to do his bit. He had dreams of sailing the world and, like the Feeny brothers, conquering evil marauders. They knew he was fervent about standing up for what was right, even if the rest of Empire Street did think he was always up to no good. Danny, with his fearless attitude, intended to fight for his country and come back to these shores a national hero. Kitty, long-suffering as she was, would be so proud.

All his life he had the urge to make good. It had not been easy, and he had narrowly squeaked out of trouble with little to spare many a time. However, he did not want to bring worry and heartache to the door, for Kitty's sake, and in respect of the memory of his much-adored mother.

Danny balled his fists and pushed them deep down into empty threadbare pockets, his cap at a jaunty angle on the back of his head. Whistling, he walked with his head held high along the dock road towards the centre of Liverpool with the urge to make good his vow at his mother's graveside that he would make this family proud of him come what may.

Even if there wasn't a war, he thought, he would join the Royal Navy anyway. He'd see the world, bring back exotic presents and tell tales of places that Kitty and young Tommy could only imagine. The voyages would be a dream come true. The best time of his life. Articulate, intelligent, Danny wanted to reach beyond the limits forced upon him by his poverty-stricken upbringing. He wanted to be successful, to provide for his family. He wanted people to look up to him, as they

143

looked up to Dolly Feeny's boys. He wanted to grab life by the scruff of the neck and live it.

Removing the tattered envelope from his pocket once more, he checked the address. This was it: the Royal Navy Recruitment Centre. His heart gave a little flutter and he felt almost breathless with excitement. This was the last stage of the enlistment procedure. The medical. Then he would get his date to start training. He could not have felt more proud.

'Good afternoon,' Danny said confidently to a matelot dressed in an immaculate navy-blue uniform, his gaiters pristine white and his boots so shiny he could see his face in them. Observing these boots, Danny could only gasp in admiration. This was it. He couldn't wait to tell everyone later at the wedding. They'd be speechless.

'Speech!' Sid Kerrigan called, sitting at the top table, tapping one of Dolly's best gold-rimmed champagne glasses. Dolly, watching him, silently flared her nostrils in disgust. Sid was making a right show of himself and, if she were not mistaken, he had been drunk before the service at St Mary's church had even begun. The Kerrigans were sitting further up the table, looking at Sid as if he were a little king. Pop had been round to see Mr Kerrigan the previous night and had made his feelings about Nancy's condition very clear, he'd said. Dolly was aware of a slight frostiness coming off both Mr and Mrs Kerrigan, but Sid had to do his duty and that was that. No point in anyone blaming anyone else. Neither Nancy nor Sid were children any more and they would just have to grow up.

Rita, sitting between her husband and her two shiny children, looked on proudly as Nancy, looking every inch the radiant bride, smiled and acknowledged the good wishes of her guests. She'll be fine, Rita thought. It was a case of having to be now, she supposed. Nancy had taken the plunge and was going to live with the consequences. She would have to put all thoughts of fighter pilots out of her head.

'I'll do the honours, Sid,' Frank said in a jovial tone, standing up and addressing the guests sitting expectantly around the room. Their Rita looked pensive and his mam looked as if she wanted to give the groom a piece of her mind, he thought as he waited for complete silence. Under the sociable surface of bonhomie and good cheer, there were storm clouds brewing and it was not just the new groom causing them. All this talk of war was doing funny things to people's nerves.

Frank had a little speech prepared. It was not a long speech as he'd known the assembled guests would be eager to tuck in, and most of it comprised good wishes and reading telegrams from absent friends and family. He enjoyed the laughter that his little jokes invited. However, unbeknown to his loving family, Frank was on stand-by. If he got the call to return to his ship it would mean only one thing. He hoped he could get through the speeches without that happening.

From his vantage point, as he spoke he was admiring the way Kitty Callaghan nipped in and out of the parlour with the huge teapot, making sure the guests had everything they needed. She

145

had done Mam proud, he thought, looking at the table with its pristine tablecloth, a pure white background on which to show off his mother's fine china, crystal glasses and silver cutlery, usually locked away in the bow-fronted glass cabinet and brought out only on special occasions.

Kitty had done a smashing job of bringing up little Tommy, Frank thought, as well as looking after the rest of her family, and, from an early age, keeping a house going on very little. She deserved a medal for putting up with it all.

Poor Rita – Frank's attention turned to his sister. She was smiling now, passing a dainty cup on a matching saucer to her husband. Charlie was laughing at something the priest was saying, totally ignoring his wife. She put the cup and saucer down beside his untouched plate while looking a little embarrassed. She certainly danced attendance on that smarmy bugger, thought Frank.

Nevertheless, it was none of his business unless his sister asked him to speak up for her, and that would never happen. What was it Pop used to say: 'Never trouble trouble, till trouble troubles you'? The wise words certainly had not done Pop any harm. Frank smiled, as he put his delicate china cup to his lips and discovered he had emptied it already.

'More tea, Frank?'

Frank turned to see Kitty standing with the huge pot in her hand. He noticed she did not wear a scrap of fake, no lipstick and powder to mar her natural beauty like some of the 'girls' who frequented the dock road ale houses.

Girls! That was a laugh. Adam was a lad the last

time some of them were girls, Frank knew. They were a common sight in every port. He had never succumbed to the charms of these doxies, no matter how much the other tars tried to tempt him.

'Thanks, Kit.' His voice was low as he caught her eye and the pink tinge that suffused her cheeks only added to her beauty when she smiled back. As honest as the day was long, Frank thought; it was a shame that life had dealt her such a cruel blow, especially when others, more worldly wise, knew how to keep the wolves from the door.

'I'll have a top-up too, love.'

Frank watched Alfie Delaney, a dock foreman, rattling his cup on his saucer, and felt an uneasy stirring in his gut. He did not like the way Alfie was looking at Kitty. It reminded him of the way a dog looked at a bone. Kitty, nodding, smiled at Alfie, and for the first time Frank realised that what he was feeling towards Kitty wasn't purely neighbourly concern. Men found her attractive. It was with surprise that he realised that he found her attractive too. He had no claim on Kitty, so why did he suddenly feel the urge to tell Alfie to keep his eyes off her?

'I'll just go and put some hot water in this pot, the tea is getting a bit strong.'

'Like me.' Alfie laughed and winked, while Kitty blushed. Frank bit his tongue to prevent a quick retort. How he would like to wipe that grin off Alfie Delaney's face. Not backward in coming forward, Delaney had always been cocksure and never short of a girl.

When Kitty returned to the parlour, Frank could not help but notice Alfie's open approval of

147

her. Her coal-coloured curls had escaped the triangular scarf knotted at the nape of her neck and, feeling strangely protective, Frank watched her work her way around the table, a smile and a friendly comment for everybody.

He liked the way she wore her naturally waving hair loose beneath the bandana and he admired her trim figure in a black skirt and cardigan worn over a perfectly laundered white blouse all covered with a white starched apron.

The stark hues of the outfit did nothing to diminish the golden glow of her perfect skin and, teamed with her dark hair and kind eyes that danced when she smiled, it gave her a European elegance. Spanish, maybe Italian, he could not make up his mind … what would it be like to hold her in his arms…?

'So, you made it home then. That was a stroke of good luck.' Delaney's crashing words shattered Frank's contemplation and brought him back to the sultry heat of his mother's parlour, and the low buzz of polite conversation. Taking a deep breath, Frank studied the beefy power of the man he now suddenly thought of as an adversary.

'Luck had nothing to do with it, Alfie. We were owed leave and we got it. Simple,' Frank laughed, giving nothing away. Under the heavy herringbone suit and brushed cotton shirt, Alfie must be melting in this heat.

A few of Frank's pals off the ship were also enjoying Dolly's hospitality. There were also a few merchant mariners present, chums of Eddy's, and their conversation took on the form of lighthearted barracking. Dolly and Pop were enjoying it immensely, not to mention Nancy, over her nerves now and more relaxed. Now she was laughing at something Sid whispered to her. Frank was amazed at how many people their small parlour was able to hold, though guests were spilling out into the corridor and beyond into the back yard where cigarettes were being smoked and views on the threat of war were being traded.

'Home long?' Alfie asked.

'Not really,' Frank said, accepting another cup of tea, which Kitty poured with a smile. He was not interested in talking to Delaney right now. Instead, he was trying to resist the urge to brush from Kitty's face the stray wisp of a dark curl that escaped her scarf.

'Just give me a call if you want another top-up,' Kitty smiled back, and her eyes lingered just a fraction longer than he ever dared hope.

Oh, I will, he thought. I'd be overflowing with the stuff just to keep you close.

A diamond in the rough, his mother had called Kitty. However, Frank knew it would not take much for Kitty's brilliance to shine. Later, when she had a minute, he intended to ask her if she fancied going to the pictures before he went back to his ship. He was not much cop as a dancer and hoped Kitty did not want to go to St Winnie's or St James's church dance. If she did go out with him, no matter where, he would make sure he gave her an evening to remember.

'How's *Anna*?' Alfie asked. 'Still bobbing along?'

'She's fine.' Frank did not want to talk about HMS *Anna* in front of Kitty, nor active service, and especially not with Delaney, who would probably find a way to dodge the war. His type always did. He was a wide boy if ever there was one.

'I bet you can't wait to get back to her,' Alfie smiled as Kitty poured a finger of whiskey into his glass.

Frank shrugged. He was telling Delaney nothing. They'd been clearly briefed time and again not to talk carelessly. These were uncertain times and secrecy was of the utmost importance if war were to break out.

'It's a wonder she manages without you.'

'Leave it out, Alf,' Frank said, but behind the light-hearted words was an almost undetectable core of steel. He knew that Alf was goading him. He was probably jealous. The likes of Alfie Delaney were more likely to line their own pockets and make money out of others' misery than fight for their country.

'Over 'ere, love.' Delaney snapped his fingers impatiently in Kitty's direction as she moved away.

Kitty tried to keep her smile bright; she had just been wondering what had happened to Danny today – he should have been at the wedding – but her worries were overshadowed when she had overheard Alfie mention someone to Frank called Anna. Was Frank seeing someone again? Was it a different one from the one she had seen Frank walking with on Empire Street? Rita hadn't mentioned it. But why should she? 'More tea?' she asked.

'A little more of something a bit stronger, if you don't mind, Kit, my love.' Alfie spoke to Kitty in a way that she didn't much like. Supplying her with a bottle of linctus for her younger brother might have saved the day, but it did not mean she and Delaney were bosom friends, as he seemed to be implying now. She vowed she would pay him for the medicine as soon as their Jack got paid next Friday.

'Of course.' Kitty was aware of Frank watching this exchange with Alfie; she could feel his eyes on her. She felt very self-conscious. Frank probably thought her clumsy and silly. It was a ridiculous idea, her being head over heels in love with Frank Feeny. He saw her as a friend, more like a sister, she reminded herself. What a fool she was to think he would ever see her as anything more. Why on earth was she getting herself upset that he might be courting – why shouldn't he? She could feel a painful tightening in her throat and the sting of tears behind her eyes and she knew she had to get out of the claustrophobic room quickly before she made a show of herself.

'Everything all right, Kit?' Frank asked, and she nodded, too full to speak and glad when somebody asked to open a window as it was very smoky in the parlour.

'I'm fine, Frank. The room's just a bit warm, that's all.' And Kitty excused herself, dashing off to refill the teapot again before Frank could say anything more.

CHAPTER NINE

Sitting in the corridor where the doctor had told him to wait after the examination, Danny could hear the low buzz of conversation within. He wondered if he was being missed at the wedding? Kitty was bound to have noticed he was gone and think that he was up to no good, but hopefully she had her hands too full to worry. He'd give them all something to talk about when he came back with his news. Listening hard, he couldn't make out what the doctors were saying no matter how much he strained to listen. Jumping slightly when the door opened, he felt his heart race and tried to calm it with a few deep breaths. *This is it.*

'Daniel Callaghan?'

Danny nodded and followed the doctor into the room. The others had already gone. Anticipation was coursing through his veins now. He felt special already. Closing the door quietly behind him he followed the doctor to the desk at the far end of the room. Danny was already rehearsing what he was going to say to everyone at the wedding tonight. They were going to be so proud...

'...Did you hear what I said, young man?'

The doctor's voice seemed to be coming from a long way off. It echoed around the large room, which suddenly felt hot. *Danny, concentrate!*

'I'm sorry to have to spring this on you, young man, but...'

The man's voice droned on but it was as if the words were coming from somewhere very far away. His blood was pounding in his head. Danny willed himself to listen. He hadn't heard it right. Surely to God he had not heard it right!

'I am sorry, I ... I didn't catch...'

'You had rheumatic fever as a child?'

Danny nodded, unable to speak. He had caught rheumatic fever after his mother died. The doctor said it was the shock. All he remembered was that he was sick and his mother was not there to care for him. Kitty did her best, but she was only eleven...

'...an enlarged heart...' The words kept circling in his head. 'I'm afraid that rules you out of joining the Royal Navy.'

Danny heard a gasp and surmised it must have come from himself. They must have got it wrong! Got him mixed up with someone else.

'It can't be right!' Danny shook his head, running his hand through his now unruly mop of dark hair before putting his cap on. Then he took it off again. No. They were wrong. His mam once said he had the heart of a young lion! She would have known...

'Get him a glass of water!' Danny heard the order and felt the cold glass being gently put into his hand and then directed to his lips but he could not make himself drink. Moments later, he looked up to see the navy doctor and an officer looking down at him with concerned expressions on their faces.

'You mean...?' His chest tightened. The air felt like it was being sucked out of his body and his heart was racing. He had always been able to make his heart beat faster. All he had to do was stop breathing for a few moments. Then he would take a deep breath and it would race along like billy-o. Who would be able to do that if they had a dicky ticker? This fella didn't have a clue.

'You can ask anyone,' Danny challenged, 'they'll all tell you... Danny Callaghan isn't scared of no one.'

'We are not questioning your bravery, Daniel,' the officer said in a kindly tone. There was something fatherly about the older grey-haired officer, Danny thought, but not like his own dad, who barely looked anyone in the eye.

'Danny, the name's Danny.' He would scupper his chances for sure if he carried on talking to the top brass in this tone of voice, but he could not stop himself. 'The only people who called me Daniel was the teachers and the Church.'

'There are other things you can do,' the officer was saying. 'But right now you have to get checked out at the hospital. We will forward the details. Someone will be in touch.'

'So, that's it?' Danny felt stuck to his chair, unable to move. They couldn't just send him away like this. It was all he had been able to think about and now he was literally sick with disappointment. Nausea rose to that dip in his throat just below his Adam's apple and he experienced the tingly feeling he got in his ears when he was about to throw up. Taking a long slow breath he swallowed hard. He could quell the nausea if he concentrated enough.

'I know this must be a blow for you but there's

154

'nothing we can do, I'm sorry...' the officer said, seeing Danny's pale and anxious face.

'No you're not,' Danny said, unable to contain his distress. To his horror, Danny found that it was not only his legs that were letting him down, but now his voice was too There was no disguising the shake in his voice. 'As soon as I'm out of here it will be business as usual. What about me? What about–'

'Bad luck, son.' The navy doctor looked genuinely sympathetic but that cut no ice.

'So, that's it then?' Danny shrugged. He felt hopeless. Worthless. All those people who had said he would come to nothing were right. Right now he couldn't care less that his heart didn't work properly. What was the point in living half a life anyway? He finally forced his legs to stand and managed to walk out of the examination room, closing the door quietly behind him, even though he wanted to slam it shut, and keep on slamming it until it fell off its hinges.

Later, he would not be able to recall the journey back to Empire Street.

'Any chance of another bottle of that beer, Kitty? I've been stood with this empty glass for ages and I'm parched.' Delaney was now outside in the back yard with the rest of the men, who were cooling down and having a smoke, and he was getting impatient.

'She'll get to you in good time,' Frank said in that quiet, authoritative tone that made the naval ratings obey without question. He never repeated himself or raised his voice to serving men, and he

155

did not intend to do so for this porcine upstart. Who the hell did Delaney think he was? The dockyard foreman had always been full of himself. Nevertheless, he had no right to treat Kitty like a skivvy, thought Frank, or take it for granted that there was beer on tap. He was a guest so how dare he snap his fingers?

'You just can't get the staff these days, hey, Frank?' Alfie Delaney laughed, but the obvious joviality did not reach his eyes.

Frank, in amiable tones for the sake of his family, said, 'Kitty's a family friend and we are grateful she offered to help out.' But the threat in his voice was there and Kitty picked up on it.

'Oh, it's all right, I'm here now. Let me take that glass, Alfie, and I'll fill you up,' Kitty said. She didn't want the men coming to blows over something silly, not on her account.

'I wouldn't have been able to do all this without her, would I, Kitty, love?' Dolly said, collecting empty glasses from the windowsill.

'I'm sure anybody would have done the same, Aunty Doll,' Kitty said, heading back into the house. 'I'll just go and put some boiling water in the pot.'

'I didn't mean anything by it; Kitty knows what I'm like, don't you, Kitty?' Delaney shouted after Kitty as she went back inside. 'She's a great girl.'

'I know that,' Frank said.

'I'll have a word later,' Alfie said lightly, not meeting Frank's steady gaze. 'Kitty's got a sense of humour, unlike some people.'

Frank shook his head. Delaney really was a waste of space.

'Hey, Kit, let me give you a hand with that. Take no notice of that Alfie Delaney; he's too full of his own importance,' Rita said, taking the tray of dirty glasses.

It was that time of the day between the afternoon reception and the evening knees-up and the guests were relaxed, if not yet merry enough for a singsong.

'I'm not bothered by the likes of him: fingers in every pie, doing a bit of this and a bit of that, ducking and diving on the dock and always got something to sell.'

'I'd give him a wide berth if I were you,' Rita said, but Kitty looked shocked at the well-meant advice.

'I wouldn't touch Alfie Delaney with asbestos gloves on, and I certainly wouldn't trust him as far as I could throw him, and that's not far at all.' She didn't tell Rita about the medicine for Tommy; Rita might not approve. 'Oh, mind your lovely suit,' Kitty said, admiring the marine colour that brought out the beautiful blue-green of Rita's eyes.

'Here, I'll take the jacket off and put me mam's pinny on and I'll give you a hand,' Rita laughed. 'To tell the truth, Kit, I could do with a breather from the party. The heat and the drink are going to the men's heads. If you didn't know better you'd think some of them would be able to beat off Hitler and his Nazi bully boys single-handed.'

'Do you think war will happen, then, Rita?' asked Kitty.

Rita paused. 'Yes,' she said after a moment. 'I'm

157

sure of it. You and I have lived round here long enough to know that something different is happening now. We've seen all of those naval ships being readied and the hundreds, maybe thousands, of men in uniform all seeming to have appeared out of nowhere. It's in the air and I don't think all the fine words of Neville Chamberlain will put a stop to Hitler. It's action, not words needed now.'

Kitty started washing up some of Dolly's fine teacups and saucers, placing them on the side where Rita got to work drying them with a tea towel, stacking them tidily on the kitchen table. 'I saw in Dad's *Echo* yesterday that some more of those Jewish children had arrived from Europe. What was it they called them, Rita?'

'I know the ones you mean, the Kinder-transport, I think they're called.'

'They looked so sad and alone, Rita. It must be awful not knowing what's happening to their parents back home.'

Rita thought of her own children. Soon to be sent off as evacuees. 'I'm sure we don't hear the half of what is going on over there, but at least those parents know their children are safe, Kitty.'

They finished washing the glasses and cups just as the kettle boiled.

'War terrifies the life out of me, to be honest,' said Kitty, placing rows of china cups onto their matching saucers before taking the huge teapot Dolly had borrowed from Father Harding and filling them. When she'd taken out the tea she and Rita sat down at the table, taking a breather and enjoying cups of tea themselves. 'Will Charlie join

158

up, d'you think?' She and Rita had been friends for so long they were like family.

'Charlie says he'll apply to be a conscientious objector,' said Rita. 'I said to him, "Charlie, you've got to have a conscience first" – he wasn't impressed.' The two women laughed.

'I'll be in the shop as soon as our Danny gives me the money he owes me and settle my bill,' Kitty said.

Rita shrugged. 'I'm not even thinking about that place today. For all I care it can fall down. Let's take our chairs out to the back yard and see if we can get ourselves a bit of a tan.'

'If our Danny hadn't been so partial to that game of pitch-and-toss, and me dad didn't like his ale so much, we wouldn't be in this mess, and now Danny hasn't turned up. What on earth can he be up to now?' Kitty wondered as she picked up a straight-backed chair.

'You know what they say, Kit, "If ifs and buts were apples and nuts, we'd have a cupboard full."' Rita laughed. 'So come on, let's not worry for tomorrow is another day.'

'My mam used to say that too.' Her mother would have enjoyed the wedding and a good old knees-up. Kitty's throat tightened when she recalled her mother. Dad would sing to his beloved Ellen every chance he got. It must be perfect to have a love so strong. There was only one man she could ever imagine being that happy with: Frank Feeny.

'We're all cut from the same cloth, Kit, and there's no use pretending otherwise.'

Unconsciously, Kitty lifted her chin. Rita, like

the big sister she never had, always managed to make things better.

Vera Delaney, on the other hand, was already out in the yard, legs like newel posts, feet planted wide apart, whiskey in hand and giving her two-penny worth of ill-thought advice to whoever would listen.

Kitty swallowed hard and looked away over the high wall where a poster on the side of the shop was advertising Camp Coffee. Although usually sociable, Kitty did not want to get involved in conversation with Vera Delaney.

Vera made no secret of the fact she had no time for the Callaghan family. Kitty suspected it was her own father's drunken performances at closing time that caused Vera, who lived almost opposite the Sailor's Rest, to push up her sash window, Dinkie curlers akimbo, and scream blue murder.

Standing tall now, Kitty tried to tell herself that it did not matter what the likes of Vera Delaney thought. However, it did not stop her cringing every time the older woman looked pointedly in her direction.

'I'll make a start on those sandwiches for later on tonight, Rita.' The party was destined to continue into the small hours. Kitty managed only a tight smile for her friend.

'Don't let her drive you inside,' Rita said, offering her face to the sun. 'Have you enjoyed yourself, Mrs Delaney?' Rita called, then whispered to Kitty, 'The old bag is listening to every word of each person present; how she does it I will never know. I was in the middle of a conversation with her the other day, and she turned to answer somebody else's question! Then she turned back to me and continued where she left off.' Rita clapped her hands and laughed uproariously. 'She's a case!'

'It's been very nice,' Vera called back. 'Lovely spread.'

'She sounds disappointed,' Rita remarked, and Kitty laughed, feeling herself relax. She had not realised she was so tense.

'Enough's as good as a feast, I always say.' Mrs Delaney sniffed loudly from the other side of the yard.

'Your Alfie looks as if he's been filling his boots too,' Rita answered, watching Alfie sway under the influence of too much whiskey.

'He's just tired, he's been working hard. He's not greedy, you know!'

'It's just as well, missus,' said Cyril Arden, the pub landlord, who had come over to the party when the Sailor's Rest had shut for the afternoon at three o'clock. He knew these good people would spend a fair whack over his bar tonight. 'There'll be no such thing as a large quantity of anything if the Boche get their way.'

Mrs Delaney tutted and patted her waved hair. 'I don't take no notice of that scaremongering talk,' she said. 'They said the last war would end all wars, and that's good enough for me.'

'What they say and what they do are two different things,' said Pop, filling the hot summer air with plumes of pipe tobacco, his eye-patch, a dark contrast to his shock of thick white hair, a constant reminder of his service with the Grand Fleet in the last war. 'You mark my words, Vera, we'll have another war, and my Rita will be back

161

where she belongs on the wards.' He was proud that his eldest daughter had been training as a nurse before she married Charlie Kennedy. 'When the enemy comes they will be crying out for good nurses. You see if they don't!'

'Don't let Mam hear you talking like that, Pop,' Rita laughed, knowing Dolly did not approve of her husband discussing politics in public, and certainly not in his own back yard.

'Every man's home is his domain, isn't that right, Cyril?' Pop looked to the proprietor of the local, who nodded amicably. 'I'll have you know,' Pop said, waving his pipe, 'it's my own decision not to talk about politics – or religion – when my good lady wife is around.' Everybody laughed, knowing Pop would never do anything to upset Dolly, if he could help it.

'We know who wears the pants in your house, Bert,' Vera Delaney said with a sniff.

'Aye, we certainly do,' replied Pop good-naturedly. 'My Dolly, every time.'

Rita rolled her eyes. She loved her old dad, who was the fount of all knowledge and wisdom. Moreover, with Empire Street nestling precariously in the docklands, she was glad her father had expertly directed the conversation away from any more worrying war talk.

It was far too early on their Nancy's wedding day to listen to negative views and the people of Empire Street were anticipating a good old knees-up. However, Rita said to Kitty, 'I can't understand why Mr Chamberlain doesn't have this lot in his Cabinet. If he wants a solution to Hitler's threats all he has to do is come here to Empire Street

162

where any one of them will be only too pleased to show him how the country should be run.'

'That girl is talking sense,' Cyril Arden laughed, ignoring Rita's sardonic tone.

'They've dug up our bowling green,' Pop said to Cyril sadly, shaking his head, 'and those big silver elephants are flying all over the docks,' he added, referring to the barrage balloons that were erected to deter low-flying enemy aircraft. 'Not to mention the sandbags around the Town Hall and those ugly great shelters being built in every other street.'

'They haven't dug up all that lovely grass?' Vera Delaney looked genuinely shocked.

'I'm telling you, missus.' Pop, was getting in the mood for a good old natter now. Rita could see trouble ahead if her mam came out. 'Furthermore,' he pressed his forefinger into the palm of his hand to stress the point, 'a factory on Derby Road has taken an order of silk and patterns for those flying elephants. I should know, I delivered them.'

'I don't believe it!' Mrs Delaney shook her head, bewildered.

'Well, you believe what you like, missus, but I am telling you,' Pop said, puffing on his pipe, filling the yard with the mingling aroma of St Bruno and timber from the nearby wood yards.

'That Heil Hitler reminds me of Charlie Chaplin with the bit of 'tache stuck under his nose,' Mrs Delaney said.

'Well, I can't imagine him doin' much harm with a face like that, can you?' Cyril's eyes twinkled, as he rolled his shirtsleeves past his elbows. A whiff of sooty smoke from the dock meandered up the

163

yard and lingered in the hot sunny yard.

'Maybe you should ask the good people of Poland if they think the same as you, Cyril,' Pop said in exasperation.

'Well, it's a long while since I've seen so many advertisements calling for men to join up as there are now,' said Cyril with a curl of his lip. 'Plastered over every wall, they are.'

'When there's no work about, what is there for a man with plenty of verve and energy to do but join up? There's a method in their madness, I'd say,' answered Pop.

Mrs Delaney did not sound too sure when she said, 'My Alfie's got a good job on the docks. I'm a widow woman...'

'Oh, well, in that case you'd better write and tell them; see if he can be spared,' said Pop with a healthy dose of astonishment. 'Not much point in having a war when Alfie's heart's not in it.' He puffed a cloud of pipe smoke into the air. *Stupid woman.*

'But don't forget, missus,' Cyril joined in, 'with all that pent-up energy going spare, young, virile men have got to find an outlet somewhere.' He tapped the side of his nose.

'I'll thank you to keep your lewd comments to yourself, Mr Arden.' Vera Delaney was outraged. 'My son is a gentleman, I'll have you know.'

'Ah, enough of this war business, let's have a singsong,' said Pop, breaking into a rousing rendition of 'Run Rabbit Run', which soon had everyone joining in, even Kitty, who was normally a bit shy. Pop seemed determined to keep up the party atmosphere.

164

For the next couple of hours as the guests wandered in and out of the Feenys' ever-welcoming household, there were singsongs and jokes told and plenty more forthright exchanges of views.

Kitty's main concern, apart from putting food on the table, was her father's welfare. He had to rely on casual work at the docks and she knew a day's work, let alone a week's, depended much on the mood of the charge-hand.

Alfie Delaney was the man who hired the workforce to load and unload the ships, and the one who did the firing. Kitty had overheard her father talking about how Alfie wasn't above lining his own pockets by taking bribes from decent men who were desperate for work. More often than not, he favoured his own cronies over other hard-working folk, but it didn't do to get on the wrong side of Alfie because most families had one or more men who relied on the employment. It wasn't so long ago that men were queuing round the block for a bowl of something hot from one of the soup kitchens. Things had improved slightly but no one was sure what war could bring.

Alfie lurched towards her now and Kitty felt a little vulnerable since Rita had gone to find her own husband, who had been missing for ages.

'D'ya fancy coming dancing with me tonight?' Alfie's eyes were all over her as he slipped a huge hand around her waist. He was quite drunk and Kitty baulked at the stale smell of whiskey and cigarette fumes. She neatly wriggled free of his grasp.

'I think you need to go home and sleep it off

165

before you try dancing, Alf,' she said amiably, knowing he might turn nasty in drink and not wanting to chance it. If it had not been for their Jack, they would have been completely beholden to the likes of Alfie Delaney. Kitty shuddered at the thought of keeping him sweet for the promise of work for her father.

'Are you all right, Kit?' Frank asked, coming out of the back door.

Kitty breathed a sigh of relief and nodded. 'I'm just going to go in to make those sandwiches,' she said quickly. Saved by Frank – again. It was funny, Kitty observed, that more than once today he seemed to have come along at just the right minute.

'More tea, Aunty Doll?' Kitty asked. She was starting to really enjoy the day now. It was hard work but very rewarding. Everybody had commented on the lovely spread, and the cake had brought gasps of admiration. Kitty felt so proud. Not much had ever come good in her life so far but one thing she could be sure of: she could always bake a good cake and knowing that made her feel a little more secure. Everybody liked cakes.

'You could certainly be a comfort to a man on a cold, dark winter's night.' Alfie Delaney's hands rubbed the thin fabric on the shoulder of Kitty's blouse as he sidled up to her in the front parlour. There was no mistaking the look of hunger in his eyes and Kitty knew it was not cake he was after. She half turned away from him but to no avail as he made a fresh attempt to put his arm around her slim waist and pull her towards him.

Everybody had been drinking and some were the worse for wear, but Kitty was stone-cold sober and she did not like being pawed by the likes of Alfie Delaney. She felt a bump and she was jolted forward slightly.

'Sorry, Kit!' Frank laughed as he swooped her into his arms. 'How's about a dance?'

'Be my guest, Frank.' Alfie's lip curled but he didn't dare challenge Frank. 'After all, we're here to have a good time.'

'Just say the word, Kit, and I will floor that bastard... Oh, sorry, Kit, I should mind my language!' Frank's slip of the tongue embarrassed him more than it did Kitty, who had never been so relieved to be whisked off her feet.

'He's drunk,' Kitty said, thrilled to be in Frank's arms for whatever reason; she did not care as long as they were close together.

'He's not as drunk as you think,' Frank informed her. 'I've seen his type before: they blame all their bad behaviour on being drunk and get away with it.'

Frank whirled Kitty round and round the room and Kitty wasn't sure if it was the heat and the smoke, or if it was being so near Frank, but she felt a little dizzy and nearly lost her footing.

'Oops-a-daisy,' said Frank, holding her firmly by the waist and steadying her.

Kitty suddenly realised that the only thing she could smell on Frank was the clean fragrance of soap. There was not a hint of alcohol... Alfie might be drunk but Frank certainly wasn't! She leaned back and looked at him now and his eyes were dancing with mischief.

'Do you think I could blame my bad behaviour on being drunk, Kitty?' he said.

'What do you mean, Frank? You're not drunk,' she answered uncertainly, but good-naturedly, carried along by the mischievous look in his eyes.

'No, Kitty, I'm not drunk.' Frank looked at her steadily, grinning, but Kitty saw something else in his blue eyes, something she had never seen before, something that made her heart beat faster in her chest and that almost took her breath away. Then, right there, in the middle of the gathered guests in his mam's front parlour, he took Kitty in his arms and he kissed her. The feel of Frank's soft, warm lips on her own gave Kitty a delicious tingling feeling somewhere near the top of her legs. It was a sensation that she had never experienced before, but it was a rush of pleasure that seemed to radiate throughout her whole body, from the tips of her toes right up to the hairs on her head. It was heavenly, but over so quickly.

Frank let her go and pulled away from her, laughing shamelessly. 'Sorry, Kit, I couldn't resist.'

Kitty didn't know where to look. Frank had only been teasing her, but now Kitty thought that the whole room must be able to see the blush that she felt sure must have crept over her face. She tried to laugh to cover her embarrassment.

Frank looked over to Delaney to see a slow, thoughtful grin widen his adversary's fleshy lips. Frank felt his blood rise when Alfie said, 'I'll sit this one out and just admire the view.' He raised his glass and took a swig of free whiskey. Frank felt that if Delaney so much as tried to go anywhere near Kitty he would tear him limb from limb!

As much as he would not normally give a damn what anyone else thought, Alfie was wary of the calculating look Frank Feeny was sending his way. He had to tread carefully here. He knew the lad, a few years younger than he, had always been quick on his feet. He boxed for the navy, now, apparently. Alfie would not take kindly to being on the receiving end of a quick dig from one of Feeny's powerful left-handers. The sailor would be a dangerous man to cross.

Raising his glass, Alfie nodded his regard to his adversary. He liked to know what he was up against in battle... However, he never could get the measure of Frank Feeny, even though he had known him all his life.

Frank knew Delaney was a fool and certainly not worth upsetting his sister's day for. He turned his attention to his younger brother, Eddy, when Kitty disappeared into the back kitchen, sitting himself at one end of the table while Eddy took the other.

'We sail next Friday, what about you?'

'Monday morning,' Eddy answered, 'off to Montreal unless the wind changes.' They both knew that he meant in the event of the announcement of war, which, both brothers had been warned, could be any day now. They were allowed leave only on the understanding they would be able to get to their ships at short notice. As luck would have it, both ships had docked at Gladstone, less than ten minutes' walk away.

However, their conversation was cut short when Mrs Kennedy, wearing a felt tricorn hat that matched the colour of her fox fur, said, 'Sailing on a Friday?' She shook her head, and grimaced at Frank. 'I've heard it's bad luck to sail on a Friday.'

'You'd better stay at home then, son.' Dolly, neatly elegant in her new blue dress, knew nautical superstition was prolific around here. 'I don't know what the Admiralty would say about it, mind.'

'Sarah, you look as if your corset's too tight,' said Eddy, the quiet joker of the family, laughing at his younger sister sitting on a straight-backed chair while the tables were being set against the parlour walls to make room in the centre for people to dance if they wanted to. Sarah looked around, making sure Nancy was not within earshot, before plucking at the sleeve of the taffeta dress. 'I want to take this off. It's cutting in,' she hissed.

Eddy smiled. 'You look lovely.'

'I'm uncomfortable and it's too hot. I'll have to go outside to cool down.'

'If she hangs on a few years, I might take her to a dance or two.' Delaney was swaying slightly now. Frank sighed. For Nancy's sake, he knew it would do no good if he threw the groom's best friend out on the street, no matter how much he wanted to.

But Eddy, the quieter of the Feeny brothers, seemed to have no such reservation when he said, 'You lay one finger on my sister and I'll swing for you, Delaney.'

'Well said, brother,' Frank laughed. Rumour had it Delaney had been dropped on his head when he was little and that was why he was prone to violent outbursts. However, Frank did not believe that. He thought Delaney was one of life's bad 'uns,

170

who got a depraved kind of enjoyment out of seeing other people suffer. It was a power thing. There were some here today who had to keep the foreman sweet for the want of a day's work, but not the Feenys. They were not in Delaney's pocket, nor would they ever be.

Frank felt he had been a decent amount of time in the parlour entertaining guests by now.

'Excuse me, ladies,' he said to his appreciative audience in that polite way his mother had instilled in him. He left the ageing aunts smiling before wandering out to the back kitchen where he considered Kitty might need a hand with the washing-up.

Standing in the doorway, he silently watched her for a moment as she removed the triangular scarf and lifted her glossy, ebony curls to allow the faint breeze to waft over her slender neck. It was a movement so unusually sensual that it made his pulse race. Frank had an overwhelming urge to go and lift those curls and kiss her on that delicate spot on her neck. However, the self-assured audacity he displayed earlier had somehow deserted him.

Frank was a man of the world. He'd had plenty of girls in his life and knew the sort of treatment they liked from men, but how was it, he wondered, that all of his confidence around women seemed to have deserted him now? Kitty Callaghan had been a mainstay in his life for as long as he could remember, from the very day when they had brought her home after her mother had died and she had sat in their parlour wrapped in his mother's arms. Frank had wanted to protect Kitty

171

then. What did he want now? Something more than all of the other girls had to offer. But Frank checked himself. It wouldn't do to race ahead of things. He was about to set off to sea and who knew when he would be back? War was coming and every man would be needed to head off the threat of the Nazis. He could be gone for months, years even. Frank could see that Kitty was caught up in her own thoughts. Her soft eyes gazed off into the middle distance and Frank thought that her features, caught in repose, had never looked so beautiful. I'll keep this picture in my head, thought Frank. No matter what the future holds, I'll think of Kitty and she'll be the face of home for me.

'Can I give you a hand with anything?' His voice came out unusually hoarse, making Kitty whip around quickly.

'I... erm... No... You mustn't,' she stammered. 'You'll get your uniform ruined.'

'It's fine. Let me get these for you; we'll have them done in no time.' Frank picked up a stack of gold-rimmed plates and plunged them into the enamel bowl of hot soapy water. 'You wash and I'll dry.'

Kitty looked at him as if he had gone quite doo-lally, and with her hands resting on her slim hips, her hair loosely inviting and her dark eyes flashing she said with the hint of a smile, 'They've already been washed and dried.' They looked at one another and a bubble of laughter rose simultaneously in their throats, rendering them both helpless with hilarity.

'Come on, Kitty,' said Frank, wiping the tears of laughter from his eyes. 'Let's ditch the shackles of domesticity and go and join the dancing.'

'This must be the hottest summer for years,' Sarah said, fanning her face with a white cotton napkin, pressed to perfection in the shape of a fan. She, too, had had enough of the stuffy, smoke-filled front room where the alcohol was loosening tongues and making some of the assembled guests maudlin, turning the conversation to war talk. She was now sitting outside on the low wall at the front of the house. 'There's thunder in the air, I'm sure of it.' She looked up at the cloudless sky.

'You're imagining things, Sarah,' said Danny Callaghan, appearing beside her seemingly out of nowhere.

'Here, where have you been?' She looked up at him. 'You've missed the wedding and the spread.'

Danny avoided her eyes. 'Not far,' he answered nonchanantly. 'Weddings aren't my cup of tea. All those maiden aunts and women getting daft on sherry. You look nice,' he added for the want of something to say, even though he thought the dress was hideous. Flicking the napkin at a passing fly, Sarah realised that for as much as she had looked forward to this day for months, she was not in the humour for it now.

'This dress is a monstrosity and the heat's giving me a headache, I wish it would rain,' she said, watching heat waves quiver above the pavement.

'Frank and Eddy look smart,' Danny said, his voice laced with envy as he watched the two men stand by the front door smoking and chatting with Alfie Delaney. How much would he give to be in their position now? Bloody heart trouble.

173

There was nothing wrong with it. He hadn't had any pains or anything. How could they say he had a bad heart?

'They could be called back any minute,' Sarah answered with a dramatic air. She and Danny had been friends since they were young. 'Thick as thieves' was how Dolly affectionately described them. Sarah thought Danny was misunderstood. She could not see any harm in him whatsoever.

'So what? Bloody war, a lot of flippin' nonsense, if you ask me.'

Sarah looked at Danny quizzically. 'What's the matter, Danny?' she asked. Sarah could tell he was out of sorts and that something was bothering him.

'Sorry, Sarah, your mam must be worried, what with the news and everything...' His voice sounded strangled and Danny cursed himself again for his stupid weak heart.

'Come on, Danny. I know you too well to be fobbed off. Something's got to you. Come on – spit it out.' Sarah could be quite tenacious when she put her mind to it. But Danny couldn't bring himself to speak.

'Just leave me alone, Sarah! It's nothing. Nothing, I tell you,' he blurted out. Danny was surprised by the force of his words and he could tell that Sarah was shocked and hurt too. He'd never spoken to her like that. She was his best friend.

'Well, if that's how you're going to be, then you're on your own, Danny Callaghan.' Sarah stood up and was about to make her way back into the house, her shoulders thrown back and her head in the air.

Danny regretted his outburst and put his hand on her arm to stop her. Sarah turned to look at Danny but was taken aback to see hot tears welling in his eyes.

'Danny, what on earth...?'

Danny sat down on the wall and put his head in his hands. Sarah, momentarily speechless, sat down next to him and rested her hand on his. She looked at his ashen face. What could be wrong?

'I'm not fit for the war, Sarah. They've said I've got a weak heart and can't go into service. I've got to sit the war out.' He looked down at his feet, unable to meet her eyes.

'Oh, Danny.' Sarah knew what a disappointment this would be for him. Danny had done nothing for months but talk about what he was going to do to get that ruddy Hitler. Sarah didn't try to offer him platitudes. She knew this was a bitter blow.

'There's other things you can do. You're clever. Can't they put that brain of yours to good use?' she asked.

'Don't be daft, Sarah. There's all those clever clogs out there that went to posh schools and the like. The likes of us lot from Empire Street won't get a look in. Besides, I should be fighting, like a real man.' His face was full of anguish. 'Anyway, no point crying over spilled milk.'

'You'll make something of yourself, Danny. You've got more heart than anyone and I know you'll surprise us all one day. You'll see.' Danny looked at Sarah. In her face he saw only honesty, conviction and total faith in him. For a moment he almost believed her, but then the crashing reality came over him again.

'You're the only one that believes that. Promise you won't tell anyone. Not a word, not even to Kitty.'

'Not a word,' Sarah promised him truthfully.

'Are you coming over later?' Sarah asked. 'Mam's asked everybody.'

'Maybe.'

'I caught me mam crying in the back kitchen when the news came on earlier.'

They both sat quietly for a moment or two, Sarah closing her eyes against the sun. Neither of them was aware of Alfie Delaney looking intently at them before stubbing out his cigarette and making his way back into the house. Danny nudged Sarah and pointed down the street. 'Look, somebody's been a naughty boy.' Sarah opened her eyes and looked up the street at an approaching police constable heading their way.

'I hope this bobby isn't coming for us. You haven't even started singing yet!' Danny laughed, and Sarah was pleased that his good humour was restored for now, while she confidently swung her legs off the low wall. However, they adopted serious faces when the police officer stopped in front of them.

'Frank Feeny?' he asked solemnly. Sarah looked up at Danny and her heart flipped. What did the police want with her brother?

'Frank! Frank, you're wanted out here!' she called up the lobby, and soon well-dressed wedding guests surrounded the police officer.

After talking to the police officer in the privacy of the hallway for a few minutes, Frank thanked him and, looking a little subdued, he gave his father a signal to go with him into the other room where it was a little quieter.

'I've got to go back, Pop.' Frank looked worried. 'I've got orders to return on board straight away. She's sailing on the midnight tide.'

'If the authorities are sending the police to round up the troops then things must be serious,' Pop said grimly. Something was starting to happen now. Moreover, that something, he presumed, was war.

'Make us proud, our Frank. I'll walk as far as the dock with you after you've said goodbye to your mother,' Pop said quietly, and Frank nodded. Each knew what the other was thinking. This time tomorrow, they could be at war. It was anybody's guess what would happen after that.

'There's someone else I need to speak to,' Frank said quietly. Why had he left it so long? Why hadn't he asked Kitty earlier?

He looked around the home he had grown up in. He could not wait to get away at one time. See the world. Make something of himself. He could hear his mam's unmistakable laugh in the parlour, and someone had retrieved Pop's squeezebox from the front bedroom where he kept it by the dressing table, and was playing a lively tune. Everyone was having a good time, oblivious of the fact that this time next week, they might have to fight for the right to sing in the street. But Frank would not be here. He would be protecting this street, this country, from the tyrants who wanted to put a stop to people having a good time and a free life.

He took a deep breath and wondered when he would see this little community again. The navy knew what to expect. They had been waiting for something to happen for months. Now it looked as if it had finally arrived.

'Hey, Kit.'

Kitty was just leaving the house. She turned, expecting to see the ready smile that usually crossed Frank's lips, but it seemed forced now. For a moment, there was no sound between them. Then he called, 'Do you think we could fit one more dance in now?' Kitty stood on the step, her spine as straight as the handle on a back yard brush. He had his kitbag over his shoulder.

She had known Frank Feeny for twenty years, and for as long as she could remember she had thought of him with a pleasure so intense it would carry her through the day. She watched him when she was younger with something akin to hero worship.

He was taller and braver than anybody she knew, except their Jack. He won medals for scoring more goals and making more runs than anybody else in the whole borough, and he had begged his proud mother to take the trophies out of the parlour window.

Frank had taken her in his arms the day little Tommy was born and, holding her closer than she had ever been held before, he let her sob on his shoulder because her mam had died. He showed her how to fold a triangular nappy because he had done it for his own little sister, Sarah. Kitty hated goodbyes. She had not said it to anybody since her mam had died. And she was not going to say it today.

He looked down at his Royal Navy regulation

shoes, as black and shiny as beetles, while Kitty fixed her eyes on the white silk ribbon fluttering in the gentle evening breeze that wafted up from the river.

'Shall we?' Frank asked, and he edged towards her, unsure. A feeling of euphoria rocketed through Kitty's chest, straight to her heart. This was going to be the most exquisite pain she would ever endure. To feel the closeness of Frank's strong, muscular arms holding her for only a short time. She wanted more ... much more.

'You've got to go right now?' Kitty tried to suppress the sob in her voice and Frank nodded, obviously unable to speak. He looked at her for a long time and she silently gazed back at him, her eyes taking in the contours of his handsome face, his dark blue, wide-awake eyes, the small scar on his left cheek where he'd once fallen from the railway wall after a dare, just to prove how brave he was. Kitty knew how brave he was and longed to tell him but words seemed to have deserted her. Only their eyes spoke now. Hers were begging him to come home safe, while his were saying a reluctant goodbye.

'Come on, Kit, just one dance,' Frank whispered at last. 'I don't know when I'll be passing this way again.' His heart was breaking at the thought of Kitty left here with Alfie Delaney. There was a sad ghost of a smile on his lips and Kitty suddenly longed to feel the gentle pressure of those lips on hers.

'Hopefully soon,' she whispered.

'I promise I won't trip you up.' Frank scooped her into his arms in full view of their neighbours, who had come out to say goodbye. He held her close, hardly moving as the sound of Gloria's melodious tones sailed through the open door of the Sailor's Rest down the street. The thought of them both making a spectacle of themselves in the street did not enter Kitty's head. She and Frank were the only two people in the world. Kitty never wanted this dance to end.

'Will you write to me, Kit?' His gentle plea was whispered through her hair. They had stopped dancing now. Each was locked in the other's gaze ... the other's heart. Frank was still holding her.

'Of course I will, Frank.'

'Come on, lad.' Pop's reluctant words shattered the moment. 'It's time to go.' The air was heavy now, and a single rumble of thunder rolled across the sky as if heralding the war to come.

'Don't come with me, Pop, I'd rather go alone. Stay here with Mam and Nancy...' Frank's smile was forced when he threw his kitbag back over his shoulder. 'Take care, Kit. I'll see you soon. Promise you'll save a dance for me.' He leaned down and placed a single, gentle kiss on her lips...

Kitty's heart was too full for her to be able to say anything. Along with everybody else, she watched Frank walking away down the street towards the dock. His back was straight and his head held high. His distinctive whistle filled the evening air. Reaching the bottom of the street, he waved without turning back. Then he was gone.

PART TWO

CHAPTER TEN

September 1939

'C'mon, son, it's time...' Rita's voice echoed in the quiet void between night and day, knowing it was far too early to rouse a child from slumber. She turned fleetingly and took in the black fingers on the round-faced alarm clock. It was almost five thirty, an ungodly hour to wake up a child, her mother had said yesterday. It must be done, though, Rita answered. Her heart was silently breaking but she had to be strong. She could not let Megan and Michael see that she did not want them to go. If they got so much as the merest hint she could refuse to let them go they would beg, plead, and finally wear her down. Then, if the city were bombed, as it was expected to be any day now, and something happened to her babies, she would not be able to live with herself.

Signing the form allowing the authorities to drag her children from the bosom of a family who desperately loved them was the hardest thing she had had to do so far. The Good Lord Himself only knew how she was going to summon the courage to say goodbye.

Standing beside six-year-old Michael's bed, Rita caught sight of the unruly mop of flame-red hair atop a reluctantly stirring little body that had been curled around the tangled counterpane and crumpled, clean white sheets. It might be a long time before she was fortunate enough to wake her boy in the morning again. How would she live without them? Her children were her reason to keep going each day.

'Come on, Michael...' Rita's hesitant tone was barely above a whisper. She did not want to waken him, but she must. Rita knew Michael, a sensitive lad, was frightened, although he had hidden it well before last night's stomach cramps made him cry.

Drawing a deep breath of warm air, Rita suspected the pain was really in Michael's heart and not his tummy. He must be ever so scared, she thought. They all were. However, she had to be resilient. She was their mother, the one person in the world they could trust unconditionally. So why did she feel as if she was betraying them? She took a deep breath. She must not buckle. She must show the children how to be brave. She must hold her head high and encourage them to do the same.

'Come on, Michael... I have to wake Megan now.' Trying to make her voice sound bright, Rita's heart broke into a million pieces as she silently pleaded to her boy, *Please, do not make this any harder...*

'You don't want to be the last one on the charabanc, do you?'

Michael did not answer though she knew he had heard.

'It'll be like goin' on holiday. Remember when we went to the Isle of Man on the ferry? We stayed in that guesthouse... You loved it.'

'I don't wanna go on a charabanc, Mam.' There

184

was a sob in Michael's voice even though he was trying hard not cry. Rita could hear it though it was muffled beneath the sheet he had pulled over his head, and her throat tightened as she watched his little body curled into a ball. 'Now come on, Michael, be a good boy for me today.' Going against every instinct she had, Rita hardened her tone to a warning note. 'I've boiled your egg just the way you like it.' If she let her emotions take over now she would never let him go. She headed towards the bedroom door. 'You've got two minutes to get out of that bed and into your trousers. So move it!' Outside on the landing she had to put her fist in her mouth to stop the sob escaping from her lips.

'Kitty, I've got a sore throat!' Tommy still sounded like a bullfrog, even though Kitty had given him the last of the medicine Alfie Delaney had brought over before Nancy's wedding last week. If Tommy's throat did not get any better, Kitty knew she would not let him be evacuated. How could she? What if he got worse? What if his new foster parents thought he had been neglected? They could report her for cruelty even though she had always tried to do her best for Tommy.

'Maybe you should stay at home until you are better,' Kitty said. 'I'll go and fetch the doctor.' In accepting that Tommy was not going with the rest of the school, another worry formed in Kitty's head. What if they were invaded by the Germans? The people of Empire Street were a close-knit community and would lend you their last penny if they thought it would help you out but what were these daily kindnesses when they would have to fight against bombs and bullets? How could she look after Tommy if war came to the city? What would she do if she had to get a job in a munitions factory and he would be hanging around the streets because the authorities had requisitioned the schools? Kitty's mind was in turmoil, hopping from one worry to another.

She passed the school on her way to the doctor's. The kids were all gathered, the older ones obviously enjoying the big adventure they were about to embark on, anxious to get away from doting mothers.

Younger ones, like Rita's, were hugging the hems of their mothers' coats and trying not to cry. The strained look on the faces of the silent mothers was enough to tell Kitty she had done the right thing. Tommy was staying put!

Standing at the back of a group of mothers, Rita waited while the children lined up to get onto the charabanc. They just looked like a group of children leaving for a school outing until you saw their respirators hanging around their necks in the stout, brown cardboard boxes, and the way they were clinging to their little suitcases or haversacks, filled with their personal necessities. Some even carried their belongings in white pillowcases.

Rita saw Megan and Michael listening intently to their teacher, who told them to wave when they were about to move off. Rita took a deep breath through her nose, trying to suppress the painful sob that threatened to make a show of her. Her children were bound for who knew where, and she could do nothing to stop that now.

One little girl was carrying a gaily coloured res-pirator box, which was being delightedly admired by the other children. Rita read the child's name on the identity label pinned to the lapel of her good-quality woollen coat, and was not surprised to see she was the daughter of a local bookie.

Children of all ages had been scrubbed and pol-ished and were being told not to worry, everything would be fine... 'Stay with your brother.' 'Don't let them separate you.' 'I'll be there as soon as you send me your address.' 'Make sure you wash your neck.' 'Don't you dare make a show of me!' *Hey, we've got chocolate!* A whoop of delight delayed the inevitable tears. A teacher began to sing 'Wish Me Luck as You Wave Me Goodbye' as the crocodile line of children inched their way onto the chara-banc.

Rita looked up to the brightening sky. It was no good; she could hold the tears back no longer. She prayed as she had never prayed before. *Dear Lord, don't let anything bad happen to my babies. Don't let them suffer.*

A foghorn sounded on the river as the early morning miasma dulled the calls of men who had been unloading the ships through the night so they could quickly turn round and cross the Atlantic to bring back supplies to replenish England's pantry. When the bombers came the larders would be worst hit, and a hungry country would quickly lose the will to fight.

Listening to the soothing clip-clopping hoofs on cobbled setts as the shire horses paraded the dock road pulling heavy loads, Rita knew her children would be well out of it. The docklands would most certainly be one of Hitler's main targets.

The evidence was all around them. Bootle Corporation had piled sandbags around the walls of the Town Hall on the other side of Millers Bridge. The community air raid shelters had brick walls and thick concrete roofs to withstand the bombs, and had been great places for kids to play when war was just a rumour. Now they stood empty, waiting, while the mothers of those children broke their hearts.

Evacuation was a precaution, the teachers had said. The children would be home by Christmas. However, Rita was not so sure. They'd said everyone would be home by Christmas in 1914. She knew it must be serious to put the kids through this, disrupting schools and communities. Mothers weren't stupid. The war was coming here for sure.

'I can't wait to see where we're goin', Mam,' Megan said brightly through the small window of the charabanc. She was standing on the seat and Rita worried her daughter would be scolded by one of the teachers. Well, not while I'm standing here, Rita thought determinedly. Just let them try!

'Do you think we'll be near the shore, Mam? Do I look all right? Do I really need me big coat, even though it's so warm?'

'It won't be warm for much longer,' Rita said without thinking. When the reality of her situation dawned on Megan, her eyes grew wide with unshed tears and her chin trembled. She held her lips together in an effort to stop them turning downwards. Rita could see she was doing her best not to cry and watched little Megan take deep breaths to stem the tears that threatened to fall as her little hands gripped the metal frame of the narrow window.

Be brave, little one... Someone else must dry your tears now.

'You'll be home in no time, love.' Rita gave Megan her widest smile while inside she felt her heart was breaking into a thousand shattered little pieces. Then, in a moment of blind inspiration, she said, 'You look like Shirley Temple with your hair in ringlets.'

'Do I, Mam?' Megan smiled through her tears. 'Do I really?'

'We'll soon be off, children. Wave goodbye to your mothers.'

As she blew a kiss to her beloved children, the engine of the bus started up, and Rita manoeuvred herself to the front of the tearful throng of mothers. She saw Michael was laughing – actually laughing – at something someone had said. Rita breathed a sigh of relief. She had been so worried he would try to get off the bus. When he turned and caught sight of her, he waved frantically, his face wreathed in smiles.

He is only going on a school outing. Rita forced herself to think nice thoughts so she could wave the children off without crying. Then she saw Michael nudge Megan, who had elbowed her way to the window again. Rita's heart slumped when she saw the tears flowing down her little girl's cheeks, her chin wobbling desperately and her bottom lip curled.

Megan had been so stoically brave until the last possible minute for Michael's sake. It was obviously too much for her to bear now, though. Rita tried to make a smiling face for her daughter's sake, but her heart was not in it. Her own eyes now brimming with scalding tears, Rita waved as if her life depended upon it.

'...I have to tell you now ... this country is at war with Germany.'

Kitty, Rita, Mrs Kennedy and a few other neighbours without the wireless had gathered around the Bakelite radio in Mrs Kennedy's back room. On 1 September, Germany had invaded Poland. The country awaited anxiously for what would happen next and now here they were two days later. It was the news that everyone had expected but that no one had wanted to hear. Most disturbing was Mr Chamberlain's warning that the country should expect air raids at once.

'Jesus wept!' Rita said to Kitty. 'We got the kids away just in time!'

Moments later the most awful banshee wail started up and the two women headed to the front of the shop where they looked out of the window to see people scurrying up and down the little street. Mrs Kennedy came hurrying from the back room, her usually immaculately coiffured hair wrapped in steel curlers.

'Oh my God,' she cried, running pointlessly around the shop. 'We're all going to die!'

Not long after, the all clear sounded and the air raid warning was obviously a false alarm, much to the relief of the women of Empire Street who had been preparing the veg or putting the joint in the oven for Sunday dinner. For weeks now there had been drills, but the awful reality that an air raid could be imminent was a shock.

Pop, in the sitting room at number three, lowered his head and experienced that stomach-churning fear he had felt the day he had lost his eye at Jutland during the Great War.

Dolly's face had turned a sickly white at the news that the first British ship had been attacked only hours into the war. SS *Athenia* was not even a fighting ship; she was a passenger liner, and she had been torpedoed and sunk 250 miles off the north-west coast of Ireland by a German U-boat. Pop knew exactly what this meant. There was no turning back now.

'It looks like Germany's up to its old tricks again, Doll,' Pop said, gripping his wife's hand. During the Great War, submarines had nearly strangled the shipping lanes of Great Britain. 'It looks like we're in for more of the same from them U-boats.'

'Oh, Pop!' Dolly exclaimed, shock etched across her stricken face. 'What about my boys?'

'They won't be boys after this, Doll.' Pop looked grave. 'You take my word for it.'

'It's like the January sales in here today,' Gloria said when she and Nancy took their break.

'I know. I'm sorry I only took a week off after the wedding. Sid said I should have taken two.'

'It was a great do though, Nance,' Gloria laughed. 'I got chatted up by one of those Canadian marines; he gave me his address and every-

191

thing.' Her eyes sparkled as she spoke.

'I thought Giles would be there,' Nancy said mischievously, knowing her best friend liked nothing better than having a boyfriend spare in case her current relationship didn't work out. They both laughed as they headed for their favourite table in the staff dining room.

'I was surprised to see you back,' Gloria said, evading the insinuation. 'I thought Sid would stop you working after you were married.'

'We're saving for a house.' Nancy's eyes wandered to the morning newspaper left by one of the boiler-suited workmen applying strips of sticky tape to the windows. A short while later a waitress brought two cups of tea and some toast.

'It says here, people left their holiday guesthouses in droves,' Nancy read from the *Daily Mirror*, 'all eager to get back home in case anything happens.'

'Well, I think it's tantamount to hysterics.' Gloria buttered a piece of toast and then applied a liberal spread of lime marmalade before breaking the toast in half and then half again.

'That reminds me, I've got to pick up some more blackout material for Sid's mam.' Nancy rolled her eyes, obviously not pleased about the prospect.

'I've got segs on my eyes, measuring and cutting all that black material,' Gloria said, 'and I'm sure it will all be for nothing.'

'Are you?' Nancy looked doubtful now. 'Our Rita's kids were evacuated the other day.'

'I saw long lines of kids going into Lime Street Station early this morning. They looked ever so little...' Gloria gently blew a stream of air onto her hot tea, wondering if her hips could risk another round of toast. 'They were really well-behaved, though, all carrying their little suitcases and pillowslips.' Gloria eyed the second round of toast and reckoned she would risk it.

Nancy nodded and her curled fringe bounced on her forehead. 'I didn't think it would get to this stage!'

'You were too engrossed in your wedding day to notice anything, Nancy. War preparations completely passed you by.'

Nancy giggled. 'I don't want another war, Glor,' she said in a low faraway voice, her hand resting protectively on her stomach. 'My Sid's a member of the Territorials and I am expecting, you know.'

Gloria rolled her eyes and sighed, aware of the low hubbub of chatter in the staff dining room. 'Of course I know you're pregnant.' Nancy had talked about nothing else since she got married. 'I'll drop the Germans a line if you like, Nance; they'll take it into consideration when they start bombing, I'm sure.'

However, even though the air raid sirens had gone off every night since war was declared last Sunday, there had been no sign of any attacks. Still, nobody was taking any chances and the air raid shelters were usually filled with people.

Gloria's mother loved it because it gave her a chance to put her feet up and have a good old natter to her neighbours for a couple of hours until the all clear went, but Dad wasn't so pleased if the all clear didn't go until after ten o'clock of an evening, by which time it was too late for 'last orders'. Gloria knew he had started locking the doors and continuing serving if there was a good crowd of foreign sailors in. Nancy's new husband was a regular when he was supposed to be doing nights on the docks but Gloria decided to keep it under her hat. She wasn't one for causing trouble.

Nancy was still reading the paper and Gloria was twisting her slim wrist this way and that, watching the light glance off the marcasite bracelet Giles had given her. It was a thank you for the pleasure she gave him, he had said. Gloria felt a little soiled by his gratitude. After all, they weren't diamonds, were they?

'Are you going anywhere tonight, Glor?' Nancy asked, folding the paper, which contained only depressing stories about Hitler and his henchmen anyway.

'It depends how busy the pub is.' She gave her parents a hand behind the bar if it was busy. Nevertheless, Gloria was restless. The hoped-for regular spot at the Adelphi had come to nothing since war was declared because all forms of live entertainment had stopped for the time being. Even the theatres had closed.

However, her belting renditions of popular songs could still be heard in her father's pub at the end of Empire Street on a Friday evening, and kept the regulars as well as the visiting foreign sailors suitably distracted. Happy customers drink more, her dear old dad was wont to say. He also said she could have a room full of corpses on their feet, clapping along in no time.

'Is that a new bracelet?' Nancy asked covetously, wishing she got presents like Gloria did. She was sure she would appreciate them much more than her best friend did.

'It's the ugliest thing I've ever seen,' Gloria scoffed. 'I only wore it because Giles said he was popping into the store this morning and as usual he let me down.' Why do men think they can keep hold of you with very small tokens of their appreciation? Gloria wondered, eyeing the bracelet with a sweep of disgust through her false eyelashes.

She did not need gifts. Her parents had given her gifts all her life; it was their way of compensating her for neglecting her. She never looked neglected. In fact, she had everything a girl could want and more – but the one thing she valued and longed for above all else was their time. A few short moments of their attention would have Gloria walking on air all day. She wanted to be loved for herself. For those so-short moments when she let her men friends have their way, she knew she had their full attention, and it was knowing she was the only one they cared about in that moment that she really liked.

'Don't be daft,' Nancy said admiringly. 'It's a lovely bracelet. It would go nicely with my pale blue twinset.'

Smiling, Gloria immediately unhooked the clasp, took the bracelet off, and gave it to her friend across the table. 'Here, take it. You will be doing me a favour.'

'You can't give your present away!' Nancy protested, knowing she would be thrilled if Sid ever gave her something so lovely. However, Gloria was not listening.

'Enjoy it,' Gloria said, wrinkling her small tilted nose.

'You don't know when you are well off, Glor, that's your trouble,' Nancy told her friend as she fastened the bracelet on her wrist. Then, offering it to the overhead electric light, twisting it so she could enjoy its lustre more clearly, she added, 'Men love you so much...'

'Want to get me into bed, you mean,' Gloria said, raising a perfectly arched eyebrow before draining the last of her tea.

'Well, he wouldn't be the first,' Nancy laughed. Gloria was so sophisticated.

'And he won't be the last either,' Gloria agreed, 'but he won't be *the one*.'

'You sound so sure,' Nancy said.

'The man I give my life to will buy me diamonds,' Gloria laughed, grabbing her crocodile skin handbag. 'Marcasite doesn't do it for me.' They both rose from the table and, catching up her handbag, Nancy quickly followed her friend back to the mayhem that was Haberdashery.

The new consignment of blackout material had arrived earlier and someone had leaked the information. Nancy was halfway down the marble stairs when she stopped, her hand on the shiny wooden balustrade, to see frantic housewives elbowing each other out of the way to get at it.

'You're lucky to be so beautiful you can choose,' she said almost to herself.

'You're too insecure, Nance,' Gloria said matter-of-factly. 'You have no faith in your feminine allure and were daft enough to get yourself caught, that's all.'

'Don't sugar-coat it, will you, Glor?' Nancy huffed. If she had to live with Sid's mother, Gloria would be insecure too. Lack of faith in her feminine allure was the least of her worries.

Pop put his arms around his wife when he told her that the ARP had been mobilised. He wanted to comfort her should she dissolve into tears at the news.

'I'd be most surprised if you hadn't joined, Bert.' Dolly usually only called him Bert when he was in hot water. Kissing her forehead, he let her go, safe in the knowledge she had accepted the news that Britain was at war with Germany even if she didn't like it one bit.

'But what if it all comes to nothing? Hmm, tell me that!' Dolly nodded.

Pop sighed and finished fixing up a pelmet to accommodate her newly made blackout curtains before putting his hammer back in his toolbox. 'Well, that will be a good thing, Doll,' he said with little hope in his heart as, at 7.47 p.m., blackout regulations came into force. He peered out of the parlour window. The street looked eerily strange with no children playing outside. He saw Cyril had blacked out the lights of the pub. The Sailor's Rest blacked out – what was the world coming to?

Rita almost fell on the postman as she saw his figure pass the front parlour window and dashed to open the door. He was just about to put a couple of letters through the letterbox.

'Is there one for me there, Bob?'

'Eh, Rita, keep your 'air on!'

Bob the postman passed Rita two letters. One looked like a bill for Mrs Kennedy but the other one was the one that she had been holding out for desperately. It was addressed to Mr and Mrs C. Kennedy and the postmark was from Lancashire. She could barely get inside the door quickly enough and her eager fingers tore the envelope.

Breathlessly she opened the letter. Inside was an official one which read:

Dear Mr and Mrs Kennedy
We are pleased to inform you that your children have been found a suitable place in a village called Freshfield with a suitable family who run a farm in the area...

Rita read on eagerly. The letter was from the children's teacher and told them that they were welcome to visit the children once they had settled in, that regular visits were permitted and there was an address provided so that they could write and make arrangements with the family that were looking after the children. Rita breathed a sigh of relief. She had heard of Freshfield. It wasn't too far away and she felt sure that there was a train that went straight there from Liverpool. Thank heavens they were close by. They could easily have ended up anywhere in the country.

There was also another letter in the envelope. Tears welled up in Rita's eyes as she recognised the childish scrawl of her son, Michael. It read:

Dear mummy and daddy. We are very safe here. There are sheeps and pigs and cows and a goat that eats everything. Megan likes the little chicks and we help the

farmer to feed the animals. We miss you very much.
Love from Michael and Megan xxxxx

Tears streamed freely down her face. She was counting the days until she saw them.

'Tommy! What do you think you're playing at?' Kitty stormed down the narrow lobby towards the front door to see a small group of women gathered outside her parlour window. Poking her turbaned head outside, Kitty was amazed to see the glass covered in sticky tape. Not, however, the nice neat regular crisscross pattern favoured by her neighbours and every other respectable resident in the area.

Instead, Tommy had chosen to cover their windows with haphazard squares, and triangles that resembled Christmas trees, even though it was only October. A huge W covered one window while another one had an M – anything, it seemed, that had caught his fevered imagination filled the bay windows.

Kitty had known Tommy would be better off tucked away in the countryside when the local bobby had brought him home for trying to deflate a barrage balloon over Gladstone Dock with a stone from his catapult.

'Where have you been?' Kitty asked. As usual Tommy looked like a bag of rags with his grey knee-length socks concertinaed around his ankles, and his mop of dark brown hair falling into his eyes as he jumped out of the home-made trolley cart. He'd made it with four pram wheels of differing sizes, the big ones at the back and the smaller ones at the front. The seat was an orange box, and the whole thing was held together with two planks of wood and its axles. The steering device was a long length of string to pull the front wheels, and was useful when Tommy went to collect the chippy orders for the foreign sailors off the ships.

'Look at the cut of you!' Kitty said, pushing him into the house. She lifted his grubby hands and inspected the dirt under his fingernails. 'You could grow spuds in those. Have they seen soap and water this morning?'

'You're soap mad. Which question shall I answer first?' Tommy eyed the bowl of soup and the plate stacked high with bread. His stomach grumbled hungrily.

'I will have none of your lip, bucko,' Kitty said. 'Did you get the gas mantle I sent you for?' Tommy suddenly remembered the errand to the chandler's.

'Well, I saw Ginger Dempsey. He thought he saw a German hiding in the coal yard,' Tommy answered, his mind working quickly in the hope of keeping out of trouble, 'so I went over to tell Mr Kennedy in case he had a gun, 'cos he wears a suit for work and all men who wear a suit carry a gun...' After he'd decorated the windows with sticky tape he'd seen a film at the pictures and he really did not want to get to the part where he told Kitty he had forgotten all about the gas mantle.

'So, what time's the war coming to Empire Street, Mister Know-All?' Kitty asked while Danny, sitting at the kitchen table, was studying his horses from the morning paper and struggling to keep a straight face.

'What war?' Tommy was wide-eyed now. 'When did the war start?'

'About two minutes from now, if you haven't got that mantle!' Kitty stood over him, hands on her hips. Tommy knew he had to be very careful when she was in this mood. She thought nothing of slave driving, and he had already scrubbed the back yard down once this week.

'It was like this, Kit,' Tommy began. 'I was walking down to Ginger's house and he said that all the teachers were coming back from evacuation and the school was opening again...'

'You told me that already.' Kitty waited; any minute now he was going to tell the truth.

'Well,' Tommy said, getting into his stride, 'I said to Ginger, "What if the school opens when we are in the chandler's?" and he said–'

'Never mind all that.' Kitty sighed impatiently.

'Just get to the bit where you forgot to get the gas mantle, then Kitty can give you a good telling-off, and I can pick me horses in peace.' Danny did not raise his eyes from the paper.

'But, Kit, I thought we were getting invaded, like they said on the news.'

'Well, you thought wrong,' Kitty answered with determination. 'I won't have you turning into a hooligan!'

Tommy eyed the soup and bread, hoping this would not take long or that she did not send him back for the mantle before his dinner.

'Right, we've got things to talk about.' Kitty dragged the chair out from under the table and her determined eyes silently invited Tommy to do the same. He sighed, relieved.

'Can we talk while we eat, Kit, 'cos I'm starving.' Tommy eyed the dwindling bread as Danny tucked in. His bowl of homemade oxtail soup smelled so delicious it was making his mouth water. Kitty took her place at the table, pouring tea into the cups.

'I'm sorry, Kit.' Tommy did look genuinely contrite. However, Kitty knew he had the repentant expression down to a fine art.

'We've got to sort out what we are going to do with you. Me and Dan have war work to do and we can't keep an eye on you as well – it's not safe.'

'You don't have to do anything with me,' Tommy said. 'If anything happens to you lot it's got to happen to me too.' He looked so determined.

'You can't stay here!' Kitty's heart raced and she took a huge exasperated gasp of air. 'It won't be safe.' Bootle docks would certainly be one of Hitler's main targets.

'If the Great War was anything to go by,' said Danny, 'Hitler will try and starve the country into submission and our Tommy can't go without his grub... And look at all the timber yards along the dock road,' he pointed out. He worked on Canada Dock, which brought in the biggest shiploads of timber. 'The London, Midland and Scottish Railway have got a depot near the hospital, with sidings to the Alexandra Dock branch line and goods station, not to mention the Brocklebank Dock and the North Carrier Dock... We're surrounded.'

'We'll be a prime target.' Kitty tried to make her young brother see that he would be in danger if he stayed here.

'I'm not going and you can't make me.' Tommy

was defiant and determined, but he did not reckon on Danny.

'She might not,' Danny looked up from his paper, 'but I will.'

Tommy said nothing.

'It's for your own good, Tommy,' Kitty said in a more persuasive tone. 'We live too near the docks for you to be safe.'

'And what about you?' Tommy asked. He was nine years old and to him everything was black and white; there were no grey areas. 'Will bombs and bullets miss you 'cos you're bigger than me?'

'Don't be daft, Tom.' Danny tried to reason with him. 'Liverpool is the most important western port in the country – it's bound to be attacked.' He stared out of the kitchen window and down the yard now. 'We won't be able to look after you all the time.'

'I can mind meself,' Tommy, with tears in his eyes, said stubbornly.

'It's not that simple,' Kitty said. Looking at him now, his eyes full of tears, she wanted to go over and hug him until he popped. However, she daren't; she would weaken and then he would have won – again.

'Can I go to Freshfield with Michael and Megan?' Tommy asked later, as Kitty filled a clean pillowcase with every stitch he possessed, which was not much. A couple of shirts, a threadbare, sleeveless gansey, a pair of grey, knee-length woollen trousers and not much more.

'No, they're settled with a farmer. You'd scare the life out of a rampaging bull, you would.' Kitty had to keep her tone firm. 'Miss Taylor, who lives with her widowed aunt in number six, has a sister who lives in Southport,' Kitty said coaxingly. 'She has two lovely little boys about the same age as you and it's all arranged. Pop said he'll take you to Southport in his horse-drawn cart. You'd like that, wouldn't you, Tommy?' *Please say you will like it.*

'Do I have to go? There's been no invasion. No bombs – nothing.'

'Nor might there be, Tom, and if there isn't I'll bring you back.'

'When?' Tommy asked, and Kitty felt her heart sink. She had hoped he would like the idea of living by the seaside; he'd loved it when they went last year. Then her thoughts drifted to the times when he felt ill and his throat was bad. Would a foster mother know how to cope? Of course she would if she had two young boys. Kitty's mind was a torment to her now.

'I'll come and see you every weekend and you can tell me all about the great time you'll be having,' she said enthusiastically, trying to drum up a smile from her little brother. 'And we can go for picnics and watch the boats on the water.'

'Can I have a boat for Christmas?' Tommy asked unexpectedly, and she knew he was trying it on now. Kitty nodded. She would save up and buy him the best boat in the toyshop. Tommy smiled and began to come around to the idea of living by the seaside. 'Can I have a pocket knife too for foraging in the pine woods?'

'Don't push it, Tommy...' Kitty smiled. 'I'll see what I can manage.' She sighed with relief. She would miss Tommy but the doctor had said the sea air would be better for him than the smoky air around the docks so she was doing her best for him. She was not fobbing him off on somebody else. Anyway, if the war stayed like this and there were no raids by Christmas he might as well come back home. Until then, the fresh air might do him some good.

Pop clicked his tongue to start the horses moving and Tommy, sitting beside him, scowled and lifted the corner of his lip. He rolled his eyes again, as if he was embarrassed at his sister's obvious display of sensitivity. However, as the cart slowly pulled away from the kerb, Kitty's smile disappeared. To her surprise and utter heartbreak, before they left the street Tommy turned and shouted, 'See you soon, Kit!'

Kitty would miss Tommy, and she would worry about him every day. Perched up on Pop Feeny's cart, he looked so small and she knew he was more scared than he let on. He had never been anywhere before, not even camping with the rest of the class, because she had not had the money to give him.

'You'll love it, it's like a holiday,' Kitty called. 'Write to me with the address.' Tommy put his hand behind his ear and made out he could not hear what she was saying, but Kitty knew he understood perfectly, and she laughed. She was glad he had not made a big fuss about the sore throat he had last night and was surprised he did not mention it this morning.

'Have you got your sweets?' she called and he nodded. 'Have you got your comics?' Tommy nodded again and rolled his eyes. *Stop being silly!*

Do not let him see you downhearted. Keep your chin up, girl.

He tilted his chin up with his forefinger before waving vigorously. Yet before they turned the corner Kitty saw the tears streaming down Tommy's little face and it tore at her heart. His over-bright words and sad eyes had been a big cover for the heartbreak he must have been feeling all week and it took every ounce of willpower Kitty had not to run down the street and bring him back.

However, she couldn't. She intended to find war work to do. Danny had his own work on the docks, and who knew what else he was up to, but she didn't dare ask, feeling it was better not to know. Somehow she had to get this family on the straight and narrow and she had to do it quick!

Dolly had offered to look after Tommy while Kitty worked, but the doctor had recommended evacuation for the good of his health as well as for safety's sake. Kitty thought she was doing the right thing. But was she?

'See you soon, Tom,' she whispered.

CHAPTER ELEVEN

November 1939

The dark nights had long drawn in and there was a powerful, bitter wind blowing in off the River Mersey as Danny Callaghan stepped out of the warm, smoky confines of the Sailor's Rest. His unsteady footsteps, meandering up Empire Street, were not helped by the blacked-out gas-lights, or the torrential rain that started as soon as the saloon doors closed behind him. Pulling his jacket collar up, Danny stumbled towards the edge of the pavement and by some pull of magnetic force he veered back towards the houses.

'Not fit to fight for King and country,' he muttered, thumping his chest with a clenched fist. 'What do they know...? Idiots, the lot of them!' Danny's head was bent low to protect him from the blinding rain and, with his cap pulled down over his eyes, it would be almost impossible to see even if there wasn't a blackout. His chin almost touched his chest and, huddled down inside the thin jacket that offered little protection against the onslaught, Danny drove his hands deep into his threadbare pockets as he lurched and staggered up the street. The sun would never shine for him again, he knew for sure.

His lifelong dreams had crumbled to nothing after he applied to join the army, only to be told by their doctors exactly the same as the navy medic had said. They might as well have said, 'You are surplus to necessity... Not worthy.'

'What is the point?' Danny said aloud to the street, which, as far as he could make out, was deserted. 'Why don't you just finish the job, give me pneumonia and kill me now?' he added to the black sky.

Sarah Feeny was hurrying to put the milk bottles out on the step and praying there would not be an air raid tonight in this weather. She shivered, terrified of what her brothers might be going through at sea on a night like this. News reached civilians via injured naval personnel and was coming in on an almost daily basis. U-boat and surface ship-laid mines continued to inflict heavy losses on merchant ships and warships alike. Only last week the minelayer *Adventure* and destroyer *Blanche* were mined in the Thames Estuary. *Blanche* was a total loss, said Cyril Arden, who had been reliably informed by a returning sailor.

Sarah thanked the Lord every chance she got that her brothers' names were not among the serious casualties, and she knew her parents were worried sick even though they tried to carry on as normal. They were going through something called 'the Phoney War', the papers said, because Germany was preoccupied with focusing their efforts on Poland. There were signs everywhere, however, that the country would be fully prepared for all-out war when necessary.

Ration books were distributed, identity cards had already gone out and Britain was now being called 'the Home Front'. On her way home from the St John Ambulance meeting tonight Sarah had slipped into St Mary's and lighted a candle for both her brothers.

She was keen to be inside to shut out the foul night when she heard rather than saw a man coming up the street, and he did not sound at all happy.

'Who'd have thought it? Danny Callaghan's got a heart... And it is a big heart... Too bloomin' big!' Sarah heard the belligerent tone but could not make out the words immediately.

'Danny?' she said in an exaggerated whisper

loud enough for him to hear.

'Is that you, Sar...?' Danny whispered back. Then: 'A big heart...' His voice rose again above the icy deluge bouncing on the hard ground. 'A heart big enough to survive a life well lived in the rough, tough streets of Bootle. But no heart to fight for my country!'

Not one to cause trouble, but not one to back down when it approached him either, Danny sounded as if he was defeated now. Sarah could hear the unsteady rhythm of his feet along the wet pavement and see him swaying towards her.

'Who'd have thought it?' Danny's voice, although low, seemed to fill the blacked-out street. 'Danny Callaghan, frightened of no man – or woman.' He laughed softly to himself and shook his head as if he could hardly believe it. 'Except our Kitty...'

'What's wrong, Dan?' Sarah whispered into the darkness.

'The country is at war but you won't see me proudly carrying my kitbag up the street.' Danny's voice was full of regret.

'You have to get used to the idea of doing something else, Danny,' Sarah said softly.

'What else is there to do, Sarah? Everyone will think I'm a coward if I don't join up, but if they find out the truth, they'll say I'm an invalid. Good for nothing that Danny Callaghan, they'll say. We knew he'd never amount to anything.'

'Oh, Danny, of course you will,' Sarah said. 'You just need to find the right thing.'

'The right thing? What's that when it's at home? No point in staying on the straight and narrow

209

now, Sarah. No one cares about me, so why should I care about meself?'

'Stop feeling sorry for yourself, Danny!' said Sarah sharply. 'There's loads of people worse off than you, you know.'

Danny stood still. 'Quite right,' he said. 'That's something else real men don't do isn't it – cry into their beer?'

'That's not what I meant...'

'I know, Sarah,' said Danny. 'It's not your fault, kid.' Danny's words were slurred and he tapped his nose. 'Best be off. Our Kitty will have the bobbies out looking for me, I haven't been in for me tea yet.' He staggered off.

Sarah, sadly shaking her head, wrapped her cardigan more closely around her slim body. With sleeves pulled securely around her clenched hands she hunched up to the doorframe, shivering, but reluctant to move in case Danny fell and needed her help. Poor Danny, she thought, one of the bravest boys she had ever known, denied the chance of glory for the sake of a weak heart.

Rita missed the sound of her children's voices terribly. She missed the feel of their little arms around her. She yearned for the trips to the farmhouse in the Freshfield countryside from the moment she left Michael and Megan until the moment they were running towards her, arms open wide. She was not allowed frequent visits because their foster mother said they were too upset after she left them.

Rita wondered how much longer it would be before this place was filled with the sound of children's voices once more. The day war broke out they expected to be invaded immediately, but they had not been. Some children were being brought back home before Christmas.

Charlie absolutely forbade Rita to bring the children home, telling her that the Germans were lulling them into a false sense of security. Rita did not know what to believe, but Charlie refused to discuss making any arrangements for Michael and Megan to return home.

'What are we having for lunch?' Mrs Kennedy asked from her chair near the blazing fire, where she had sat all morning, complaining that her leg was playing up and giving herself a mottled, corned beef-coloured rash from sitting too close to the flames. If she sat any closer, Rita thought, she would cook.

'I'll just finish this.' Rita was aware of the indignant tut behind her because she did not jump up and do Mrs Kennedy's bidding straight away. Vigorously, she circled the sideboard door with her Mansion Polish-covered cloth and smiled to herself.

'Do you have to do it now?' Mrs Kennedy's whining contributed to the increasingly oppressive atmosphere. 'I used to have my housework done first thing in the morning,' Mrs Kennedy's voice was thick with censure, 'when I was able.'

One day that halo will fall down and choke you, Mrs Kennedy.

'Was that the letterbox?' Mrs Kennedy said from her armchair, although she made no move to get up. Rita had heard the sound too and hurried outside to the vestibule between the sitting room and the shop. Her heart leaped when she saw the official-looking envelope with her name on it sitting on the coir matting.

Ripping the letter open, she could feel the thrum of her heartbeat in her throat as her eyes quickly zigzagged the lines of words. She tried to contain the small gasp of joy. Her name had been added to the list of the Civil Nursing Reserve weeks ago, after her successful interview, and now here was the date on which she must report to the matron of the local hospital.

Holding the letter close to her body, Rita could not wipe the smile from her face. This was just what she had been longing for. At last she had something to look forward to.

She did not want an invasion, but it seemed inevitable, going by the heightened talk on the wireless. The newsreel at the Sun Hall picture house even showed awful pictures of the ships being attacked in the Battle of the Atlantic. Merchant ships carrying food from America and being escorted by Royal Navy warships were being blown out of the water by German U-boats. The sight brought tears to Rita's eyes. She knew now that this war, like the one that ended twenty-one years ago, would not be over by Christmas. The Germans were trying to starve them into submission.

Nursing and all that it demanded of her would keep Rita occupied and stop her from fretting. As the sitting-room door opened behind her, Rita stuffed the letter into her overall pocket.

'Rita?' Mrs Kennedy said. 'Is everything all right? You look quite flushed.'

'I'm fine, thank you, Mrs Kennedy, nothing to worry about.' Rita did not want to discuss the letter with her mother-in-law. It was going to be difficult enough trying to get through to Charlie.

Rita couldn't quite make sense of what she was seeing in her little red Post Office book. The money in their account had disappeared. The last time she had looked at it there had been hundreds of pounds in there. Now there were barely a few pounds left.

'Charlie, do you know what happened to the money in the Post Office? There must be some mistake.'

Mrs Kennedy hadn't sat down to dinner yet and Rita knew this would be her only chance to tackle Charlie. Charlie was reading the *Echo* and didn't look up.

'Charlie, are you listening to me?' Rita stood in front of Charlie, challenging him to respond. 'Something must have gone wrong at the bank. I'm going to go in there tomorrow and find out what has happened.'

'Nothing has gone wrong at the bank, Rita.' He still didn't look at her, keeping his eyes on the paper in front of him.

'Then where is it?' An uneasy feeling had started to creep into Rita's stomach. That familiar clench that now materialised any time she and Charlie had something to discuss.

'It's gone.'

'Gone where? There are hundreds of pounds missing – nearly all of it. That money was for our new house.'

'There'll be no new house, Rita. The money's gone.'

'I think at least you owe me an explanation.' Rita couldn't keep the shake from her voice. It had taken them years to save up the money and now they were back to square one. She could hardly take it in.

'I owed money to Harry Calendar.'

'Harry Calendar? But he's a criminal, everyone knows that. Why on earth would you owe him, of all people, money?'

For the first time, Charlie looked up from his paper, his eyes full of contempt for her. 'Why do you think, Rita?'

All of the whispers that Rita had half heard and chosen to ignore started to come back to her now. She'd enter a room and people would stop talking and Rita would have to pretend that she hadn't heard the hints and rumours; that Charlie had a gambling habit and that he was too fond of women and drink. Rita had chosen to close her ears to such talk, knowing it would be another nail in the coffin of her marriage. But Charlie didn't need any help in that department, he was doing a pretty good job of killing what was left of their marriage all by himself.

'How could you, Charlie? That money was ours. I'd saved every penny I could, letting the children go without, thinking that it would all be worth it in the end.' Rita was on the verge of tears, but this time, they were tears of anger and rage, rather than hurt and disappointment. She'd felt those emotions too many times already, but this news was almost too much to bear. How

214

could she ever love Charlie after this? But a quiet voice at the back of her head told her, *you've never loved him, Rita, have you? Not like Jack? Never like Jack.*

'No, Rita,' Charlie goaded her. 'That money was never yours. You're just chattel, *for better for worse, for richer for poorer* – remember that, do you? *With all my wordly goods I thee endow.* That money was mine and I've done exactly as I pleased with it.' Charlie mouth was twisted in an ugly sneer. 'Now be a good wife and keep your mouth shut. I can hear Mother on the stairs. I don't think we need to upset her with any of your histrionics, do we?'

How Rita managed to keep even a mouthful of her dinner down she didn't know. The boiled ham and pease pudding had gone cold on her plate and she pushed it away.

'You're not going to waste that, are you?' said Mrs Kennedy, shrilly. 'We've never let good food go to waste in this house and we're not about to start now.'

Mother Kennedy had scraped her plate clean and proceeded to scoff down the remainder of Rita's dinner. All throughout the meal, Rita had had to listen to Mrs Kennedy on her usual tea-time rant, running down the neighbours and other blameless people on Empire Street. Rita had tried her best to appreciate her mother-in-law, but this evening, watching her sneer at everyone, Rita was reminded just how alike her husband and his mother were, and how much she despised them both. The only thing that kept her going was the thought of the bombshell she was

215

about to drop on their heads.

'I've heard from the Infirmary,' she said calmly. 'They want me to report for duty. They need all the trained and trainee nurses they can get.'

'You're not going,' Charlie said firmly as he finished his own plate. 'Write and tell them you have an obligation to look after a member of your own family before you go looking after strangers.'

Rita could hardly believe her ears. For seven years Mrs Kennedy had given her nothing except a hard time and ridicule. She had tried to belittle Rita at every turn. She had complained about non-existent illnesses and now Charlie wanted Rita to stay at home and care for her when brave volunteers, those defending the Home Front, might be kept waiting for the want of a good nurse. She looked up from her plate and the determined look in her eyes told her husband that this time she would do as she wanted, not what he told her to do. Why should she? What had this family ever done for her except cause heartache and misery?

'I have an obligation to do my duty for my country.' Rita's dignity and the set of her face silently dared him to challenge her. How dare he tell her any longer what she could and could not do? Her children were gone; as far as she was concerned there was nothing stopping her doing exactly as she pleased.

'What about me and Mother?' Charlie asked.

Rita looked at him. His arrogance and selfishness defied belief. He had only just given her the dreadful news about their savings. They now had no nest egg and Rita's longed-for home of her own was an unattainable dream. However, that was not the worst of it. In the two and a half months the children had been away, Charlie had not visited them once. He had not even asked how they were doing. It was simply unforgivable.

'What about you, Charlie?' she asked quietly. 'Do you honestly think I care? I'm going to do my bit in this war – do what I know I can, what I'm trained to do – and if you have any views on this I suggest you look to your own conscience.'

Mrs Kennedy opened her mouth as if to speak, but Rita had the satisfaction of seeing her shut it again. Rita's countenance brooked no argument and both Charlie and his mother were, for once, struck speechless.

'There's a factory on Derby Road making barrage balloons. They're looking for workers.'

'I hope it stays fine for them,' Dolly said as she sat beside her husband at the tea table, 'but listen to me good and proper, Bert Feeny. If you think our Sarah's going to work in some barrage balloon factory you can think again!'

'I didn't say that, Doll,' Pop defended himself. He was just about to tell his wife that things were looking serious when Dolly interrupted him.

'And if you come into my house again wearing a gas mask, Bert,' Dolly waved her knife and looked fierce, 'you can turn around and go right back out...'

The gas mask had been his little joke, but Pop, realising she was worried, laughed and gave her shoulder a customary squeeze.

'I've got the message loud and clear, Doll,' he

said as Dolly gently shrugged him off.

'You've gone all pink, Mam.' Sarah laughed, and Dolly gave her youngest daughter an old-fashioned look. Even after twenty-six years of marriage, Pop's tactile show of affection in front of the children still embarrassed her. Rita, who just then came through the kitchen door, enjoyed seeing her parents so close. Her own marriage might be a sham but there was nothing like coming from a loving family.

'I brought a couple of tins of those sardines Pop likes,' Rita said, sitting at the table to enjoy the cup of tea her mother had just poured for her.

'I'll put them in the chest with the other tinned stuff, just in case.'

'In case of what, Doll?' Pop asked, giving his wife a smile, knowing she had been saving tinned goods since the war began.

'In case we're invaded in our bed,' said Dolly, shrugging her burdened shoulders.

'There'll be no invading going on in our bed, old girl,' Pop laughed. 'I'll make sure of it.'

'Just you make sure you've always got your clean combinations on, Pop.'

Rita and Sarah laughed, watching them now. They were like a double act.

'I'd die of shame if we were invaded, and you got shot in yesterday's long johns!'

'Perish the thought, Doll.' Pop gave her a little unabashed hug.

Rita knew her father, now in his mid-fifties, was out in all weathers working every hour God sent to keep his family well fed and a decent roof over their heads. He often said that their love was the only comfort he needed – except for a little jam tart now and then.

Rita's dependable mother and father loved each other as much, if not more, than the day they married. It was obvious. They showed it in a thousand different ways: those little smiles, the looks they gave each other when they thought nobody was looking, and his inability to pass his wife without that split-second brush of his hand.

Those little things that made the years fall from her mother's caring face clearly showed the girl Pop had fallen in love with. Rita could only dream of such a love. However, life was not built on dreams, she thought sadly.

She had tried so hard to emulate the love her parents shared. However, when it was not a two-way thing, it became harder. It was her children Rita pitied most of all. They were the innocent party caught up in the middle of the silent warring that had become part of everyday life.

'How much do I owe you?' Dolly asked, taking her purse from the pocket of her flowered cross-over pinny, the familiar attire of the women around Empire Street.

'It's one and sixpence for the tinned stuff.' Rita knew Winnie Kennedy charged more than any other grocer around the neighbourhood. 'I could always put your name in the book.'

'Indeed you will not.' Dolly's lips puckered with indignation. 'I won't have that Mrs Kennedy talking about me.' Then, turning to Pop, she asked, 'Would you lend me one and six until next Friday?'

Pop could not stop the smile from creasing his

weathered, nut-brown face as he handed over the silver shilling and sixpenny piece to his wife. 'Keep the change, Doll,' he chuckled.

'Chance would be a fine thing,' Dolly said, laughing.

Watching them together now, Rita knew theirs was a love story being lived to the full. The warmth and loving emotions that should be a part of everyday family life were anathema to Charlie.

Rita could not recall the moment Charlie began to treat her like an unpaid servant. Nor could she remember when he stopped loving her. However, it wasn't Charlie's refusal to make love to her that hurt Rita the most. What made her feel worthless was the way he looked at her with almost lip-curling scorn. That look confirmed his mother's attitude and told Rita she was only here because she had made the huge mistake of conceiving in the first place. Mrs Kennedy had made it plain in the early days that she thought Charles had married beneath him.

Nevertheless, Rita was determined she would show them what she was. *It will not always be like this. One day things will change.* Rita wished she felt the conviction of her words. But for now, there was a war on and she was determined that she was going to do her bit, whether Charlie liked it or not.

Gloria Arden looked in the mirror of her built-in wardrobe. She took the silk scarf and folded it into a triangle, dipping her head forward and wrapping the long end around the nape of her neck. She then flicked her head back and knotted the scarf, tucking in the short pointy bits at the front before expertly ruffling the blonde coiled fringe. 'Would you look at the kip of me?' She roared with laughter as Nancy, four months pregnant, sat in her printed smock, admiring her friend.

'I can't be bothered working in a shop when there is much more money to be made in the munitions factory, Nance,' Gloria said. 'It's not the same since you left to have the baby.' She also knew that since the nightclubs closed at the beginning of the war, there were now morale-boosting singing competitions in the munitions factories during something called 'Workers' Playtime'. 'And,' said Gloria, 'they are judged by people in the profession. I could get a singing spot on a troopship!' She threw back her head and let out a peal of laughter.

'I'm sure you'll make it, one day, Glor,' Nancy said distractedly. She was worried about Sid, he being in the Territorials, she was anxious about having the baby and she was depressed about the war and living with Sid's mother. She'd thought married life would be fun, the kind of gentle daily fun her parents enjoyed. It was turning out to be far from the case.

Dressed in her smart red duster coat and straight black skirt, Rita had taken extra care over her appearance this morning.

'Going somewhere special?' Mrs Kennedy asked, folding the morning paper she had just taken off the top of the pile in the shop. Rita shook her head; giving Mrs Kennedy the means for a morning's gossip was not a priority.

She wasn't going to let on to Mrs Kennedy

where she was heading. Nothing was going to stop her now. This family had held her back long enough. Since she'd told them she had joined the Civil Nursing Reserve, nothing else had been said. She did not feel the need to remind Charlie or his mother that she was starting her job this morning.

Pushing the thoughts from her mind, Rita made her way out of Empire Street, along the dock road, and up Church Street. She would just nip into the church and light a candle. Her beliefs gave her the strength to face the worst that life had thrown at her – the threat of invasion, her children living away from home and her husband's betrayal when he lost their money – and she said an extra little prayer to give her the strength to stay in this loveless marriage instead of doing what she longed to do and get as far away from it as possible. She also refrained from praying that Charlie, like most men of his age, would be called up very soon instead of wasting all their money on illegal gambling. She didn't feel it would be a very Christian sentiment, though she was sorely tempted.

She lowered her forehead to her joined hands, resting on the pew in front, and she prayed. *Please, Lord, keep my children safe. Do what you will with me, but spare them.* She paused, lifted her head and, looking straight at Jesus on the crucifix, she said aloud, 'As for Charlie Kennedy, Lord, make him see the error of his ways. For the sake of his children if not for me. And, Lord, please forgive me for my sin. I know I don't deserve it, but I am trying to make things right.'

Rita stood up, moved into the aisle, genuflected as she made the sign of the Cross and then went to Our Lady's grotto beside the main altar. There was only one empty candleholder, as if the candle had been saved just for her.

The clink of her copper coins dropping into the collection box told Rita that many other mothers had been here today already. With shaking hands, she took the long, thin taper and lit the white candle before placing it next to all the others. Then she kneeled down to pray. After a while, she stopped shaking, filled with new strength.

'Today is going to be a new beginning, Rita,' she said, straightening her spine and pushing back her shoulders. Her words resonated around the church and bounced off the sandstone walls and stained-glass windows. Her determined footsteps echoed in the beautiful place of worship, her sanctuary. She imagined the spirit of all that was strong surrounding her now, and as she walked down the main aisle to the ever-open door, she knew there was still a lot to do.

When she came out of the church and breathed in the chill of the morning air, she recognised a figure walking towards her. She would know that walk anywhere. The uniform of the Royal Air Force was not so familiar on him, though.

'Jack!' she gasped in surprise. 'Is that really you?'

'Your mam said you would be here. I didn't want to interrupt you when you were...'

'I was lighting a candle for the children ... for everybody, really...' There was a moment's awkward silence before they both spoke together. Their ensuing laughter was uneasy and strained. He had been in Warrington for the last six weeks doing his training.

'You first,' Jack said, turning his cap between both hands. He looked so smart and a little uneasy in his new uniform, like the first day in long trousers at senior school, Rita thought, and her heart swelled. He was even more handsome now, standing tall and proud. His dark hair was tousled in the light wind that was blowing in off the river, but Rita barely felt the cold when his dark eyes looked at her with such concern.

Suddenly the memory of a moment from the past flashed into her mind and she wanted him to tell her that she was the only girl he would ever love – just as he had years ago when they were so young.

Then another memory came to her. Of Jack's face the first time he had seen her with Charlie – and two little children in a pram – after he returned from his training in Belfast. Rita's face had burned as she saw the look of shock and pain that flashed across his face. But there was nothing she could do. She couldn't undo what had happened and this was her punishment. She had sinned and now she must pay the price. But Jack's look had haunted her then and it still haunted her now.

Rita remembered her engagement tea in Charlie's mother's sitting room behind the shop. Rita had got drunk on the port and lemons Charlie kept pushing into her nervous hands. Rita had seen the look on her parents' faces and knew that they were baffled by this sudden turn of events. Her mother and father knew that she was expecting. Her mother had even offered to take the babe on as her own. To send Rita away so that no one would know and Rita wouldn't have to marry

Charlie Kennedy. But Rita declined, knowing that in Empire Street the gossips would have the last word. It was better this way. The banns were read and Rita and Charlie were married three weeks after that. How Rita wished she had taken her mother up on the offer.

Now Charlie was ducking and diving, trying to avoid the conscription, and here was Jack willing to give his life for his country.

'When did you get home? Have you seen Kitty?' Rita hardly knew where to begin.

'I'm only passing through,' Jack said, and Rita felt her heart slump with disappointment. 'I can't tell you where we are going, but now basic training is finished we can be posted anywhere in the world.'

'Shall we go and have a cup of tea in that little café by the hospital?' Rita asked, surprising herself for being so forward. She would never normally do such a thing. However, these were not normal times ... and Jack was a family friend. There was no harm in it.

'I can't think of anything I'd like more,' Jack answered, 'but my train leaves at ten. If I miss it they'll have my guts for violin strings.' He gave a short laugh but there was no humour in it. His eyes locked into hers. 'I just wanted to come and say ... well, you know, as I told you first, I thought it was right that I should let you know I...' He took a deep breath. 'What I'm trying to say is, look after yourself, Rita.'

'Aye, Jack, and you.' There was that awkward silence between them now as he looked around him, as if trying to memorise the place for later.

'Right, well, I'll be off then.' Jack smiled but he did not move.

'Me an' all,' Rita replied. 'I've got a job at the Infirmary. It's my first day. Wish me luck.'

'You'll walk it, Rita,' Jack said.

'Thank you, Jack,' she said, smiling.

'Right,' said Jack briskly, 'time for me to go.' He leaned over and kissed her cheek as he would his own sister, and Rita managed to stem a little gasp of excitement. 'Take care, Jack, and come back safe, promise?'

He nodded and hurried to board an oncoming tram. Rita was glad he did not hang around otherwise he would surely have noticed the tears in her eyes.

Saturday dinnertime, the dock road was heaving with vehicles of all shapes and sizes. Men and women in every kind of uniform could be seen on foot and hanging out of the back of khaki-coloured lorries heading towards the ships harboured in the dock.

'Mrs Wetherby sent this over,' Pop said, glad to have got his horses off the busy roads and stabled for an hour or two, handing Dolly a bolt of heavy white material. 'She asked if you can do something with it on your sewing machine.' Pop looked a little embarrassed. He was a fully fledged member of the Air Raid Precautions now, but although there had been air raid warnings there had been no raids. People were beginning to ignore the ARP warnings, seeing them as a bit of a joke. Even the black and white diamond shape painted at the side of the front door, telling people that this was the home of a warden, got Dolly all of a dither.

'What does she want me to do with that?' Dolly asked. Mrs Wetherby was part of the Women's Voluntary Service. Things were changing so fast around here, with men coming and going, women joining this and joining that – going out to work! That was the latest thing. *They*, being the wives of serving men, said it was their duty. Dolly thought they were having a fine old time while the cat was away.

'She wants you to make shrouds,' Pop said quickly, and hurried out to the back kitchen.

'Shrouds! Oh, my giddy aunt!' Dolly could not believe her ears. 'What do they want shrouds for?' She refused to believe that the Germans would have the audacity to fly over Empire Street and drop bombs. 'This war's an excuse to go a bit doolally, if you ask me,' Dolly said, putting the extra sugar, flour and tinned stuff she'd purchased earlier in the chest she had set aside especially. 'I don't know what the world's coming to, I really don't.' She locked the chest and put the key in her pocket. 'Mrs Kennedy said Vera Delaney had been in the shop six times this morning and each time she went out with an extra quarter-pound of tea and a two-pound bag of sugar. Now that is just pure greed, if you ask me. Something has to be done.'

'You helped me deliver the leaflets about rationing last night, Doll,' Pop said, and was amused to see the outraged look of surprise on Dolly's face.

'Rationing?' she asked, as if she had not quite heard. 'Is that what they were for? We've got ration books already and we have to register with certain shops. Winnie Kennedy is thrilled to bits.'

'That's right. You said yourself something had to be done. Some foods will start to be rationed after Christmas.'

'Well, that's a fine how-do-you-do, I must say.' Dolly could hardly believe her ears. 'How are we going to manage on two ounces of butter and half a pound of sugar a week?'

'We will have to get used to it, Doll.' There was the sound of running feet on the linoleum in the long narrow passageway and moments later Nancy, breathless and with a tear-stained face, ran into her father's arms and began to sob.

'Oh, Pop! Sid got a telegram!' she cried. 'He's got to report for duty immediately.'

'He's part of the Territorials, Nance,' Pop said as gently as he could. 'We knew this was going to happen at some time.' He produced his handkerchief and wiped her tears, as he did when she was a little girl.

'But, Pop, he's doing work of national importance; he's in a reserved occupation. Why didn't someone do something to stop him?'

'When he joined the Territorials he knew he could be called up to fight. Only certain key skilled workers are exempt from conscription for now.'

'But they need men to load and unload the ships!' Nancy cried. 'Surely that's a key job.'

'It is, love, but Sid signed that piece of paper saying he would fight if needed and it looks like he's needed now.'

'Oh, Mam!' Nancy wailed, as tears flowed down her cheeks. 'What am I going to do?'

'We've all got to be brave, love,' Dolly said.

'We'll always be here for you, Nance, and you're only in the next street.'

Sid had only a few days to settle his affairs and ready himself for being sent off for basic training. The speed with which he was called up and sent away was astonishing. Nancy had dealt with the news in her usual way and had spent most of the intervening time crying and wailing in the arms of her mother while it fell to Mrs Kerrigan to make sure that Sid had everything he needed. The time for tearful goodbyes arrived in no time.

Sid had gone round to say goodbye to his in-laws. Dolly's heart went out to both Nancy and Sid. It was such an uncertain, terrible time for everybody.

'Well, ta-ra, Sid.' Dolly gave him a hug and Pop shook his hand.

Sid nodded as if too full to say anything.

'Come on, love, let them go now.' Nancy was going to Lime Street Station with Sid to see him off. 'You look after yourself, Sid,' Pop said, and then to lighten the sombre mood a little he added, 'And don't get in the way of anything sharp or explosive.'

Not one of life's natural heroes, Sid definitely looked paler than usual.

'I won't lie, Pop,' he said. 'I'm not looking forward to whatever's in store for me.'

'You will be fine, Sid,' Pop said. 'You'll come back a different man.'

'That's if I come back at all,' said Sid, which sent Nancy into a fresh flood of tears.

CHAPTER TWELVE

Just inside the double doors of Bootle Infirmary, Rita took a deep breath, drawing in the over-powering smell of disinfectant, which permeated the whole building. To the left of her were winding stone steps that led up to the wards, on the right-hand side was a closed door with an opaque window. She stood looking at it for a moment. Should she knock or should she wait until some-one came to her aid?

She was early and the senior member of staff who was supposed to meet her had not arrived yet. The long shiny corridor ahead of her was swarming with nurses in stiff, rustling uniforms, pulling beds or pushing wheelchairs. The place was a hive of activity. Porters were wheeling patients in bath chairs while other patients were being helped by young St John Ambulance volunteers.

Turning quickly as the entrance door catapulted into the wall inches from where she was standing, Rita saw a slight, delicate-looking girl with busy freckles and complicated tendrils of red hair escaping from a navy-blue tam-o'-shanter. The girl, huffing and puffing, proceeded to drag a heavy suitcase across the immaculately polished floor.

'Cheeky bugger!' she said loudly, allowing the door to close behind her.

'I beg your pardon?' An astonished porter about the same age as Pop stopped pushing an empty iron bed to see what the commotion was.

'Not you, mister.' The girl had an Irish accent, a wide-awake look and a cheeky smile, Rita noticed. 'That eejit of a cab driver watched me drag this audacious thing from the cab.' She nodded to the suitcase. 'He did not even try to help me, but his choice of vocabulary was not that of a gentleman when he did not get a tip!'

'Well!' exclaimed the porter drily. 'Have you ever heard the likes?'

The impervious window quickly slid to one side.

'Who is making that racket?' A stern-looking sister in a navy-blue dress and frilled cap leaned forward, glaring disapprovingly at the Irish girl's heavy-looking suitcase. 'And I would advise you to try to carry that thing,' she said. 'Matron will not be pleased if you mark her clean floor.' With a thud, the window shut tight. The girl made a face, as if she had a bad smell under her nose. Then she let out the most raucous laugh. Rita's eyes widened. It would be difficult to miss a laugh like that.

'Hello,' the girl said, thrusting a gloved hand towards the nurse who, carrying a list, had just come from the office. She refused to shake the girl's hand.

'It wouldn't hurt her to crack a smile, would it, now?' Apparently unfazed, she turned her smile to Rita, her voice low. 'Would you be starting today too?'

Rita could not help but smile. This girl was like a breath of fresh air and caused her anxiety to disappear when she took her hand and gave it a hefty shake.

'How're ya? I'm Mary-Josephine Kerrigan,' she said, passing a letter to Sister, 'but everyone calls me Maeve.' She turned her attention to Sister now. 'Did Matron not tell you I was coming?'

'It must have slipped her mind, but that might be because there are ten of you starting today,' Sister said as her eyes scanned the letter. Then, without another word, she began to walk down the corridor. 'Follow me.'

Rita was relieved. However, she soon realised Maeve, who was valiantly trying to hold on to the heavy suitcase, would probably receive more than her fair share of attention from the senior staff if she didn't tone down her vibrant personality a little. She looked and sounded more suited to being on the stage of the Metropole than here in a place of recovery.

'You two are the first,' said the nurse.

'Well, aren't we the lucky ones?' Maeve whispered, dropping her suitcase on the floor with a thump. The nurse gave her a withering glance before telling them to wait in the dining hall.

'I am sorry, Sister, it's just me way,' Maeve said. 'You'll get used to me.'

'And you might even get used to me,' said Sister, 'but I doubt it.'

'I bet you expected a heifer of a girl from the back of beyond?'

'I did not, and certainly not in a coat like that,' Sister said. Rita tried hard not to laugh now.

'D'ya like it?' Maeve twirled unashamedly in the middle of the room where the smell of boiling cabbage and potatoes filled the air. 'My dad said when I take it off there will be a tiny body inside, because I'll have shrunk with the heat!' She gave a burst of effervescent laughter. 'It belongs to me sister... She lent it to me for the summer.'

'That was kind of her,' the nurse said as Maeve took off the coat and slung it over the back of a chair. Rita thought the nurse a bit sour, knowing it cost nothing to be civil. But it didn't seem to bother Maeve in the least when she replied, 'I have to admit it is a bugger when you're running for the bus...'

'Young ladies do not run, especially in this hospital,' replied Sister primly. 'And they certainly do not use bad language.'

'Do they not?' asked Maeve, her brows meeting in a disbelieving crease.

'Matron would cut you off at the knees if she caught you running.'

'I'd better practise walking then, hadn't I?' said Maeve. 'I run everywhere at home.'

'You are no longer at home. And I don't want to hear any more swearing coming from your lips, or there will be consequences.' Sister went to fetch a straight-backed chair to sit on.

'Isn't she the tetchy one?' Maeve whispered out of earshot. 'I bet she'll ask to borrow me coat one o' these fine days or my name's not Precious O'Toole!'

'But you said your name was Mary-Josephine Kerrigan,' Rita said.

'So I did,' Maeve sighed theatrically. 'Precious O'Toole is me stage name.'

'You entertain?' Rita asked, wondering if this girl really was a nurse or if she was a patient who had escaped from the psychiatric ward. *Kerrigan?*

Rita wondered if she was any relation to Sid. However, she did not have time to ask.

'You will call me Sister Brown,' said the efficient senior nurse carrying the list of names. 'I am very busy this morning, and I do not want to waste time here. Patients are being discharged or moved to safer hospitals. I'll tick you off my list as present.'

'That's nice,' Maeve said brightly.

Rita was increasingly bewildered at this young woman, who hurtled into the hospital, turning it into something resembling the stage of a low-grade music hall. Maeve, with hand on hip, leaning on the table, waited for the nurse to finish examining the list.

'Ahh, there you are: Mary-Josephine Kerrigan. I wonder how long it will be before we are striking your name off this list altogether. Nursing is not for everyone, you know. It takes a certain sort of strength.'

'I come from a long line of nurses,' said Maeve, 'going right back to Florence Nightingale.'

'I'll go and see if Matron is ready to see you,' Sister Brown said, raising her eyebrows and giving Maeve a tight smile.

'That smile didn't suit her,' Maeve said, watching her leave the hall. 'She looked like she was practising for a photograph.' She winked at Rita, who could not help but laugh.

'You'll get yourself into trouble,' Rita said, feeling Maeve was instantly likeable as long as you were not Sister Brown.

'Jaysus, if she was a bar of chocolate she'd eat herself!' Maeve declared.

'Ahh, you've arrived, I see,' Matron said smiling, meeting Sister at the door. Matron had a natural authority which brooked no nonsense and Rita noticed that Maeve quietened somewhat. She could behave herself when she had to.

'Tell me, why do they call you "Maeve"?' Matron asked.

'Sure, wouldn't I have a hump on me back carrying a name like Mary-Josephine around with me all day?' Maeve gave the matron what she hoped was a winning smile but Matron was stony-faced in return.

'Well, now,' said Sister as a horde of chattering girls entered the room, in Bootle Infirmary you will be known as Kerrigan. I hardly think anybody will even know your Christian name.'

'Ah, here's the rest now.' Matron waited until everybody was seated at the long wooden forms along the tables before commencing. They were told that their normal day's work started at seven thirty a.m. and finished at eight p.m. They would get three hours off sometime during the day, and they were allowed a half-day off every week.

'That's grand,' Maeve said in a voice barely above a whisper.

'I'm glad you approve, Kerrigan,' Sister said in a sharp tone. Maeve sunk visibly into her seat.

'Your main duties today will be moving patients,' Matron continued, 'and you will be wherever you are needed.'

'I wanted to bandage people up; I can do that,' the irrepressible Maeve whispered to Rita, who imagined she and Maeve would become firm friends.

'D'ya think we'll get a chance to nurse on the male ward any time soon?' Maeve said with a gleam in her eye. 'Sure, wouldn't I be thrilled if I had a male bed-bath to look forward to?'

'Nurse Kerrigan,' Sister's strident voice echoed across the room, 'your duties are in the sluice room today.'

'Yes, Sister.' She sat quietly next to Rita and there was a few moments' silence.

'Are you waiting for a special invitation to the sluice room, Kerrigan?' Matron asked in a quiet voice and Maeve jumped out of her seat as if it was hot. 'Would you look at me sitting here like pith on a rock bun?'

Rita watched as her new friend then dragged all her belongings out of the dining hall and clattered down the long corridor outside.

'Go and help her, Nurse Kennedy,' Matron said in a tortured tone. 'When you have done that I want you to help mobilise as many patients as possible into ambulances, buses, or anything that will transport them as far away from the docks as possible. We've had word that there could be raids and we're moving as many out as we can as a precautionary measure, in case of an influx of servicemen.'

'Yes, Matron,' Rita answered, knowing, after a word from Sister Brown, that those who could not be discharged were to be sent up to the Corporation Hospital for Infectious Diseases in Linacre Lane.

'Kitty, you've got to come quick!' Danny called up the lobby. 'Dad's had an accident on the dock!'

Terrified, Kitty threw on her coat even though the hospital, was only along Derby Road.

She rushed after Danny but her footsteps grew increasingly heavy the more she tried to hurry. She needed to whip along the busy main road unheeded but her feet refused to move with the same speed she was used to. As they rushed, Danny told her what had happened at the docks. 'Dad was offered an afternoon's work unloading a Yankee boat, but by then he had already had a dinnertime session drinking in the Sailor's Rest. He didn't see the open hatchway as he was moving backwards. He stepped right back and fell.' Kitty, panting now, listened carefully. The docks were dangerous at the best of times. She knew her father would have had to be extra vigilant after a skinful.

Kitty felt the stab of a stitch shooting through her ribcage and taking her breath away. She had to slow down.

'You go ahead of me, Danny. I'll be there as fast as I can.'

She watched as he raced off and she trotted, panting, in the same direction, thinking of her father. She knew he never did do things the way he was expected to. But he was built like a brick outhouse and was strong as a bull. He was going to be fine. She was being dramatic again! He would call her Bette Davis and say she made a scene out of everything.

He wasn't really a bad father, she thought. Just a haphazard one who sometimes forgot that his kids needed the money that he drank for food and rent. However, he could also be a loving dad; there were no two ways about that. He would sing daft songs and make them feel like laughing. He would croon old love songs and make them feel sad. He would sing 'Rose of Tralee' and make them want Mam. He had his moments.

The large, soot-blackened sandstone hospital came into view and Kitty gasped through the pain in her side as a voice suddenly popped into her head, though why, she could not fathom. Today was a goodbye day, it said. Kitty got a second wind and put on a spurt. The winter sun was shining. The cloudless sky was calm and blue.

'I'm nearly there, Dad!'

When Kitty entered the hospital she could see Danny already pacing up and down the highly polished corridor. The air was thick with the pungent smell of disinfectant. His expression was grim.

When he caught sight of her, Danny made a little motion with his head, an almost imperceptible shake. Looking at his colourless face Kitty could see he was in shock. Her heart lurched. She could not face him! As long as she didn't talk to Danny, everything would be fine. She did not want to hear what he had to say. If she left the hospital, she could be home in five minutes. She could not bear the thought of losing her father, too. *Please don't tell me!*

But Danny was coming closer. He didn't have to say the words. The sadness in his eyes told her what she already knew. Slowly he shook his head and then said the words anyway.

'He's gone, Kit.' His voice fractured. 'I got here just before...'

'He's gone?' Kitty didn't want to hear it. She certainly did not want to believe it. 'He was fine this morning. He was up, talking, making plans for when he came home. He said he would change his ways, and leave the drink alone... He was looking so much better...'

'He wasn't on his own.' Danny put his arms around her now and held Kitty close. She should cry, if only to make Dan feel better. However, she could not. For some unfathomable reason the tears did not come even though the burning sting of pain was behind her eyes.

'I want to see him,' Kitty said in a low whisper and vaguely registered that Rita was standing with them. She was in uniform.

'I'm so sorry, Kit.' Rita had been trained to give bad news without emotion, but these people were her friends. This was different. Compassion and concern took over now. 'If there is anything I can do, just say.'

'Thanks, Rita.' Kitty stood plucking at the skin on her fingers. 'What am I going to tell Tommy?' she cried.

'We'll talk about it later. I'll have to get in touch with Jack, but I don't know how,' Danny said.

'Leave it with me,' Rita said. 'I'll sort it all out.'

Danny thanked her; he didn't have the first clue where to start. He had never had to deal with anything like this before. The important stuff was usually dealt with by Kitty or Jack. Jack wasn't here now and Kitty was in no fit state.

'Soon there'll be nobody,' Kitty said quietly. 'Tommy's evacuated, Jack's in the air force, and you...' Kitty looked at Danny, '...what about you? When will it be your turn to go and leave me?'

'I'm going nowhere, Kit. I'll look after you,'

Danny answered. He had told nobody but Sarah that he had been turned down for the Forces. There was no way on earth he was going to worry Kitty now with news about having a faulty heart.

'He'll be safe in Mam's arms now, Kit.' Danny put his arm round her shoulders and the thought gave Kitty comfort.

She reached up and took his hand. 'Tommy doesn't need to be disrupted.' Her voice was barely above a whisper.

'Come on, Kit, let's get a nice hot cup of tea inside you,' Rita said, linking Kitty's arm.

CHAPTER THIRTEEN

'I hope you won't be offended, Kit,' Rita said when she called into number two after the rosary, which was said by Father Harding from St Mary's Catholic church the night before the funeral.

'What is it?' Kitty asked, taking the package wrapped in brown paper and unwrapping it carefully to save the paper for the paper drive. When she opened it out she was surprised and thrilled to see a plain black, square-necked woollen dress with long sleeves. 'It's perfect,' she gasped. She had not given much thought to what she would wear tomorrow. The only provision she had made was a few coppers from the funeral money, which Rita had lent her, to buy a black lace mantilla to cover her head.

'Don't say another word,' Rita said.

When Kitty took hold of her hands in gratitude she gave a small, self-conscious laugh. 'Mine are always freezing cold lately,' she said.

'Cold hands, warm heart, Kit,' Rita said, 'and in your case it's true. I've never known anybody go through as much heartache and still keep going.'

'What else can I do?' Kitty asked. 'It's not like I have a choice.'

The following day was a Friday, four weeks before Christmas. Kitty was up early to put on the dress Rita had given her. She had taken in the side seams so it fitted properly. Even though it was black, the neckline flattered her slim neck and the puffed sleeves made her shoulders look wider and more robust than they really were.

Almost the whole street came to pay their respects and Kitty was humbled by their community spirit. It was a shame Jack could not make it. The official Danny had spoken to on the telephone said he would pass the message on and Jack would be in touch, but Kitty had heard nothing since.

She felt Jack's absence keenly. He was her mainstay and she missed the calm, assured way he had about him when there was a crisis. He might even have stayed away on purpose, if he was still in this country. Jack and Dad had never hit it off since Mam had died nine years earlier. Jack had felt their mother's death deeply and thought that, for as much as he loved his wife dearly, Dad was useless as a husband and could barely provide for his family above subsistence level.

There were times when Mam went without food to give it to her children. She would stand by the range and make sure they were all fed, but Kitty rarely saw her eat. Was it any wonder she did not have the energy she needed to sustain her throughout a healthy pregnancy? Was it any wonder she did not survive? Was it any wonder Jack stayed away?

It had been a simple ceremony without fuss. It was almost dark when Kitty and Danny buried their father three miles away at Ford Cemetery. With them were Rita, Dolly and Pop, the people who had done the most to keep the Callaghan children fed and warm when Sonny's behaviour was at it's worst. They were family too. The tranquil surroundings of trees and fields reminded Kitty of a peaceful haven in the heart of the countryside and, in spite of everything, it was the perfect reunion for him with their mother.

Tommy had not been told about his father's death. He was unsettled enough with living away from home and Kitty did not want him any more upset. She hoped she had done the right thing.

'Hello, Kit,' Jack said, standing in the doorway of her home after the ceremony. Kitty had been filling cups with tea and, she turned to see her older brother standing there, kitbag over his shoulder, looking a little sheepish. 'I'm sorry I couldn't get here sooner.'

'Jack!' Kitty put down the pot and she flew into his arms. For the first time since her father had died the floodgates opened and she cried until she was too exhausted and too empty to carry on.

Later, when they had all mopped their eyes and regained their composure, they agreed that what

Dad would have wanted was a good old knees-up in the Sailor's Rest.

'He'll turn in his grave if he knows you're drinking tea!' Jack said, and as they closed the front door to make their way down to the bottom of the street a huge rumble of thunder rolled across the sky. Many people ran for cover, thinking the Germans were here.

'That's Mam giving him what for,' Jack said, saluting the sky. 'Goodbye, old man. God bless.'

'Is Charlie working today?' Kitty asked Rita a short while later. She'd noticed that neither Charlie nor his mother had been at the funeral, but she was grateful she had her friend to support her.

'He is always late home on Fridays. It's one of his collection nights. Sometimes it has gone midnight when he gets in,' said Rita. It sounded plausible when she said it, but deep down, since the discovery of the missing Post Office money, Rita was never really sure what Charlie was doing any more.

Charlie met Amanda Smallfield at the crowded Central Station in Liverpool, where she told him she had a little Christmas shopping to start while she was in town. That meant that instead of dinner at the Adelphi and then up to a room, as he had planned, the evening would be cut short. Charlie was not pleased, especially when she expected him to carry the myriad of Christmas shopping bags around Liverpool and she continually bemoaned the fact that there were no lights on in Church Street because of the blackout. Charlie could not care less about Christmas lights although he agreed, not wanting to sound churlish. He was also calculating how much time he would have to finish his rounds.

'After I've finished shopping we can get the train back to Southport,' Amanda said. 'My husband is away on business until tomorrow.'

Charlie smiled. Her palatial Edwardian villa would save him the cost of a hotel room. All thoughts of doing any more collecting today went right out of his head.

'I am enjoying this war so far, Charles, are you?'

Dressed in a black satin négligée Amanda Smallfield was a feast for the eyes of a starving man. Charlie knew she had brains as well as beauty.

'Come back to bed, my darling.' He sprawled naked on top of the silk eiderdown, with one hand behind his head, resting on the silk pillow. He blew lazy smoke rings to the ceiling while Amanda smiled at him seductively reflected in the looking-glass of her dressing table. Charlie was spellbound by the way her breasts strained against the silk of her gown and the way the contour of her shapely hips and tiny waist were accentuated by the wide satin belt.

He was thrilled at the clandestine afternoons. He had pleasured many women over the years, usually rich, bored housewives whose businessmen husbands were away a lot. But Amanda was different. The anticipation was always there. He never tired of Amanda as he did some other women. She was not needy like the others. She made him feel as if he was being rewarded. Sometimes the telephone would ring in the office, and he would be summoned with the promise of an afternoon of unbridled lust. How could he possibly refuse? Since he had had a promotion a few weeks ago he was freer to come and go as he pleased.

Turning from the mirror, Amanda moved like a sensually stretching cat and slid onto the silk-covered bed beside him. Taking the cigarette from his lips, she placed it between her own freshly painted lips, inhaling deeply. Then she threw her head back and exhaled a long stream of smoke before grinding the cigarette into the ashtray. Charlie's fingertips outlined the sensual curves of her silken breasts, his breath coming in short bursts now. He must have her one more time.

'Isn't it ironic, darling,' she said in a low, sixty-a-day gravelled voice, 'we actually need this war to be free?' Her elbow on the pillow, she supported her beautiful oval face with the palm of her left hand, looking down at him now. 'Do you think we are destined to be lovers for always?' she asked as her crimson talons zigzagged down his chest and circled the tip of his rigid manhood.

Charlie gasped and grabbed her hand.

'I promise you, my love,' he murmured, 'we will be together soon.'

Her tone changed. 'I think not. I'm leaving for the country tomorrow. You have left it too late.'

Charlie did not know this. Surely, one didn't just up and leave at a moment's notice? He grabbed her hand and she pulled it free, daring him to try again. He relented. They had been lovers since the day he had come for the first payment on the premium. And what a payment it was. She was all he ever needed. He had no need of Rita from that day on. Amanda taught him more that day than he would have thought possible.

Charlie gently brushed a wisp of blonde hair from her face. She was perfect in every way. He caressed her cheek as she nuzzled the palm of his hand. The aftermath of their lovemaking was always the same. She would threaten to end the affair, he would pacify her, undress her, make love to her again, reassure her again...

However, this time was different, he knew. His fears were confirmed when he saw the expensive-looking leather suitcases standing in line at the other side of the room.

'Kitty is made up you managed to get home, Jack.' Rita took his empty teacup and refilled it from the large teapot at the end of the table. The others had all stayed on at the Sailor's Rest but Rita had told Kitty she would go back and wash the cups and tidy up a bit, as Kitty herself had done many times for Dolly. Kitty and Jack had gone with her. When something like this happened, everybody mucked in together. Kitty took a tray of used crockery out to the kitchen to wash while Rita poured milk into Jack's cup.

'She didn't tell Tommy,' Jack said quietly, 'and rightly so, I think.'

'It would unsettle him,' Rita agreed, 'and your dad wouldn't have wanted that.'

'I didn't come home for Dad,' Jack said, taking the fresh tea from Rita. The cup looked tiny in his hands. 'I'm here for Kitty. Dad's better off out of it, by the look of things.' Jack hesitated. 'And...'

'And...?' Rita felt her heart pounding in her chest. She felt that she and Jack were on the verge of something, but it was madness for her to think that there could be something between them. She was a married woman, for heaven's sake. 'I'm sorry, I shouldn't be so nosy! Ignore me.' Rita quickly apologised and began to clear the table.

'How could I ever ignore you, Rita?' Jack said it in a way that only increased the pounding of her heart. *Don't speak*, she silently willed Jack. Whatever he was about to say, it couldn't be unsaid. Rita shifted and for a moment there was a heavy silence between them.

'You know how I feel about you?' Jack's deep, gentle voice was barely audible and Rita was not sure she had heard him properly. 'I have never cared for anybody the way I care about you, Rita.'

'Don't say that, Jack. You're grieving.' Rita could hardly believe what she was hearing. 'You don't know what you're saying.'

'I know exactly what I am saying, Rita.' Jack put the cup down on the table and he looked at Rita in a way that had once been familiar to her. He did not say another word and for a few anxious moments Rita thought he was going to come over to where she was standing and take her in his arms. She doubted she would have the strength to resist. Instead, with a great effort, he turned and, with his hands in his pockets, he looked out of the small sash window overlooking the back yard.

'I was a fool to ever leave Empire Street,' he said, staring down the yard, 'and an even bigger one to let you marry Charlie Kennedy.' Jack said her husband's name as if it caused a bad taste in his mouth. 'He might be your husband–' Jack's voice was barely above a whisper, as if talking to himself – 'but you will never be his wife in the same way you would have been mine.'

Rita could only stare at the man who had been her sweetheart.

'Why didn't you wait for me, Rita?' Jack said, and Rita shook her head, not sure what she should say.

'I tried to wait for you, Jack. Truly. After you left, I wrote you a letter...'

It was Jack's turn to blush. Rita thought it only made him more desirable, to see that bashful and modest side of him.

'Rita, I never told you this at the time, because I was ashamed. I never learned to read and write. I always seemed to spend more time out of school than in it, looking after Mam.'

Rita thought back to their time together and things fell into place. Jack always let Rita choose for him if they went for a bite to eat in a café or if they chose a film to watch at the flicks. It was all starting to make sense.

'Oh, Jack, if only I'd known. But I can't believe my letter didn't reach you. In it I explained...'

'I lived with the foreman, Bob, and his wife. They were so good to me, Rita. Bob's wife taught me my letters. They believed in me and wanted me to make something more of myself – to succeed. And I have, but it means nothing without you, Reet.' Jack looked at her; his eyes full of love for her.

Rita thought back to the contents of her letter and what it said. She had sent it care of Harland

248

and Woolf and she could well imagine it passing eventually to Bob or his wife; of them opening the letter and reading its contents. Who could blame them if they kept it from Jack? The truth it held could have spoiled Jack's future for ever. Rita was suddenly struck by the emotion of his words, but also by the cruel twist of fate that had kept them apart.

'What did the letter say, Rita? I wrote to you too, when I'd learned to, to tell you I was coming home.'

Rita remembered getting Jack's letter, telling her how well he was doing and that he would soon be back. But by then it was too late. She and Charlie were already married and the die was cast.

It was almost too much to bear and Rita suddenly felt that her legs weren't able to hold her up any longer. Jack saw her sway unsteadily and was around the table in a flash, steadying her; helping her into a chair and sitting beside her.

'Oh, Jack, you've no idea...'

'What, Rita, what was in the letter?'

How could Rita tell Jack now? What was the point, she thought, desolately. There was nothing that could turn back time; she was destined to be with Charlie and not with Jack. She was punished for being wicked and now it seemed they must both pay the price.

Better for Jack to think that Rita had let him down than for them both to live with the constant ache of what might have been.

'Let's leave the past alone, Jack. What's done is done.'

'If you don't tell me now you never will and it

will haunt us both for the rest of our days – however long that may be.'

'Oh, Jack, don't say that. The war will be over soon and then we will all get back to normal.'

'You don't understand, Rita – the war has hardly begun!' Jack looked serious. 'People on the Home Front haven't got a clue!' He gently took her by the shoulders as he would a child and he lowered his head. 'Some people around here think the war will be over quickly because that is what they have been told to think – but we are far more intelligent than that, Rita. We have to love for today, for who knows what tomorrow will bring?'

Rita stifled the urge to tell Jack what was really in the letter. Knowing wouldn't help either of them now. Telling Jack a lie would be better for both of them in the long run.

'Jack, I wrote you a letter to tell you … to say…' she could hardly get the words out. She took a deep breath and rushed the words. 'To say that I had fallen in love with Charlie and that we were getting married. I didn't want you to be surprised when you came back.' Rita kept her head down, her eyes on the floor as she said the words.

Jack's voice was trembling with emotion as he said, 'Rita, is that true?'

'Yes, Jack,' she whispered. 'I'm sorry, but it is true.'

'I won't believe you until you look me in the eye and say it.' Jack gently lifted her chin and Rita met his steady brown eyes with her own green ones. A single tear escaped and rolled down her cheek. 'It's true, Jack.'

Jack didn't say anything, but tenderly wiped the

tear away with his fingertip. He held her gaze and gave her a smile. A smile that seemed to hold for Rita all the love that was missing from her life.

'I'm no fool, Rita. I know that you're not telling me the truth. But I'll wait and one day, when you're ready, you'll tell me what was really in that letter.'

'Oh, Jack.' Rita felt that her heart was breaking.

'I've always loved you, Rita. You know that, don't you?'

'Yes, Jack. I've always known.'

'I may not be your husband, Rita, but I'll always be your friend. And you won't find a better one. Remember that.'

Something in the air shifted. They both knew they had said too much, but even though Rita should feel guilty, she didn't. It felt like a weight had been lifted from her shoulders. Knowing that the love that she and Jack felt for each other hadn't changed had given her hope. Hope for what, she didn't know, but it was something that Charlie and his mother couldn't spoil. It was for her and Jack, and no one could take it away from her. Not ever.

Jack stood. 'I'd better nip up and change this shirt. It's filthy after the journey.'

'Yes, and I'd better be getting back to the Sailor's Rest. Charlie may have come back and wonder what has happened to me. Goodbye, Jack.' She held out her hand, and Jack took it in his own, holding it for a moment before letting it drop.

Suddenly, Rita was shocked to hear a loathsome voice behind her.

'No need for me to wonder, Rita. I can see exactly where you are.'

251

Rita's head whipped round to see her husband standing in the doorway just as Jack had let go of her hand. Rita wondered how much he had overheard.

'Hello, Charlie, I didn't expect you,' Rita said, looking from one man to the other.

'Obviously,' Charlie rasped in a low voice. 'I just came round to pay my respects to the family. I'm surprised to see you here.'

'I just came back to tidy the house for Kitty. Jack has just arrived.' Rita was damned if she was going to let Charlie intimidate her.

Charlie glared at her, then taking Jack's hand, he said in a tight, strained voice, 'My condolences, Jack.' With that he left.

'I've stayed too long,' Rita said. 'Tell Kitty I'll see her later.' And with that she left the house, and didn't dare to look back.

'What was he sniffing around for?' Charlie said through gritted teeth. He was nursing a small glass of brandy, and by the look of the bottle he had already scuppered quite a lot of it.

'Charlie, what's wrong?' Rita asked, glad the children were not at home to see their father behaving like this. Mrs Kennedy had already left for her sister's house in Crosby, where she was spending a long Christmas holiday, coming back on Boxing Day. 'That's a terrible thing to say. Jack was not *sniffing around*. He buried his father today, don't forget.' Rita felt uncertain; Charlie smelled strongly of drink and she had not seen him in this mood before.

'I arrive to pay my respects to the Callaghans

and instead I find my wife in a cosy chit-chat with another man.' Charlie pointed his finger at her accusingly. 'What would I have found had I been ten minutes earlier?' His tone was argumentative now. 'My mother has gone to her sister's for Christmas and we have the whole place to ourselves. Isn't that what you've always wanted? But I see my wife has had her Christmas present early – gratis from the RAF!' Amanda had started something she did not finish. He had hoped his wife would do the honours. 'You whore!'

Rita could not have been more shocked if he slapped her. 'I beg your pardon!'

'You can beg all you like, bitch!' Charlie was in a foul mood and Rita knew she had to be wary. She had come across drunken belligerent men at the hospital and they had to be treated very carefully indeed.

'Charlie, you've made a mistake. I wasn't alone with Jack!' she said desperately. 'Didn't you hear Kitty in the back kitchen; she was washing dishes out there?' Her voice sounded light, but inside her emotions were torrents of rage and humiliation. However, Rita knew better than to argue with a man when he was drunk.

'Don't try and wriggle out of it now,' Charlie said angrily. 'I know what I saw. And I know what you're after.'

Rita managed to force a stiff smile. She had seen Charlie like this before, when he'd had a bad day at work, or if he'd lost money on a horse. She didn't remember him being as drunk as this before, though. The look in his eyes told her what was on his mind. For years, Rita had prayed that they could have a normal life in the bedroom, but now the idea of it made her physically sick.

'Come home to give my wife an early Christmas present.' Charlie finished his brandy in one gulp and Rita could feel the muscles in her stomach tighten.

'Come on, Charlie,' she coaxed tiredly. She had been on duty the night before and had hoped for an early night. 'There's no need to be like that.'

'I'll be any way I damn well please in my own house, Rita.' Charlie went and filled the short glass with more brandy then half emptied it in one go. Rita refrained from reminding him that this was his mother's house. They didn't even own a single teacup in it.

'Do you know something?' Charlie said, waving the glass and pointing at her now. 'There is not one woman on this earth I would trust and shall I tell you why, Rita?'

'I have never given you any cause to be suspicious of me,' she said. 'I am a good wife and mother.' Charlie scoffed at that and she was disgusted to see the white saliva gather in the corners of his lips like foam.

'Well, let me tell you why I don't trust a single one of you, Saint Rita.' He finished his drink and poured another. 'When I was just a little boy my mother took me to the countryside for a little holiday, she said, away from my father who was looking after the shop, she said...'

Charlie stumbled slightly as he made his way to his mother's chair by the fire. He lovingly stroked the arm of the chair in a way he had never stroked her. Rita, for some reason she didn't quite under-

254

stand, gauged how far she was from the door.

'She thought I was asleep. I could hear her talking to somebody. She was laughing softly... I got up from my bed and went to the next bedroom... She was in bed with a man. A man who was not my father. But a stranger, pawing at her, touching her...'

Rita gasped in surprise as her hands covered her open mouth to try to conceal her shock. The look in Charlie's eyes was terrifying, mad even.

'I know, who would ever have thought the high and mighty Winifred Kennedy could be such a slut?'

'Charlie, you must have been mistaken. Maybe you–'

'I dreamed it, is that what you are saying?' He threw his head back and laughed until he choked. 'Have you never wondered why she will not hear a word said against me? It's because I know, Rita, I know what she is really like and she's terrified that one day it will all come back to haunt her!'

'What will come back to haunt her, Charlie?' Rita was all at sea now; what did Charlie mean about his mother?

'I'm tired, Charlie, let's go to bed.' She was pleading now; if she could get him into bed, surely the drink would take over and he'd be snoring in seconds.

'Bed, is it, Rita? You always were a wanton slut. That first night you seduced me, you were like a woman possessed; not so enthusiastic now, are you? All of you are the same. You just get what you want out of men and then please yourselves,' he said belligerently.

255

Rita looked at him, her brows pleated. She realised now that Charlie didn't want them to be happy, and all of the effort that she put in to try and make things better was wasted. Charlie wasn't capable of love, not even for his own children.

'Come on, Charlie.' Rita reached to undo his tie. 'You've just over-indulged. Perhaps you should have a nap.' She tried to keep the shake from her voice.

Charlie moved her hand from the silk tie. 'Haven't you had your fill with lover boy? I saw the way you looked at Jack Callaghan.' His lips curled into a sneer. 'Do you think I don't notice the way Callaghan seduces you with his eyes and you, like the harlot you are, you reciprocate in kind, humiliating me? I must be the laughing stock of the street.' Charlie banged his fist on the arm of the chair and jumped up so fast Rita felt genuinely frightened for the first time in her life. Before she knew what was happening, Charlie pushed her forcefully down onto the sofa, roughly lifting her skirt and tearing at her underwear.

'No, Charlie, not like this!' Rita cried. 'Charlie, stop it!'

His hand covered her mouth. 'Shut your mouth, you stupid bitch, do you want the whole street to know what a whore you are?' He pushed her head to one side so he could whisper crude words in her ear. 'Do you like it like this, Rita? Is this what you want...? Yes, it is, you love it!' All the while he was forcefully thrusting himself into her, grinding his body against her. This was as far as you could get from making love; this was full of hate.

'Charlie. No!' Sobs racked Rita's body as Charlie

buried his face into her breasts, nipping her with his teeth. Rita's stomach heaved. Charlie was her husband – he was supposed to love her and to cherish her – yet he was capable of this!

'No, Charlie! No!' Rita's anguished cry sounded like someone else's voice, even to her own ears. She grabbed his thinning hair and pulled his head up. All Rita could feel was pain. As his head came up he had venom in his eyes. In seconds he was spent, limp on top of her, and Rita found the strength she needed to push him off.

He stumbled slightly but quickly steadied himself. Towering over her, Charlie looked down at her in a way she did not recognise. His eyes were cold, distant. And his next words chilled her to the bone. 'You were never my choice of a wife, Rita.'

He turned and walked away. Rita felt ashamed, exposed, humiliated. How could she ever look at Charlie after this? Her stomach churned as she quickly jumped up, trying to cover herself. She could barely comprehend the circumstances. How could Charlie do that to his own wife? She had seen the results first-hand when women, battered and bruised, had been brought into the hospital because they had said no to their husbands. Rita shuddered to think she was just like those poor women now. She jumped when the bedroom door slammed shut.

Quickly she ran to the freezing-cold scullery and grabbed two large pans off the shelf. After filling them with cold water, she struck a match and lit two gas rings. Rita's bruised arms encircled her tired body. Pacing back and forth along the kitchen she tried to quell the memory of what had just happened. But it was impossible.

She closed the kitchen door and slipped the snip across, thankful that it still worked. Then she dragged the table up against the door and, gasping now, she leaned against the wooden draining board, slowly rocking back and forth to try to ease the ache of shame and humiliation, momentarily uncertain what to do next. A dog barked in the distance and she jumped, her nerves in shreds.

Hot tears streamed silently down Rita's cheeks as her trembling shoulders curled inwards. She could feel the nausea rising, finding it impossible to swallow as the water in the pans began to bubble. After pouring the boiled water into an enamel bowl, Rita added just enough cold water to allow her to dip her hands. She needed to be clean. Really clean.

Slathering a clean cloth in carbolic soap, she began to scrub her body thoroughly from top to toe. What if he came back and wanted to have another go? He was her husband. He said she had no right to stop him. Please God, she prayed, don't let him near me again. Could she go home? Take the kids back to Mam's? Yes, that was it. She didn't have to stay now; he'd betrayed her, hadn't he? Then she remembered. This was her punishment. There was no going back and she must suffer the consequences of the choices that she had made. She continued washing. The water soothed her bruised arms but did nothing to calm her troubled mind.

Thank the Lord the children were not here to see him like that, Rita thought as she dried her glowing skin, now red raw to the touch. Is this how it was to be now? No more pretending; just angry, twisted sex. Well, that was the last time Charlie would ever do that to her, she vowed. Although still feeling soiled, she told herself that next time she would be ready for him ... punishment or not, there were limits to what she could take. She and Charlie would never share the same bed again. While the children were away, she would sleep in Megan's room at the back of the house.

CHAPTER FOURTEEN

The diamond frost glistened underfoot as Kitty hurried towards the dock road. She secured the woollen scarf under her chin before pulling up the high collar of the coat she had got from Rita, who had been going to throw it out. She was shivering as sleet began to fall in the murky light of dawn, drenching her feet as the cardboard that covered the hole in the sole of her shoe became more sodden with every step.

Kitty stopped to lean on the railway wall, known to all as 'the ralla', and pulled the flapping cardboard from the hole. As soon as she got her first pay packet, she promised herself, she was going to Cazneau Street market to get a second-hand pair that had soles! The icy water was making her toes numb, but there was no time to worry.

Even at this ungodly hour, the dock road was alive with men, horses and lorries. Kitty hurried on past the carters, their heads and shoulders covered with hessian sacking, loading flat-backed wagons with crates and bales straight off the ships. She felt sorry for the patient horses standing motionless and unflappable on the quayside, exhaling plumes of white vapour.

The canteen was still in darkness when she got there. Hugging the wall close to the door, she tried to protect herself from a westerly squall blasting in off the river. After a few minutes, aware she was inviting curious stares from carters and passing lorry drivers, she moved further into the shadows of the canteen doorway, hoping nobody got the wrong idea. If they did they would soon get their eye wiped, she thought.

From here she could see directly across the busy dock road to the enormous battleships, their huge superstructures seeming to glow against the pewter sky. Men, maybe days away from being called to war, were loading and unloading.

This view of sea-going traffic, lying at anchor in the busy dockyard, was a familiar sight, although new to Kitty recently was the evidence of war wounds on some ships that were there being mended. At this hour, it looked strangely eerie.

Hitler will not beat Liverpool, she thought proudly. This was one of the busiest ports in England, she knew, but it would refuse to be beaten.

The port looked to be thriving now but she recalled the times when it had stood silent, when men went on strike for better conditions. It had taken a war for them to get anywhere near the dues the men deserved and Kitty wondered if they would still get them after the war was over.

After Tommy had been evacuated she had seen a notice in the employment exchange advertising for women – or men who were exempt from fighting – to join the newly opening Navy, Army and Air Force Institute on the dock road, NAAFI for short. It was run on the lines of a co-operative society controlled jointly by the three services. NAAFI waitresses were not classed as war workers but as civilians attached to the services. Thank goodness for that, Kitty had said; she was not cut out for square-bashing or saluting. Her supervisor, Rene, who had interviewed her and told her punctuality was imperative, was now late.

Looking to her right and then to her left, Kitty was not sure from which direction Rene would approach the canteen. She stamped her feet to try to get some life back into them and wondered if she had got the time wrong. Maybe Rene had said eight o'clock and not seven. She did not know how long she'd been standing here, probably not that long, but in this weather it seemed like ages.

'Have you got the time, please, mister?' Her voice carried on the cold wet air to a passing carter, who gave her a guarded look. Immediately Kitty realised she had worded her question in such a way it could have been misinterpreted.

'Y'all right, there, love?' The carter's muffled voice was full of concern. Below the flat cap pulled down over his eyes and a couple of thick, woollen scarves wound warmly around his neck and hiding the lower half of his face he was unrecognisable. 'Is that you, Kit?'

Kitty took a closer look and realised it was Pop!

She should have known. He did not wear a hessian sack covering his head and shoulders like some of the carters. Instead, he wore a good-quality Crombie overcoat and, encased in thick woollen gloves, his hands were probably a good deal warmer than hers were right now.

'Hello there, Pop.' Kitty shuffled a bit in the cold. 'I'm starting work here today and I'm not sure I got the time right.' Just then, she noticed a bustling figure hurrying towards her, and by the amount of freezing air she was wheezing, Kitty could tell she had been moving at a fair lick.

'Hello there, girl!' Rene gasped. 'So sorry, we overslept this morning.' She stopped a while to catch her breath. 'I said to my fella, "That poor girl's gonna be frozen to the bone" – on yer first day an' all!' She paused and peered at the passing carter, recognition lighting her eyes.

'G'mornin' there, Pop.' Rene gave him a friendly wave. 'Lend us yer scarf – it's Baltic freezing this morning. I see your Dolly's been at the knitting needles again.' Rene let out a raucous laugh that split the morning air and convinced Kitty that it would wake her dad if the supervisor were any closer to Ford Cemetery.

'Aye, she's good with the old needles, is my Dolly,' Pop said cheerily from his lofty perch.

'D'you think she could knit me a millionaire so I don't 'ave ter come out in this weather?' Then she let out another disorderly laugh that ended in a fit of coughing as she scrambled in her bag for her keys.

'If she does I'm first in the queue,' Pop called back, laughing at his own witticism. Kitty laughed too for what seemed the first time in ages. She had hardly laughed at all since Tommy went away.

'Here, we got a letter from our Frank this morning, Kit. Dolly's made up. You can't sit her down she's that excited, especially after hearing about the poor buggers who lost their lives on the *Royal Oak* at Scapa Flow.'

A warm glow suffused Kitty when she thought of Frank. She missed him like crazy. The Royal Navy had taken such a battering protecting the people back home.

'I'll try and drop him a line tonight,' Kitty said. After all, she had promised, and even if she was just a neighbour it certainly had not felt that way when he had danced her around Empire Street at his sister's wedding.

'He asked to be reminded to you!' Pop waved as he moved off to do his daily work.

'Ta-ra, Pop, see you later!' Rene called as she bent down to ram the key in the rusting lock. These people were far too cheerful first thing in the morning for Kitty's liking. It was not natural. Dragging her fingers from the confines of a warm pocket, she gave a little wave.

'Pop's lovely,' Rene said, 'a true gent.'

Kitty shifted from one foot to the other, wishing Rene would hurry up. The NAAFI canteen wasn't opening for another few days. They were here to clean the building, which had been closed for years, before they could even start serving food to the men of the Forces. Rene had been supervisor at various other NAAFI establishments and knew just how these places were run, and by whom.

'When we get cracking on this cleaning we'll

soon warm up.' Rene's voice was twenty-a-day scratchy above the noise of the cranes and wagons as she pushed open the canteen door.

Kitty made to enter the building, grateful to get out of the freezing air, but Rene held her back with her forearm. She flicked an electric light switch and the canteen was suffused with a dull yellow light from low wattage bulbs.

'What was that?' Kitty jumped back, imagining she saw something skitter along the wall. Then she noticed another greyish flash. And another! When her eyes adjusted to the light, she gasped at the sight of bugs skidding across the walls, their antennae quivering ahead of them as they whipped into the cracks.

'Jesus wept! I've seen crawlies before but none the size of those buggers.'

'Don't be scared, girl.' Rene shuddered visibly. 'You'll soon get used to them.' She waited a moment before continuing. 'They're silverfish. Always around an urn first thing. So make sure you put fresh water in it every morning.'

'Is that my job?' Kitty grimaced, following close behind Rene in the delusion that this would prevent anything dropping on her head.

'Well, you don't think I do it, do yer?' Rene gave her a withering glance. 'Don't use the water from the day before, whatever you do. They come out at night to eat, but sometimes they like a drink as well, and we don't want the customers knowing they're not the first to drink their daily cuppa.' Rene laughed again and Kitty shuddered. 'Nor do we want the customers thinking they are getting more than their fair share.' Kitty felt her stomach heave. She had put up with bugs in number two – every house had them – and she had even creosoted the walls to get rid of them.

'Haven't you had the bug man in?' Kitty asked, and Rene laughed.

'I'll tell you what, girl, you tell the chief cook and bottle washer when he comes in, and he'll tell you what you can do with the bug man.' Rene took a box of matches out of her overall pocket. 'He's a conchy,' Rene said, meaning a conscientious objector. 'Tighter than a crab's backside ... and that's watertight.'

'I take it he runs this salubrious establishment?' Kitty scoffed, not sure if she was staying yet, knowing she could resign at a week's notice. She followed Rene to a small room at the back, where they took off their coats and hung them on a nail behind the door. Kitty wasn't too keen to leave it unattended in case the bugs took up residence in her pockets.

'It'll be fine here,' Rene said, showing Kitty how to drain water from the urn. Kitty wrinkled her nose, looking at the sink full of dirty crockery.

'Oh, behave yourself, you'll see much worse than that before you're done.'

After refilling the urn, Rene turned on the gas tap. It hissed and spat and she gingerly introduced the lit match. The geyser plopped. Then it whooshed into life! Flames like an angry dragon shot from its mouth.

'That'll have someone's fringe off one o' these days,' Rene said, quickly stepping back. The whole place now reeked of gas. 'It'll be a wonder if we don't poison someone. Mr Cropper says he'll fill in a chit and give it to the requisitions people. I asked him when we took the place on, but he is so dozy – anyone would think it was coming out of his pocket.'

'I'm not touching it!' Kitty exclaimed, her eyes wide. 'It's lethal.'

'We'll have to get used to it, until a new one comes in,' Rene said. 'Mr Cropper will be in soon. You can tell him if you like.' She laughed, watching the urn until it settled down. 'He'll probably put you on a charge, like.'

'He can't do that – we're civvies!' Kitty argued, and Rene shrugged.

'He pleases himself more or less.'

While waiting for the water to boil Rene went to retrieve a packet of five Woodbines from her coat pocket, took one out, broke it, lit half and blew out a long stream of smoke. 'If you mention he has to do anything official you don't see him for a week.' She put the unlit, broken cigarette back in the packet, and put the packet on the shelf above the sink.

Kitty had no choice. If she wanted to pay Rita back for helping her pay for her dad's funeral she had to put up with the danger. Leaking geysers, although lethal in the wrong hands, must be ignored. So must the bugs.

However, she knew she would not be able to put so much as a cup to her lips until this place was scrubbed from top to bottom. It was not a case of just wiping down the tables. If the building was not fumigated then hot soapy water, and plenty of Lysol, would have to be the next best thing.

Looking around, Kitty noticed brown drip

marks cascading from the brown grease-mottled ceiling and wondered who had worked here before to let it get into this state. She didn't come from Buckingham Palace, but this place was downright filthy. No stranger to a scrubbing brush, she could not wait to get going.

'I'll make a start.' She pulled on the overall Rene gave her and, rolling her sleeves to her elbows, she filled a galvanised bucket with hot soapy water. Every surface was covered in a tacky residue that would have to be scraped off with a knife, she noticed, and that was before she attempted to put a scrubbing brush near it!

'This place was probably condemned before the NAAFI got hold of it,' Kitty muttered to herself. The customers must have had cast-iron stomachs.

'I do my best to keep on top o' things, once we get going,' Rene said later. 'But apart from you there's only Mona and me. And she's as useful as a wax fireguard!' Rene poured two teas into surprisingly clean cups. 'I've never seen anyone who's got so many ailments in one body.' She took a long puff on the cigarette permanently hanging from the corner of her crimson lips. 'She's been bloody neurotic since the beginning of the war.'

'Has she got anybody away?' Kitty asked, and Rene told her that Mona's son was in the Eighth Army. 'But we don't get our pick of staff,' Rene said. 'Let's face it, what girl wants to be up to her elbows in dirty dishwater every day?'

'Well, you've sold the job to me,' Kitty laughed, 'but beggars can't be choosers. You've got to take what's going, I suppose.'

'Aye,' Rene said. 'Mona will only be here when she feels like it.' She stopped for a moment as if pondering her next statement. 'One thing I will say, though, don't let her persuade you to run messages.'

Kitty's brow creased into a furrow. *What messages?* But Rene did not elaborate.

'I don't suppose you work in a place like this for the lovely view,' Kitty said, her voice holding a cynical note. She looked out of the steamed-up window to the dock road where grime and noxious fumes flew in off the river.

'It's a job,' Rene said nonchalantly, picking up a bucket of hot water. In no time at all the two women were scrubbing for all they were worth.

At the end of the morning Rene said, 'I'll tell you what, Kit, you can't half shift yourself with that scrubbing brush.'

'I might come from Empire Street but I'm not working in filth.'

'Good on you, girl,' Rene laughed. 'You'll do for me!'

But will this place do for me? Kitty wondered.

As the conflict continued, the nursing staff at Bootle Infirmary began to relax when there was no sign of attack or invasion of the city.

'I wish something would happen,' said one of the probationer nurses training alongside Rita. Many patients had been moved out to make way for the hordes of wounded civilians and servicemen who had not yet materialised. Most of the staff were standing around twiddling their thumbs and trying to look busy when Matron did her rounds.

'I was on Men's Surgical, last week,' said Maeve, 'and when an appendicitis case came in, the nurses practically threw themselves at him!' She laughed. 'He had never been so pampered.'

'I don't suppose that will last if we get invaded,' Rita said. 'We are the nearest hospital to the docks.'

'At least when we were run off our feet we weren't bored.'

'Be careful what you wish for, my dear,' Rita said with a smile.

Kitty had been working at the canteen for nearly a week and the place was now open and flourishing.

'Even the bugs have been polished,' Rene laughed as the dockers queued for their midday meal.

'She's what you could call an asset,' a sailor in Royal Naval uniform said. 'You'd better not let her slip through the net.'

'Hey, be quiet, you,' Rene laughed. 'She'll be expecting a rise in her wages at this rate.'

Kitty took it all in her stride. She was here to earn the money to pay for her dad's funeral. When that was paid, she would consider moving somewhere else. The munitions factories paid much better money than this job did. The only thing stopping her was that she could not stand the noise of the factories. How those girls put up with that racket all day she'd never know.

It was a six o'clock start every morning. Rene liked to get the canteen open for the early birds. They had both fed so many servicemen, Kitty had lost track. Nevertheless, woe betide anyone who outstayed his welcome. Rene had a novel way of discouraging lingering at the table in the steamed-up canteen. She would fling a floor cloth, which usually landed around the unwelcome party's ears. He soon got the message when she warned him this was not a dosshouse.

'I hope you'll stay, Kit. You've done a great job,' Rene said when they got a break one afternoon.

'I'd like to see the appreciation in my wages, if it's all the same to you.' Kitty knew compliments cost nothing and you could not feed your family with them.

'You can tell that to Mr Cropper. He'll be in later.'

Kitty had heard that before, but there had been no sign of the manager. 'I thought you said another woman worked here,' she said, wiping down the L-shaped counter that ran half the length of the canteen, the floor space on the customer side being crammed with uncovered tables of every shape and size.

'She's got her hands full with Mr Cropper's business,' Rene said.

'It's nothing to do with me,' Kitty said. The less she knew, the better. What the eye did not see and all that. 'I'm only here to earn me wages. No more, no less.'

'We'll get on just fine, then,' Rene smiled as the canteen door opened and a corpulent man, almost as round as he was tall, came waddling into the canteen, filling the steamy atmosphere with pungent smoke from the cigar clenched between his teeth.

''Ello, Mr Cropper, me old tater,' Rene called cheerfully, scraping tarred remains from a huge cast-iron frying pan. 'Come and meet Kitty.'

'So this is the new girl, is it?' Mr Cropper said, holding out a podgy hand to Kitty, who was carrying a heavy tray full of dirty crockery. However, she thought it wise to greet the manager properly. Putting the tray on a nearby table, she wiped her hand on her pinny and took his clammy digits in hers.

'Has Rene been looking after you?' he said. He didn't wait for her to answer. 'Good, good...' He seemed distracted, looking out of the window, grimacing and rubbing his barrel chest.

'Give me something for heartburn, Rene, love,' he said, undoing the buttons of an expensive camel-coloured cashmere overcoat, and heading to the till. 'And a nice cup of tea. None of that stewed stuff you used to serve, mind.' He half turned to Kitty.

'Are you planning on staying here?' he asked, surveying the canteen and holding a wad of pound notes that he had taken from the till. 'I see you've given these walls a lick of a cloth already.'

'We did that last week, Mr Cropper,' Rene said conversationally.

'Where's that Mona today?' the large man asked. 'I need an errand run.'

'She'll be in soon,' Rene said quickly.

'Don't be letting her pull the wool over your eyes. She's a sly one, that Mona. And watch what she slips under the counter.'

Kitty looked at Rene, not knowing what to say. Experience had taught her to say nothing. Mr

Cropper sat heavily on a chair at a table nearest the counter and Rene rolled her eyes before taking him a fresh cup of tea.

'I can manage with Kitty here, Mr Cropper,' Rene said. She sounded a bit nervous and Kitty wondered if she was afraid of the large man. 'Mona won't be long so–'

Mr Cropper raised his hand. 'I'll stay until Mona comes in.' He rubbed his chest. 'Get me something for this indigestion.'

'Won't be a minute, Mr Cropper,' Rene said, heading to the back room, followed by Kitty.

'He must have an important order coming,' Rene said, getting liver salts from the staff room. She added in a low voice, 'A word to the wise, Kit. Whatever you see or hear in here stays in here. D'you understand?'

Kitty nodded.

'I'm not saying I agree with it, mind. But it pays to keep your opinions to yourself.'

'Shall I take the medicine out to Mr Cropper?' Kitty asked, and Rene nodded just as the canteen door opened.

'Oh, here goes,' said Rene. 'Look what the cat dragged in.'

A tall thin woman sauntered in, dressed in a loose-fitting wrap coat that might have seen better days ten years ago, judging by the balding fur collar and cuffs.

'Afternoon, Mona,' Rene called from behind the counter.

A cloche hat covered Mona's head, so Kitty could not make out the colour of her hair. Her feet were encased in black, Mary-Jane shoes that reminded Kitty of a pair her mam once had.

The woman, looking from under the scalloped rim of her hat, eyed Mr Cropper and said in a low voice, 'Is 'e gonna be 'ere all day?' She didn't wait for an answer as she sashayed into the staff room, undoing the single coat button at her hip.

Kitty gave Mr Cropper his glass of Andrews Salts before picking up the loaded tray of dirty dishes and carrying it to the sink in the back room, where the woman was hanging her coat behind the door.

'I'm Mona,' she said, unhooking a grubby-looking white overall and slipping it over her black skirt and buttoned-up cardigan. 'You must be Kitty.' Then she lit a cigarette, laid it in the groove of a Bakelite ashtray and filled the sink with cold water. Kitty emptied the tray on the wooden draining board and after a while Mona turned off the tap, emptied the water from the sink, and put the plug in again. Kitty couldn't work out what the woman was playing at. She hadn't been here all week and she suspected that Mona was trying to fool her boss that she was putting her back into it.

Although she engaged the same darting movements as the silverfish Kitty had seen when she first arrived, Mona did not do much in the way of work. She seemed to use up an awful lot of energy making no progress whatsoever.

'Don't get comfy; he wants you to run a message,' Rene told her.

'I didn't think he'd come in to cook.'

Rene put the dishes into the sink. What were these 'messages'? Kitty wondered.

'I've seen more waitresses come an' go over the years than you've 'ad hot dinners.' Mona's voice had a note of irritated world-weariness that suggested she didn't believe Kitty would be staying long either. She made no move to wash the crockery. Kitty set to work.

'I'll wash and you can dry if you like.' Kitty noted Mona's look of disgust.

'I cook and run messages,' Mona said. 'I don't wash dishes.'

That put me in my place, Kitty thought as she washed the greasy plates, but noted that it was she and Rene who had been doing the cooking all week.

'I see the canteen has been washed,' Mona said, puffing on the cigarette. 'When I saw it when 'e took it on I thought it was only the muck holding it together.'

Rene came back in looking concerned. Leaning towards Mona, she said in a low voice, 'He's waiting for a delivery.' She sounded annoyed. 'He said the stock is running out too quick.'

'Don't look at me,' Mona said defensively. 'I didn't eat it all!' There was an awkward silence and the two women eyed each other like cats after the same mouse.

'I hope 'e doesn't think it's me,' Mona said before taking a long, nervous drag on her cigarette. Rene didn't answer, Kitty noticed. She was glad she had nothing to do with whatever was going on. It did not take a genius to see that there was trouble brewing. Food shortages were already on the increase; it would be very tempting to offload a bit of sugar here and bit of bacon there.

274

Especially if the price was right.

Rene's deadpan expression altered when she raised her black-pencilled eyebrow. It was obvious to Kitty that she did not believe Mona, but she kept her head down. She was paid to work, not gossip.

'The order won't be here till tomorrow,' Mona said. 'I'd better go and tell him.'

'We need supplies in here,' Rene said. 'The last time that fat was changed Mr Chamberlain was still in short trousers.'

Kitty shuddered, having seen the brown sludge in the fryer. She dreaded to think what the food tasted like and avoided it herself.

'Best keep anything you hear under your hat; loose lips and all that.' Rene nodded towards the tall cabinet near the window. 'I wouldn't say this to a new girl usually, but I trust you, Kitty.' She looked at Mona before continuing, 'Mr Cropper has *an agreement* with a couple of suppliers.' She nodded her turbaned head. 'But he gets greedy. At first it was a bit of butter here, some meat there—'

However, her revelation was cut short when Mr Cropper waddled into the room.

'Right, let the dog see the rabbit,' he said without preamble. 'Rene, you are using far too much tea. Cut it by 'alf per pot.'

'But it's like midden water now, Mr Cropper. We'll get lynched if it's much weaker.'

'You'll manage.' There was a warning note in his voice. 'Knowing you lot, I'm sure you are extremely generous with supplies.' Mr Cropper, panting now, wiped his face with a huge handkerchief before saying impatiently, 'Get me a drink

275

of water.' His face was purple as a plum. Rene threw a tea towel across the kitchen and it landed on the draining board as Kitty gave the boss a cup of cold water.

'If you don't mind,' said Rene, 'I've got pies to bake while they're still affordable.'

'I'll clear these dishes,' Kitty said. Then she heard Mr Cropper's heavy bulk slump onto a straight-backed chair with a thud, making the legs creak. Rene's black eyebrows met in the middle of her forehead. Kitty turned to see Mr Cropper, his head lolling forward, his chin resting on his chest. They exchanged questioning glances but nobody moved until Kitty took the tea towel and dried her hands. The other two seemed stupefied.

'Are you all right there, Mr Cropper?' There was a hint of panic in Rene's voice as she edged towards him, hunching down so she could see his putty-coloured face at close range. Mr Cropper did not attempt to answer. She patted his cheek and poked his arm, but still there was no response. She looked at the other two and shrugged her shoulders.

'What should I do? He's spark out.'

Kitty went over and looked at the man, who did not seem that old at close quarters. She lifted his ample chins and his head flopped back. She jumped, alarmed that his staring unseeing eyes were directed at the ceiling.

'Jesus, Mary and Frank!' she exclaimed. 'He's dead.'

CHAPTER FIFTEEN

'I got a terrible fright!' Kitty said, sitting at the table with Danny at teatime.

'You must have something about you if you give a fella a heart attack on your first meeting,' Danny said, tucking into his tea.

'It's not funny, Dan.' Kitty was put out that he should not give the sad circumstances their due respect. 'He wasn't very old.'

'I'm not laughing at the situation, Kit,' Danny said, 'but you must admit, five minutes after meeting you, he dropped down dead! You'd be a boon to the Government if they sent you over to meet Hitler.'

Kitty shook her head. She knew the job was too good to be true. Now presumably a new manager had to be appointed.

'Mona went to pieces and then fainted clean away.' Kitty's brow wrinkled. 'I half expected the ambulance man to cart her off too,' she tried hard to suppress a smile, 'but instead he shoved her head between her knees and told her to behave herself.'

'That's a bit harsh,' Danny said.

'You should have been there,' Kitty scoffed. 'She was milking it for all it was worth.' Kitty, mimicking Mona, put the back of her hand to her brow and turned her head to the side. '*Oh, woe...*' she wailed. 'Then Mona had a good look round to make sure she had a soft landing and realised the chair was just out of reach,' Kitty began to laugh, 'so she staggered over to it like she'd been shot!' The howling laughter around the table made the cups rattle.

'I think he had some sort of black market racket going on. I didn't ask questions but it was obvious they were up to something. What with all the rationing coming in.'

'Well, where there's a demand, some will find a way to supply,' Danny said with a dangerous twinkle in his eye.

Kitty gave him a stern look. 'You'd better not be up to something like that yourself, Danny Callaghan.'

'Stop fretting, Kitty. There's nothing to worry about.'

Kitty was serious now. 'I hope not, you've been spending far too much time with that Alfie Delaney and everyone knows he's as bent as a nine-bob note.

'I wonder how our Tommy's getting on,' Kitty said, changing the subject. She knew Tommy would have been full of questions about today's events. 'I hope he's behaving himself and not getting up to mischief.' She missed her younger brother more than she ever would have realised.

Kids were gradually coming back to Liverpool from the countryside even though the Government urged mothers not to be too hasty. Kitty had been sorely tempted to bring Tommy home for Christmas, but they all knew he would never go back again afterwards so it was best that he stay in safe hands for now.

The following week Kitty was thrilled to receive a letter offering her the job as manager of the canteen. Apparently, Rene had put Kitty's name forward after turning down the position. From dishwasher to manager in a fortnight! Maybe her luck had turned.

'Get those greens ate, Thomas. I do not want that sister of yours complaining.'

Kitty did not complain, thought Tommy, looking miserably towards the plate of Spam and sprouts he had been given. This was the fourth time this week he had been given sprouts and Mrs Hood knew he didn't like them.

'Kitty doesn't make me eat sprouts even when my throat isn't sore,' Tommy said in a croaky voice. If he tried to eat those he would do himself a mischief, he was sure. Mrs Hood made him eat everything she put in front of him, whether he liked it or not. Usually he did not like anything she cooked, and neither did her two boys, but they just piled the food they did not want onto Tommy's plate, and he had to eat it otherwise the oldest boy, Ronald, would give him a Chinese burn by twisting his skin in both directions at once.

'Come on, eat up.'

'I can't... My throat is sore... Our Kitty doesn't make me eat when my throat is sore.'

'Well, *your Kitty* isn't here ... and I'm not forking out good money because you are malingering, so eat.'

'I can't eat it.' Tommy stabbed a sprout with his fork. He was close to tears now and he stared at the awful green orb with something akin to revulsion. His stomach heaved.

'You will not get down from the table until you eat every one.' Mrs Hood was a harsh, hostile woman who ruled her evacuee with fear. She made him go outside first thing and sweep the yard every day, rain, hail or snow, and would not let him back in until it met her exacting standards. He also had to run all of the errands, sweep all of the rooms out and clean the loft where Mr Hood kept his pigeons. If he complained she just gave him a clip round the earhole and drove him even harder. No one in his own home had ever raised a hand to him. He'd learned to keep his mouth shut normally. No wonder his throat was sore, he thought miserably. She never talked to her own boys like she spoke to him. She was sweetness and light to them. But every time she looked at Tommy she scowled, like he was something the dog dropped and she had stepped in.

'I'll report you to the authorities,' Mrs Hood said between clenched teeth, and Tommy was tempted to tell her that her threat did not scare him; their Kitty was always saying she would report him to someone or other and she never did. He did not look up at Mrs Hood, in her black coat, like a vulture waiting to pounce. Instead, he kept his eyes firmly on the offending plate. Why could he not have a bit of meat and mashed potato with some of that lovely gravy, as her boys did? The only thing she gave him was Spam and vegetables, sometimes not even Spam.

Suddenly he felt a familiar tingling in the back of his throat and down his ears, his mouth filled with bitter water and he could feel his stomach lurch and heave. Without further warning the meagre contents of his stomach landed on the scrubbed linoleum.

'Now look what you have done. You naughty little boy!' Mrs Hood's angry words accompanied a barrage of stinging slaps on his bare legs. 'You did that on purpose,' said Mrs Hood, dragging him up from the chair by his collar, 'all over my nice clean floor.'

Tommy battled to suppress the tears. The lump in his throat made it ache even more. He wanted to tell her that he was very sorry and ashamed, but the words would not come. They were stuck behind the next avalanche of vomiting.

'Oh, you wicked, wicked little boy!' Mrs Hood looked very angry now. Turning to her children, she said, 'Leave the table, boys.' Her two sons scurried from the room holding their noses. Tommy could see by their downturned mouths they were not impressed.

'You will not get away with this, boy,' Mrs Hood said through gritted teeth. 'Mr Hood will give you a damn good thrashing when he gets home, that's for sure. Now get the mop and bucket and clean it up!' She left the dining room with a flourish, slamming the door behind her. Moments later she returned. 'I want it cleaned before I get back and I want it spotless.' Then the front door slammed and the house was silent save for little sobs as Tommy cleaned up the mess he had made on the floor. As he did so he could feel his stomach lurching again.

'Not again, please,' he said aloud. Then, as the nausea subsided, he took the mop and bucket outside, and tipped the whole lot down the outside drain. Then he went up to the room he shared with the two boys. He needed to lie down.

After a few minutes, when sleep eluded him, Tommy kneeled on the bed, looking out of one of the little square windows towards Liverpool. Way past the sand dunes, he could see the frothy white horses rolling in on the rough sea to meet a leaden sky.

Was that water still the Mersey, he wondered, realising that, any other time, he would have gone to ask one of his brothers, or even Pop. However, there was nobody he could ask here. They all thought he was stupid and they took every opportunity to tell him so.

Kitty's first job on becoming manager was cleaning the premises properly and ordering in the bug man. She and the other new NAAFI girls she had recruited did not mind pulling it apart and scrubbing it from top to bottom: walls, floors, fryers, even the cooker. It looked brand new after they had taken it to bits. Every nut, bolt and screw, every pipe and burner. Everything was soaked overnight in a solution of caustic soda that could strip the skin from your bones. It brought everything up a treat when they took the parts out of the galvanised bin.

'You've done a great job, Kitty.' Mrs Cook, a jolly woman in her late forties, stood back to survey their handiwork.

It did not take long for Kitty to get into the swing of things and she had to admit that it was much better working with women who knew what they were doing. She thrilled at the compliments her baking brought and she could not be happier.

'We're running like the Adelphi Hotel kitchen,' she laughed. It looked like things were on the up now.

CHAPTER SIXTEEN

December 1939

'It is perishing cold out there,' Dolly said, bringing in the milk, obviously frozen, judging by the half-inch of ice popping out of the bottle tops. 'I can't remember when it was so cold.'

'The papers say it's a worldwide chill, and it's stopping essential supplies getting through,' said Pop.

'Sid mentioned that in his last letter,' Nancy said, taking it out of her handbag. 'He says that it has been so cold the ground is frozen and they can't dig in.'

'Must be bad if soldiers can't even dig trenches,' said Pop, pouring fresh tea into three cups.

'He said men who have been in France since September were allowed to go home to spend Christmas with their families,' Nancy said sullenly. 'He missed it by a few weeks and it feels like he has been gone for years.'

'I know exactly how you feel, love,' Dolly answered, recalling the Great War, when Pop had to leave her alone and pregnant with Frank. 'But he will get home as soon as he can.'

'Did I tell you Sid's mother fell off the kerb in the blackout and has to have a walking stick?' Nancy asked. She and Sid's mother did not get on so Nancy came around to her mother's house early every morning. Dolly was delighted as she liked nothing more than looking after her family. 'It isn't broken but very badly sprained, the doctor said.'

'I've heard of so many accidents since the blackout,' Dolly said, 'and you can't get a battery for love nor money.'

'When I went into the chandler's he said I had to buy a whole torch,' Pop answered. 'I said to him, "Look, mate, I'm ARP. It's your duty not to make money on those in need." He told me he was in need as well. It looks like we're all in the same boat.'

'I thought our Rita would be here by now. I'm taking her out to Freshfield on the cart, to see the children.'

'Oh, Pop, I forgot to tell you, Jack Callaghan's getting a lift back to the air force base at Acklington and his friend said he'd take a detour for Rita.'

'Tell her I'll go and pick her up after she's had a few hours with the kids,' Pop said.

'I asked Kitty to call over at tea time,' said Dolly, sitting down to a piece of toast. 'She's made us a lovely Christmas cake and some bun loaf – she started work in the NAAFI on the dock road a few weeks ago, Nancy.'

'Has she heard from Tommy?' Pop knew Kitty felt guilty for sending Tommy away.

'He's been complaining in his letters home, doesn't seem to like the family he's with. Keeps saying he doesn't like Spam and sprouts!' Dolly replied. 'Kitty is worried. She wants to bring him back home.'

'Do you think he's just trying it on?' Pop scratched his chin. 'You know what a young rascal he can be, Doll.'

'I couldn't say, Pop, all I do know is this: not one single bomb has dropped anywhere near Empire Street. I'd be on the next train out to fetch him back.'

'You always did have a soft spot for the lad,' said Pop smiling. If he had his way he'd go and fetch him too.

Rita, dressed in her best, heavy woollen coat, was tying a scarf around her throat, which was still showing some bruising from her husband's attack. Charlie had made himself scarce since then and Rita, who hardly saw anything of him, was glad. When she had seen him on the landing, her arms were full of her clothing, which she was transporting to the chest of drawers in Megan's room.

'Rita, how long are you going to keep this up? Every marriage has its little disagreements.'

Rita's voice was coldly efficient. 'Hear this: Charlie, you will never lay your hands on me again.' She continued along the landing and, stepping down to the back bedroom, she closed the door behind her and leaned against it, her heart beating so strongly she could feel it in her throat as relief flooded through her. She would not be held responsible for what she would do if Charlie tried to touch her, even benignly, ever again.

Rita was relieved that there was no awkwardness between her and Jack. In fact, she felt closer to him than she had ever done. It was a dangerous way to feel, but after Charlie's behaviour, Rita felt reckless.

Jack's pal, who had to be back at Acklington airfield too, was picking up Rita. It seemed such a shame these young men were missing Christmas at home because they had to be on duty.

'You wouldn't say that if we were suddenly invaded in the middle of your Christmas pud,' Jack said, laughing, and Rita had to agree. She wondered what her own brothers were doing right now. She did not even know where they were. It seemed so long since they were all together.

'This is Giles Betterton,' said Jack, as they climbed into the luxurious convertible sedan, although thankfully the hood was up. 'He's a friend of Gloria.'

'Hello, Giles,' Rita said, thankful for a lift in a motor car today. 'Small world.' With petrol rationing in force, it was almost impossible to drive out as far as Freshfield. However, she did not spend too long worrying about Giles's petrol; she was far too excited. It had been eight weeks since she'd seen the children and if it had not been for returning to her nursing job she felt she would have gone mad without them. It had been a glorious day that time, and they had gone for a picnic. The children had seemed to be having a wonderful time on the farm and though it was dreadfully sad saying goodbye, Rita at least knew that her children were in good hands.

Rita took out her small compact and flipped it open. She wanted to look her very best for them both.

The journey seemed to take for ever although it was less than an hour away from the dockside. Rita's foot tapped impatiently and no matter how hard she tried to stop the annoying habit she could not. Biting her lip, she wondered if the children had forgotten her.

Her stomach suddenly growled and she could feel the hot colour of embarrassment rush to her face, but the two men in the car were far too courteous to comment, thank goodness. She had been too excited to eat breakfast and only now realised she was starving. However, Rita doubted she would be able to eat anything, even now. Moments later the car came to a halt and she saw they were by the gate of the farm where her children were staying until the threat of invasion passed.

'Well, thanks for the lift,' she said, getting out, so grateful for it on such a cold morning. Even inside the car, she could see the cloudy vapour from her lips when she breathed.

'Here, let me get the presents out of the boot,' Jack said, getting out of his side, going round and opening the boot. As he passed her the gifts, he reminded her to save the brown paper and string for the Spitfire fund.

'I will,' Rita laughed, and was secretly although pleasantly surprised when he leaned over and kissed her lightly on the cheek. It was as natural as breathing though it felt as if a hundred butterflies were fluttering around in her stomach.

'Well, take care of yourself, Jack, and come back home soon,' she said.

'You can be sure of it, Rita, and remember what I said,' Jack replied in a low voice and then, as the sound of children's excited voices filled the country air, he laughed. 'Here they are, all pink and shiny for Christmas.' He took some coins out of his pocket and offered them to Michael and Megan when they had finished being hugged by their mother.

'Here you go,' he said. 'Get yourselves some sweets or a comic each.'

A deep contented sigh escaped Jack's lips when he saw the children skip happily away, each holding on to their mother's hand.

'Thank you, Uncle Jack!' they called back in unison. Even though they were no longer looking he lifted his hand and half waved. Their only interest now was their mother, as it should be.

Jack wondered if that bastard Charlie Kennedy knew how lucky he was.

'Bye, Rita,' he whispered, knowing that any day now he would receive his orders and God alone knew where they would take him. 'Look after yourself...'

'Is that the River Mersey?' Tommy asked Kenneth, the quieter of the Hood boys. He had to know. Kenneth shrugged his shoulders, just as Ronald entered the small back room and Tommy repeated the question. Ronald, not as gentle as his younger brother, threw back his head, opened his mouth and forced a laugh so false that Tommy wondered if he was having a fit.

'You nincompoop,' Ronald said in a haughty voice. The same age as Tommy, he was without a doubt, Tommy thought, much cleverer. He did not hesitate to inform Tommy of the fact every day, calling him names and ridiculing his accent. Tommy was surprised; he didn't even know he had an accent until he came here.

'That is the Irish Sea! The Mersey stops at Formby Point.'

'Oh,' Tommy said, still looking out of the window. Although prepared to be educated, he was not too fond of being called a nincompoop. If he were back at home, he would not let anybody call him names. However, he had promised Kitty he would stay out of trouble, and he was doing his best. He really was. Although, given the choice, Tommy knew he would never get sick of rearranging that smug look on his tormentor's face.

He wondered what Kitty was doing now. Thinking back fondly, he recalled the times he watched the ships, big and small, sailing up the Mersey. He had marvelled at their ability to slip perfectly into the dock, like that pane of glass fitted into the frame, all snug as if that was where it always should be.

'Look at his silly grin,' said Ronald. 'Did you find that by the River *Mirsey?*' He roared with laughter at his imitation of Tommy.

'Funny,' Tommy said drily, clenching his fists and praying to whomever was listening to let him keep his temper in check.

'Come along, Kenneth, let's leave him to his water gazing.' Ronald tugged Kenneth's sleeve and they left the room. Tommy was ever so glad they'd

289

gone because he might have had to break his promise to Kitty to behave himself.

That Ronald really was a trial: prefect of the class Tommy had been shoehorned into, and too full of his own importance for Tommy's liking. Nevertheless, he thought, a promise was a promise, and Tommy intended to keep it. He didn't want their Kitty coming all this way to apologise for him. Anyway, he thought, how long could the war last? Nothing was happening.

The days were getting much colder now as December drew on. It would be Christmas soon and Kitty hadn't been here for a few weeks now. Looking far out to the misty sea, he wondered when Kitty would visit. The Hoods were going carol singing later, Tommy remembered, hoping Mrs Hood wouldn't make him go.

He was not feeling too good this morning. His throat hurt. There was nothing unusual in that; he always suffered from wonky tonsils. But he was also feeling sick inside, he was hot all of the time and his legs ached.

'Get your coat on. You are coming with us and I will hear no more about it.' Mrs Hood was determined Tommy was going carol singing and he was equally determined he wasn't. While her back was turned and she was organising her sons, Tommy went outside for a breath of bracing air.

'I've had enough of this,' he said aloud, taking big gulps of seaside air. Here, chimneys puffed sedately and houses were the same colour now as the day they were built. Unlike the wonderful soot-covered buildings that belched noxious fumes, which he longed to see again.

The buildings, like him, were rough and ready. He didn't belong here. He didn't fit in with the two ninnies who couldn't climb a tree or skim a flat stone across the water. No, he belonged in Empire Street and, Tommy thought, taking a deep breath, feeling the searing pain slice his throat, he was going back there right now.

The only thing he had in his pockets was a hole. He didn't possess a penny piece, as Mrs Hood never gave him any of the money she was given for his billet. There was nothing for it, he thought, if he did not have his fare home he would go on foot.

He turned left and made his first step home.

'We went along to the pine woods, Mum,' said Michael, who was now the talkative one. The outdoor life suited him, by the look of it. He had filled out and there was a rosy glow that he didn't have back home. 'We saw the red squirrels. They were gathering hazelnuts for the winter. Aunty Joan said they come as far as the farm some days, so I've been looking out for them.'

'That's lovely, Michael,' Rita said, thrilled he had settled, yet trying to quell the feeling of helplessness. He had called her 'mum' – not 'mam', as he usually did. Rita suddenly and inexplicably felt as if she was losing them.

'And what about you, Megan, what have you done since I saw you last?'

'Cried to go home,' Megan said in a sad voice and Rita felt a stab of alarm rush through her.

'I know, it is tough for all of us. I miss you both so much,' she replied, taking her little girl in her arms. Megan's hair seemed lighter now and she had the same glowing complexion as her brother, but there was not the same sparkle in her eyes.

'You know I will bring you home just as soon as it is safe, and look,' Rita said, pointing to the end of the lane, 'there's a telephone box! I will leave some pennies with Aunty Joan and the telephone number of the shop, and each night, before you go to bed, you can ring me or I can make arrangements to ring the telephone box.' Suddenly her daughter's face lit up. 'I am only at the other end of that phone, my little love.'

'Mrs Kennedy, how lovely to see you,' said the round, jolly-looking woman of indeterminate age. 'The children have talked about nothing else but your visit all week. Even Father Christmas didn't get a look in!' The woman the kids called 'Aunty Joan' laughed now. 'Come in, come in, we've just come back from morning Mass. I'm just cooking breakfast. Uncle Seth is setting the table. The chickens have been fed – now it's our turn.'

'Do you want your eggs fried, poached, scrambled or boiled?' asked Aunty Joan's husband, Seth. Rita inhaled the tantalising aroma of freshly cooked food, and her eyes widened appreciatively when she saw the huge plate of bacon in the middle of the table alongside another heaped plate of thick toasted bread dripping in home-made butter.

'Hello there, Mrs Kennedy. Come in, tuck in!' Seth said, ladling all manner of eggs onto the plates. The children sat up to the table after washing their hands and Rita was glad to see that some things hadn't changed.

'We can hardly get bacon any more,' Rita said. 'We have to queue for most things now.'

'I've heard it will be really scarce after Christmas,' Seth said, tucking in and encouraging everybody else to do the same. 'We'll open our presents at Christmas.'

Rita felt a thrill of contentment. She had thought she would burn with jealousy because another woman was raising her children. However, she could think of nobody else she would want to take care of them – except Mam and Pop, of course. The children had not once asked where their father was, either this time or on Rita's previous visits.

'You remind me so much of my own mother and father,' Rita said, smiling, as they took a walk through the frosty fields after breakfast, taking in the cutting freshness of a winter morning.

'We were not blessed with children of our own but we love them so much,' said Joan. 'As soon as we set eyes on Michael and Megan we knew they were for us. Michael took to country life like a duck to water, but Megan misses her mum.' Rita watched her daughter running without a care in the world through the wide expanse of fields. 'But I think she's going to settle down eventually.'

'I promise I will try to get here as often as my hospital shifts allow. It's not too bad now but ... if anything should...'

'I know,' said Joan, patting Rita's hand. 'We know how difficult it is, but hopefully Megan will be fine.'

Rita would have felt her departure more keenly than she did, had it not been for the kind and loving nature of her children's foster parents.

'Are you sure you can't stay for lunch?' Michael and Megan pleaded, and Rita felt the first pull of separation. She was going to miss them even more now.

'I will next time,' she told the children, then, turning to Joan she explained, 'I promised Mam... My brothers are somewhere in the Atlantic... She feels it with Christmas coming.' Joan nodded and patted her shoulder and, his arm around his wife and the two children at their side, Seth waved her down the lane where she was meeting Pop near the Copper Kettle pub. The weather was closing in, and the sky was dark with the promise of snow. It had been a wonderful morning and, looking at her watch, she noticed that she was in good time for her lift. She didn't want him hanging around all afternoon waiting for her. It would only upset the children if they saw Pop too. Seeing the children had eased her mind. They were with good people, but Rita didn't think that she would ever have true peace of mind until Michael and Megan were back home in Empire Street – where they belonged.

Tommy knew he was in Formby when the sound of the sea drew him to the famous wide, sandy beach, now deserted, and the sand dunes behind. The sea looked grey and sinister in the winter light. There was not a soul in sight. He was freezing cold. The short jacket he wore was the same one he'd had all year and his short trousers did nothing to keep the cold out either. The urge to sleep was very strong but Tommy knew that if he did, he might not wake for hours and then it could be dark. Even though his feet were blistered, he knew he had to carry on. He dragged himself to his feet and headed off.

Hoping he was going the right way he came to a crossroads and noticed an old hall he'd seen on the way into Southport. 'Stanley Hall' was engraved in the high sandstone gateposts and Tommy's heart sank. He was still miles away and knew he had a long way to go yet.

'Here!' An old man with a shotgun over his arm shouted to him now. 'Come here, boy!' Tommy felt his courage seep from him and he wondered if Mrs Hood had reported him missing. But he did not have the strength to run right now. The old man leaned down close to his face, as if Tommy would not understand what he said.

'Are you all right, boy?' he asked. 'You're as white as a sheet.'

Tommy could not say a word.

'Stay where you are until I get back.' With that, the old man went in the direction of a large field at the end of which was a farmhouse. Is he going to fetch help? Tommy wondered. Or is he going to fetch a policeman to take me back? There was no way he was going to risk it.

'I don't need help, thank you,' Tommy said politely, but the man was already heading towards the farmhouse.

Tommy picked up his feet as much as he was able to and trudged on. A couple of hundred yards down the lane, he was thrilled to see a flat-backed cart pulled by two shire horses coming his way. He hid in the hedge as it approached and then he summoned all of his strength and scrambled onto the back of it as it passed him.

Hiding under the hessian sacks stacked at the back of the cart, he stayed there until it had gone dark. The rest had helped him feel a little less tired so, as the cart pulled into the yard of a little country pub, Tommy waited for the driver and his female companion to go inside before jumping down and making a run for it. Tommy was grateful for the ride, knowing it had cut many hours from his journey, not knowing the treacherous land through which he was clambering. Darkness had long descended, and a hoar frost was settling on the ground. His brief rest earlier was long forgotten and his feet were too cold and sore to run any longer but he limped painfully on.

He could see the icy frost hovering in the bitterly cold air as a rolling mist covered the fields and hedgerows, giving a gothic eeriness to the land. A pheasant scooted across the dirt road almost frightening the life out of him. The black sky felt as if it was on top of him. His heart soared when he spotted a small group of cottages further up the lane. Dragging himself through yet another field, Tommy came to a T-shaped junction. Crossing the narrow main road as an Arctic wind swirled around him, he noticed a blacksmith at the nearest building, shoeing a horse. Tommy edged closer to the smithy so he could get warm but he was careful not to be seen. The thin jacket he was wearing gave little protection and he was sure he would succumb to the cold if he stopped moving for too long.

The blacksmith stopped what he was doing and

locked the double doors, blocking off the heat that came from his brazier. In the black wilderness, Tommy heard voices and managed to make his way towards them.

He could just make out a building called The Cabbage Inn and he wondered if he should go inside to ask for a drink of water. However, on second thoughts, he dare not. He was a runaway and the authorities would surely be looking for him by now.

Tommy's mind became filled with awful thoughts. What if the police found him and locked him up? Kitty would never know where he was. The bitterly cold wind cutting into him was a blessing now as he was burning up. He put his hand to his throat and was horrified to feel that his neck had swollen to what felt like twice its normal size.

When he got to the pub doorway, little Tommy lost his nerve. The low murmur of voices inside the pub belonged to local farmers, he realised. His body began to shiver and as he looked through the window, he saw the farmers sitting around a blazing fire. It would be nice and warm by that fire, he thought. Nevertheless, he could not take the chance. If he wanted to get back to Empire Street tonight, he would have to keep moving.

The ruts in the ploughed fields were rock hard, making his journey more hazardous, and Tommy felt the cold seep into his bones. Exhausted, he longed to lie down, curl up and go to sleep. However, the way he was feeling now, he knew if he fell asleep, he might not wake up.

His Kitty would be at home. He needed to see

her. She would know what to do about his sore throat. It was burning so badly now he could hardly swallow, and the tiny amount of saliva that he did manage to produce did nothing to wet his dry lips.

It took him a long time to reach a place that he soon discovered was a cemetery. A rook cried in the distance and Tommy pulled up his collar and began to hurry. The swish of tree branches whispered in the night air, filling him with such fear he wanted to scream. Just as he was about to give up an owl swooped from a nearby tree, its powerful wings almost touching his head, and Tommy found the strength to run.

Barely able to see his hand in front of his face, he dragged himself across the fields. He was hardly able to breathe now and the fresh flow of tears made him realise that his few months in Southport had turned him soft. He had never cried when he lived in Empire Street.

Tommy heard the low, mournful wail of a foghorn in the distance and knew he was near his beloved River Mersey. Not long now, he thought. Almost there.

'I'm coming home, Kit,' he gasped as another wave of nausea engulfed him.

CHAPTER SEVENTEEN

Determined to get home to the warmth of her fireside after staying behind at work to bake some pies for the next day, Kitty marched up Empire Street as the tantalising smell of the steak and kidney pie wafted to her nostrils. Well, she had to sample her own cooking and Danny was a good judge of pies. Her stomach growled and she hoped he had the fire going and the kettle on. She was parched.

Reaching inside the letterbox, covered by the lion's head knocker, she felt around in the darkness for the key that hung on a piece of string inside the door.

'Kitty, is that you?' Danny called as she closed the front door behind her and pulled the thick curtain across to keep out draughts and cover any light that may be visible in the blackout, giving Pop Feeny no cause to give vent to instructions to 'Put that light out!'

'Of course it's me, Danny. Did you think we were being invaded?' Kitty hurried along the narrow passage as the kitchen door quickly opened. 'What have you been up to this time, Dan?' she said in a low voice, knowing her brother had irons in many fires. However, she did not really want to know about them. What the eye didn't see the heart could not grieve over. He did look uneasy, though, she mused. Her heart plummeted.

'What is it, Dan? Are you ill? You look awful.' Kitty was almost too afraid to ask.

'Come and have a look at this, Kit,' Danny said, standing aside to let Kitty into the kitchen. Kitty gasped, completely unprepared for the sight that met her eyes. The room was freezing and there was no fire in the grate. Quickly she hurried to the couch to see her young brother covered in Danny's overcoat.

'Tommy!' she cried. 'Oh my word, what's happened to him, Danny? Why is he here?' Tommy lay so pale and still that Kitty feared he was not even breathing.

'I found him out in the back yard when I came in from work.' Danny's voice cracked as he looked down at their nine-year-old brother. It was difficult to tell if he was alive or dead.

'Oh my God!' Kitty exclaimed. 'Where has he been?'

She saw only the filthy condition of the child huddled under the coat and, bending, she scooped Tommy's thin body into her arms. The heat that rose from his shattered little body was quite at odds with the freezing atmosphere of the austere room.

'He's been sick all over the yard, Kit.' There was a sob in Danny's voice. 'I didn't know what to do.' The child was almost weightless, and Kitty looked down into his stricken face, his sunken eyes remaining closed as she held his emaciated body close. His breathing was frighteningly shallow now, and Kitty knew that she'd have to move fast.

'Danny, see if Rita's home from the hospital!'

Danny was already out of the door and he

returned moments later with Rita.

'Good God!' Rita said. 'Has he been attacked? Look at those bruises on his face!'

'Rita, please tell me he's going to be all right!' Kitty's face was soaked with tears and she was visibly shaking.

'What happened?' Rita asked as she opened each of Tommy's eyelids in turn. 'Kitty, we have to get him to hospital right now. Danny, go and get Pop. Tell him he needs to get the horse out of the stable straight away.'

'I'll go and get a blanket,' Kitty cried, and hurried up the stairs. She would die if anything happened to her brother, her baby boy whom she had raised since the day he was born.

Kitty dragged the heavy grey blanket from the bed and took the stairs so fast she almost fell down them. When she entered the kitchen, Danny was back with the news that Pop was getting out the horse and cart, and Rita was cradling Tommy in her arms.

'Get me some water, Danny, hurry.' Rita's voice took on the professional tone she used at all times at the hospital. 'I've got to cool him down as quickly as possible.'

'What shall I put it in?' Danny asked desperately.

'Anything!' Rita did not mean to sound harsh, but she had to be firm as their fear was making them oblivious to anything else but Tommy. 'I have to break this fever.'

'He's been asleep since I found him,' Danny wailed, hurrying into the stone-floored kitchen. 'He was sick on me as I carried him in, and he still didn't wake up.'

'It's all my fault,' Kitty said.

'No it's not, Kitty,' Rita said firmly. 'You could never have prevented this.'

'I should have paid attention to his letters, he tried to tell me that something was wrong! And I never went to see him. He must have thought I'd forgotten him!'

'No, Kitty.' Rita sighed and tried to make her friend listen. 'I'm sure he didn't, but we haven't got choices any more. We have to do as we are told now.'

'Kit,' Danny said, a little calmer now, 'you know we would have moved heaven and earth to get to Southport if we'd known he was sick.'

Rita opened Tommy's mouth and, with the small torch she carried in her uniform pocket she peered again down his throat. Danny stroked the translucent skin on his brother's cheek.

'Don't worry, Tom, we're here now, we'll look after you.'

'May God forgive you, Mrs Hood,' Kitty said through clenched teeth as Rita placed the cool cloth on Tommy's forehead, 'because I never will.' Little Tommy did not stir and Rita's heart went out to her friend.

'I got a letter from Sid this morning,' Nancy said, thrilled that Gloria had called round with some matinée coats and a dozen towelling nappies as a present from some of the girls she worked with at George Henry Lee. 'He said to keep looking for a place of our own... I've been doing nothing else,' she added, looking to make sure the parlour door was closed.

'Why?' Gloria asked. 'Isn't she easy to get along with?' She nodded to the wall that separated the parlour from the kitchen where Sid's mother lived.

Nancy had lived in the parlour since they married and it was obvious by the wrinkling of her nose at the mention of Mrs Kerrigan's name that they did not get on.

'She's glued to the wireless listening to Lord Haw-Haw spouting about how many aircraft the Germans have shot down or ships they've sunk,' Nancy said. 'It's all lies and propaganda but she will not have it. She loves the drama – and probably has a glass to the wall as we speak.'

'You can't half pick them, Nance,' Gloria laughed.

'She's miffed because Sid sends his pay to me and not her; she says she should have it because she has the house to keep so it's only right she should get the housekeeping. Miserly old witch.'

'Tell her where to go, Nance. I would,' Gloria answered, sipping the tea Nancy had made.

'She's sitting in there with a face on her that's enough to give you nightmares,' Nancy laughed.

'She could be England's secret weapon: send her over to Hitler and scare the pants off him!' Gloria answered, and the two of the squealed with laughter.

'Oh, Glor, you are a tonic,' Nancy said, wiping tears of laughter from her face with her handkerchief.

'I needed a bit of cheering up.' Gloria told her that as Giles's leave had finished she was at a bit of a loose end and had come round to ask if Nancy wanted to go to Midnight Mass a bit later.

Nancy suspected she was only going because she enjoyed singing the carols.

'It's lucky you caught me in... I should give Mrs Kerrigan Sid's allotment money, and if it carries on I'll have to give her my new ration books after Christmas, too,' she said jokingly.

They chatted almost nonstop for another hour and then Gloria said she had to go.

A few minutes after Gloria left, Mrs Kerrigan, a tall, thin woman, limped with her sprained ankle into the parlour without knocking. She had a tea towel in her hand, which she kept folding and unfolding.

'Is everything all right, Mrs Kerrigan?' Nancy asked, retrieving her knitting from behind a cushion.

'You didn't say you were looking for a place of your own.' Mrs Kerrigan looked most put out. 'I thought you were settled here. We could be company for each other while Sid and Mr Kerrigan are away.'

Nancy had been living here for over three months and Sid's mother had never invited her into the kitchen to listen to the wireless once. After Sid had gone away, the nights were so long and lonely as she was left on her own, while Mrs Kerrigan listened to Tommy Handley or a play, so Nancy took to nipping through the narrow alleyway to Empire Street to listen to her mam and dad's wireless instead.

'We've always wanted a place of our own, Mrs Kerrigan,' Nancy said politely. 'We can't impose on you for ever.' *To be nagged to death, no fear.*

'Well, I think you should wait until Sid comes

home. I do not think he would like the idea of you gallivanting off getting your own place without his say so.'

Without you being able to interfere, you mean. Nancy said nothing. It was not her place.

What more did this girl have to go through? Rita wondered. She had not had it easy over the years, and now, so soon after her father's death, she had Tommy's illness to contend with, too.

'How could Mrs Hood let him get into this state?' Danny said. 'We should go round there and give her what for.'

'Why didn't she get a doctor for him? Surely she could see he was ill?' Kitty asked, shaking her head. 'This could not have come on him today.'

'By the looks of him,' said Rita, 'I'd say she had no intentions of letting a doctor see poor Tommy. A doctor would report her for this!' Rita was so angry she felt as if she would burst at the effort of staying calm. However, she couldn't let them see how worried she was, too.

How could any woman and mother let this happen to a child? She really did not know.

Danny sat on the chair, watching Rita carefully wrap Tommy in the blanket.

'I'm telling you, Kit,' Danny was so angry he thumped the arm of the chair, 'he is never going away again.'

'You are not wrong there, Danny,' Rita said determinedly. 'If the worst should happen and we do get invaded by the Jerry, we will all go together.' The child stirred and Kitty kissed his scorching cheek.

'Why didn't Mrs Hood send for me?' Kitty's voice was hoarse with fear. 'I even gave her the number of the NAAFI. She could have telephoned me there.'

'I'd have gone to fetch Tommy,' Danny said. 'I'd have carried him home on my back. It would have been no trouble.' Danny's words tore at Kitty's heart. She gave her brother's shoulder a squeeze.

'It's a good thing he got here when he did, Kit,' Rita said sadly. 'Danny, go and see if Pop's ready yet now, quick!'

Danny jumped up from the couch. 'Let me know if he wakes up.'

'He's not asleep,' Rita said grimly, barely able to keep the horror from her voice. 'He's unconscious.'

Kitty, horrified, grabbed hold of Rita's arm. 'Tell me what it is, Rita!'

'I think he's got diphtheria, Kit,' Rita said, 'he's in grave danger and we must get him to the hospital right away.' If her suspicions were confirmed, Rita knew Tommy did not have much time. As well as being a highly contagious and notifiable disease, diptheria was one of the leading causes of childhood death.

Pop Feeny was on his way when Danny collided with him in the blacked-out fog.

Pop followed Danny at a run into the house and was horrified when he caught sight of the stricken child. He'd never seen a child look so ill. In no time he was leading Kitty, who was carrying the young lad, out into the street.

'Let's get this around him, Kit,' Pop said briskly,

tucking another blanket over both of them. Rita, sitting beside her, took Tommy's feeble arm to check for a pulse, while Danny sat next to Pop.

'I don't know much about these things,' he said grimly, 'but I'd say our Rita's right. He needs the hospital straight away.' He could see there was much less of Tommy now than there had been when he left the street three months ago. If he ever got hold of those people who were supposed to be looking after Tommy, he'd throttle the life out of them. His face set in grim determination, he motioned for the horse to set off, careful to move quickly without jolting Tommy too much.

'How did he get home?' Pop asked, flicking the reins and concentrating hard on the road.

'I dread to think, Pop,' Kitty answered, holding Tommy's still body to her chest as she listened anxiously to his rasping breath.

The flat-backed cart that usually lugged bales of American cotton and logs from as far away as Canada came to a halt outside the borough hospital carrying the most precious person in Kitty's life. Jumping down from the cart onto the pavement, Pop went ahead, saying he would get a doctor, while Danny lifted his arms to take Tommy.

Kitty passed little Tommy into Danny's strong, capable arms and followed at a run when his long strides quickly covered the distance.

'Doctor! Can I have some help here, please?' Rita was ahead of them all as she hurried through the doors, her words bouncing off the tall side windows as her feet hardly conferred with the highly polished terrazzo floor.

'What is all this commotion?' an imposing and capable-looking sister demanded, hurrying from a side room. Kitty's troubled gaze took in the stiff navy-blue uniform, rigid white cuffs and collar, her scraped-back hair hidden under a starched cap and a scowl to stun at thirty paces. Kitty was right behind Pop.

'It's the lad, Nurse.' Pop wasn't intimidated.

'Sister,' the nurse corrected him and he gave a slight nod as she opened a side door and pointed into the adjoining room. Danny took Tommy in as she followed. Then she stopped as Kitty and Pop tried to follow.

'Stay right there!' Sister commanded before disappearing into the room and closing the door firmly behind her. In a couple of minutes Danny came out again. Kitty decided not to make a scene in front of Danny; she was sure it would not help Tommy if she was or was not in the room. Instead, she guided Danny to a long bench in the corridor and swallowed a desperate urge to cry when she caught sight of the desolation on his face. His need for reassurance was far greater. Danny wasn't out of his teens yet and was still a lad himself. She had to be strong for both of them.

Kitty persuaded Rita and Pop to go home. They had done all they could for now and there was nothing for Kitty and Danny to do but wait. They sat for a long time. The ornate fingers crawling around the face of the huge round clock, the quiet tick-tick-tick were getting on Kitty's nerves. People came and went while they waited impatiently for some news. However, nobody would tell her what was happening behind the closed door of the side ward.

'If I don't get some news soon I'm going in there,' Kitty said. *Please get better, Tommy.* She dreaded the thought of losing him. If only Jack had been here now, instead of training for some stupid war that nobody wanted.

Kitty sighed deeply and stood up. She could not sit still any longer. Pacing the length of the long corridor she counted every step.

'One... two... three...' she said, turning, and then counted her way back. She had to do something, anything to keep from thinking the worst. Finally, she reached Danny, sitting on his hands, vacantly staring into nothing. He lifted a hand and began nibbling furiously on stubby nails, a sure sign that his patience was now wearing thin. Kitty could have wept.

'Kitty, is Tommy going to be OK?' he asked her when she eventually stopped pacing and took her seat beside him. 'Is he, Kit?' His face was the colour of cold, grey dough and Kitty did not have the heart to worry him any more.

'He's in the best place, Danny.' She hoped the words would comfort him, but they didn't seem to do so. Kitty's desperation was obvious now as huge tears washed down her face. Apparently oblivious, she did not wipe them away.

Danny hugged her close. Each minute was like a lifetime, each hour an eternity, and still they waited, each lost in their own thoughts.

Kitty had stopped looking at the clock so she didn't know what time it was when the ward sister finally came over to her and Danny. They both stood quickly, anxious for news. Danny's face was ashen and Kitty pulled nervously at her handkerchief.

'The doctor is coming to see you now,' she said, her face a mask.

Moments later, a tall, dark-haired and handsome man came towards them. He was wearing a white coat and he held a folder in his hand.

'Are you Thomas Callaghan's mother?' he asked Kitty.

'No, Doctor, I'm his sister, Kitty, and this here is his brother, Danny. Oh please, Doctor, is Tommy going to be all right?'

There was something reassuring about the young man and Kitty thought he had a kind face; like someone who really cared about making people better.

'My name is Dr Fitzgerald. I won't soft-soap you, Kitty. Tommy is very, very ill. But he is young and strong. We're doing everything we can to make him better.'

'What's wrong with him, Doctor?' Danny asked.

'Nurse Kennedy was correct. Tommy has contracted diptheria, which is very dangerous, but we are treating him. The next few hours will be critical. You should be very grateful to your friend for getting him here so promptly.'

Kitty asked, 'Doctor, can we please wait here?'

The doctor looked behind him at the brusque ward sister. 'Sister doesn't normally let relatives stay out of normal visiting hours, I'm afraid.' Kitty's face dissolved into tears and Dr Fitzgerald took pity on her. 'But I think we can make an exception in Thomas's case.'

'Oh, Doctor, thank you. We won't get in the way, will we, Danny?' Danny shook his head.

'Very well. Stay in the waiting room and we'll let you know as soon as we have any more news. He really is in the best place and I'm determined to do whatever I can for him.'

The next few hours were agonising and interminable. The ward had fallen into darkness and Kitty thought that it was like waiting for your heart to stop beating. Danny had fallen into a fitful slumber beside her on the bench and she could see the grey fingers of dawn creeping over the horizon from the window beside her.

But Kitty couldn't sleep. Not until she knew that Tommy was safe. She cursed herself; this was all her own fault. She should have kept Tommy at home, she knew he had a weak chest and no one can really take care of you like your family can.

Her thoughts were interrupted by the ward sister, who was coming towards her, her face still unreadable.

Dear God, she prayed, please don't let her tell me that Tommy is dead. If you let Tommy live, I'll do anything, I'll pay you back somehow, I don't know how exactly, but I will.

'Miss Callaghan,' said the Sister. 'Please come through.'

Kitty's legs were shaking but she rose up from her seat. Danny was still asleep. Leave him, she thought. If it is bad news, I don't want him to suffer it too.

Kitty followed the ward sister into a little side room. Through the window separating them, she saw Tommy. He was surrounded by all sorts of machines and tubes. Kitty, didn't know what they were but she saw immediately that Tommy was conscious. Standing next to him, monitoring his pulse, was Dr Fitzgerald.

'Oh, Tommy! Thank God!' She hesitated. 'Doctor, can I give him a hug?' They were able to hear each other through the glass partition.

'I'm afraid not, Kitty. Tommy is highly infectious and I'm taking a risk letting you this close.'

Kitty could see that Tommy was still very swollen around his neck, but he looked much better than earlier and he gave her a small wave. With tears streaming down her cheeks, Kitty gave him a wave back and blew him a kiss.

Kitty couldn't believe her ears when Tommy croaked out some words. 'They gave me sprouts, Kitty! Sprouts, I tell ya!'

Kitty laughed through her tears and said, 'I promise, Tommy, that you'll never, ever have to eat sprouts again.' Tommy smiled, then drifted off to sleep again; a normal sleep.

'How can I ever thank you, Doctor? You've saved his life.'

'Tommy has a strong heart, Kitty, and a huge appetite for life.' He smiled at her kindly. 'Now I think it is time for you to get some sleep.'

'Yes, Doctor.' And Kitty made her way back to the waiting room.

She gave Danny a gentle nudge and he was wide awake immediately.. His face lit up when he saw hers. 'Come on, Danny, we can go home now.' And arm in arm they walked back to Empire Street.

It was almost Christmas when Kitty, Danny and Jack, who was home on compassionate leave, were allowed into the isolation ward of Bootle Infirmary, as long as they wore protective white cotton masks over their noses and mouths. Tommy had been too sick to be moved to the Hospital for Infectious Diseases, and had been watched day and night. They were lucky that the dedicated staff had the time to tend him so well. The invasion everybody was expecting had not yet occurred.

'No, it isn't because all of the patients have been moved elsewhere and we have more empty beds than we know what to do with,' Maeve said as she bustled around Tommy's bed, enjoying waiting on him hand and foot. Some nurses were so bored they had taken to knitting balaclavas for the navy in the Atlantic. Nobody was taking anything for granted, however, except Tommy, who was thoroughly enjoying his recuperation.

'How are you feeling today, Tom?' Kitty, Danny and Jack asked in unison. Jack had brought Tommy a replica of a Swordfish bi-plane such as he actually flew. 'The lads in the workshop made it,' Jack said proudly. 'There isn't another one like it.' Tommy was thrilled to see it on his bedside table and was smiling now. They had been at Tommy's bedside for about half an hour and had been told by the little Irish nurse that 'her boy' was not to be tired out.

Jack and Danny laughed, winking at Tommy, who was now very red in the face.

'It looks like you have your own private nurse there, Tom!'

'Get away with you!' Tommy said bashfully.

'Erm, Kitty,' said Nurse Kerrigan, 'can I have a word?'

'Is anything wrong?' Kitty could feel the panic begin to rise and hoped Tommy was really doing well.

'No, Matron wants a word,' the nurse said. 'Her office is down by the main doors.' Kitty thanked her and told her brothers she would not be long.

'Tommy is now well enough for discharge,' Matron said kindly, and Kitty smiled. It would be good to have him home at last. 'However,' Matron continued, and her face looked quite formal as she sat on the other side of her desk, 'there may have been some complications with Tommy's heart caused by the diphtheria. We will have to keep a close eye on him. He's in good hands with us.'

'I'll do likewise,' Kitty promised. Although how she was going to manage looking after Tommy and working in the NAAFI was another matter.

'There is one other thing I wanted to tell you.'

'What is it, Matron?' Kitty asked nervously. She hoped there was no more bad news.

'When we became aware of the circumstances of Tommy's arrival in hospital, we were rather shocked.'

'What do you mean?' Kitty was even more nervous now.

'We understood that Thomas was being billeted as an evacuee outside the city. Thomas clearly had a right to expect better treatment than he received from the Hoods, Miss Callaghan, and I can assure you that they will shortly be receiving a visit from the authorities. Her own children will

314

now be in danger of infection too.'

Kitty smiled. She didn't have a vengeful bone in her body, but it would serve the Hoods right. Tommy had nearly died. Something should be done.

CHAPTER EIGHTEEN

Christmas Day 1939

Rita, after coming home from the hospital when her duties were over for the day, had told her mother that Tommy was making good progress, and was now out of isolation. Dolly made the sign of the Cross on her chest and whispered a few prayers to help him.

'Kitty will have a tough time of it with Jack being away.'

'Danny's there to help, too.' Rita sounded hurt on Danny's behalf. They were sitting at the table peeling parsnips for their Christmas dinner.

'Jack is the sensible one, though,' Pop said mischievously. Rita felt every nerve in her body stiffen at the mention of Jack and although she and Jack had opened their hearts to each other, Rita knew that as a married woman it must never happen again. Most importantly, she thought guiltily, Charlie must never ever find out.

If his outburst after Sonny Callaghan's funeral was anything to go by, she could not even imagine how he would react if he thought Jack and she had a private friendship going on. Any respect she once had for Charlie was now dead, but she still had her principles and it wouldn't do for there to be any hint of gossip. She couldn't risk it for the children's sake. No, they had said their piece, but now it was time to draw a line under it. Charlie had made some excuse this morning about having a serious head cold and not wanting to pass it on to everybody so he would not be at her mother's for dinner.

Rita wondered if he was ashamed at what he had done after the funeral and didn't want to face her family. She hadn't said a word to them, but she knew that Charlie might suspect otherwise. She was happy to let him think that others knew what a hateful man he was and hoped he was stewing in his shame, but she doubted it.

'Was that a knock, Pop?' Rita joined in peeling vegetables as her father got up from the table. He had been gone a few moments before returning and announcing proudly, 'Better peel some more, Doll. Look who's come to see us!' Pop sounded elated as he opened the passage door wider.

'Eddy!' Dolly's squeals of delight filled the room and had Nancy covering her ears. Dolly jumped up from the table when she saw her younger son. 'Oh! My boy! My boy! Why didn't you tell us you were coming home?' The flurry of paper hats, which Sarah had made from old copies of the *Echo*, fell to the floor as she took Eddy in her arms and hugged him until he laughed.

'We've just limped into Gladstone Dock, battered and bruised but not out yet!'

'What do you mean, battered and bruised?'

316

Dolly asked, the colour draining from her face.

'I'm only having you on, Mam.' Eddy, always the joker, hugged her close while over her head he looked at Pop and slowly shook his head, a sign he didn't want his mother to know the worst. Pop nodded. Tomorrow the news would be out that Eddy's ship had taken more than a glancing blow from a U-boat, but for now he was going to enjoy Christmas with his family.

'Oh, there's just one thing... I've brought someone with me. He's just gone into the pub for some cigarettes. He's a bit shy, so please make him welcome.'

'That goes without saying, son.' A few moments after Nancy answered the knock at the front door, another sailor edged his way into the room and everybody welcomed him in, sat him down and talked at once.

'I don't know how far that chicken will go,' Dolly worried. 'The butcher said it was a young one but it looks like an old boiler to me.'

'Don't worry about me, Mam. I'll get something at the hospital. I'm on duty later.' Dolly gratefully patted Rita's hand and promised her a bigger portion of Christmas pudding.

'So, Nathan, what part of Canada do you come from?' Dolly asked the Canadian sailor.

'Ontario, ma'am,' he said politely, and everybody nodded. The Feenys knew danger was faced every day by the Canadian merchant fleet, whose transport ships carried desperately needed equipment, fuel and food to Britain. They had a vital job to do and their ships were prime targets for the enemy.

'Well, you are welcome here any time, Nathan. You can stay here with us. We will always make room for our friends from overseas.'

'That's good to know, ma'am. It gets a bit lonely at sea sometimes,' Nathan smiled.

'You call me Dolly, son; everybody else does.'

Nathan nodded. 'And you call me Nat ... Dolly.' That sorted, they all got to know each other very quickly and later Pop enjoyed swapping naval stories of the days when he was at sea. It was all very good-humoured and Nat even donned a Robin Hood-style newspaper hat.

Eddy and Nat kept to themselves the news that wolf packs of German submarines were preying on merchant shipping. They caused heavy losses to the merchant fleet, which was why Nat was here on Merseyside instead of back home in Canada for Christmas. His ship had been torpedoed a couple of weeks ago and he had been rescued with some of his shipmates from the freezing Atlantic water.

'My brother is in the Royal Canadian Air Force. He's coming over here soon – he's being posted to a place called RAF Acklington. Do you know it?'

'Oh, that's where Jack Callaghan is!' Nancy squealed and, after a warning glance from her father, she realised what she had said. There were posters all over the place telling people that loose lips sink ships! Nancy's eyes widened in mortification. There were warnings about people called 'fifth columnists' who seemed like friends but spied for the enemy. Who was to say what a fifth columnist looked like? Nancy accepted the warning look from Pop. Nat could be anybody.

'Well, any friend of Eddy's is a friend of ours,' Dolly said, trusting her son's judgement completely, although, catching Pop's look, she thought it did not do any harm to remind Nancy that she needed to keep some information to herself. 'Your brother's most welcome to come here too, when he's got time off!'

'That's good to know, ma'am. I'll tell him.' Nat's ready smile brightened up the day a treat. Eddy informed him that this might be a small street but it had a big heart.

'Oh, doesn't he talk lovely?' Nancy said, turning her attention to Nat. 'Do you know anybody famous? Is Canada anywhere near Hollywood?' Pop rolled his eyes to the ceiling. Even at five months pregnant, Nancy was incorrigible.

'Listen ... the King is going to give his Christmas message,' Pop said, getting up from the table and turning up the wireless.

They listened to the King's message to the nation and Dolly looked around at her family and thought of the ones who were not here: Frank, somewhere in the Atlantic, no doubt; and Sid in France. She wondered if they would all be together next year. The family circle might be smaller now, but her heart was full with love for all of them.

The food was not as plentiful as it had been the previous year and Dolly worried that they hadn't got enough. She could think of nothing worse than being stingy with food. To feed her family was her greatest pleasure. She also knew if she queued long enough she could usually find something tasty to give them.

Dolly said a little prayer of thanks that she had hung on a bit longer at the butcher's on Saturday. Somebody had told her the chickens were all gone and there were only sausages left. Most women scurried off to see if they could find another butcher selling something that might be vaguely festive. However, Dolly knew that as long as they were all together it did not matter what they ate. So, after being catapulted to the front of the queue, she discovered the butcher had one last chicken. It was a bit of an old boiler, she realised, but she had done the best she could with it...

The National Anthem broke into her thoughts and everybody stopped talking. They all listened intently as King George VI, in his hesitant manner, gave his first speech of the war.

'...I said to the man who stood at the gate of the year, "Give me a light, that I may tread safely into the unknown." And he replied, "Go out into the darkness, and put your hand into the Hand of God. That shall be to you better than light and safer than a known way..."'

'Wasn't that lovely?' Rita sighed rapturously and repeated, '"Give me a light that I may tread safely into the unknown" – that lifts you up, doesn't it?'

A few moments later there was an air raid alert, quickly followed by the all clear.

'The air raid precautions are still having a few teething problems,' said Pop, who had donned his tin hat, which had big white letters 'ARP' on the front. He took off the tin hat and they all resumed their place at the table.

'This is why they call it "the Phoney War", Pop,'

Nancy said, not thinking.

'There's nothing phoney about it where we come from.' Eddy looked serious, all jovial banter gone now. 'The phrase is anathema to those of us in the Royal and Merchant Navies who see at first hand ships being blown up.'

'Sorry, Ed,' Nancy offered, and Dolly shook her head.

'*Athenia* was blown up a few hours after the declaration of war – a warning if ever I heard one,' Eddy said. 'Then HMS *Courageous* was torpedoed... The aircraft carrier lost over five hundred men, but do you know what our biggest worry is – the pocket battleships, so powerfully equipped they are a daily threat to the British fleet.'

'I'm sorry, Eddy, I didn't think,' Nancy said. 'I open my mouth and something stupid pops out.'

'I'm not having a go at you, Nance,' Eddy said, giving her a hug. 'Just don't believe everything you read in the papers...'

'I don't think Nancy meant to upset you, son,' Pop said calmly, knowing Eddy was hiding a lot of torment.

Dolly realised a bit of levity was called for otherwise the whole afternoon would descend into maudlin melancholy. 'This queuing lark will only get worse if the Germans don't stop playing silly buggers,' she said with a comic sigh and a wink.

'Have a word when you get back, Eddy,' Pop laughed, silently agreeing with his lovely wife that the talk was taking a serious turn. It did not worry him how much war talk there was around the table, but he could see his Dolly was becoming agitated, and that meant she was worried ... and on Christmas Day. Not a good sign.

'I'll go and see the skipper, Pop... Tell him my mother does not like queues.'

'I had to queue in three shops last week before I got a loaf,' Dolly said, bringing in the Christmas pudding with great ceremony.

'Hang on a minute, Mam.' Eddy jumped up from the table and, going to his kitbag lying behind the parlour door, he cried jubilantly, 'Wait till you see what I've got.' He pulled out a bottle of brandy and held it up like the FA Cup while everybody cheered.

'You'll not be pouring that over the Christmas pudding!' Pop was horrified.

'Just a little bit, for the sake of tradition?' Dolly said, taking the brandy from her son and cracking it open, but Pop had other ideas.

'Well, give it here,' he said, taking a sniff and blissfully closing his eyes. 'I'll do the honours.' He poured just enough brandy to give off a weak flame when it was lighted. 'We don't want the fire brigade out... And, more importantly, we don't know when we'll get our hands on any more.' Everybody laughed and waited with spoons at the ready while Dolly gave them all a piece of the Christmas pudding she made last summer... It seemed so long ago now.

'You're doing a fine job, lads,' Pop said. 'And we are grateful, although some people haven't got a clue that our food comes from overseas and don't care as long as they get it.'

'Aye,' said Eddy. 'We'll see the difference when

322

we can't get food any more.'

'It won't come to that, surely?' Nancy did not listen to the news if she could help it.

'A woman in the queue said they don't eat bacon in their house,' Dolly offered, 'but she said she's going to buy it any time she can now, because it's getting scarce. I ask you!'

Pop poured them each a brandy to toast 'the King, the Navy and the Family'. 'Here you are, love. You sit down with this. The lads and me will do the dishes.'

Dolly could not believe her ears. Then she heard Sarah, who had been helping out at the hospital, coming in through the back door on a flurry of freezing air. Sarah had finished school now and was keen to go into nursing, like her sister Rita. They had too many nurses at the hospital at present but Sarah was keen to show willing and had joined the St John Ambulance and was often called on to volunteer when staff were short.

When she went to fetch Sarah's dinner from the oven Dolly noticed her young daughter's colour deepen when Eddy introduced Nat.

After hanging up her coat, Sarah placed the back of her icy fingers against Pop's cheek. He flinched theatrically. 'Get in with you!' he laughed as Dolly and her youngest daughter went back into the parlour. Dolly presumed the sailors had something they wanted to talk about that wasn't intended for 'dainty' female ears.

Afterwards, they were all settling down nicely. Eddy had put some jazz music on the wireless and they were about to roll back the mat in front of the fire and have a little dance when there was another knock on the door.

'Pop!' Dolly cried when she went to answer it. 'It's Mr Kerrigan and he's got a telegram!'

Nancy fell backwards onto the armchair when Mr Kerrigan, Sid's father, brought round the telegram that said Sid was missing in action over in France. She almost fainted and the family were worried that in her condition, the baby might be brought on. She was encouraged to lie down on the sofa and was comforted by her mother and Sarah. Mr Kerrigan looked crushed. 'I'm sorry to bring the news to you like this, today of all days.'

'Here, have a drop of this,' Pop said, handing Mr Kerrigan a drop of brandy. 'It's good for shock.'

'Thank you, Bert,' said Mr Kerrigan, and he sat in a chair at the table. He looked shattered, and Nancy was inconsolable, reduced to floods of tears. 'I read in the paper, the Prime Minister told the House that heavy fighting was in progress in Belgium. It reminded me of when we were in Arras back in 1918.'

'He'll come through it,' said Pop with more confidence that he felt. 'They didn't say he was dead.'

'Of course he will. Look at us: we came through the last one. It's a nightmare...'

'How's Mrs Kerrigan taking it?' Dolly asked, pouring tea. The news had really rocked her. How would she take it if the news had been about one of her boys? And the Kerrigans only had their Sid. It was dreadful news and Mrs Kerrigan would be devastated.

'The doctor gave her something to help her sleep,' Mr Kerrigan said.

Dolly looked shocked. 'When did you get the news?' It would take a while to get a doctor out on Christmas Day.

'Mrs Kerrigan didn't want to spoil Nancy's dinner. She said to leave it until later.'

'I should have been told first!' Nancy jumped up from the chair, unable to contain her anger and disbelief. 'She had no right to take the telegram.'

'I know, love, and I'm sorry, but when Mrs Kerrigan told the lad she was Sid's mother he automatically gave it to her and–'

'And she took it on herself to keep the news from me!' Nancy was beside herself with fury. How dare she? 'Well, you can tell her from me that if she thinks I'm going back to live in the parlour on my own, she can think again!'

Dolly raised her eyes to heaven. Even in terrible times like this, you could always rely on Nancy to miss the point.

It was weeks later when Mrs Kerrigan came round to Dolly's to see Nancy. She did not want to rush round, she said, in case Nancy was still upset. She could not bear to see people upset. Swamped in a bottle-green coat, two sizes too big, and wearing a matching green hat, Mrs Kerrigan looked as if she was too exhausted to breathe. Instead, she sighed a lot.

'Please, sit down, Mrs Kerrigan,' said Dolly. 'You look done in.'

'I wanted to see how Nancy was doing,' Mrs Kerrigan said in a thin, high-pitched voice. 'We haven't seen anything of her since ... since...'

'She did call round a few times but you weren't

in. Mr Kerrigan said you were at the doctor's.'

'I have to go for my nerves; they're not good now.' Mrs Kerrigan adopted a martyred expression and shuffled on the edge of the sofa. 'When your boy has been killed you will know what I mean.'

'Nobody said that Sid had been killed, Mrs Kerrigan.' Dolly was shocked that this woman, who bore her air of torment like a banner, could say such a thing. 'There is always hope. You have to believe that.'

'I am a mother, Mrs Feeny, I know these things. I feel it deep in my heart... I would certainly know if my Sid were alive – I would know it.' She sighed melodramatically.

Her statement brooked no argument and, having two sons of her own battling in the middle of the Atlantic, Dolly gave her the benefit of the doubt.

'I don't suppose we will see you again,' Mrs Kerrigan said to Dolly as she left the house, 'not until the baby is born, at least.'

'I'm sure Nancy will come and visit as much as she can and you are welcome to call around any time you want to.'

'I'm not one for visiting.' Mrs Kerrigan's pained expression turned into a tortured smile. With a heavy sigh she said, 'Maybe Mr Kerrigan will, but I don't have the strength any more.'

CHAPTER NINETEEN

April 1940

After a bitterly cold winter, Germany turned its attention to Western Europe where, in April, it swiftly invaded Denmark and Norway. British and French counter-attacks in Norway failed to extricate the aggressors.

However, none of this meant a thing to Nancy, who was now lying with her feet in stirrups while she pushed and screamed for all she was worth.

'No wonder the baby is early with all she's been through,' Gloria said to Dolly, who gave a sympathetic nod, while Mrs Kerrigan sat stiffly on the chair outside the delivery room of Bootle Maternity Hospital in Balliol Road. After eighteen hours of labour, Nancy delivered an eight-pound nine-ounce baby boy, whom she called George.

'I thought you would have called him Sidney,' Mrs Kerrigan whined, 'after his poor departed father.'

'I prefer George; it is patriotic – after St George, patron saint of England,' Nancy offered, after she and the baby were both washed, polished and decently presented.

'You've done us proud, love,' Dolly said to Nancy while still gazing lovingly at the pink, plump cheeks of her third grandchild. 'Pop will be thrilled with this bonny bouncer.'

'I would hate to think what size he would have been had he been full term,' Mrs Kerrigan said, and Dolly, sensing a dig, gave a withering stare.

'Don't you want to come and have a look at him?' Dolly asked.

'I'm too emotional. He reminds me too much of my poor Sidney,' Mrs Kerrigan replied.

'I would have thought that would be a good thing,' Dolly answered, knowing the other woman was too wrapped up in her own misery to look at the child properly. 'I'm sure Sid will be so proud.'

'He would have wanted a son to carry on his name, I'm sure.' Mrs Kerrigan dabbed at her dry eyes.

'We do not know for sure that he is dead, Mrs Kerrigan.' Nancy, feeling highly emotional, was on the verge of tears. She would have loved her husband to be here to see his new son.

'I know,' Mrs Kerrigan said ominously. 'Believe me, I know.'

Kitty sat with a nice cup of tea and the paper on her lap after finishing work in the NAAFI. Opening the paper, she let out a little squeal of delight, surprised and thrilled to see Frank's handsome face staring up at her. She gazed at the picture for a long time. He was standing to attention on the deck of an unnamed ship in blazing sunshine.

The photograph must have been taken a long time ago, she reasoned, because he had been serving in the North Atlantic for the last seven months, to her knowledge.

Frank was taller than most of the crew who were being inspected by Lord Louis Mountbatten.

Kitty laughed softly when she remembered the perfectly magical dance they had had together on the day of his sister's wedding. She gave a small, sad sigh, aware that at that time she imagined Frank had a soft spot for her.

'Aunty Doll!' Tommy's voice carried from the front room to the back kitchen where Dolly was at the gas stove. 'Come an' 'ave a look at this. You are gonna cry your leg off.' Dolly had offered to look after Tommy when he came out of hospital, while Kitty and Danny were at work. The arrangement worked very well and Tommy was happier than he had been since last September.

'I'm out here, Tommy,' Dolly called. She loved looking after Tommy. Even with her part-time voluntary work with the WVS, she had plenty of time on her hands, leaving the proper war work to the younger ones. Dolly liked helping people out; it kept her busy and stopped her brooding. Having Tommy here while Kitty was at work in the NAAFI also kept him out of trouble. She had found him to be a great help, especially since Nancy had come out of hospital with young George.

'Don't touch that blackout material, Tommy, or I'll have your guts for garters,' Dolly called from the kitchen.

Tommy shrugged and eyed the samples of dark material. He was feeling restless and wondered if he should go to meet Kitty from the canteen. Then he remembered she said she might be working a bit later because there was a dance on. He grimaced when a deluge of midsummer rain lashed against the windows.

'That rain would go right through you!' Aunty Dolly called in that warning kind of voice that told Tommy not to even bother thinking about going out. He would leave meeting Kitty for tonight, knowing he would only get a lecture about how sick he had been and the chance he might end up back in hospital with pneumonia.

Picking up the evening paper, he read that German forces had pushed through the supposedly impregnable Maginot Line in Eastern France. The Allied troops, diverted to the north as another German army group swept through the Ardennes, then changed south into France. Tommy felt his excitement grow when he read that the British Expeditionary Force, who had landed in France last October, had been trapped in the narrow pocket near the Channel coast. Under heavy bombardment, a flotilla of ships and small boats had evacuated over 333,000 men from the beaches of Dunkirk. Tommy read the news and wished he were old enough to go and fight for his country. There was nothing going on around here.

'Nothing has happened!' he said. 'We have not been invaded or anything.' Idly he fingered the squares of material and decided that, apart from making some nifty little parachutes, the material was of no interest to him whatsoever.

'What's for tea, Aunty Doll? I'm starving.' Tommy, like one of the family now, sauntered out to the back kitchen where Aunty Dolly ruffled his shock of thick, jet-black hair, like that of his older brothers and Kitty. Sniffing the air appreciatively, he gave her a kiss on her upturned cheek. In his hand he carried the latest edition of the *Evening Echo*.

'You didn't touch that material with those grubby fingers, did you, bucko?' Dolly knew that it had taken a fair bit of bargaining to acquire the fabric. She liked haggling, and could now see why Danny Callaghan was so good at it. He had shown her how to keep a straight face to get the best deal.

'What's for tea, Aunty Doll?' Tommy asked again. Dolly lovingly pushed the hair out of his eyes.

'Remind Pop you need a haircut on Saturday. He'll take you.'

'Do I have to?' Tommy knew he was well looked after in the Feeny house and, apart from his own home with Kitty and Danny, did not want to be anywhere else ever again. 'I hate getting my hair cut. It makes my neck all itchy, and I can't get the hairs out of me vest.'

'Well, maybe a nice bit of braising steak will take your mind off it.' Dolly winked and gave Tommy one of her conspiratorial smiles.

'Braising steak on a Monday?' Tommy could hardly believe his ears, knowing you could not get a good piece of steak since rationing came in. Usually all that was available in the butcher's was offal, which was not on the ration, or sausages that tasted like sawdust.

'We're having it with mashed potatoes, carrots and minted peas from Pop's allotment. We would have had Yorkshire pudding too, but I ran out of eggs and there's a shortage,' Dolly said.

Tommy let out a low whistle of appreciation and smacked his lips. 'I can't wait.'

'I know a good butcher.' Dolly sighed. Being a local helper and doer of good deeds, she was usually 'in the know' when anything was going spare.

'Do you think the others will be long?' Tommy asked as the delicious smells tantalised his senses and made his stomach growl.

'Pop's only gone to stable the horses, and Sarah has an early finish at the St John Ambulance meeting because she promised to do a bit of night duty at the hospital to help out, so it shouldn't be too long,' Dolly said, knowing that Tommy loved nothing more than to sit down at the table and eat the hearty meals she provided. The boy's presence reminded her of the days when her own lads were young. Dolly swallowed hard. She hoped Frank and Eddy were safe out there. Wherever 'out there' might be.

'I know it's one of the house rules that we wait until everybody is sitting around the table before we eat,' said Tommy, 'but I just wish my belly understood it too.' Dolly laughed that easy chuckle that made him feel safe and secure. Apart from his own family, he could not think of a better place to be in the wide world than here with the Feenys.

'Well, that's my rule. Even Pop sticks by it.'

'There's no changing your mind when it's made up, is there, Aunty Doll?'

'You got that right, Tommy boy.' Dolly ruffled his hair again before pushing a fork through the boiling potatoes and giving them a nod of approval. Tommy knew Aunty Doll, a canny woman in her fifties, thought that to provide well for her family was to show them her highest affection.

Tommy had no problem returning her love. Her family, himself included, was better fed than anybody else's around here.

'I can't see why my family should not have the very best I can lay my hands on,' Dolly said, 'but even so, Tommy, you will have to wait like everybody else.'

Dolly thickened the rich gravy with a bit of cornflour. 'There, it'll stick to your ribs and put hairs on your chest.'

Tommy laughed and peered under his woollen jerkin, thick plaid shirt and good vest, reporting that he couldn't see any signs of a hairy chest just yet. 'And I'm sure that our Sarah won't want one either.'

'Don't be impudent,' Dolly laughed as she put the big black kettle on the gas ring to boil.

'Aunty Doll, you forgot to look at this.' Tommy tapped the paper he had brought.

Deep in thought, Dolly knew that if it was not for the goods she managed to buy from people less fortunate then life would be much different.

She was glad Pop's wages kept them reasonably well provided for. Many women, whose men had gone to war, and who had been left only a small amount of money every week, were now working in the munitions factories and were becoming more independent. She was fortunate that she did not have to do that because with the money her sons sent through the Post Office every week, along with Nancy and Sarah's housekeeping, Dolly knew she was not doing too badly. Women, strangely enough, were proving they could do, just as well, the jobs usually done by the menfolk.

'Aunty Doll, are you listening?' Tommy asked, getting the cutlery from the drawer.

'What's that, sunshine?' Dolly took five plates out of the cupboard. One each for her, Pop, Sarah, Nancy and Tommy. Hopefully, she thought, ignoring Tommy's plea for attention, Frank or Eddy might get some leave soon, and they would enjoy the food she would laden their plates with.

'Have you seen the paper?' Tommy asked, tapping it with his index finger.

'I'll have a gander in a minute.' Dolly was only half listening. The navy was doing a valiant job getting supplies through and the docks were heaving with ships on quick turnaround, with crews ready to risk their lives to supply the country with food and necessary supplies. What did annoy her, though, were the get-rich-quick spivs who were getting fat off this rationing business – and not only the spivs, Dolly noticed.

Mrs Kennedy now had 'select' customers who tried to keep on very good terms. People who would never give her the time of day before the war were now paying over the odds for stuff that was hard to come by. Well, Dolly thought, cheating was not her way. What she had she shared, and what she came across by way of a little deal here and there, she passed on to others less fortunate. Sometimes she had to add a copper here or there but not like Winnie Kennedy.

Charlie, Dolly noted, had managed to stay out of the war up to now, but soon there would be nowhere to hide. He'd have to go and fight men, real men, men unlike himself; a bully who picked on those weaker than himself.

Dolly knew he had mistreated Rita even though her daughter never said a word. Rita would do anything to save face. Instead of crying to her family, Rita threw herself into her work at the hospital and kept her thoughts to herself. Dolly admired her stoic ways even though she would have liked Rita to confide in her.

However, as she was not one for wearing her heart on her sleeve, Dolly was grateful that Charlie could no longer duck out of being called up for much longer.

'Was that the back gate?' Dolly asked in anticipation of her husband's arrival.

'It's Pop,' Tommy said, looking out of the window. 'Maybe he will be interested in what's in the paper.'

'Hello, my love,' Dolly said, holding up her cheek, which Pop dutifully kissed.

'What's that, Tom?' Pop asked as he wafted in on a breeze of summer evening air. Lifting the pan lid, he took a hefty sniff of the delicious food bubbling away on the stove.

'Here, Pop, have a look at this!' Tommy said, eagerly thrusting the paper into Pop's hands.

'What am I looking at, Tom?' Pop asked, hanging a horse harness behind the kitchen door.

'Page two!' Tommy could hardly contain his excitement. 'Right at the top of the page, look!' He tapped the paper while his mongrel dog scrambled up Pop's leg.

'Get down, Monty.' He gave the stray a welcome scratch behind the ear and Monty swished his tail. Tommy had saved the little dog from being put down shortly after he'd come out of hospital.

Tommy had then adopted the stray. Kitty thought having a pet of his own would help him get over the news of the death of his father.

'Get that fleabag out of my clean kitchen now.' Dolly pushed a salt-and-pepper wisp of hair from her damp forehead.

'Don't go thinking that you're cleaning those harnesses on my best damask tablecloth that our Eddy brought home from his last trip, because you're not.' She was proud of the fact that she owned a damask tablecloth. Some folk could not run to a tablecloth; for them it was oilcloth or newspaper. She was a very lucky woman.

'Aunty Doll, let Pop read the paper,' Tommy cried as Pop brought Dolly's attention to a box of fresh eggs laid only that morning.

'Kitty said these might be on the turn but was sure you could find a use for them,' Pop said, putting them on the table with a wink of his eye.

'Fair dos,' Dolly smiled, taking the plates to the table, which Tommy had set. 'I can make some of those nice cakes they like in the canteen.'

'I hope you know what you're doing, Dolly,' Pop said in an unusually serious tone.

'Fair exchange is no robbery,' Dolly said, putting a plate on the table in front of each chair. 'I get fresh eggs and make nice cakes for the serving men and save a few for us! What harm can I do?' Her surprised-looking eyes were wide. 'I can sell those eggs much cheaper than Winnie Kennedy.' She looked at the clock and sighed. 'I hope our Sarah isn't too much longer. I could eat a horse between two mattresses.' Dolly closed that subject, and gave a coquettish giggle when her husband's huge arms circled her ample waist.

'Ahem!' Tommy said. 'I am still here, you know, waiting to talk about the newspaper article.'

Dolly disentangled herself and continued with the tea.

'So, what's all the fuss about, Tommy boy?' Pop asked, taking his place at the table.

Nancy came down to join them, carrying George in his carrycot, which she parked next to her chair so she could coo over her beautiful baby. Mother and son were totally besotted with each other.

'Wait till you see what's on page two.' Tommy handed Pop the paper and waited for the bomb to drop.

'OK, let's have a gander.' Pop ceremoniously opened and straightened the evening paper. His exaggerated expression suddenly changed to one of amazement! His good eye grew wide.

'Dolly! Come and have a look at this!' Dolly, who had disappeared, hot and bothered, to the back kitchen came bustling in with a dish of braised steak, which she put down in the middle of the table.

'Throw your peepers around that, old girl,' Pop said with a broad smile.

Dolly took the paper whilst Tommy picked up a spoon, but resisted helping himself to a big slurp. 'I'm watching you,' Dolly warned him with mock severity and Tommy dropped the spoon.

'Now, Doll,' Pop said cautiously, 'do not have a cat when you see...'

'Well, I'll be a dancer on a dustcart!' Dolly's blue eyes widened, making her spectacles slip as she scanned the local paper. From the top of the page, a large photograph of her handsome elder son, Frank, smiled up at her. Flushed with pride and emotion, Dolly stared transfixed at the beloved face she had not seen since Nancy's wedding.

'It's my Frank,' she whispered, dragging her gaze from the page and staring around the room in wonderment. 'Tommy, why didn't you tell me?'

Tommy's eyes rolled in the direction of the ceiling as Nancy crowded round to see as well. The evening meal forgotten now, Dolly looked to her husband.

'I'll have to go and show Kitty when she's back from the NAAFI!'

Dolly spent a long time reading and rereading the article.

'It says here,' her voice cracked with emotion as she read the words, 'our Frank is light-middle-weight boxing champion of his unit.' Her eyes grew wide.

'I know.' Pop pushed out his proud chest, and his rugged, handsome face held an unabashed grin. 'My lad,' he said, shaking his head. 'Who'd have thought it?'

'Well,' Dolly said through pursed lips, her voice stronger now, 'you just wait until "your" lad gets home – I'll have his guts for garters!'

'You don't mean that, Doll,' Pop said as he regarded his indignant wife.

'I most certainly do,' she cried. 'I'll have no son of mine boxing like a common ruffian.'

'Dolly,' Pop roared with laughter, 'it's a highly respectable sport – honourable, even.'

'Then you can take your *honourable* sport and

shove it in a cupboard.' Her voice softened slightly as she stared back at her bemused husband. 'Our Frank could get hurt.'

Pop rolled his eyes heavenwards. How could he possibly tell her what he had learned now?

His elder son had been part of the convoy escorting merchant ships through dangerous Atlantic waters. The letter had arrived when Pop was on his way out of the door this morning. He had managed to get it just before the postwoman put it through the letter box. The news wasn't good. Frank had been injured and was being transferred home.

'He hasn't been playing tiddlywinks in the Atlantic, you know. He's been dodging U-boats.' Pop omitted to add, 'And trying to dodge death too.' His voice was unusually stern and Dolly looked at him with puckered brows.

'All I know is that I sent a good lad out into the world and I want him back safe and sound.' If Pop could have bitten back his words, he would. Dolly's nerves must be in shreds. She was not stupid. She knew what was going on... Better than most, he imagined.

Pop patted his wife's hand, knowing how fiercely proud she was of her offspring – all of them. He also knew she might drop the steel façade in front of the rest of the family if she found out that her son was injured. So he decided to keep the news to himself until he knew what was going on. There was no use having his Dolly going to pieces when there might be no need.

He could only hope and pray now.

'The women of the WVS knitted gloves and

balaclavas to send out to our boys,' Dolly said. 'But I haven't got a clue how they'll get to them in the middle of the ocean.'

'They have got a special postman,' Pop said, watching every move of his wife's hand as she filled the plates, and making Tommy smile. Then, as she slowly poured gravy over the meat, potatoes and vegetables, Pop said, 'My stomach thinks me throat's been cut, I'm that hungry.'

'Eddy and Frank must miss this, Aunty Doll,' Tommy said as Dolly gave him his plate.

'Cooking is her way of coping, son,' Pop whispered. 'Best leave her to it.'

'I know you all think I'm daft as a brush,' Dolly sniffed into a hankie she retrieved from the sleeve of her cardigan, 'but I can't stand the thought of my boys being cold in all that water.' She dabbed her eyes. 'I'm sure they could have arranged to stay nearer to Liverpool.' Dolly tucked the hankie up her sleeve and spread best butter onto fresh bread. Nancy reached over to pat her arm.

'They could have done the Mersey ferry run across to Seacombe,' Pop said drily, knowing that if Dolly could have wangled it for her sons to be close to home she would have been the first to try. 'But then, they would not have been sailors doing the job they love, would they, Doll?'

'I suppose not,' Dolly conceded, and began to cut the meat on her plate.

'That's right, tuck in, you'll feel better,' Nancy said. The back door opened and Sarah came into the kitchen.

'Ahh, come on in, love. I've just served up.' Dolly beamed at her daughter, accepting a kiss on her dimpled cheek.

'Wait till you see the paper, Sarah,' Tommy said through a mouthful of food.

'Yes, love, come and see the paper,' Pop said, glad to keep his mind on happy thoughts.

'I know it might sound unpatriotic and I shouldn't say it, but I wish our Frank had never gone to sea.' Dolly passed the paper to Sarah. 'Do you think he'll be OK, Pop?'

'He's a strong lad, Doll,' Pop answered with more conviction than he felt, knowing that his Dolly might come across as being made of the same stuff as the air raid shelters, but he knew better.

'Oh, Mam,' Sarah sniffed appreciatively, 'something smells lovely.' Sarah pulled off her gloves with her teeth and shoved the slumbering dog away from the fire. 'Move your bum, Monty, you mangy fleabag. It might be spring but it is not warm yet.'

'Don't say "bum", Sarah,' Dolly said. 'It's not very ladylike and it is certainly not the type of language a girl who resembles Princess Elizabeth should use.'

'Don't encourage her, Doll, she thinks she's royalty as it is.' Pop smiled as he offered the paper to his daughter, but the smile didn't quite reach his eyes. 'Turn the page, Sarah, and see who's on page two.'

'Wow!' exclaimed Sarah. 'It's our Frank, and he's won a boxing competition!

'It says here...' Sarah announced in her best King's English, 'Petty Officer Francis Valentino Feeny–'

'Valentino?' Tommy squeaked, his eyes wide in amusement. 'You'd have to be able to handle yourself round 'ere with a name like that. Who gave him that soppy handle?'

'Aunty Doll.' Pop's face showed a pained expression.

'...is seen here being given the Captain's Cup for boxing...' Even though everybody knew what the article said they listened again.

'I'll tell you what, Sarah,' Pop said, trying to keep the mood light, 'you could read the news on the wireless with a voice like that.'

Sarah beamed, taking her seat. Nancy, laughing, pulled a snooty face, her nose in the air.

Tommy grinned. He knew Pop would not have a sombre mood at his table. He said it was bad for the digestion.

Pop decided not to tell Dolly their son was being transferred to Bootle Infirmary in a military ambulance. She would only worry.

'Nice picture.' Pop gave Dolly's hand a little pat.

Just as she was about to speak again there was another knock. 'It's like Lime Street Station here tonight,' Dolly laughed. Moments later she came back into the kitchen and her face was grim. She said to Nancy, 'It's the telegraph boy for you.'

Pop followed his daughter to the front door and he watched hardly daring to breathe as she opened the telegram. Nancy's eyes flew across the paper, taking in every word.

'He's alive, Dad!' she screamed. 'Sid's alive! He was at Dunkirk.'

'He's been made a prisoner of war,' Pop told Dolly, who was hugging her crying daughter.

342

'Oh, love, what a relief!' Whatever would Mrs Kerrigan do for an encore after this?

'Mam,' Nancy said, pulling away from her mother now, 'there's your third piece of good news today.' They all laughed. Even Pop managed a taut smile as he subconsciously touched the official letter in his pocket.

'I hope that the next piece of news will make them all just as happy.'

CHAPTER TWENTY

Kitty was taking an order over to the hospital when, just ahead of her there was a bit of a rumpus. A navy-blue military ambulance had arrived, full of uniformed servicemen who were being transferred to the hospital.

It was nothing new to see uniformed men around the dock road now. However, the evident urgency of this situation brought a moment of distraction. Kitty stood to one side, allowing the sailors to wheel the stretcher and wheelchairs inside the hospital. She was bringing over some meat pies left from this morning. They would not go to waste at the hospital.

'Kitty, is that you?' A weak voice beneath the blankets made her turn and she walked over to take a closer look while the medics went to the frosted window to give details.

Kitty recognised the familiar voice at once even if it was only just above a whisper.

343

'Frank?' It could not be! Peering over the heavy blankets, Kitty gasped in surprise. He was a lot thinner than the last time she had seen him, at Nancy's wedding, when he had danced her down the street and whispered in her hair. Was that really ten months ago? It felt like a lifetime! His dazzling, cerulean eyes stood out against the golden glow of his skin and his cheekbones were more prominent than they once were. Nevertheless, he was still the same handsome Frank Feeny she had known all of her life.

'Hello, Frank,' Kitty said almost shyly. Time stood still for a moment as they stared at each other and a wonderful smile hovered around his beautiful lips. Kitty's heart raced so fast she could feel it in her throat.

'Mind your backs, please.' A man dressed in Royal Navy uniform broke the spell as Kitty hastily pulled herself together.

'What brings you here?' she asked, wondering if Pop knew his son was home.

'Can't tell you, I'm afraid,' Frank answered weakly, and suddenly reached for her hand in his usual friendly manner. Kitty unconsciously pulled away when the medic gave her a stern look, and she moved back from the stretcher thinking she had done something wrong. Frank's eyes were like buttonholes; he could hardly keep them open. Then he said with a thin smile, 'It's OK, I'm not contagious.'

Kitty wasn't sure what 'contagious' meant, knowing only that at this moment she felt an awkward elation at seeing Frank Feeny again.

'I'm sorry I didn't write,' she said.

'It's all right, Kit. You're a sight for sore eyes.' Frank smiled weakly, still struggling to keep his eyes open and she wanted to ask how he was here, in Bootle Infirmary. Frank caught the sleeve of Kitty's coat and Kitty bent down to hear him better. His voice was very weak. As she looked close; Kitty could now see that Frank was very ill. His skin had taken on a sallow hue, in contrast to his usual ruddy rude health. There was a slick of sweat on his brow and she could see he was finding it hard to focus on her.

'Kitty, will you do me a favour?' Frank's woozy voice caused Kitty to lose the power of speech and she merely nodded. 'You won't tell anybody I'm here, will you?'

'Not if you don't want me to, Frank,' she said quietly, her heart breaking for him. What had he been through, she wondered, and what if he didn't make it? What horrors had he seen? 'Don't you even want Pop to know?'

'Someone will be in touch with him.' Frank was fighting to stay conscious now. 'We'll also keep Mam, out of it for now.' His smile, though frail, was still there lighting up his adorable blue eyes. His gaze never left her face, making Kitty feel an overpowering wave of emotion that later she would recognise as love. She turned to see the naval orderlies handing over responsibility for Frank to the waiting doctor.

'We'll take over from here,' the doctor said.

'Don't forget me, Kit,' Frank called out.

Kitty said a silent prayer for him. She could not bear it if anything happened to him. Suddenly her throat tightened as tears stung her eyes. Reports on the wireless said the war in the Atlantic was raging and the U-boat menace was a real problem.

Please stay safe, Frank, she silently prayed. Please get better soon. However, not too soon, she thought, knowing that while he was only a short distance from the NAAFI she could come and see him any time.

The family had all gone off to do their own things. Nancy and Sarah were listening to the BBC Home Service on the radio, on which Gracie Fields was belting out a rousing rendition of 'Wish Me Luck as You Wave Me Goodbye'; Sarah and Nancy were singing along lustily, baby George seemingly oblivious to the din. Tommy was out in the back yard, playing with his scruff of a dog. Dolly was tidying up the last of the dinner things and Pop headed into the kitchen to give her a hand.

'Lovely dinner, Dolly. You've done us proud as always.'

'Nothing I like better than cooking for my brood. If I could, Pop, I'd cook us out of this war.'

Pop picked up a tea towel and started to dry things and put them away. 'I know you would, Dolly. We'd all like to try and find a way out of this war without folk being sent away to fight. Decent boys like our Eddy ... and Frank.'

'It isn't right, Pop. All of those young lads. Some of them have never even had a twenty bob note to blow in their pockets on a Saturday night. Why do they have to send them away?'

'You know why, Doll. It isn't old duffers like me that are up to facing down Hitler and his bully boys. We need strong young men and plenty of them if we're to win this war. It'll be hard and it will get harder still.' He hesitated. 'We'll all have to face up to some bad news.'

Something in his voice caused Dolly to look up from her scrubbing of the draining board. 'What is it, Pop?' Seeing Pop's face, always smiling and with a twinkle in his eye, suddenly so serious, the colour drained from her face.

Pop came over to Dolly and put his arms around her. 'I need you to be brave, Dolly.'

'Oh, Pop, it isn't...'

'No, Dolly, it isn't the worst. But our Frank has been injured, his ship attacked by U-boats. He has been transferred to Bootle Infirmary and they are operating. He could be there now.'

A hundred different emotions seemed to cross Dolly's face as she took in the news. How could this be? Surely not one of her boys? Frank's life could be hanging by a thread.

Pop searched her face and could feel her whole body trembling underneath his arms. How would she take the news? He knew that Dolly buried herself in other things because she was terrified that reality would come calling and shatter her perfect view of the world. Everyone was good, neighbours could rely on each other, families stuck together and if you loved your kids hard enough, nothing bad would ever happen to them – if this cosy picture was shattered, he worried for her state of mind. Could she cope?

Dolly leaned into him, but didn't make a sound. If she had burst into tears he could have understood it more, but he didn't know what to make of her silence. For a few moments they stood together like that, the strains of Gracie Fields filtering into the kitchen from the parlour.

Dolly stirred and raised her head, looking her husband in the eye. Pop could see tears there, but also a look of determination and strength, the very things that he had been hoping for.

'If one of my sons is ill and in hospital, then he'll need his family around him.' Dolly was already removing her pinny.

'Get me my coat, Pop. We'll have to hurry. I don't want Frank to be on his own one moment longer than he needs to be. Now go and tell the girls what's happened while I gather a few things together for Frank.'

Pop was bursting with pride for his wife. 'That's my Dolly. With women like you on the Home Front, Hitler doesn't stand a chance.'

Frank slowly opened his eyes a few hours later and caught sight of Kitty looking through the window. He beckoned her into the recovery ward. Kitty was glad to see he was alone.

'You're a sight for sore eyes, Kit.' He smiled sleepily. 'I wish I wasn't stuck in here. We could go for a little dance in the walled gardens at the back of the hospital.'

'Not in your pyjamas, you won't!' Kitty said, overwhelmed by a bout of bashfulness. Suddenly she could not think of a word to say. She stood silently at the foot of Frank's bed.

'I thought you were a figment of my imagination, standing there...' He smiled and patted the bedclothes. 'Come and sit here, let me look at you.'

'I can't sit on your bed; Matron will have me frogmarched out of here and shot!' Kitty smiled. 'Not long out of the operating theatre and you're joking already.' She smiled, enjoying his impudence very much. However, it would not do to let him know that. 'Did they remove your manners, too?'

'They must have, Kit. Sorry, there is a chair over there. I would get it for you but...' Frank gave a low rumbling laugh.

'Don't laugh, Frank, you'll hurt yourself,' she said hurriedly, anxious that her presence wouldn't cause him any more pain.

'Too late,' Frank winced, his hollow cheeks giving a little lift as he tried to make light of it. Kitty could see he was not making the best job of hiding the pain and her heart went out to him. He had been through so much more than she could ever imagine. His mind as well as his body needed time to heal, she was sure.

'You're in the best place, Frank... I'll go and tell the nurse you're awake,' Kitty said.

'No! It's fine, you haven't got much time... They'll be ringing the bell soon.'

'But you're in pain.' It was a wonder he was even awake, let alone talking. It was agonising watching him like this. If she could take his pain away, she would.

'I'll live.' Frank managed a weak smile, obviously tired now. 'I feel so much better for seeing you.' His eyelids were heavy and it was an effort for him to keep them open. 'I can't think of a better tonic.'

'You daft ha'p'orth, what did you say that for?'

Kitty smiled.

'I thought you'd like to know.' Frank gave a tortured laugh, just a little one, but clearly agonising.

'Are you sure you don't want me to call the nurse?'

'No, Kit, I just want to look at you,' Frank answered, and Kitty realised that he was still under the influence of the anaesthetic; he must think he was talking to someone else.

'Well, you just concentrate on getting better.' She had been here too long, Kitty knew. The nurses must have forgotten she was here in this little room alone with the only man who had ever taken up space in her heart. In her wildest dreams, Kitty had never imagined the two of them together in this way. What a strange twist of fate that he should be injured and she should be the only one with him. Even though Frank was in dreadful pain she couldn't help but feel privileged and blessed to be here alone with him.

However, it was cruel to keep him from his recuperation. A stab of guilt unsettled her. She had to admit it was nice to know that he had asked to see her though, imagining a familiar face was always welcome. Kitty smoothed her hair, knowing it always looked a fright after she'd been in the NAAFI kitchen all morning.

'You must be...' She faltered, unable to tell him she had worn him out.

'Handsome?' Frank offered. 'Wonderful?'

'Yes, all of those, O modest one,' Kitty laughed.

'Tell the truth, I look like someone who's just been cut in half,' Frank said now, his eyes heavy. His smile was only an echo of the ones she had seen before. Kitty dreaded to think how Dolly would feel when she saw him.

Kitty straightened the sheets and then pressed them gently with the palm of her hand as Frank fought to keep his eyes on her all the time. It was an effort for him to lift his hand, she could tell, and she knew she should leave now, but she could not drag herself away. He had been gone so long.

Frank took her hand in his and he said, 'It's nice of you to care, Kit,' before his lids gave up the fight and closed. 'You won't tell anyone I'm here, will you?' A lazy smile lifted his handsome features. She could not take her eyes from him. He looked so perfect...

Kitty felt a strong rush of warmth flood her face and neck when Frank said in a sleepy voice, 'I'd like it if you could call in now and then, though.'

'I'll call in every day,' Kitty whispered. 'I'll bring you something nice to have for your afternoon tea.'

'You make the best scones...' Frank let out an appreciative sigh.

'Scones it is then,' Kitty whispered and, taking a furtive glance around, wondered if anybody would notice if she stole a kiss. One small, friendly kiss to show he was not alone... She was captivated by the rhythmic rise and fall of his chest; certain he was now fast asleep.

Leaning over the edge of the bed, she placed a gentle kiss on Frank's warm cheek. He smelled of anaesthetic but she did not care as her finger traced the outline of his full, sensual lips. She made a gentle dot on the tip of his strong chin, before leaving him in peace.

As she turned to leave, his fingers suddenly hooked hers and Kitty's heart felt as if it would leap from her chest. Just as quickly, he relaxed. Sighing softly, she crept from the ward, leaving Frank to sleep ... and to heal.

CHAPTER TWENTY-ONE

'Are we nearly there, can't you go any faster?' Dolly Feeny fretted as her husband pulled the reins and steered the horses towards Derby Road. The sun was starting to set and the sky was a vibrant riot of oranges and purples. The day had been a glorious one and it was set to be another one tomorrow – who knew what it would bring?

'Don't be so impatient, Doll,' he said before stopping in front of the Infirmary. He pulled the horses to a stop and helped his wife to the ground. Once inside she took out a lace handkerchief and put it across her nose to eliminate the heady smell of ether and disinfectant.

Pop and Dolly approached the reception desk and said who they were and why they were here. The receptionist asked them to take a seat and they both sat down, Dolly wringing her hands. Pop didn't like hospitals, he hated the smell and the closeness of death ... he banished the thought...

'Come with me.' A young nurse smiled at them both, and Dolly found her smile reassuring. The woman's rubber-soled shoes squeaked down the long shiny corridor and she led them through a door marked 'Men's Surgical Ward'.

As they entered they saw, flanking each side of the long ward, a row of iron beds, and Rita was there smiling at her parents.

However, Dolly was only interested in one occupant.

'Here he is, large as life and twice as handsome,' said the nurse.

Dolly caught her breath. She couldn't believe it. Her Frank, battered, bruised and not in great shape, but all in one piece at least! She was at his bedside in no time at all.

'Hiya, Ma, how y' doin'?' Frank was drowsily trying to lift his hand in salute. Dolly could see the effort was too much as it fell onto the pillow.

'Oh, Frank!' Dolly said. 'How are you, son? When did you get home? Rita, when did you find out about this?'

'Don't be cross, Mam. I knew he was coming back, but Frank had sworn me to secrecy until he'd had his operation. We couldn't tell you, Mam. You'd have gone out of your mind with worry.'

'You gang of artful dodgers,' Dolly said, tears of joy rolling down her cheeks.

'I didn't want you to see me like this, Mam.' Frank gave her a lazy smile while Dolly shoved her daughter out of the way and hugged him to her ample bosom.

'She'll suffocate him.' Pop rolled his eyes to the ceiling. 'He's been through enough already.' Pop gently prised his elder son from Dolly's tenacious grip and sat her in a straight-backed chair.

'Oh, look at him,' she said, straightening his

353

bedclothes and smoothing his hair. 'Those bloody Germans.' Then the relief at seeing Frank got the better of her along with the effort of keeping a stiff upper lip and she burst into tears.

'Mam, please don't cry,' Frank pleaded. 'I'll be right as nine-pence soon.'

'I'm sorry, love.' Dolly wiped her tears and did her best to pull herself together. 'It's just the shock. I've got a million questions.'

'And there'll be plenty of time to ask them when he's feeling stronger.' Pop knew he had to get her out of there soon as they were getting unsympathetic looks from the nurse.

'I'll have you home in no time,' Dolly promised. 'I'll get a nurse to come to the house every day. I will pay the doctor. I'll pay the surgeon...' Pop put his finger to his lips and she promised to sit quietly, stroking Frank's head until he nodded off again. It reminded her of when he was a young boy. 'He belongs here by the Mersey, not in the middle of the Atlantic being tossed around like a cork in a bottle.'

'I'm sorry, but it's time for visitors to leave now,' the young Irish nurse with frizzy red hair was telling them.

'But we've only just got here!' Dolly was adamant she would not move. 'I'm his mother, he needs me!'

'You can see him again tomorrow, Mrs Feeny.' The nurse was just as determined. 'Frank needs all the rest he can get after his operation.' Her voice softened, and she continued a little more gently, 'Maybe you could bring his clean pyjamas later this afternoon. I'll have a word with Matron.'

'But I've brought some with me already...'

The lively nurse gave her an exaggerated wink.

'Ah!' said Dolly, comprehending. 'I'll do that very thing.' Dolly realised matters were beyond her control and she bent to kiss her son. 'I know you will do your best.'

'Thank you, Mrs Feeny.' The nurse stepped aside to allow the family to leave, but still Dolly was reluctant to go.

'I'll be back later, son,' she gave the nurse a pointed stare, 'and I'll bring lots of fruit to build up his strength.' Dolly sniffed and said again, 'We'll have him home in no time.'

'I am sure you will, Mrs Feeny,' said Maeve, who recognised a feisty woman when she saw one.

'Thanks, Ma, you're the best.' Frank's eyes were already closed. 'See you, Pop.' Pop shook his son's hand but knew he was already asleep before they even reached the bottom of the bed.

They kept him in their sights until the very last second and then each was lost in his or her own thoughts.

It was Pop who broke the silence when he said to Dolly, 'He looks better than I thought he would.' Dolly was so wrung out with conflicting emotions she had to sit down outside the ward to take it all in.

'I'll bring a good dinner next time.'

'They wouldn't allow it, old girl,' Pop said. 'I am sure they can feed him well enough...' he hesitated, 'although maybe not as good as you can.' Dolly gave a little sniff and dabbed her eyes.

'He won't be worrying about food for a while, though, Dolly.' Pop rubbed her hand.

'Oh, Pop,' she pulled her hand away, 'there but for the grace of God go we.'

Scooping her from the chair, he steered her down the corridor. As they made to leave, they heard a well-spoken voice calling after them.

'Mr and Mrs Feeny? May I have a word?'

Dolly and Pop turned. He introduced himself as Dr Fitzgerald and told them that he was one of the doctors looking after Frank.

'He's doing well, isn't he, Doctor?' Pop commented.

'Well, that is what I wanted to speak to you about.'

This was going to be the hard bit, the doctor thought. Dolly and Pop looked at each other, both wide-eyed with dread.

Dr Fitzgerald continued, 'A piece of shrapnel is lodged in his thigh bone. We've done everything we can to remove it but unfortunately, the wound has become infected and caused blood poisoning.'

Pop understood immediately, but Dolly was struggling to take in this horrible turn of events and was in no fit state to receive the news. She shrugged off Pop's arm place protectively around her shoulders and grabbed Dr Fitzgerald's arm, stricken.

'Doctor, I want you to tell me the truth now, is he going to die? You have to tell me. I've got to know!' Tears streamed down her cheeks.

'I hope not, Mrs Feeny, but the next twenty-four hours are critical. Even if we manage to halt the infection in its tracks, the damage already done to his leg could have a serious impact. He may lose it, I'm afraid.'

Dolly and Pop were speechless. This was terrible news. The thought that their strapping lad Frank could lose his leg was an awful thought.

'Everything depends on how your son reacts over the next day or so.'

'My lad's strong. He's an athlete. The boxing champion of his unit. Of course, he's going to make it.'

'All of those things will help a great deal, Mr Feeny,' the doctor agreed.

'Anyway,' Pop said, with more bravery than he felt, 'what God would want to face my Dolly's wrath on Judgment Day if anything happened to her lad? Of course our Frank's not going to die. God wouldn't dare!'

CHAPTER TWENTY-TWO

July 1940

Frank's condition had worsened. He slipped into unconsciousness and the doctors had battled for forty-eight hours to save his life. The Feeny family had never been closer; even Nancy, unable to leave baby George had selflessly held the fort at home. Dolly kept a vigil at her son's side and only left when the matron insisted that she go home and rest. But no rest was forthcoming for any of them.

Finally, Dr Fitzgerald delivered the news that they were dreading.

'In order to save Frank's life, we've taken the

357

decision to amputate beneath his knee. It was the only way. He is stable and his vital signs are already showing signs of improvement.'

In their marriage, Pop had always been the strong one, but the news that his son had lost one of his limbs reduced him to tears. It was Dolly who was the strength for them this time.

'Where there's life, there's hope, Pop – isn't that what you always say?'

'Yes, Doll.' Pop wiped away a tear. 'Will he make a full recovery, Doctor?' he asked.

'All being well, with plenty of patience and time, Frank should be as right as rain in all other respects. Since the last war, great strides have been made in designing new limbs for unfortunate men such as your son.'

Dolly stood and faced the doctor. 'Thank you,' she said with passion. 'You've given my son another chance at life and I'll never forget that.'

As well as the Feeny family, the other stalwart at Frank's bedside was Kitty. Every lunchtime, on her break from the NAAFI canteen, she could be found at the hospital. Due to being in isolation because of the infection, Frank's visits were limited to just his very close family. Kitty wasn't allowed in to see Frank, but she patiently waited for news with the family, ferrying cups of tea backwards and forwards and keeping their spirits up.

'That Kitty has been a godsend, Pop,' observed Dolly, as Kitty went off to fetch her a glass of water as they sat waiting for news in the hospital's visiting room. The hospital staff were very strict about who could see Frank and when, but Dolly had made friends with Nurse Kerrigan, who had turned out to be a distant cousin of Sid Kerrigan, and she was occasionally allowed in when the ward was quiet and Matron and Sister were elsewhere. 'I think she might be soft on our Frank. Can't think why I haven't noticed it before.'

'I don't think either of them could do better, Doll,' concurred Pop. 'But Frank is proud. With the loss of his leg he'll have a lot to face up to.'

'Love finds a way, Pop,' said his wife, sagely. 'Love finds a way.'

'D'you like the navy, Frank?' Tommy said as they sat looking at photographs of Nancy's wedding, which Dolly had brought into the hospital to show Frank. The schools were not open just yet but there were unsavoury rumours that it could happen soon.

'The sea is in my blood, Tom. I can't imagine doing anything else...'

Pop had been right. Frank had made a good recovery and was making excellent progress, but the loss of his leg had hit him hard. Frank had always known exactly what he wanted to do with his life, but now he couldn't see the future any more. He thought of himself as a seafarer first and foremost, but that career was denied to him now.

'Kitty said she was coming to see you this afternoon, whether you like it or not,' said Tommy.

Frank had been refusing all visits, except for his mother and father and his sister Rita. He was dreading the pitying looks that he was bound to get. He couldn't bear the thought that anyone would feel sorry for him. Especially Kitty. Tommy

was the exception to this rule. His youthful inno-
cence and inquisitiveness were a tonic and Frank
never felt patronised by the boy.

'I still don't want to see anyone. I don't feel up
to it,' Frank insisted.

Tommy frowned. He knew Frank was smitten
by their Kitty, but why didn't he want to see her?
He looked out of the window at all the ships lined
up in the dock, the battleships and the sloops, the
tugs and the tankers. He loved them all, and
vowed that he was staying put. Their Kitty would
have to drag him kicking and screaming to evacuation next time. If there ever was a next time!

'Did your mam tell you that she has a Canadian
lodger? He's in the air force. His brother served
with Eddy after Christmas,' Tommy said with a
gleam in his eye.

'She must have forgotten to mention it,' Frank
said, looking for a piece of jigsaw, his brow fur-
rowed. What was Tommy up to?

'His name is Ethan. Isn't that an unusual name?'

'It is around Empire Street,' Frank answered,
the jigsaw piece raised, waiting for Tommy to
speak again.

'I think he's got his eye on our Kitty,' Tommy
said impishly. 'He said he saw her when he was at
the NAAFI dance last week.'

Well, he is in a better position than I am, thought
Frank. What would Kitty want with a chap who
had only one leg? They took it off to save his life
and he could only dream about dancing with Kitty
now. Kitty was young and full of life, with her
whole future ahead of her. Now he was useless and
he would only drag her down and hold her back.

360

It was time to put all thoughts of Kitty away. Anyway, he felt sure that she only wanted to see him because she felt sorry for him, just like everyone else would.

'I'd make sure Kitty was mine, if I were you, before the Canadian makes a move,' said Tommy. 'I think Kitty might be pleased if she thought you really liked her.'

'Stop talking daft, Tommy,' said Frank. 'You don't know anything about it.' His voice sounded harsher than he'd wanted it to. But he wished Tommy would shut the hell up.

At that moment, Nurse Kerrigan popped her freckled face around his door.

'You've got a visitor, Frank,' she said cheerfully.

'I don't want to see anyone, I told you before,' he said gruffly.

'Nonsense! It's time you stopped wallowing in misery and this visitor is bound to cheer you up – you're a lucky chap!'

Frank didn't have time to protest before the nurse had gone and come back almost instantly with the one visitor that he couldn't face seeing. This was the person he had really been trying to keep away. Kitty Callaghan.

'Hello, Frank,' Kitty said shyly as she came into the room. Frank didn't think he had ever seen her look more beautiful. Kitty had finished her shift early at the NAAFI canteen and had rushed over to the hospital. Her cheeks were flushed and stray bits of her dark wavy hair had fallen out of their pins, giving her a windswept look. Frank thought she was so radiant that he could barely look at her.

'Hello, Kitty.' Frank was rarely lost for words, but he was now.

'I've waited ever so long to see you, Frank. How are you?' she asked, her face full of concern. Her eyes took in Frank's pinched features. He looked well, but there was a tightness behind his eyes that she didn't remember ever seeing there before. Without being able to help herself, Kitty felt her eyes being drawn down the bed, to the space where Frank's lower leg should be, but where it was no longer. Frank followed her gaze as it settled on his stump. He shifted uncomfortably.

'Oh, you know, Kitty. I'm getting by.'

'The doctors say that Frank could be out quite soon, don't they, Frank?' said Tommy, chattering excitedly. 'I heard them say you could have a wheelchair. That'd be brilliant – could I push ya?'

Kitty saw Frank flinch at the mention of a wheelchair. 'Tommy,' she said quickly. 'Go and fetch me a glass of water, there's a good lad. I'm parched.'

Tommy dashed off and left the two of them alone together. The silence was heavy between them. Kitty couldn't make sense of it. There had never been any awkwardness between them before and Frank had always been the one to make everyone laugh. Having his leg amputated must have affected him worse than anyone thought. Kitty couldn't bear the thought that Frank was unhappy in her company.

'Frank, I–'

'Look, Kitty.' Frank interrupted before she had a chance to speak. 'I've got something to tell everyone and I want you to be the first to know.

The doctors have offered me a special place to recuperate, far away from here. Down south, in fact. It's a special hospital; one where they help people ... men like me.'

'But what about your family, Frank? What about...' Kitty was going to say, what about us? But what was she thinking? To Frank, she was just the girl next door, no more to him than one of his sisters. She'd been fooling herself to think that there was anything between them, she could see that now. Of course, he must go and get himself better the way he felt best. It was a stupid idea to think that he had any feelings for her that might keep him here. It was just her silly overactive imagination, as usual.

'It's for the best, Kitty. You'll see.' Yes, he thought. It's for the best that you don't end up saddled with a useless cripple for the rest of your life.

'Good luck, Frank.' Kitty was heartbroken, but determined not to show it. Her love for Frank was a silly girlish dream; castles in the air. It was time she grew up, there was a war on and the time for childish fancies was over.

'I'm a bit tired, Kitty,' said Frank. He was desperate for her to go now. This was the hardest thing he had ever had to do in his life; to send away the girl that he loved like no other. But he had to do it – for her sake. It would be selfish to do otherwise.

'I'm sorry Frank. I'll leave you now.' She stood to go, buttoning up her coat which she hadn't even had time to remove. But something in the room held her there. She looked at Frank and their eyes met, but just as quickly she looked away, not able fully to comprehend what she had seen in those blue eyes.

'I'll write,' she said firmly. 'You can't stop me.' And as Kitty left the room, she banished from her mind as daft any idea that what she had seen in Frank's eyes were tears.

Rita didn't normally smoke. She thought it was unladylike and hated the way the smell clung to her clothes and hair. But every now and then she indulged herself and this afternoon she had begged one of Maeve's Chesterfields. She had finished her shift and was giving herself ten minutes before she had to head home. The thought of Charlie and Ma Kennedy waiting for her at home in the gloomy back room of Ma Kennedy's shop literally filled her with dread.

There seemed to be no good news. The Channel Islands had been invaded by the Germans – British territory – and the Welsh city of Cardiff had suffered terrible raids by the Luftwaffe. It seemed that the war was getting ever closer to Empire Street. All of these thoughts were rattling around her brain when she saw Kitty Callaghan come scurrying down the steps of the infirmary. She waved over at Kitty, who headed her way, but Rita was concerned to see that Kitty, her friend and someone who she considered as good as family, was flushed and seemed to be on the verge of tears.

'Whatever's the matter?'

Kitty told her about what had just transpired between her and Frank. Rita drew thoughtfully

364

on the cigarette. 'Fancy a puff?' she offered Kitty the Chesterfield, but Kitty shook her head.

'No thanks, they don't agree with me, Rita.'

Rita had heard from the doctor that the hospital in Hampshire was a possibility. But this was the first she had heard that Frank had definitely wanted to go. She suspected that Kitty's visit had something to do with his decision.

'You're sweet on him, aren't you, Kit?' Rita asked gently.

Kitty was too shy to answer, but she nodded her head a little.

Rita put her arm around Kitty's shoulder. 'If there's one thing I've learned about men, Kitty, it's that they're a different species – even my own brother!'

The two women exchanged looks and then both laughed.

'Frank is proud and he's had a rough ride. Give him time. It's a great healer. Some wounds aren't just skin deep you know, Kitty, and they can take a lot longer to heal.'

Kitty nodded. Thinking of her mam and dad and of Tommy's close shave, she thought she understood what Rita meant.

'I don't think I'll ever understand men, though, Rita.'

'I don't think we're meant to,' answered her friend. 'I think we're just supposed to endure them!' She was only half joking and Rita didn't expect Kitty to sympathise, she was still only a young lass. There were barely a few years between them but Rita felt old before her time.

'I overheard someone at the hospital saying that

there had been some terrifying raids over the south coast.'

'Yes, me too,' said Rita. 'They're calling it the Battle of Britain. Lots of our nurses and doctors have been transferred south to where they are needed.'

'What's going to happen, Rita?'

'I don't know, Kit. But while we've got brave men like Jack and Eddy and Sid and Frank doing their duty, we'll give Hitler a run for his money yet.'

Stubbing her cigarette out, Rita came to a decision. 'Enough of this gloomy talk, Kitty! Nancy said Gloria's singing at the Adelphi again tonight and Mam's offered to babysit George. Sod Charlie, sod Ma Kennedy and sod bloody Hitler – shall we get our gladrags on and join them?'

Kitty's smile was all the encouragement she needed and the two women linked arms and headed to Empire Street, singing 'Wish Me Luck' as they went on their way.

The publishers hope that this book has given you enjoyable reading. Large Print Books are especially designed to be as easy to see and hold as possible. If you wish a complete list of our books please ask at your local library or write directly to:

Magna Large Print Books
Magna House, Long Preston,
Skipton, North Yorkshire.
BD23 4ND

This Large Print Book for the partially sighted, who cannot read normal print, is published under the auspices of

THE ULVERSCROFT FOUNDATION